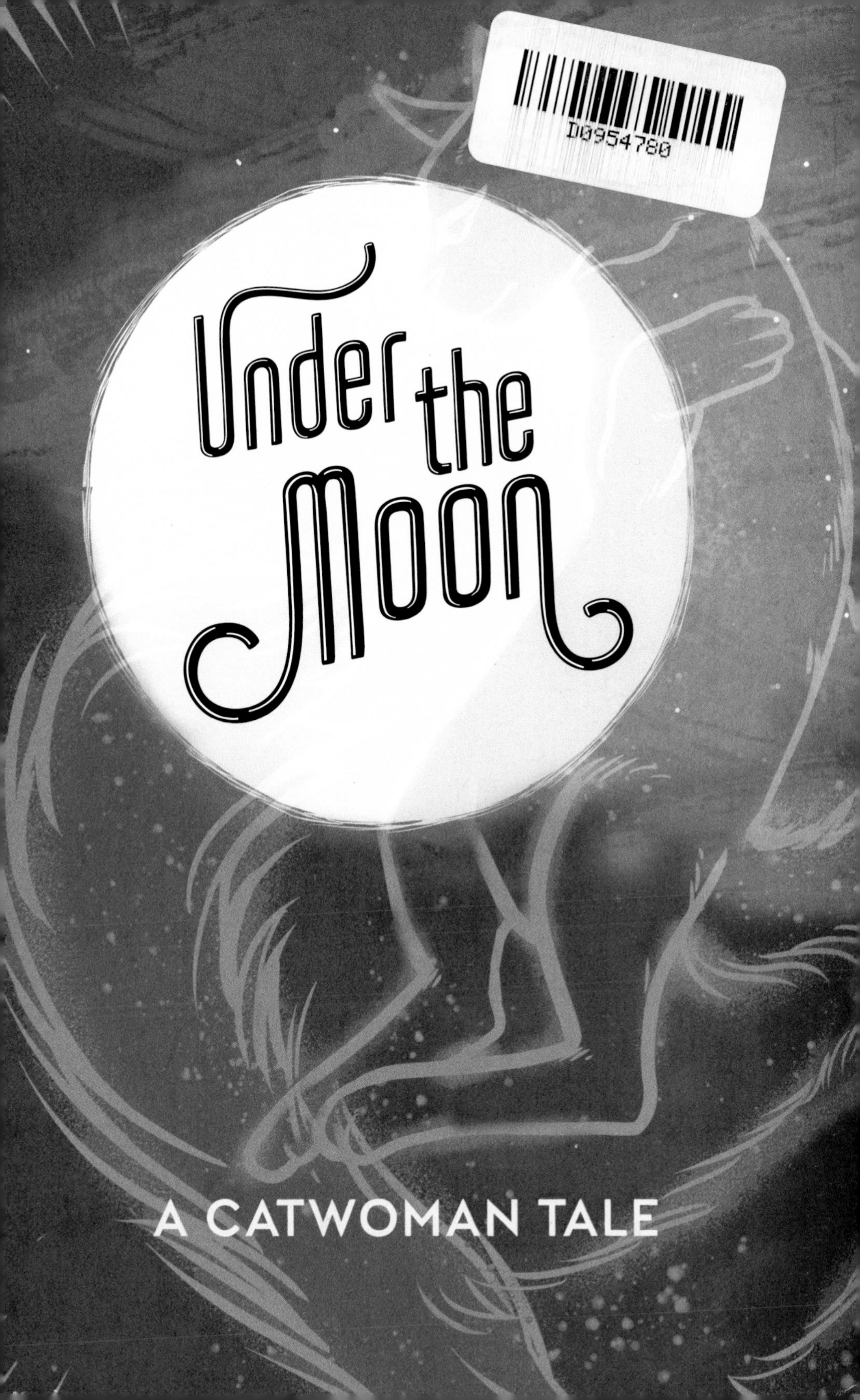
Under the Moon
A CATWOMAN TALE

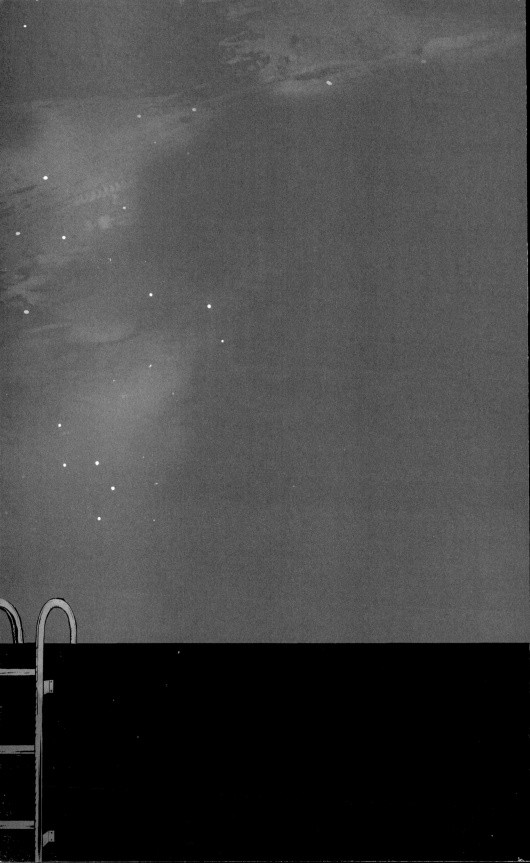

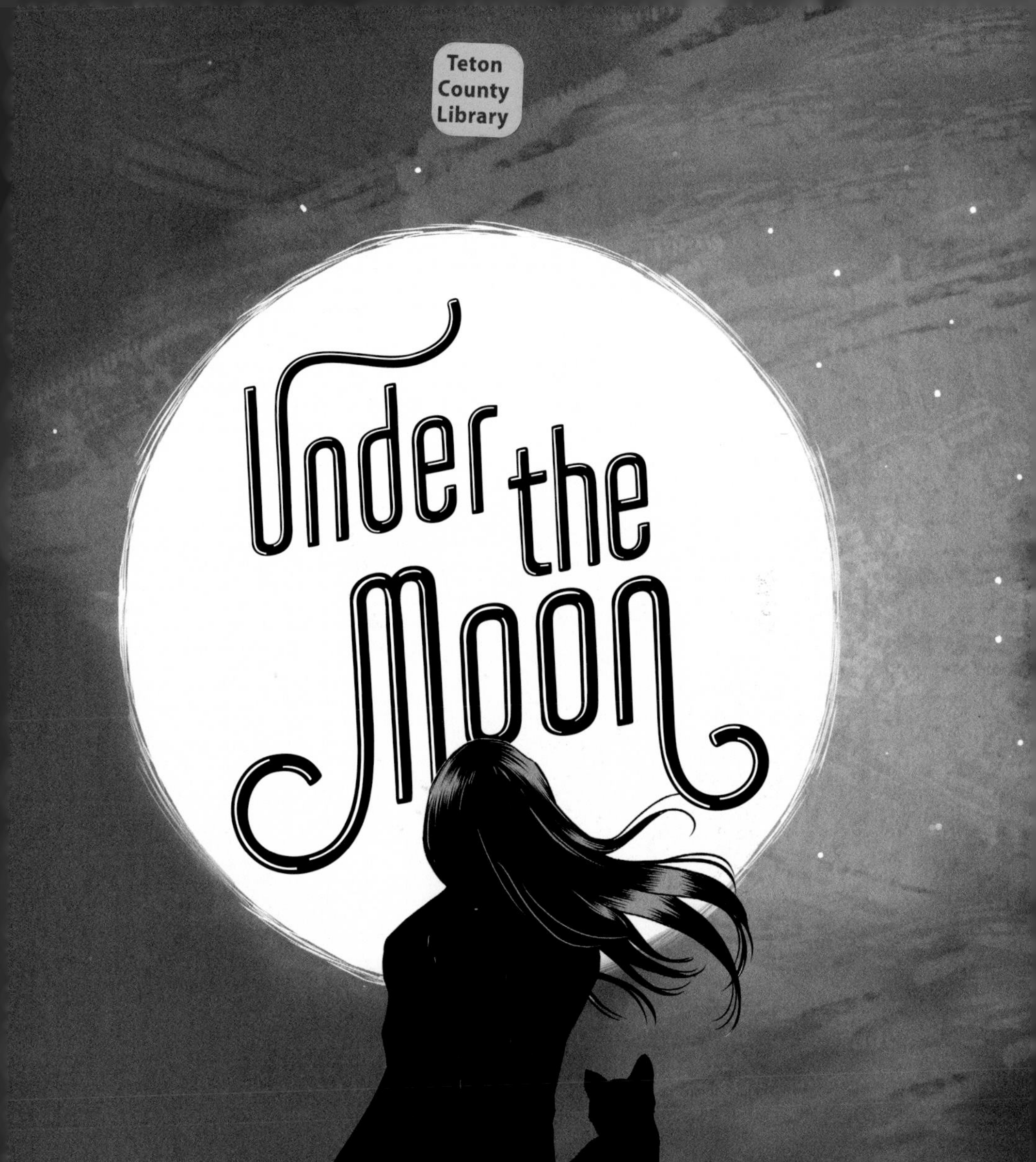
Under the Moon

A CATWOMAN TALE

Written by LAUREN MYRACLE
Art by ISAAC GOODHART

JEREMY LAWSON *Colorist*
DERON BENNETT *Letterer*

UNDER THE MOON: A CATWOMAN TALE
Published by DC Comics. Copyright © 2019 DC Comics. All Rights
Reserved. All characters, their distinctive likenesses and related ele-
ments featured in this publication are trademarks of DC Comics. DC
INK is a trademark of DC Comics. The stories, characters and incidents
featured in this publication are entirely fictional. DC Comics does not
read or accept unsolicited submissions of ideas, stories or artwork.
DC Comics, 2900 West Alameda Ave., Burbank, CA 91505
Printed by LSC Communications, Crawfordsville, IN, USA.
3/29/19. First Printing.

ISBN: 978-1-4012-8591-3

PEFC Certified
This product is from
sustainably managed
forests and controlled
sources
PEFC/29-31-337   www.pefc.org

Library of Congress Cataloging-in-Publication Data
Names: Myracle, Lauren, 1969- author. | Goodhart, Isaac, illustrator.
Title: Under the moon : a Catwoman tale / written by Lauren Myracle ;
illustrated by Isaac Goodhart.
Description: Burbank, CA : DC Ink, 2019. | Summary: When living with her
mother's abusive boyfriend becomes unbearable, fifteen-year-old Selina
Kyle, the future Catwoman, runs away and struggles to find her own
identity while living on the streets of Gotham.
Identifiers: LCCN 2019004779 (print) | LCCN 2019007049 (ebook) | ISBN
9781401293963 (e-book) | ISBN 9781401285913 (paperback) | ISBN 1401285910
(paperback)
Subjects: LCSH: Graphic novels. | CYAC: Graphic novels. |
Supervillains--Fiction. | Identity--Fiction. | Runaways--Fiction. |
Homeless persons--Fiction.
Classification: LCC PZ7.7.M98 (ebook) | LCC PZ7.7.M98 Un 2019 (print) | DDC
741.5/973--dc23

table of contents

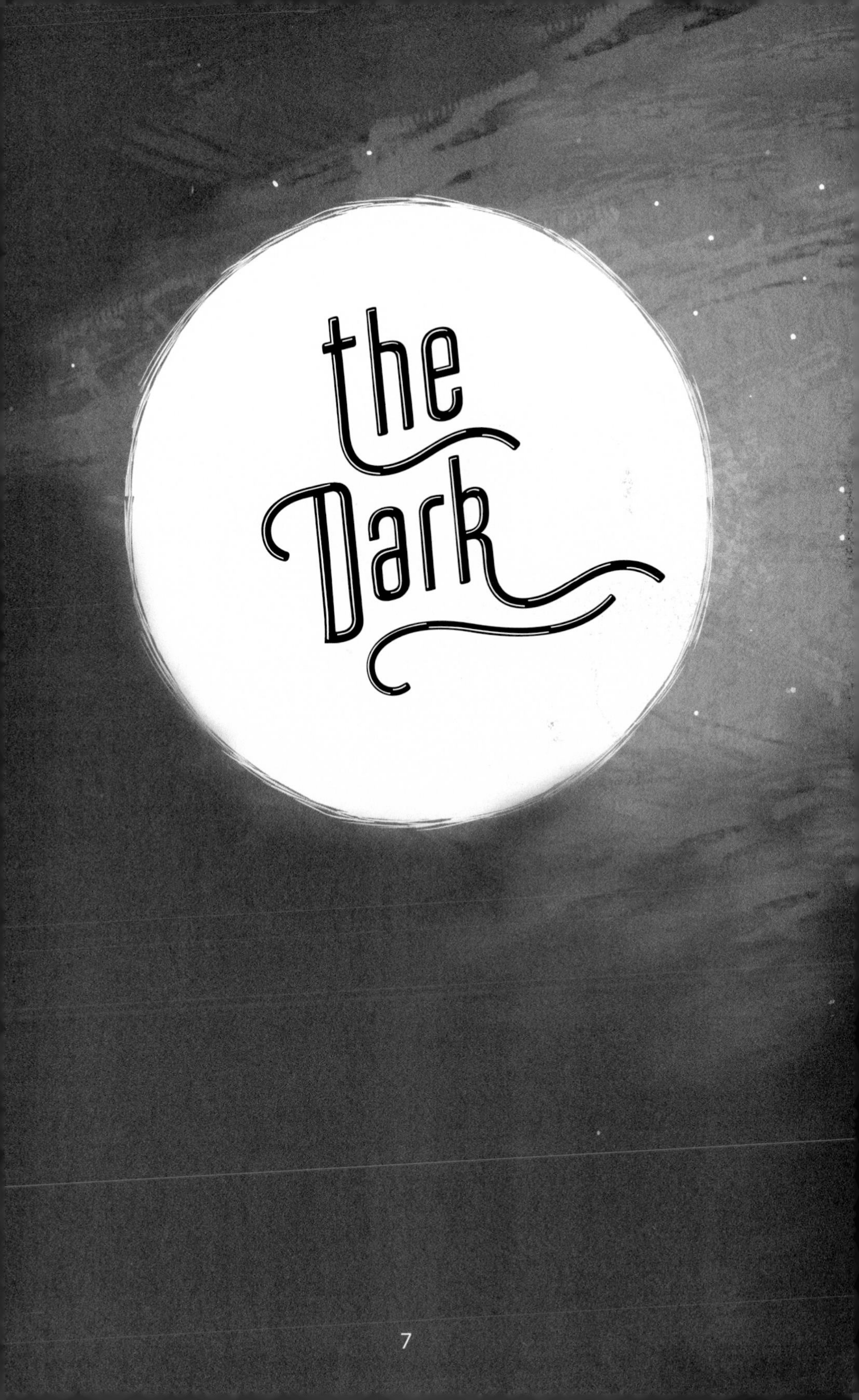

the Dark

LIFE IN THE LITTER BOX

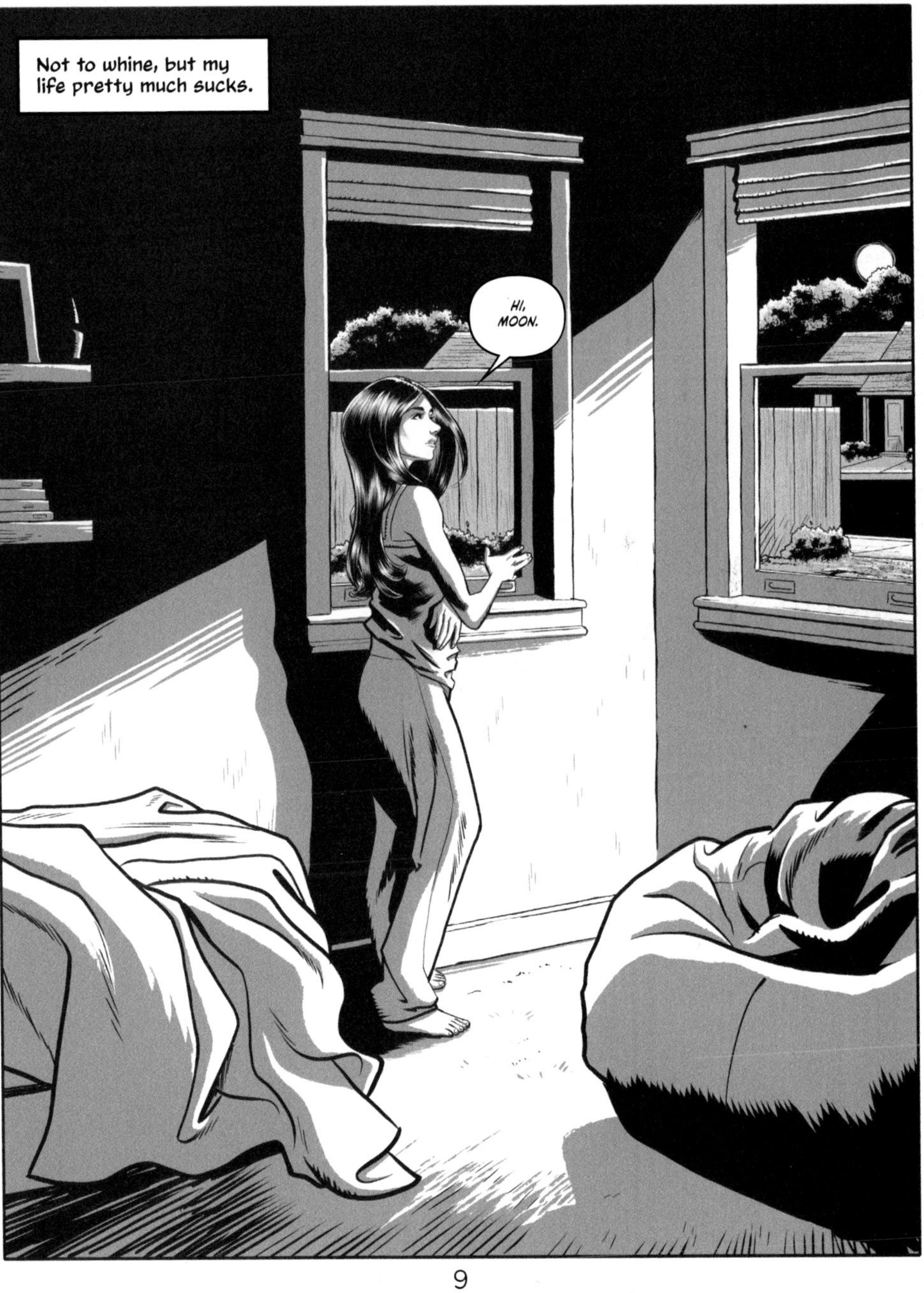
Not to whine, but my life pretty much sucks.
HI, MOON.

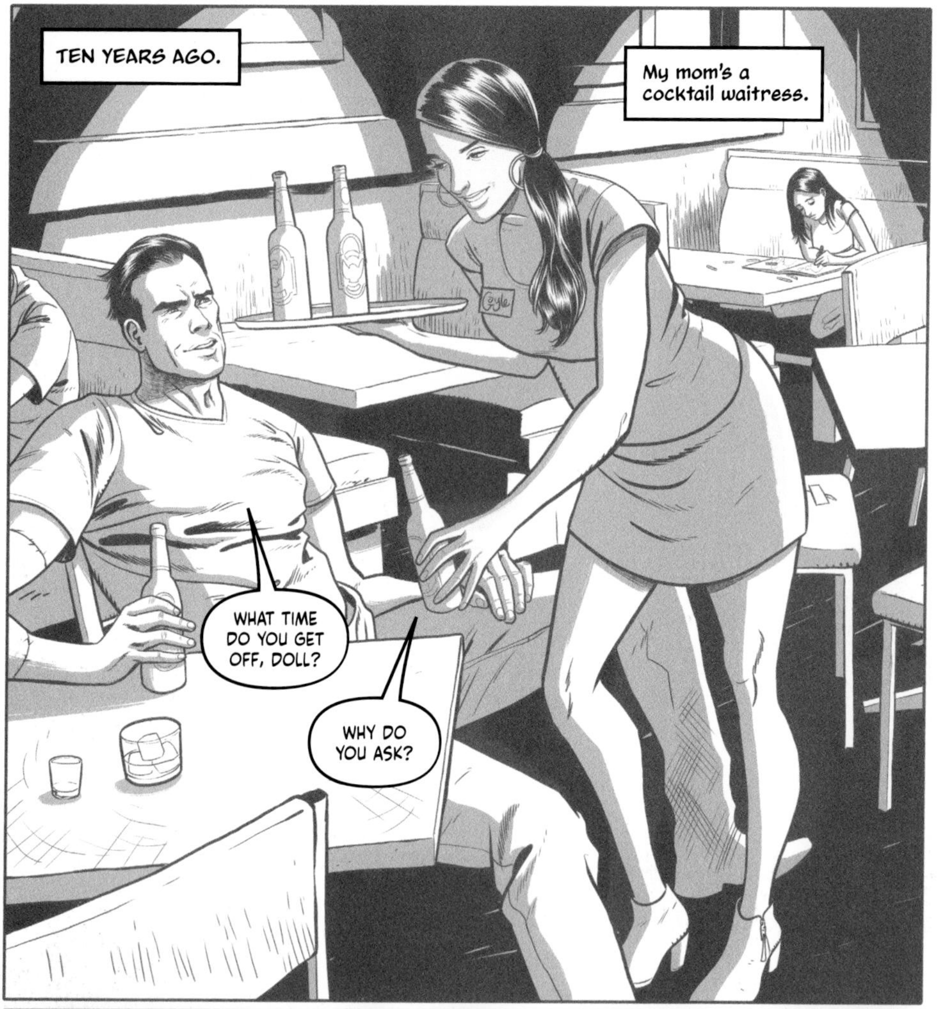
TEN YEARS AGO.
My mom's a cocktail waitress.
WHAT TIME DO YOU GET OFF, DOLL?
WHY DO YOU ASK?

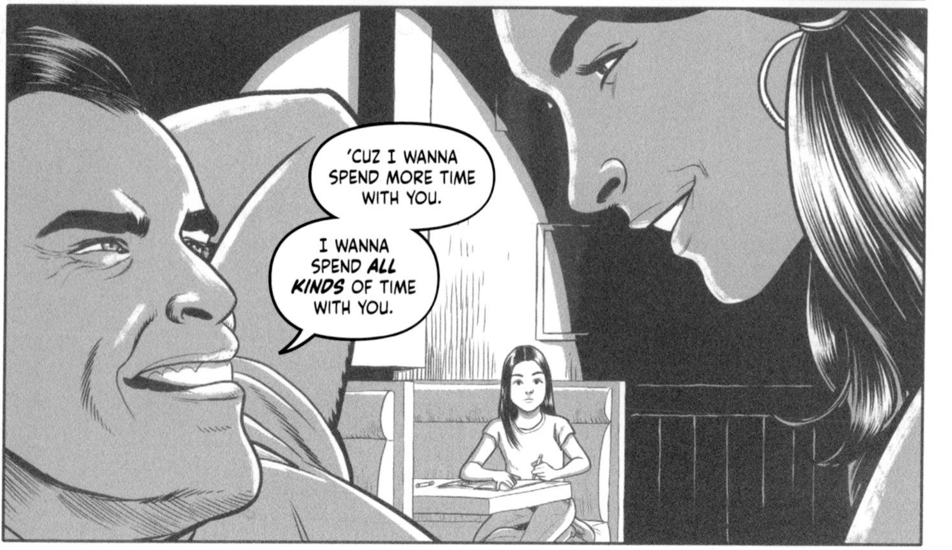
'CUZ I WANNA SPEND MORE TIME WITH YOU.
I WANNA SPEND ***ALL KINDS*** OF TIME WITH YOU.

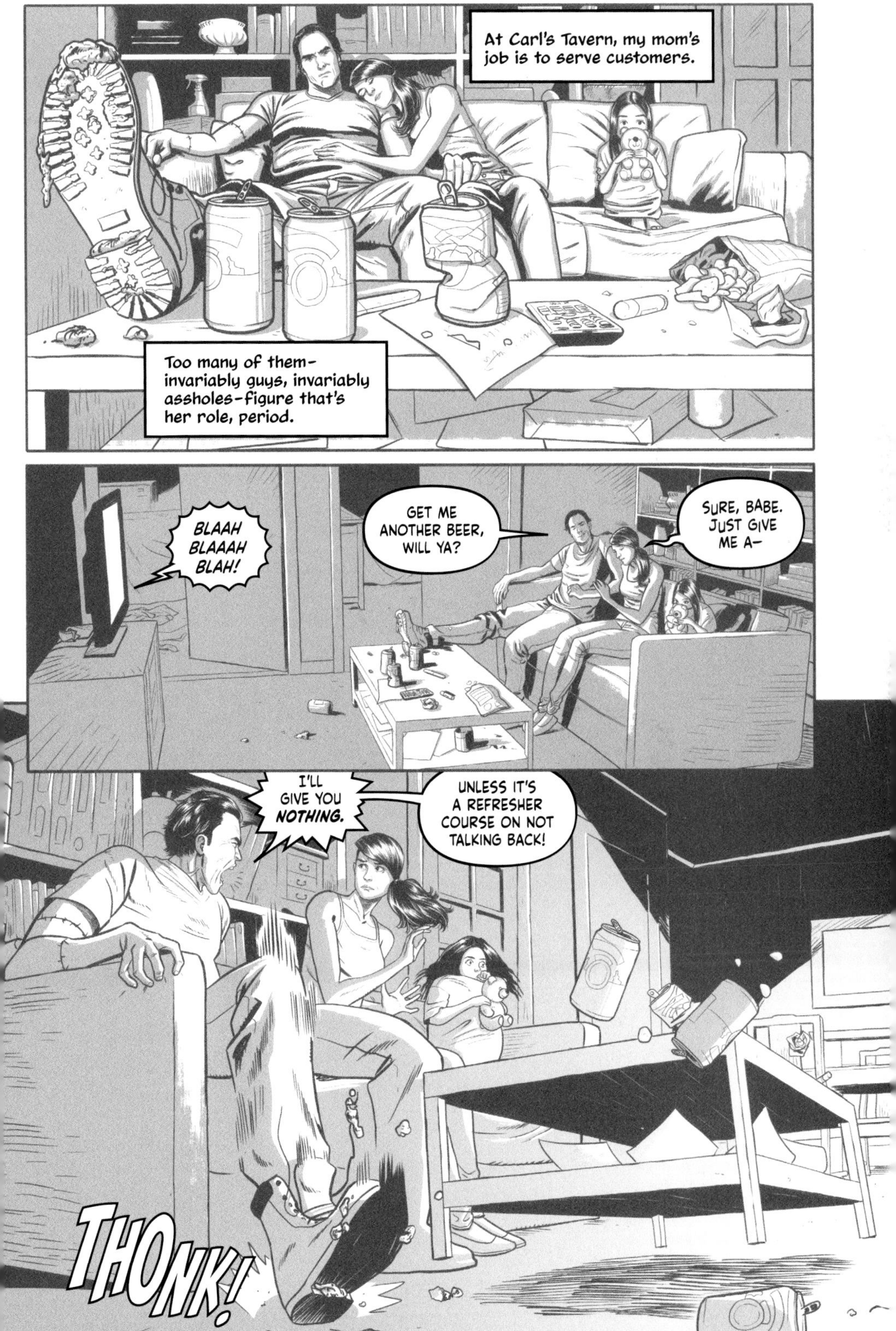
At Carl's Tavern, my mom's job is to serve customers.
Too many of them–invariably guys, invariably assholes–figure that's her role, period.
BLAAH BLAAAH BLAH!
GET ME ANOTHER BEER, WILL YA?
SURE, BABE. JUST GIVE ME A–
I'LL GIVE YOU NOTHING.
UNLESS IT'S A REFRESHER COURSE ON NOT TALKING BACK!
THONK!

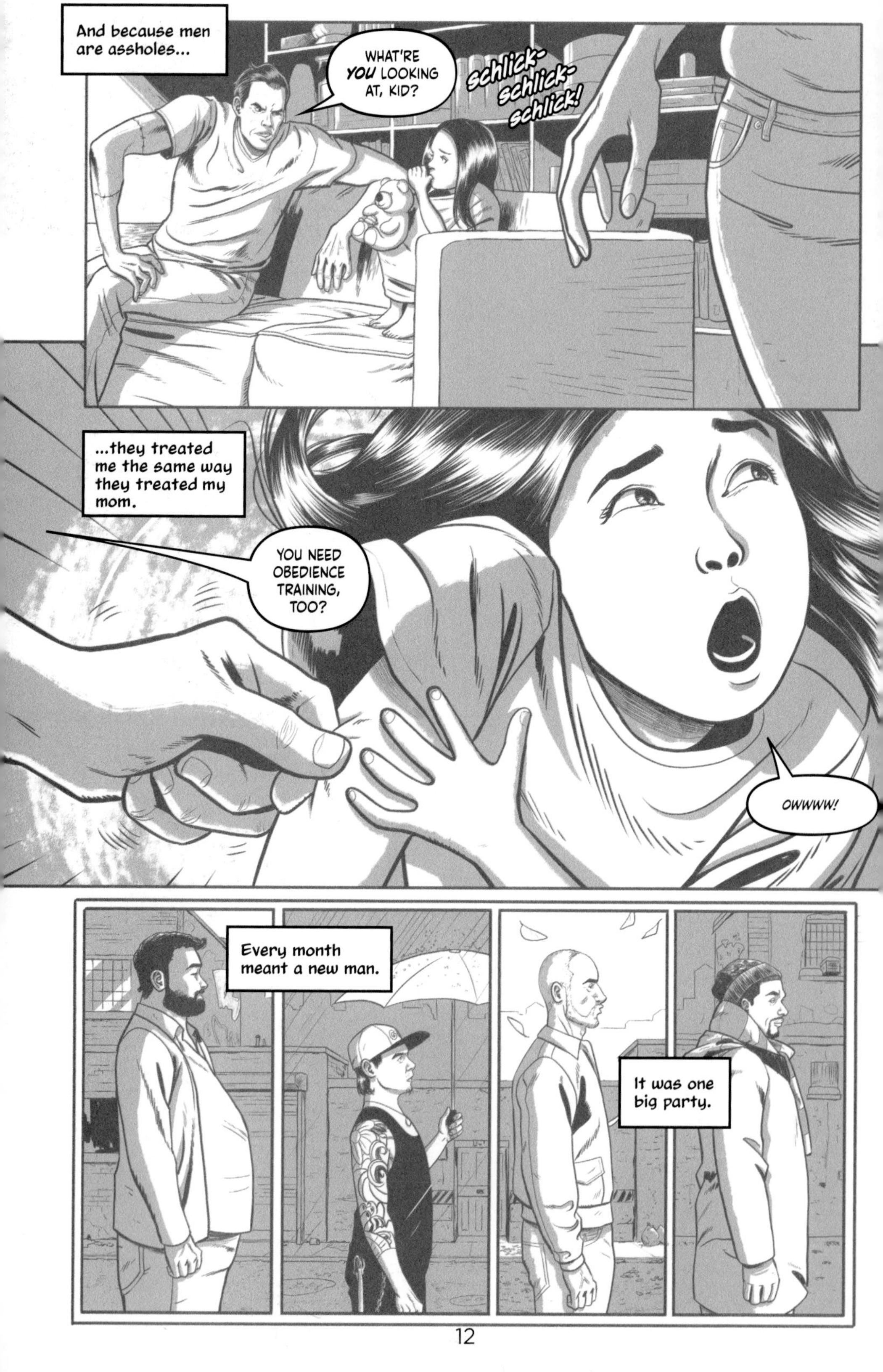
And because men are assholes...
WHAT'RE YOU LOOKING AT, KID?
schlick-schlick-schlick!
...they treated me the same way they treated my mom.
YOU NEED OBEDIENCE TRAINING, TOO?
OWWWW!
Every month meant a new man.
It was one big party.

MY PAL, DERNELL

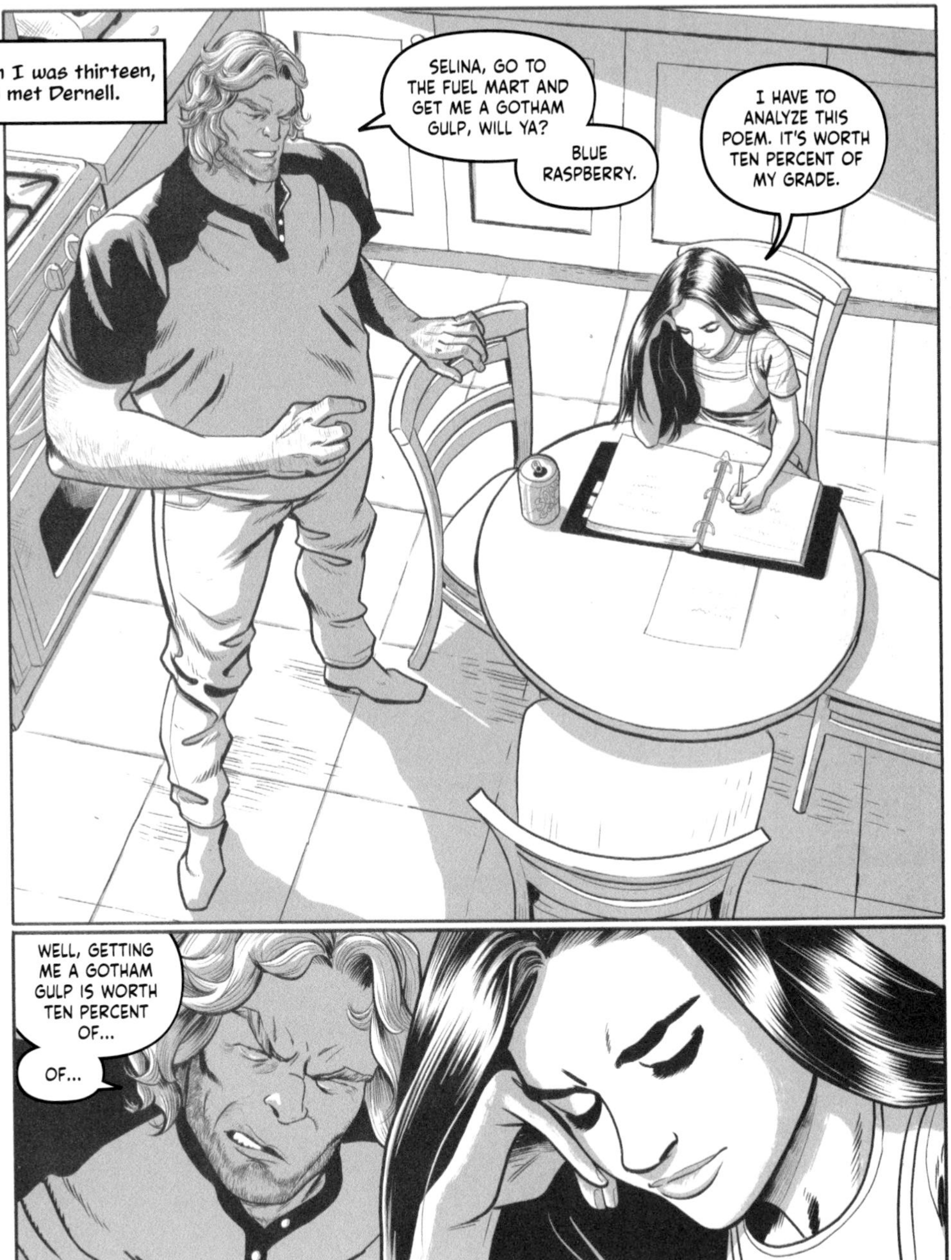

hen I was thirteen,
om met Dernell.
SELINA, GO TO THE FUEL MART AND GET ME A GOTHAM GULP, WILL YA?
BLUE RASPBERRY.
I HAVE TO ANALYZE THIS POEM. IT'S WORTH TEN PERCENT OF MY GRADE.
WELL, GETTING ME A GOTHAM GULP IS WORTH TEN PERCENT OF...
OF...

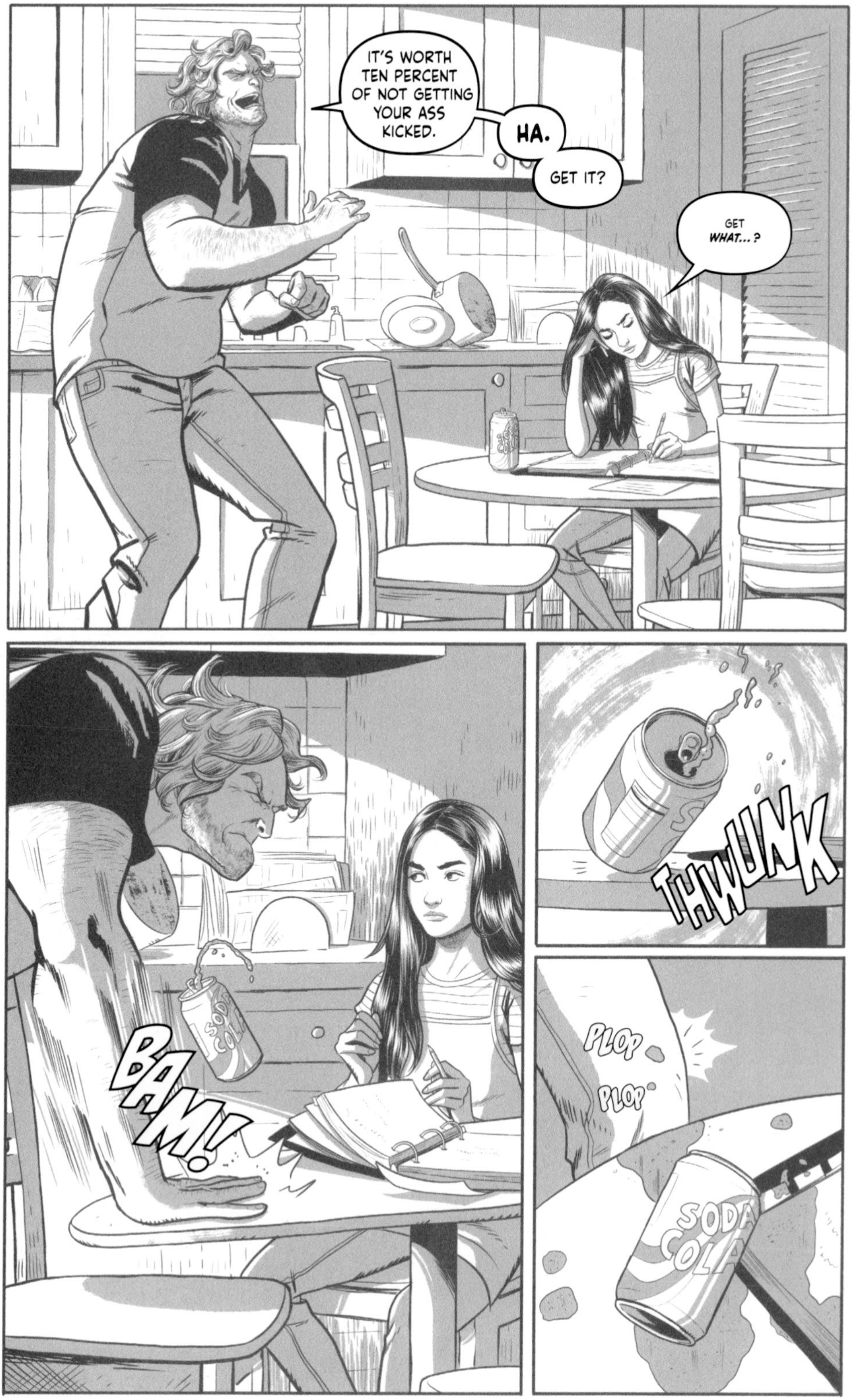
IT'S WORTH TEN PERCENT OF NOT GETTING YOUR ASS KICKED.
HA.
GET IT?
GET WHAT...?
BAM!
THWUNK
PLOP
PLOP
SODA COLA

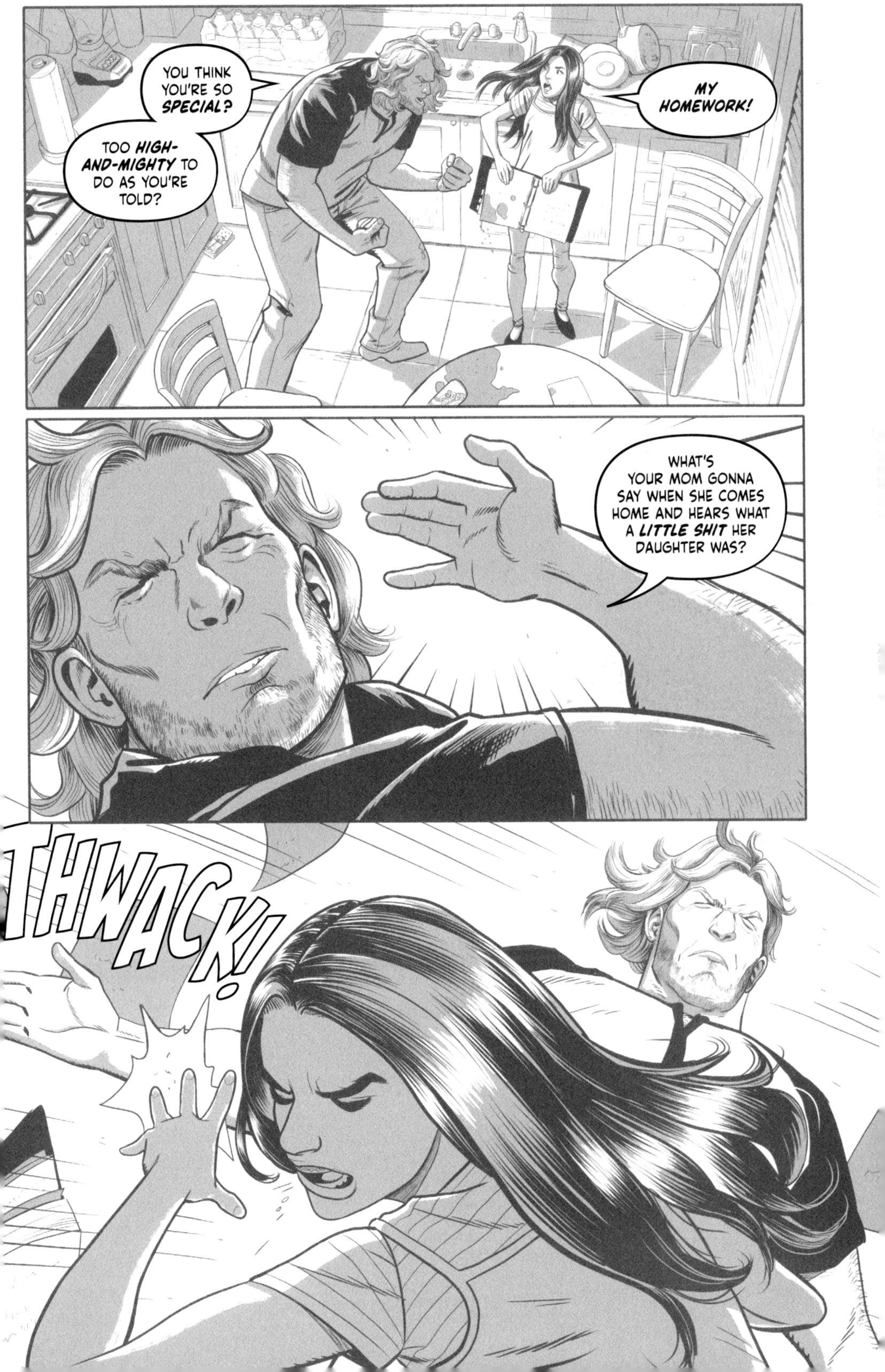
YOU THINK YOU'RE SO *SPECIAL?*
TOO *HIGH-AND-MIGHTY* TO DO AS YOU'RE TOLD?
MY HOMEWORK!
WHAT'S YOUR MOM GONNA SAY WHEN SHE COMES HOME AND HEARS WHAT A *LITTLE SHIT* HER DAUGHTER WAS?
THWACK!

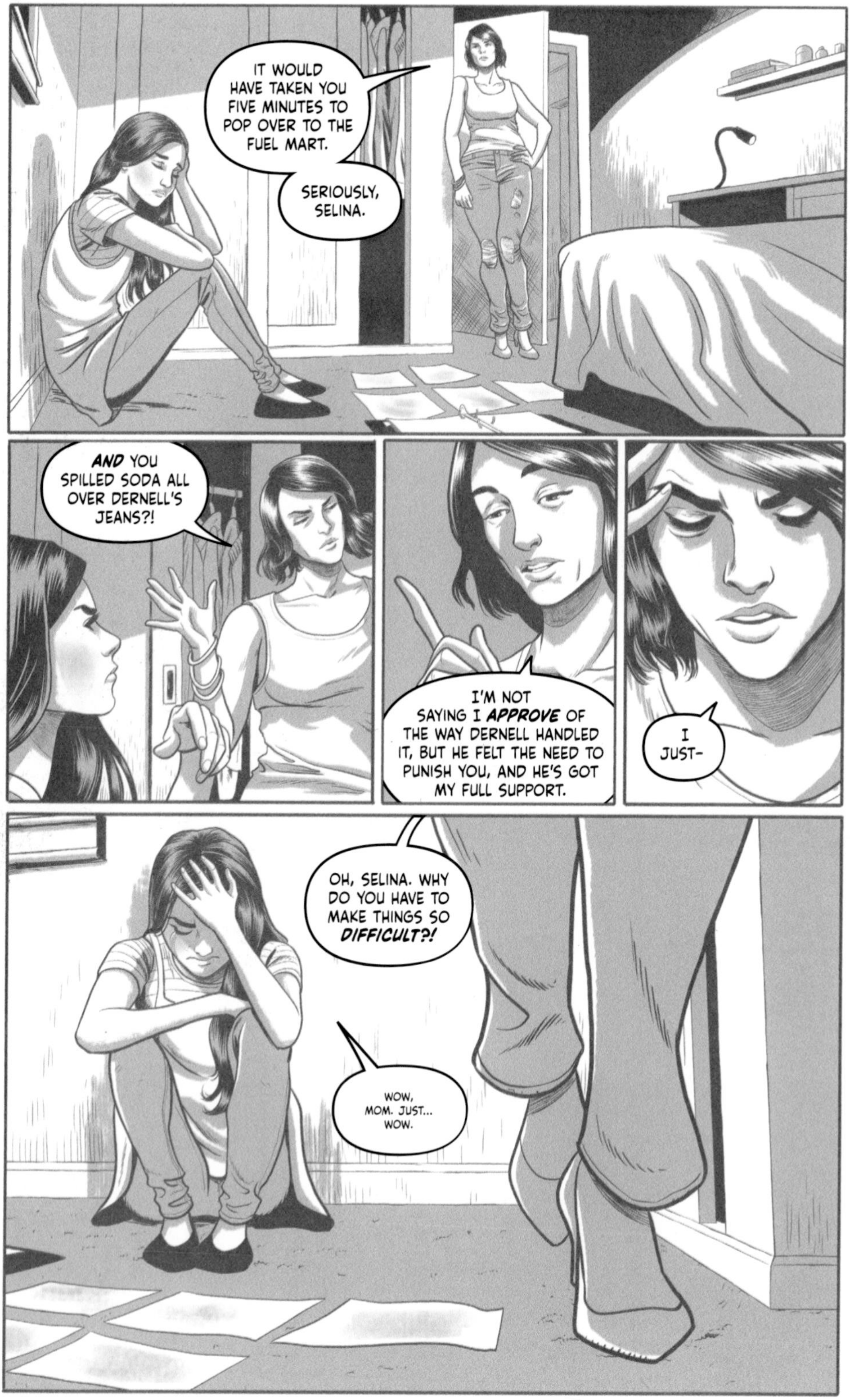
IT WOULD HAVE TAKEN YOU FIVE MINUTES TO POP OVER TO THE FUEL MART.
SERIOUSLY, SELINA.
AND YOU SPILLED SODA ALL OVER DERNELL'S JEANS?!
I'M NOT SAYING I **APPROVE** OF THE WAY DERNELL HANDLED IT, BUT HE FELT THE NEED TO PUNISH YOU, AND HE'S GOT MY FULL SUPPORT.
I JUST–
OH, SELINA. WHY DO YOU HAVE TO MAKE THINGS SO **DIFFICULT?!**
WOW, MOM. JUST... WOW.

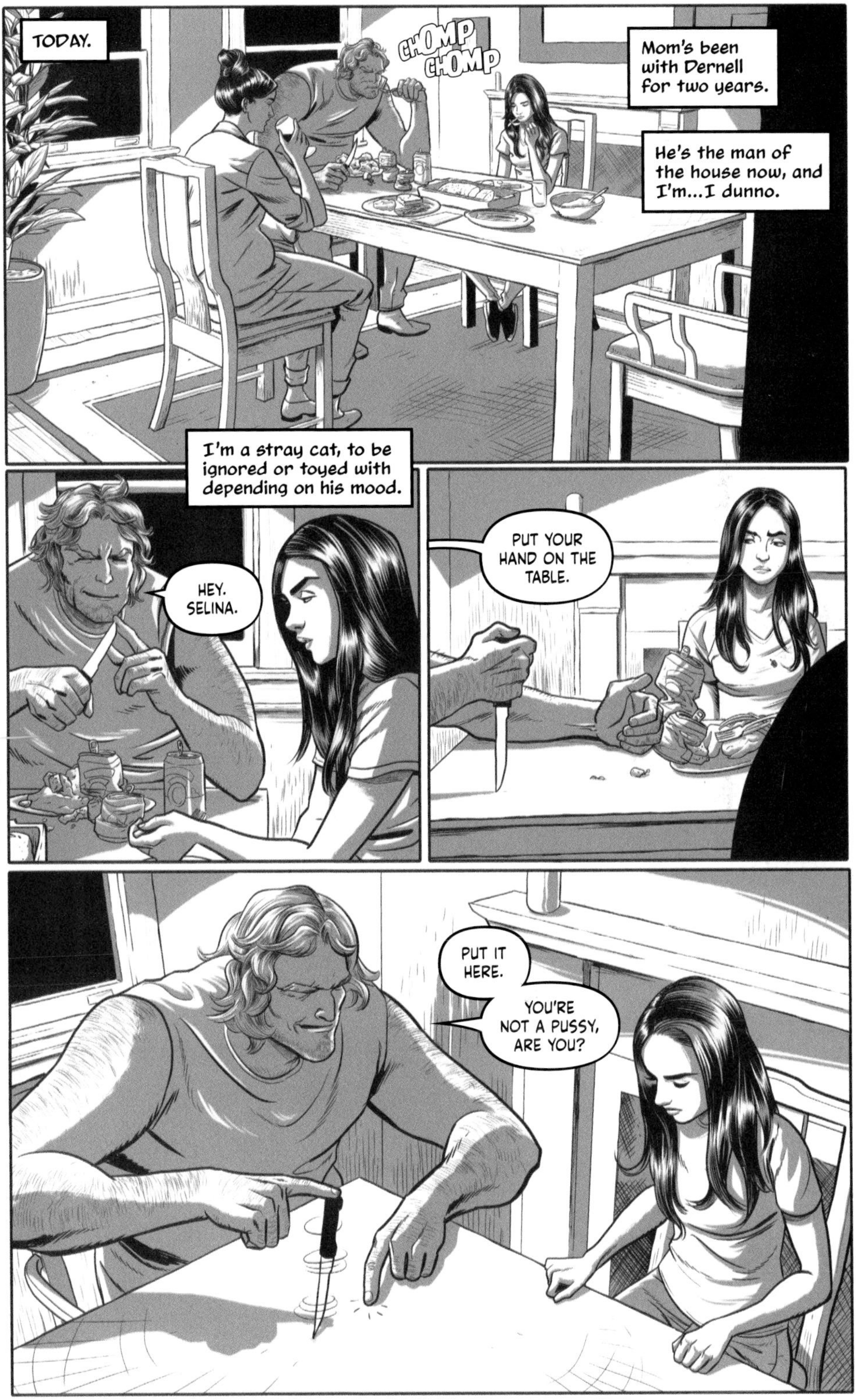
TODAY.
CHOMP CHOMP
Mom's been with Dernell for two years.
He's the man of the house now, and I'm...I dunno.
I'm a stray cat, to be ignored or toyed with depending on his mood.
HEY. SELINA.
PUT YOUR HAND ON THE TABLE.
PUT IT HERE.
YOU'RE NOT A PUSSY, ARE YOU?

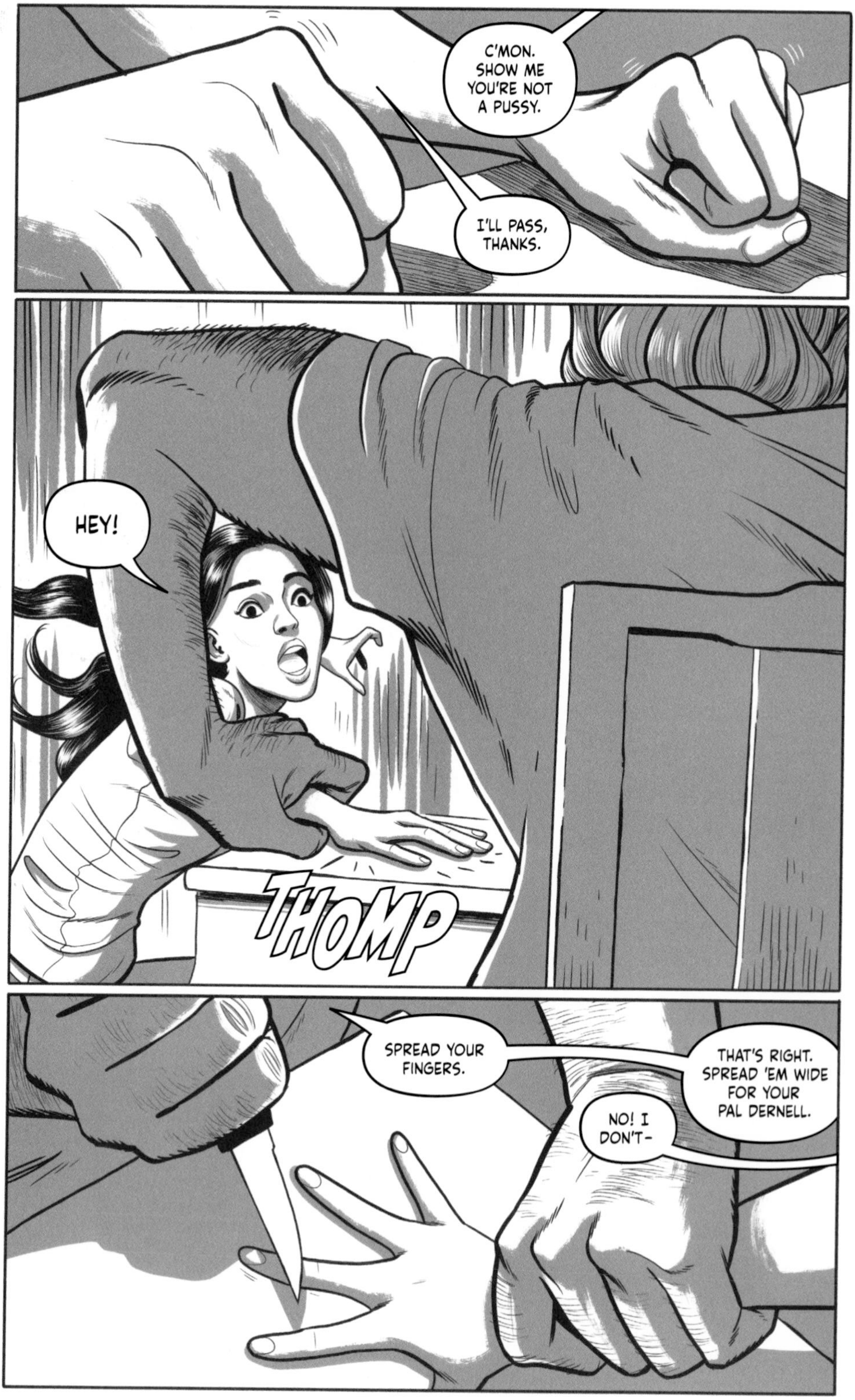
C'MON. SHOW ME YOU'RE NOT A PUSSY.
I'LL PASS, THANKS.
HEY!
THOMP
SPREAD YOUR FINGERS.
THAT'S RIGHT. SPREAD 'EM WIDE FOR YOUR PAL DERNELL.
NO! I DON'T-

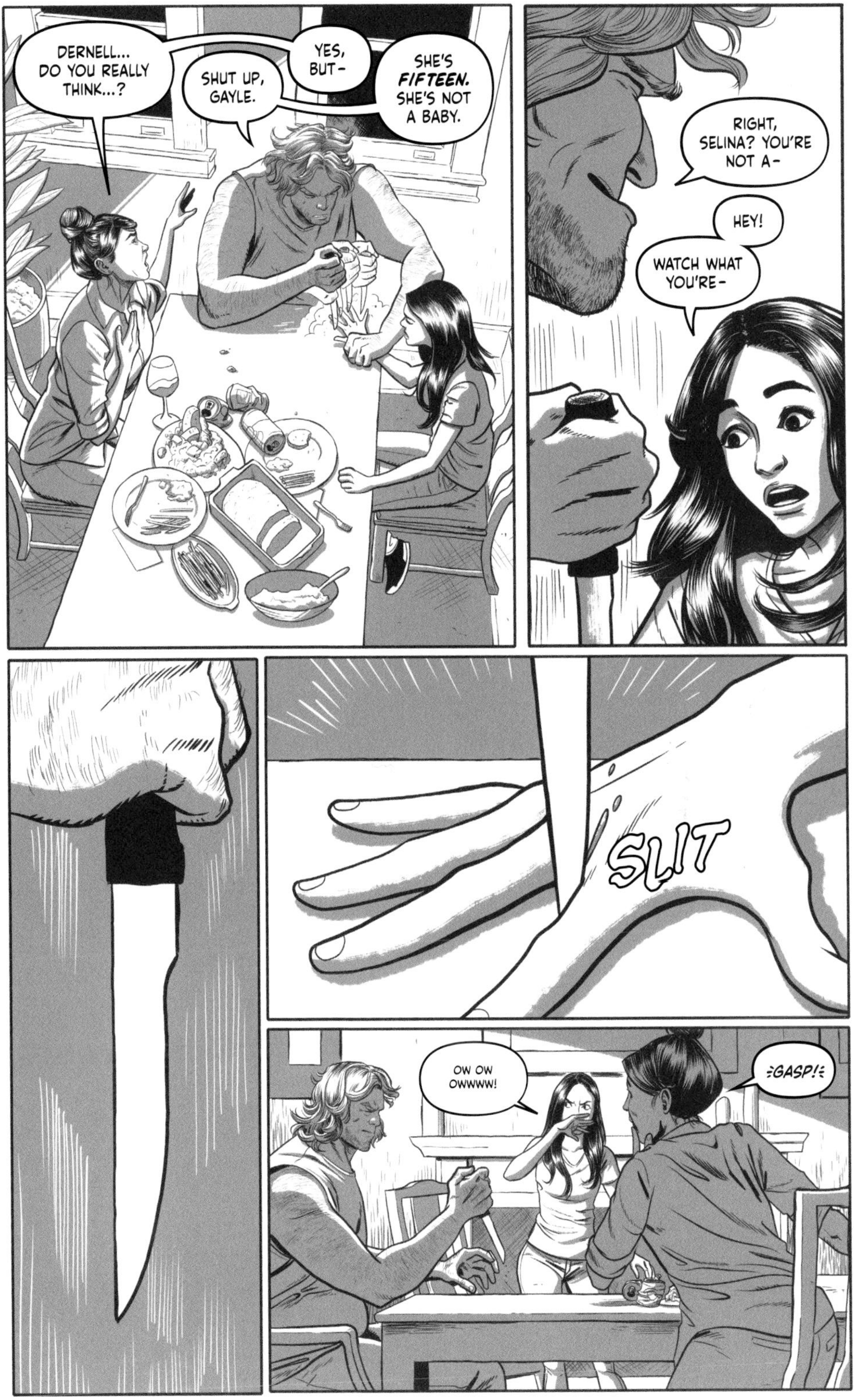
DERNELL... DO YOU REALLY THINK...?
YES, BUT-
SHUT UP, GAYLE.
SHE'S **FIFTEEN.** SHE'S NOT A BABY.
RIGHT, SELINA? YOU'RE NOT A-
HEY!
WATCH WHAT YOU'RE-
SLIT
OW OW OWWWW!
GASP!

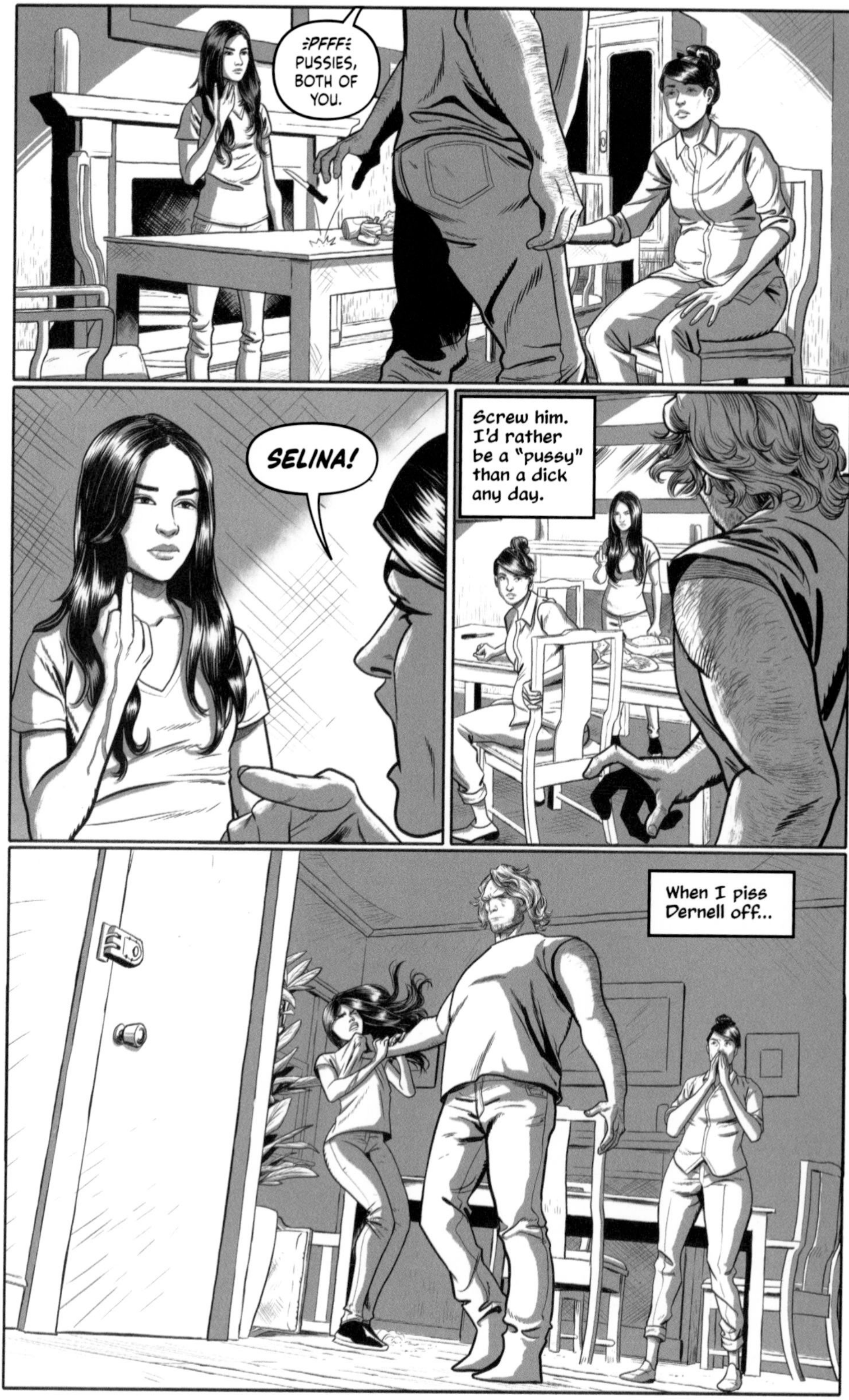

PFFF
PUSSIES, BOTH OF YOU.
SELINA!
Screw him. I'd rather be a "pussy" than a dick any day.
When I piss Dernell off...

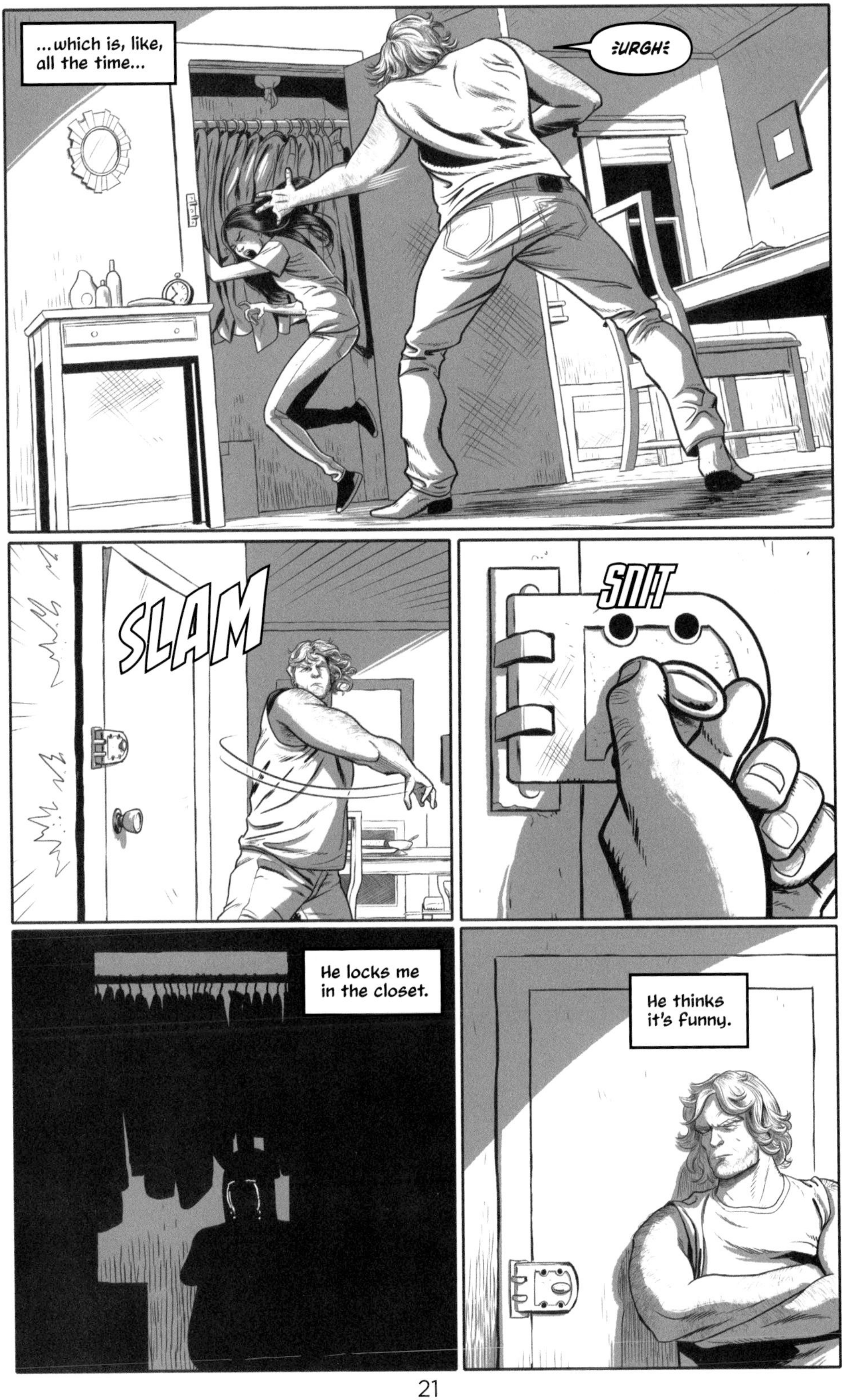
...which is, like, all the time...
URGH
SLAM
SNIT
He locks me in the closet.
He thinks it's funny.

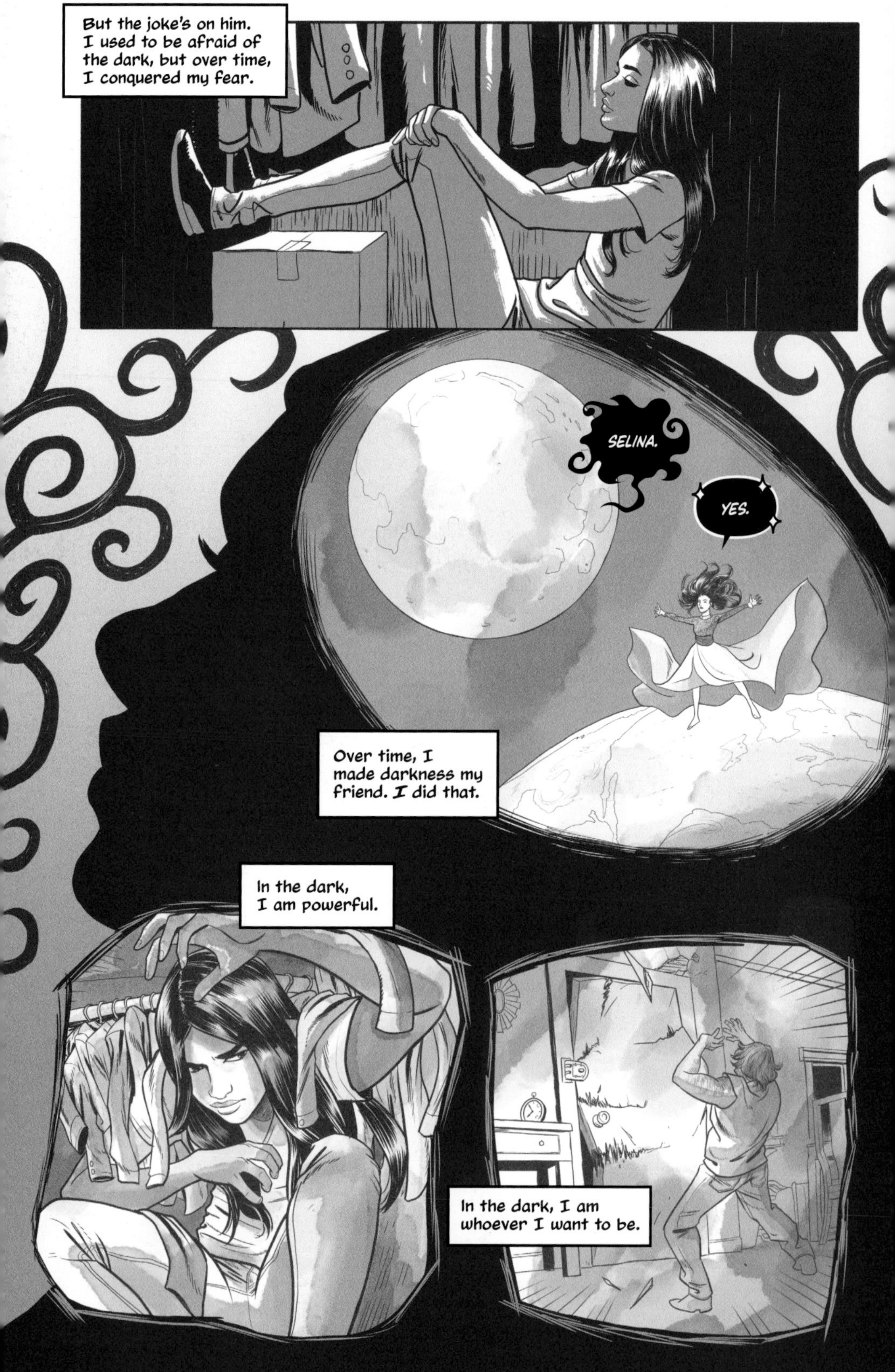
But the joke's on him. I used to be afraid of the dark, but over time, I conquered my fear.
SELINA.
YES.
Over time, I made darkness my friend. I did that.
In the dark, I am powerful.
In the dark, I am whoever I want to be.

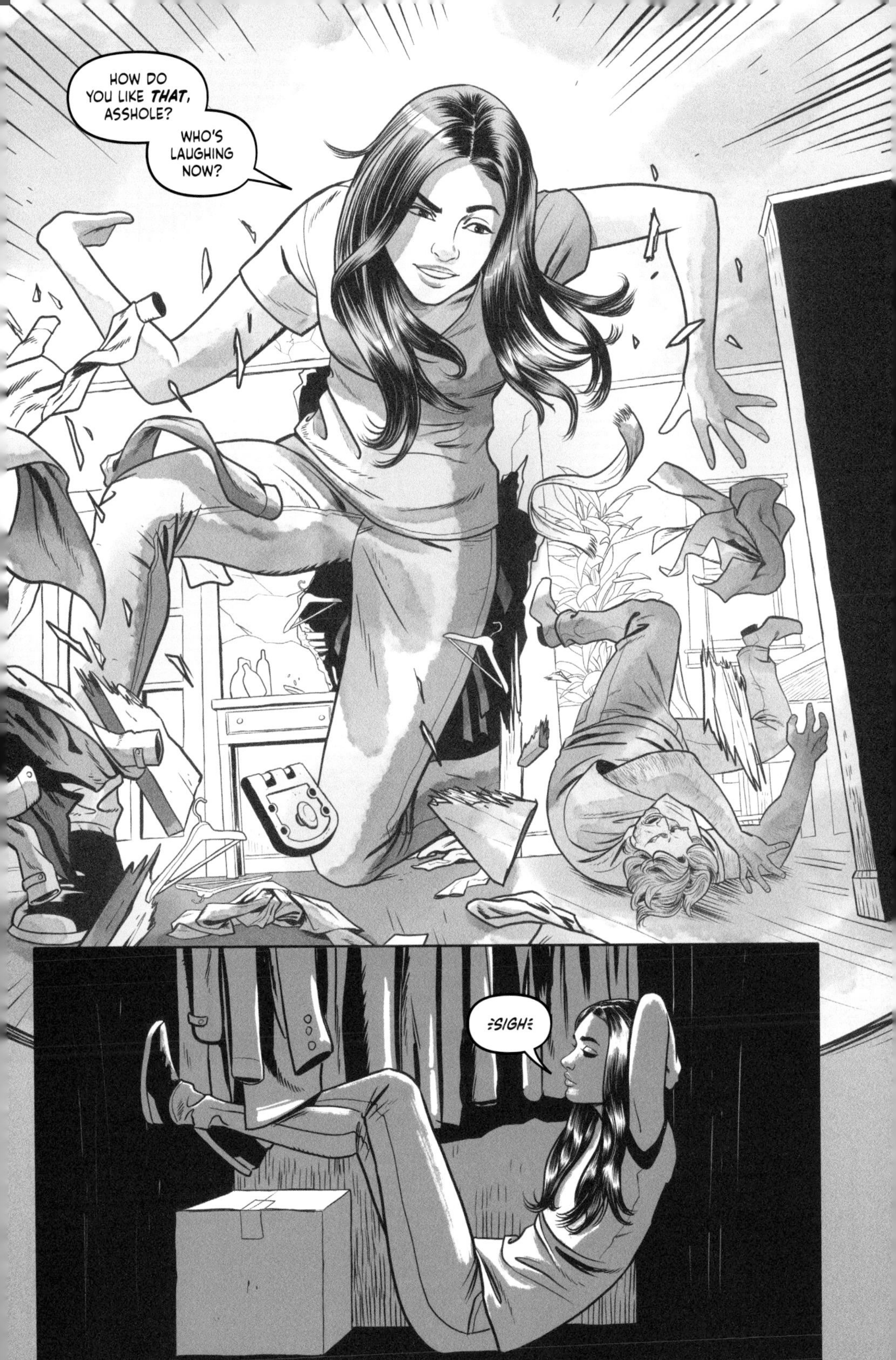
HOW DO YOU LIKE THAT, ASSHOLE?
WHO'S LAUGHING NOW?
SIGH

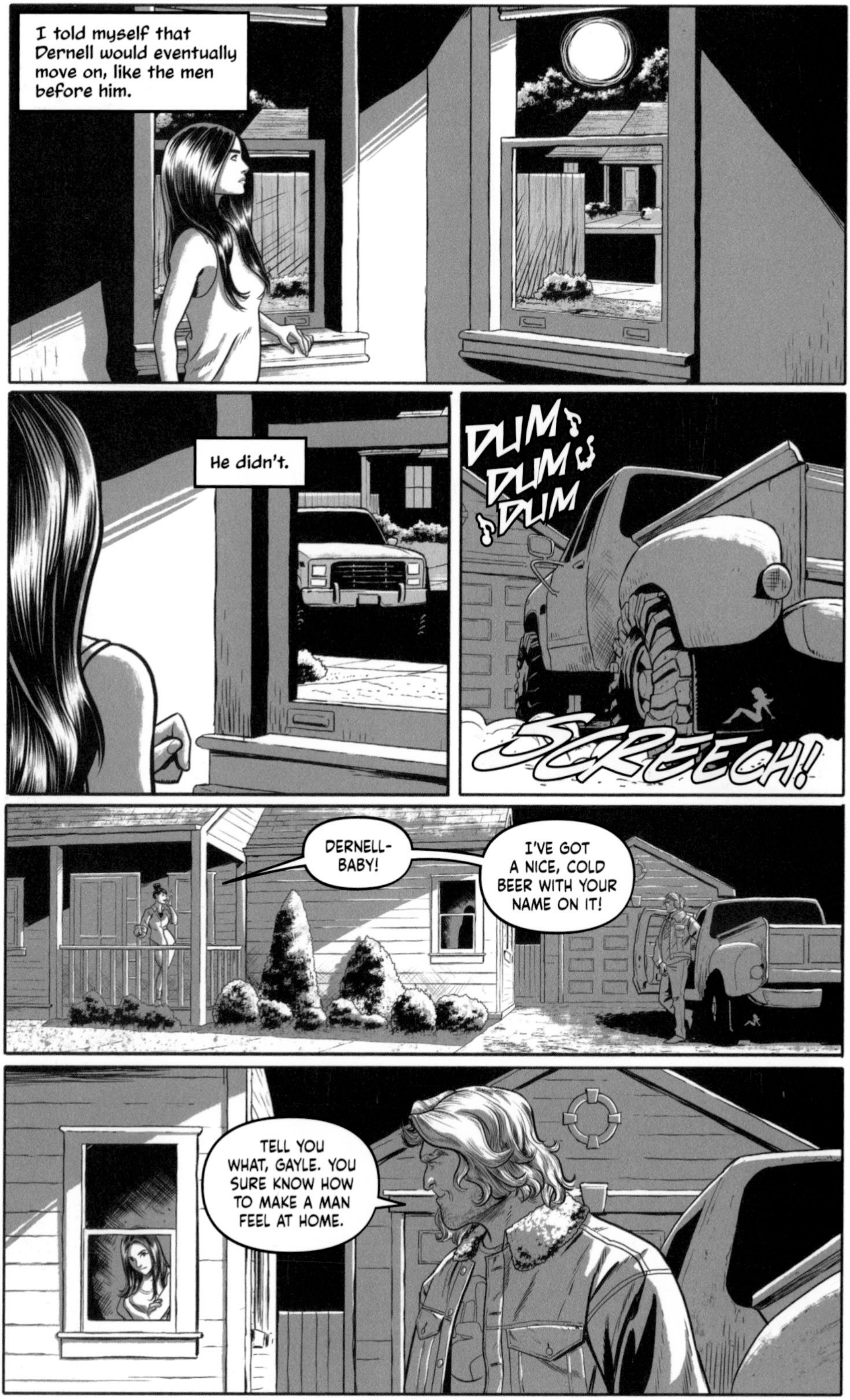
I told myself that Dernell would eventually move on, like the men before him.
He didn't.
DUM DUM DUM
SCREECH!
DERNELL-BABY!
I'VE GOT A NICE, COLD BEER WITH YOUR NAME ON IT!
TELL YOU WHAT, GAYLE. YOU SURE KNOW HOW TO MAKE A MAN FEEL AT HOME.

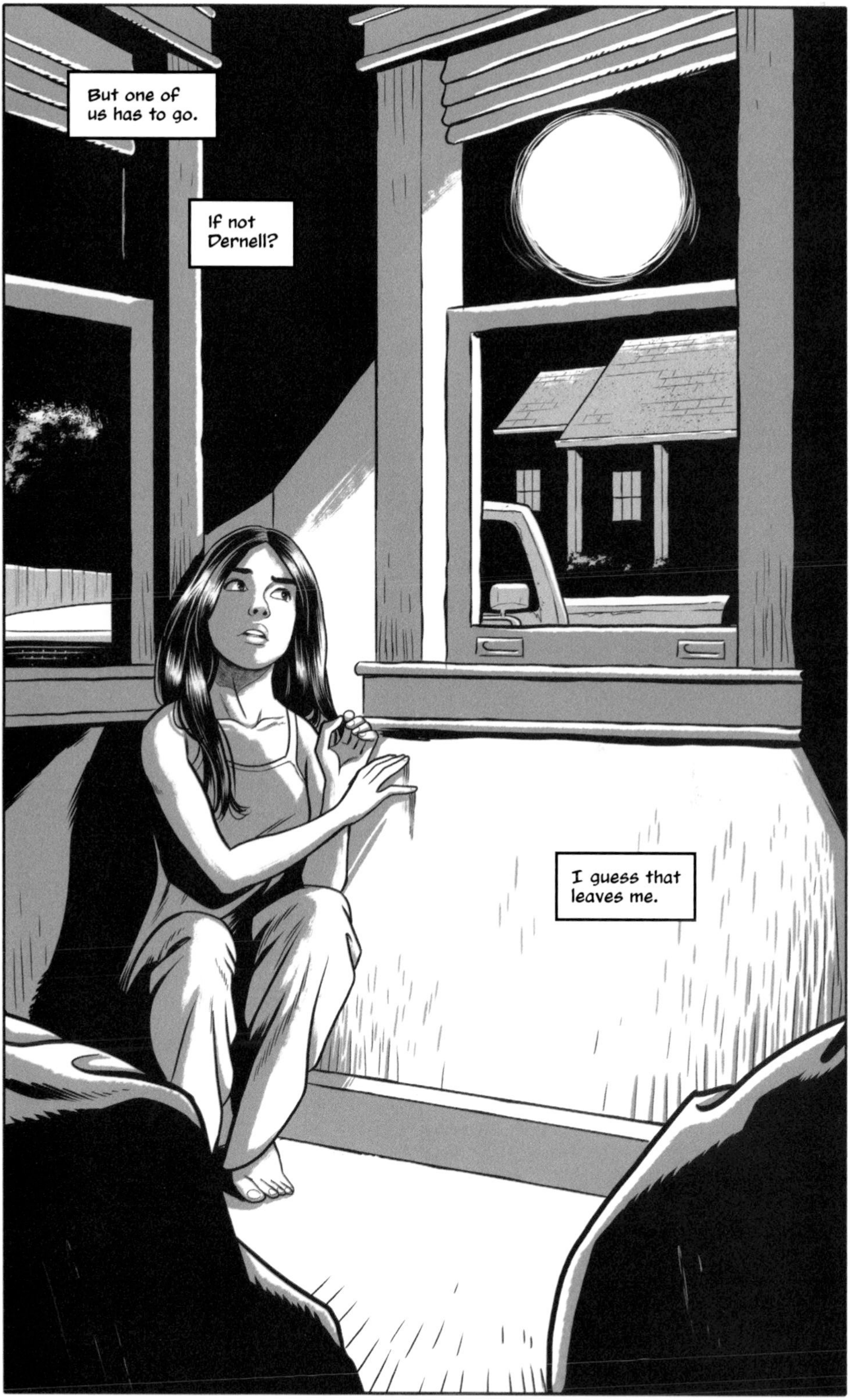
But one of us has to go.
If not Dernell?
I guess that leaves me.

ANOTHER BRICK IN THE WALL

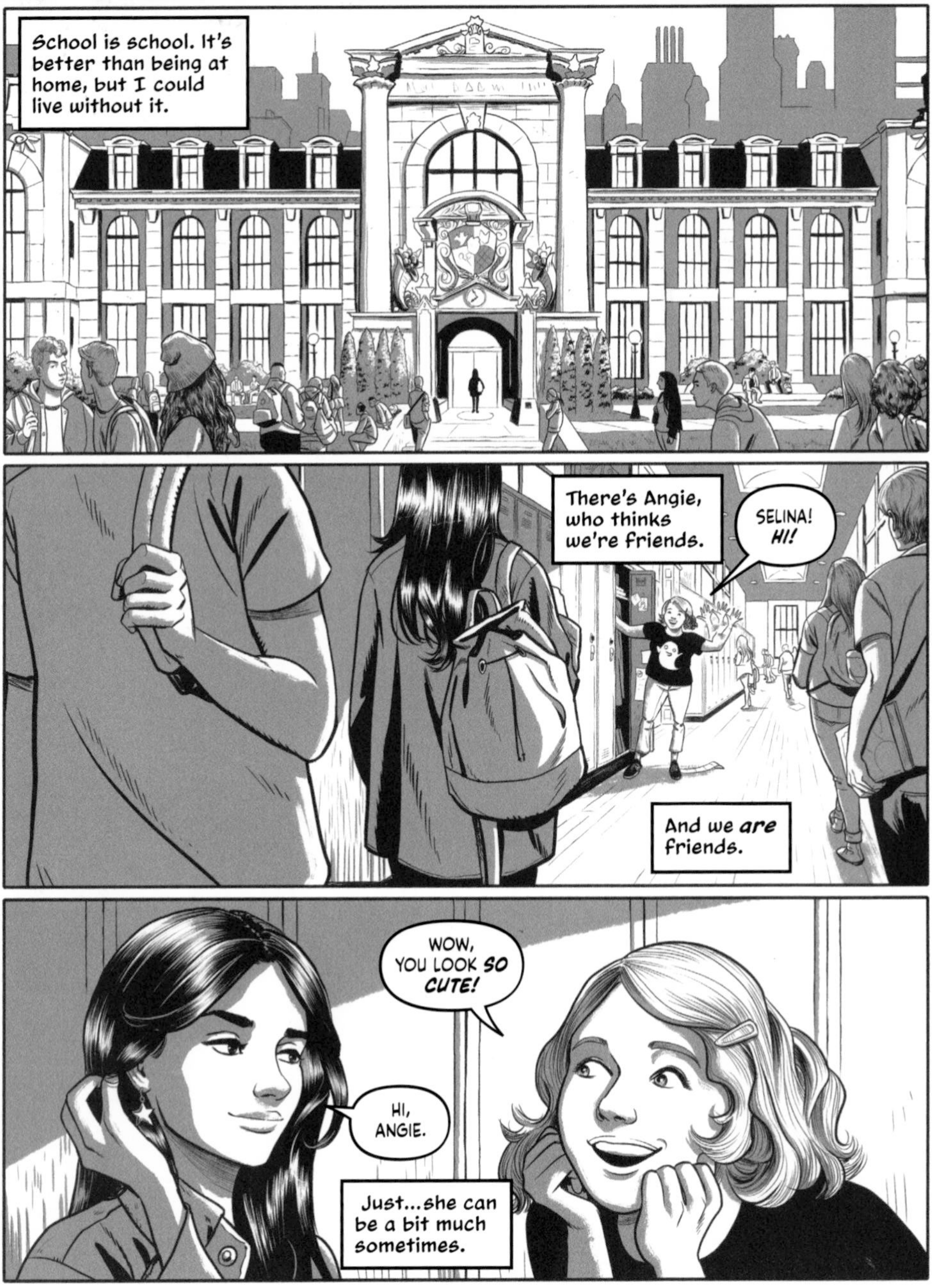
School is school. It's better than being at home, but I could live without it.
There's Angie, who thinks we're friends.
SELINA! *HI!*
And we *are* friends.
WOW, YOU LOOK ***SO CUTE!***
HI, ANGIE.
Just...she can be a bit much sometimes.

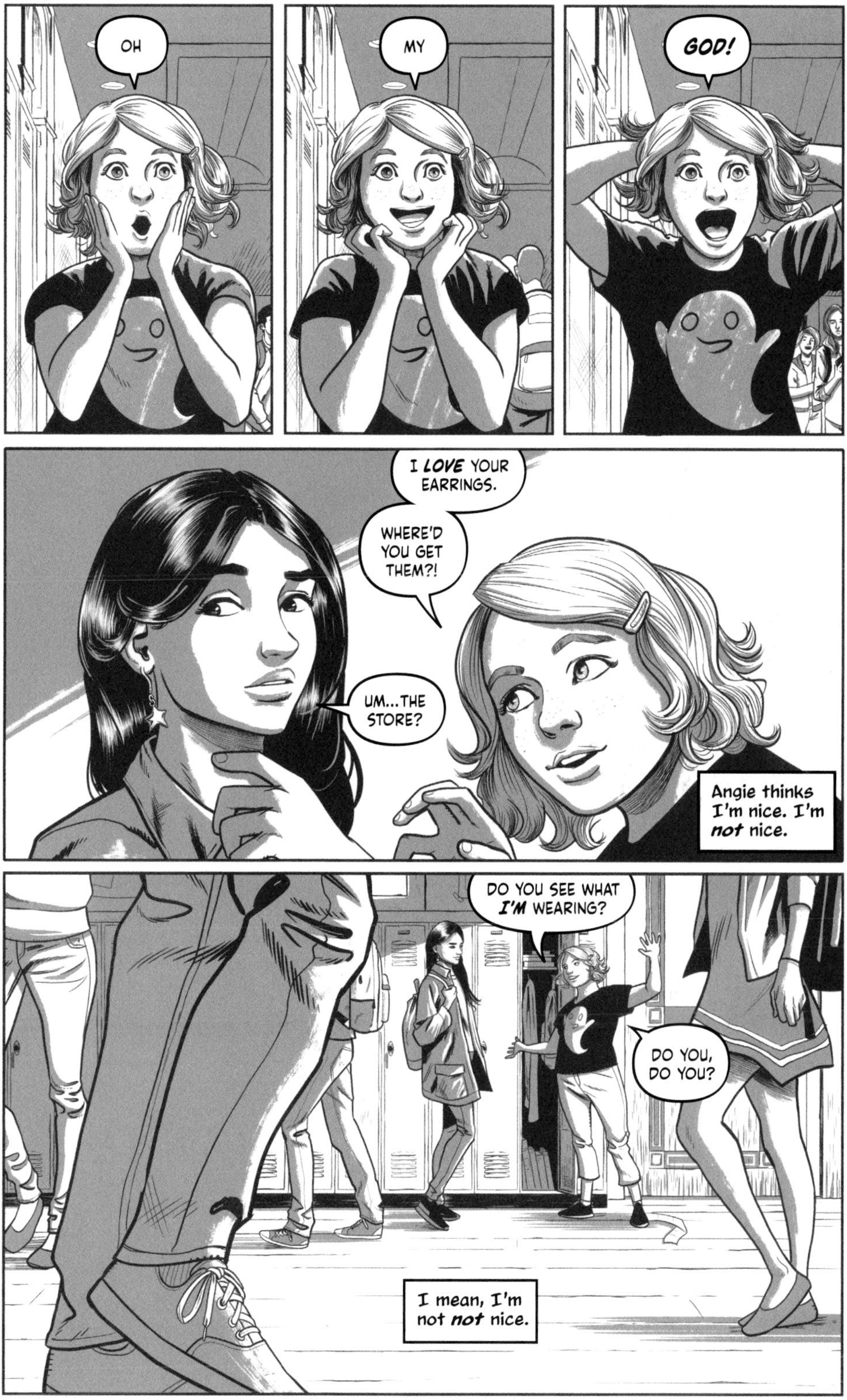
OH
MY
GOD!
I LOVE YOUR EARRINGS.
WHERE'D YOU GET THEM?!
UM...THE STORE?
Angie thinks I'm nice. I'm not nice.
DO YOU SEE WHAT I'M WEARING?
DO YOU, DO YOU?
I mean, I'm not not nice.

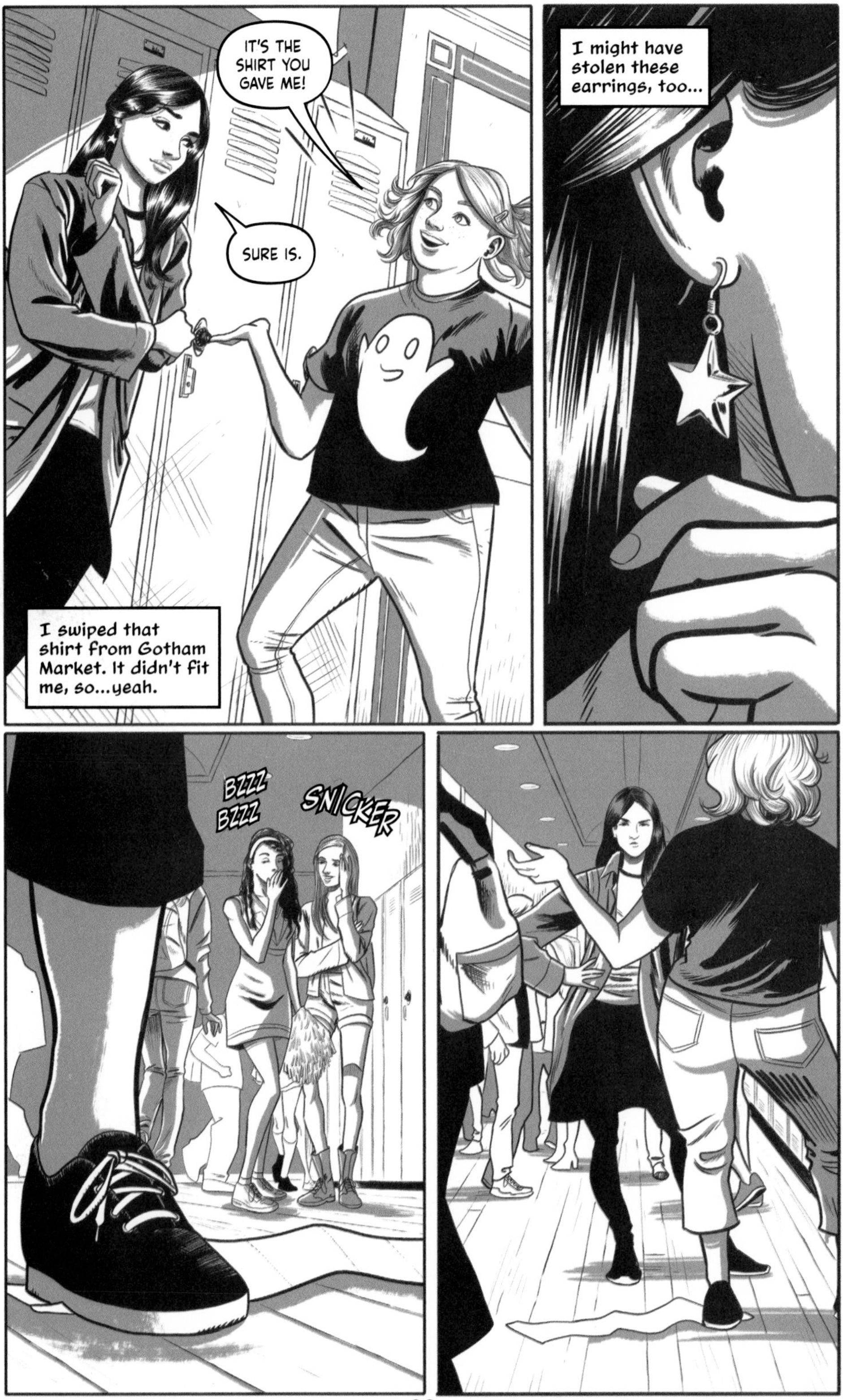
IT'S THE SHIRT YOU GAVE ME!
SURE IS.
I swiped that shirt from Gotham Market. It didn't fit me, so...yeah.
I might have stolen these earrings, too...
BZZZ BZZZ
SNICKER

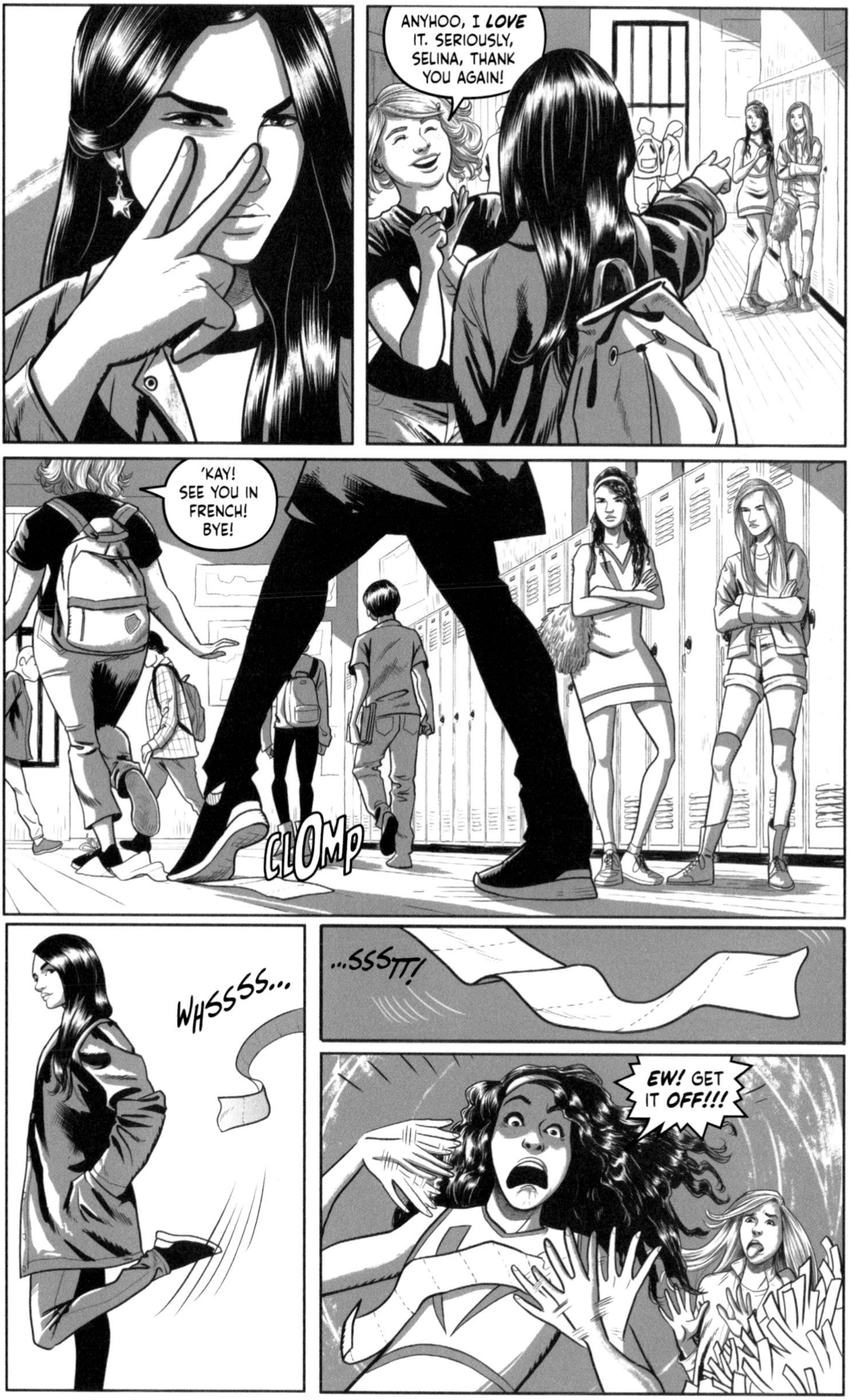
ANYHOO, I LOVE IT. SERIOUSLY, SELINA, THANK YOU AGAIN!
'KAY! SEE YOU IN FRENCH! BYE!
CLOMP
WHSSSS...
...SSSTT!
EW! GET IT OFF!!!

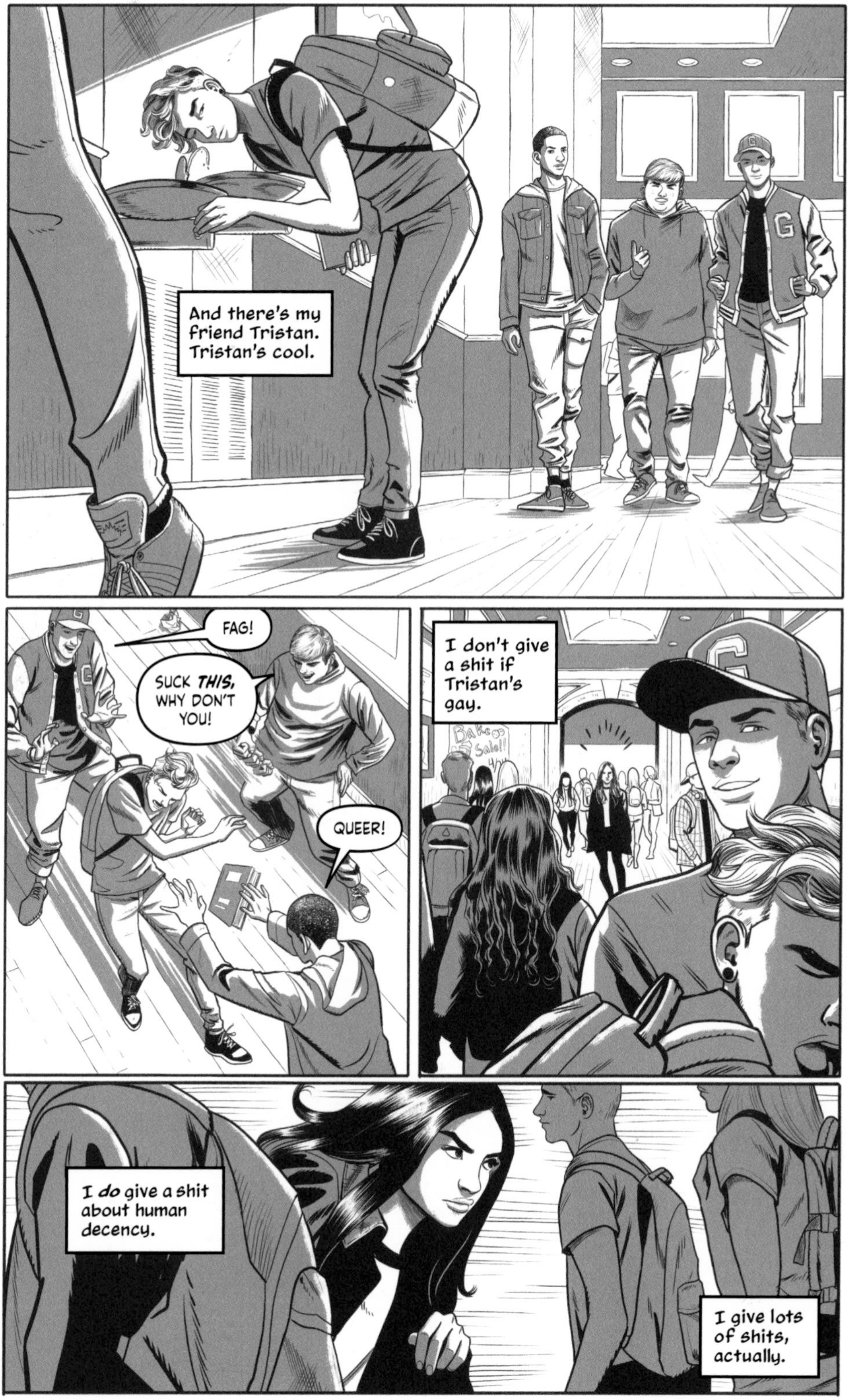
And there's my friend Tristan. Tristan's cool.
FAG!
SUCK *THIS,* WHY DON'T YOU!
QUEER!
I don't give a shit if Tristan's gay.
I *do* give a shit about human decency.
I give lots of shits, actually.

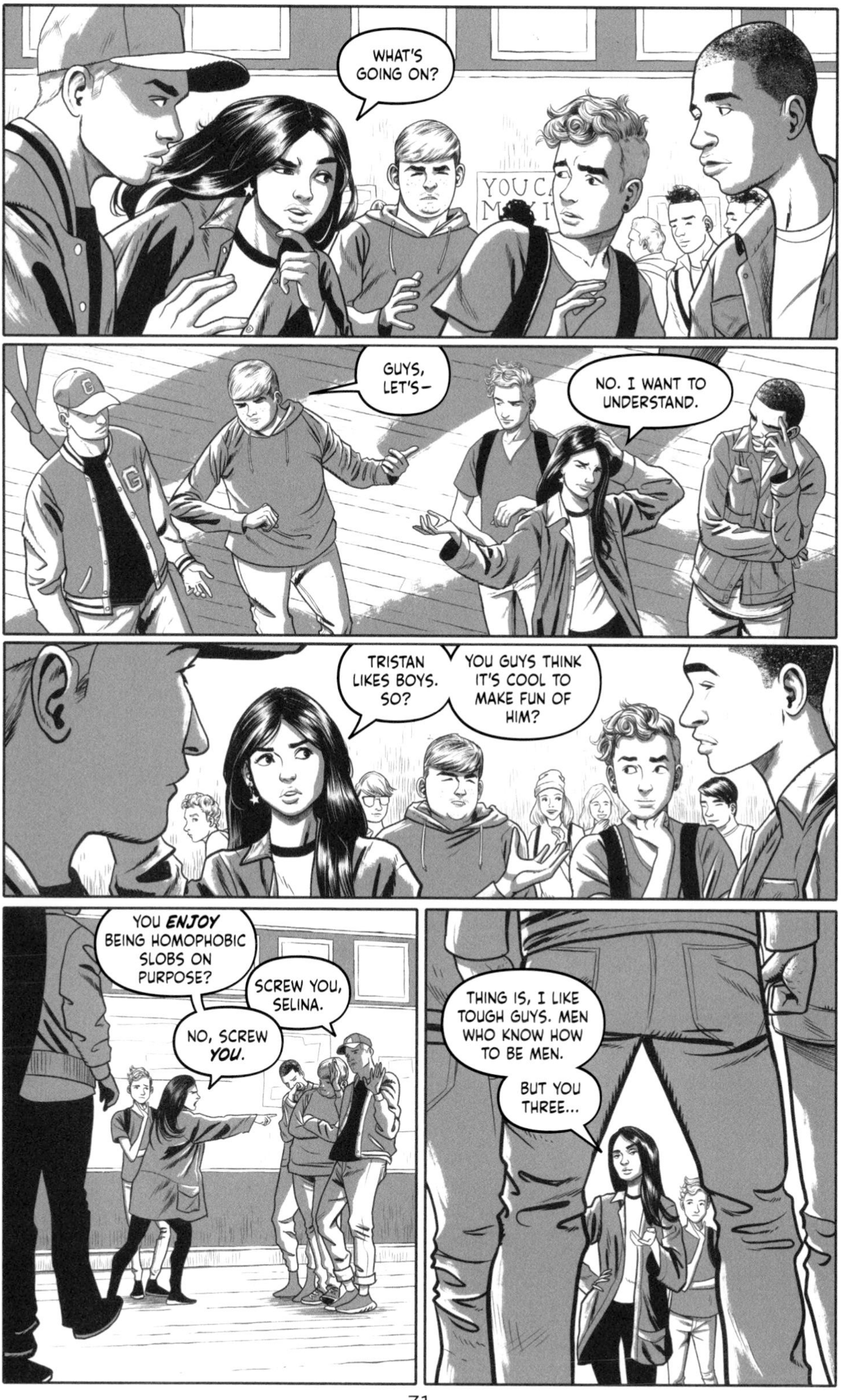
WHAT'S GOING ON?
GUYS, LET'S—
NO. I WANT TO UNDERSTAND.
TRISTAN LIKES BOYS. SO?
YOU GUYS THINK IT'S COOL TO MAKE FUN OF HIM?
YOU ***ENJOY*** BEING HOMOPHOBIC SLOBS ON PURPOSE?
SCREW YOU, SELINA.
NO, SCREW ***YOU***.
THING IS, I LIKE TOUGH GUYS. MEN WHO KNOW HOW TO BE MEN.
BUT YOU THREE...

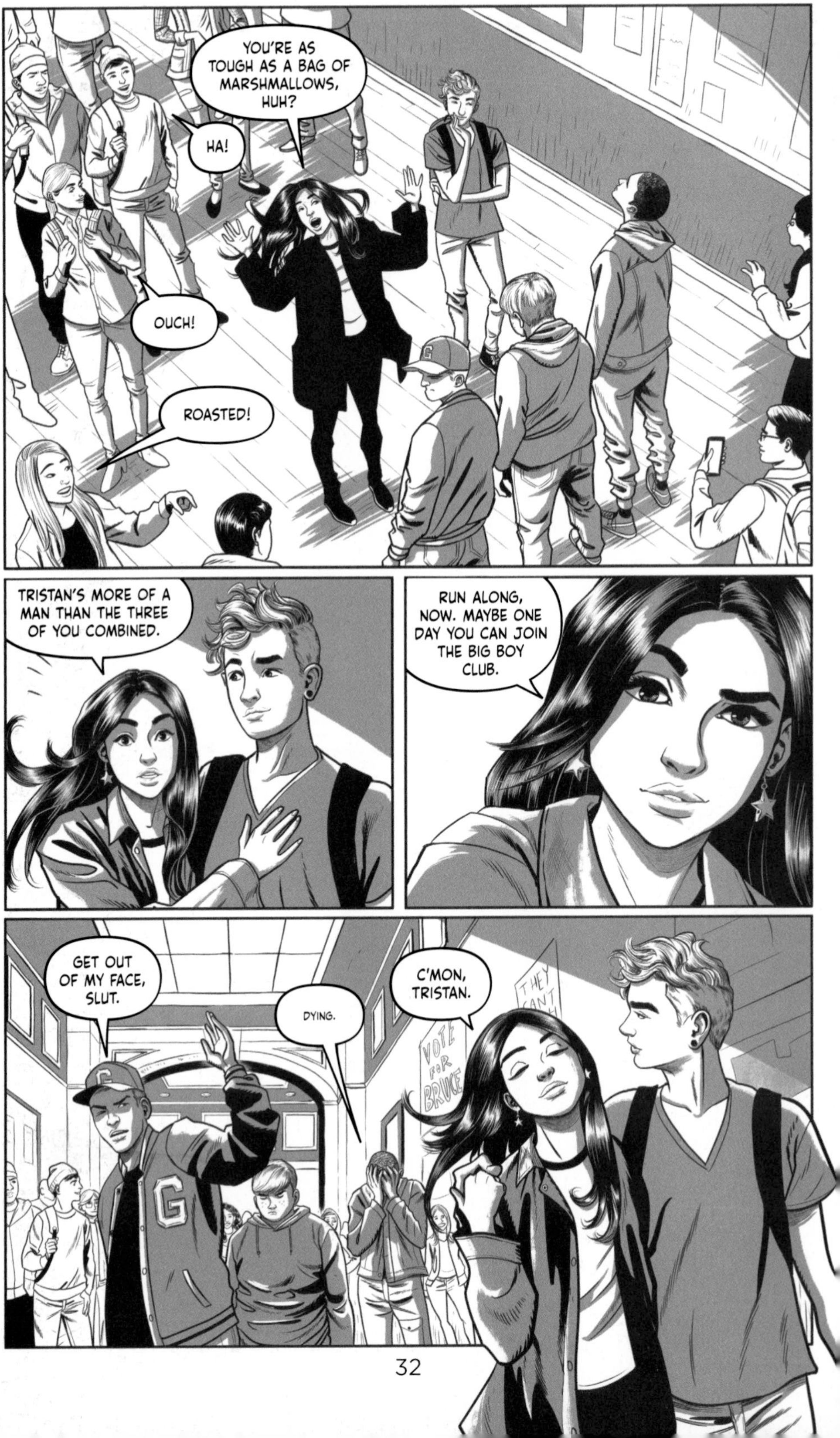
YOU'RE AS TOUGH AS A BAG OF MARSHMALLOWS, HUH?
HA!
OUCH!
ROASTED!
TRISTAN'S MORE OF A MAN THAN THE THREE OF YOU COMBINED.
RUN ALONG, NOW. MAYBE ONE DAY YOU CAN JOIN THE BIG BOY CLUB.
GET OUT OF MY FACE, SLUT.
DYING.
C'MON, TRISTAN.
VOTE FOR BRUCE

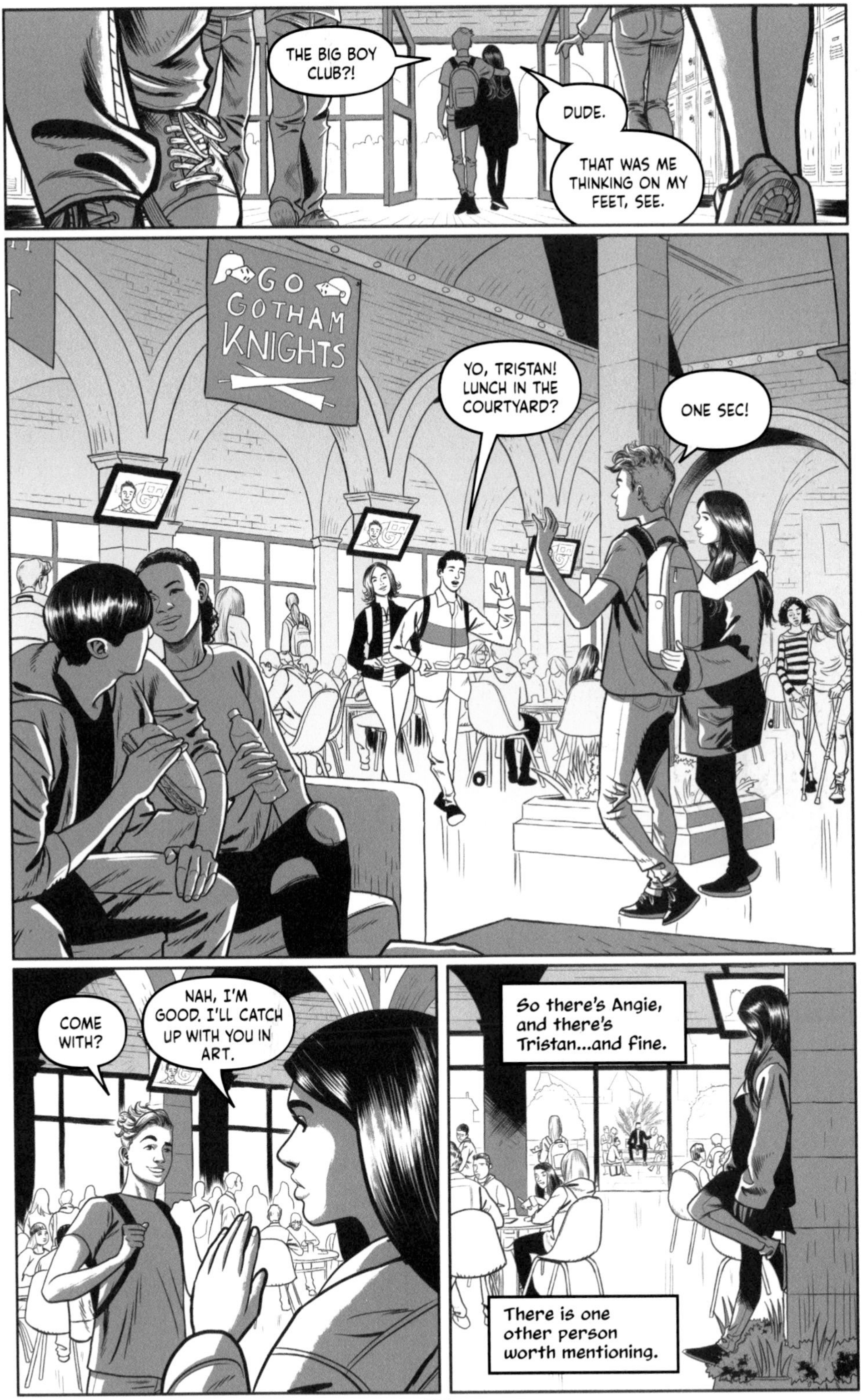
THE BIG BOY CLUB?!
DUDE.
THAT WAS ME THINKING ON MY FEET, SEE.
GO GOTHAM KNIGHTS
YO, TRISTAN! LUNCH IN THE COURTYARD?
ONE SEC!
COME WITH?
NAH, I'M GOOD. I'LL CATCH UP WITH YOU IN ART.
So there's Angie, and there's Tristan...and fine.
There is one other person worth mentioning.

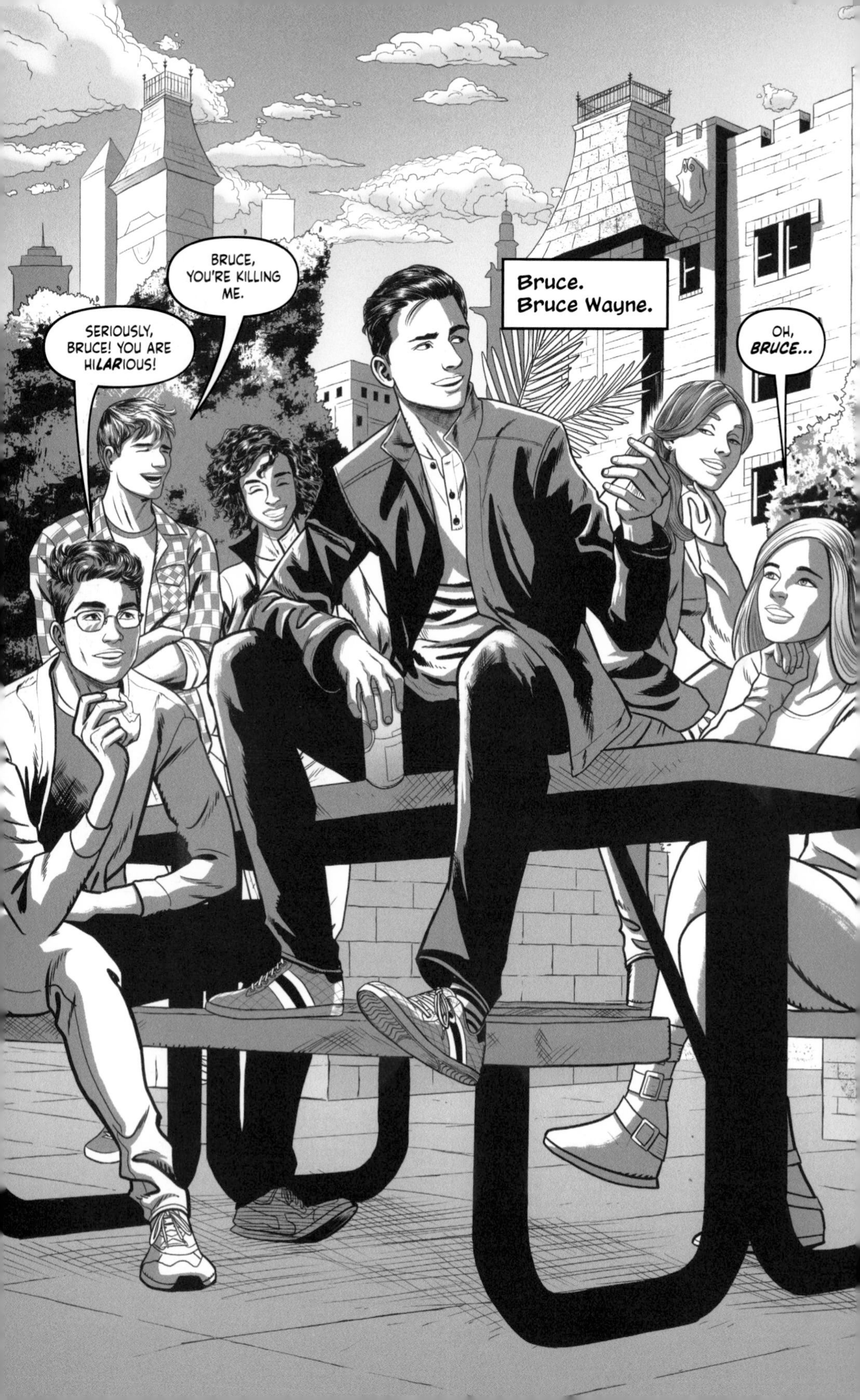
SERIOUSLY, BRUCE! YOU ARE HILARIOUS!
BRUCE, YOU'RE KILLING ME.
Bruce. Bruce Wayne.
OH, BRUCE...

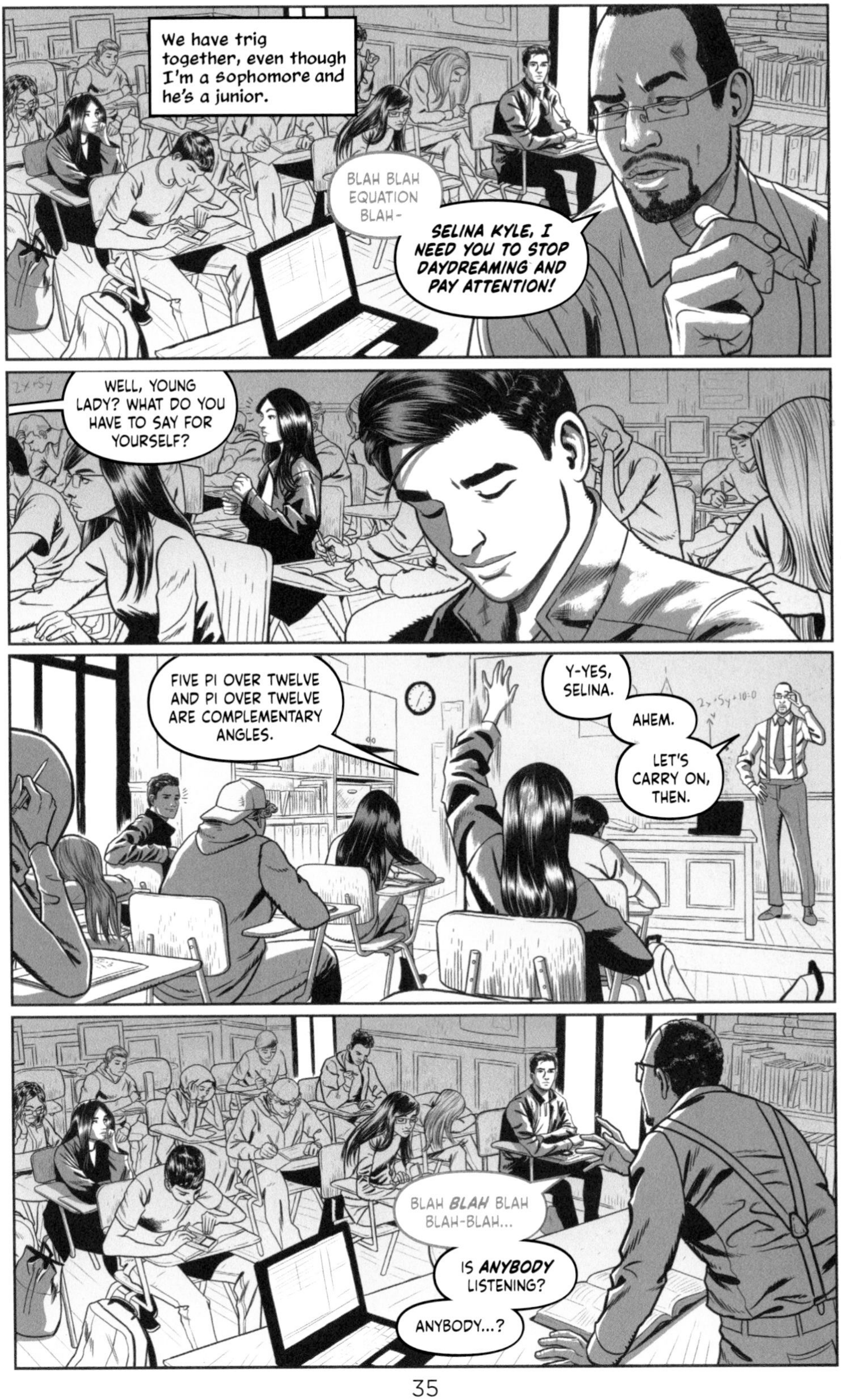
We have trig together, even though I'm a sophomore and he's a junior.
BLAH BLAH EQUATION BLAH-
SELINA KYLE, I NEED YOU TO STOP DAYDREAMING AND PAY ATTENTION!
WELL, YOUNG LADY? WHAT DO YOU HAVE TO SAY FOR YOURSELF?
FIVE PI OVER TWELVE AND PI OVER TWELVE ARE COMPLEMENTARY ANGLES.
Y-YES, SELINA.
AHEM.
LET'S CARRY ON, THEN.
BLAH BLAH BLAH BLAH-BLAH...
IS ANYBODY LISTENING?
ANYBODY...?

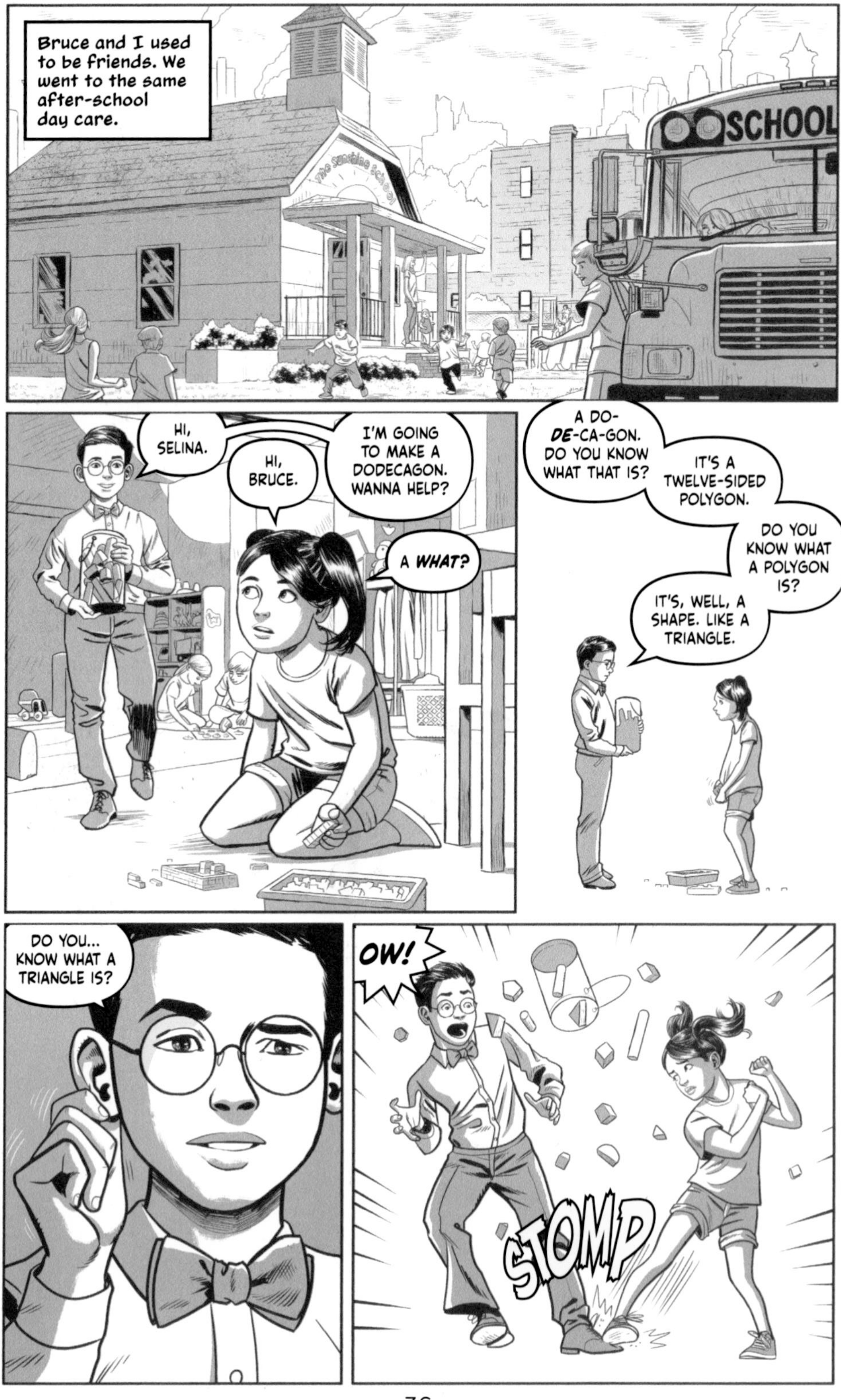
Bruce and I used to be friends. We went to the same after-school day care.
SCHOOL
HI, SELINA.
HI, BRUCE.
I'M GOING TO MAKE A DODECAGON. WANNA HELP?
A *WHAT?*
A DO-*DE*-CA-GON. DO YOU KNOW WHAT THAT IS?
IT'S A TWELVE-SIDED POLYGON.
DO YOU KNOW WHAT A POLYGON IS?
IT'S, WELL, A SHAPE. LIKE A TRIANGLE.
DO YOU... KNOW WHAT A TRIANGLE IS?
OW!
STOMP

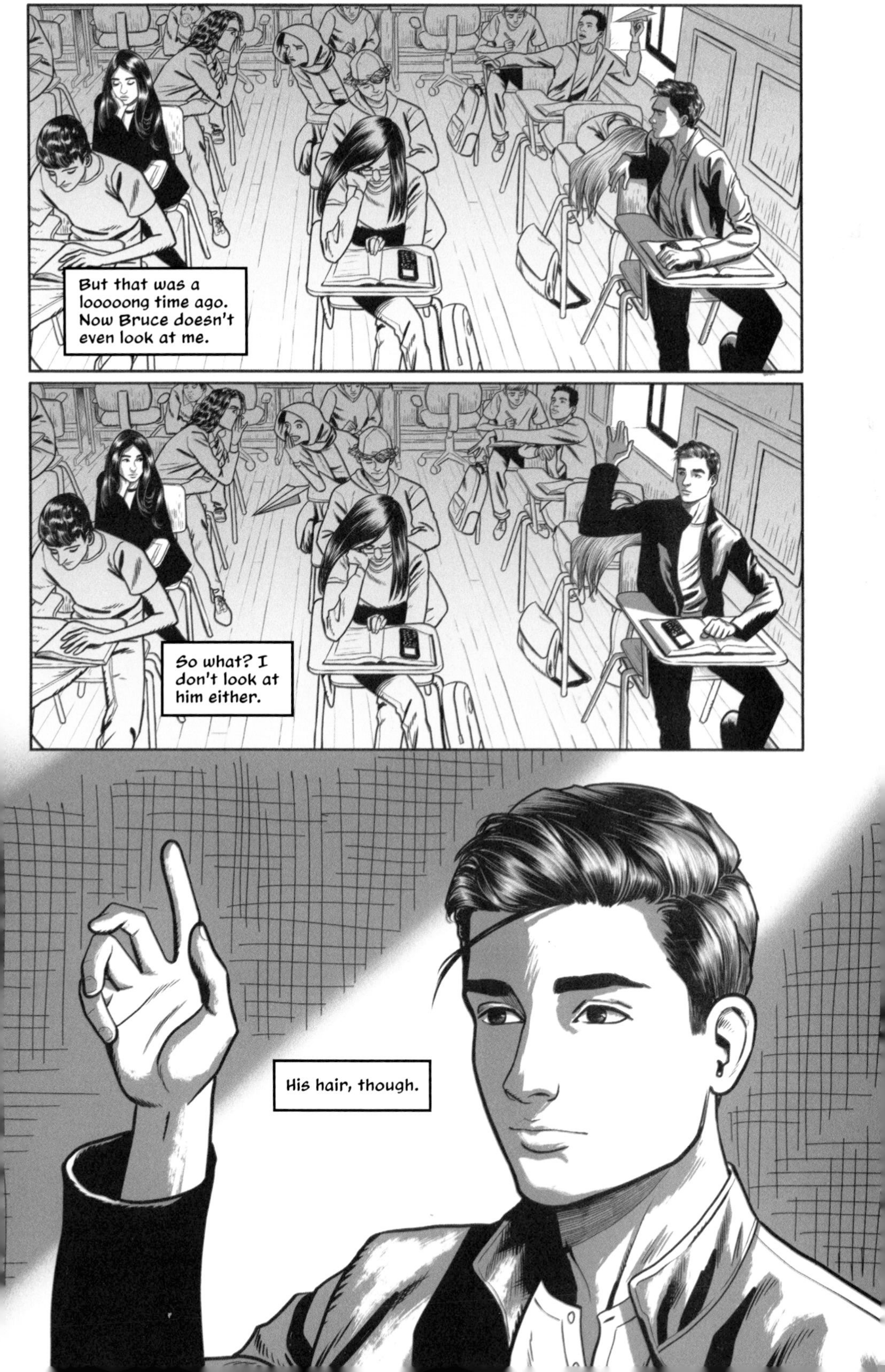
But that was a loooooong time ago. Now Bruce doesn't even look at me.
So what? I don't look at him either.
His hair, though.

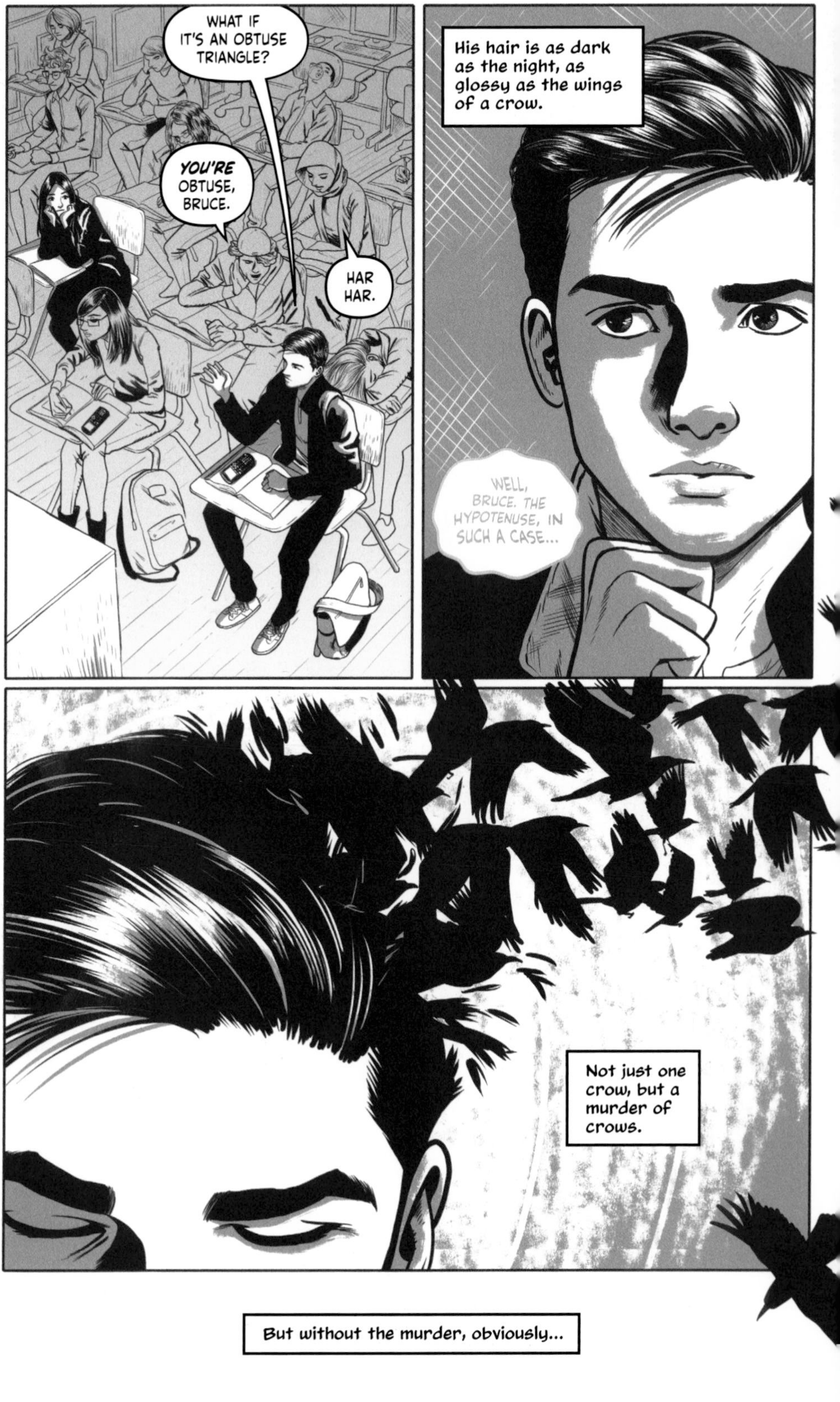
WHAT IF IT'S AN OBTUSE TRIANGLE?
YOU'RE OBTUSE, BRUCE.
HAR HAR.
His hair is as dark as the night, as glossy as the wings of a crow.
WELL, BRUCE. THE HYPOTENUSE, IN SUCH A CASE...
Not just one crow, but a murder of crows.
But without the murder, obviously...

DOG EAT DOG WORLD

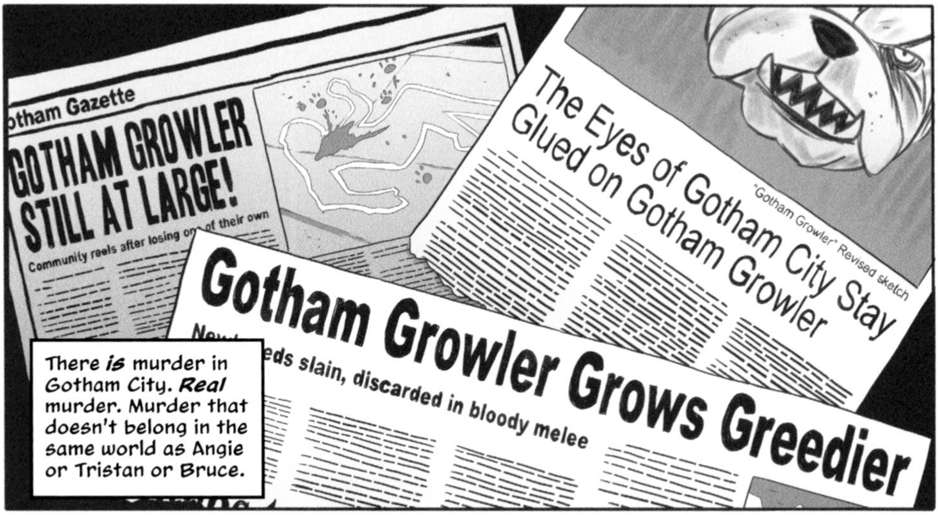
Gotham Gazette
GOTHAM GROWLER STILL AT LARGE!
Community reels after losing one of their own
The Eyes of Gotham City Stay Glued on Gotham Growler
"Gotham Growler" Revised sketch
Gotham Growler Grows Greedier
eds slain, discarded in bloody melee
There *is* murder in Gotham City. *Real* murder. Murder that doesn't belong in the same world as Angie or Tristan or Bruce.

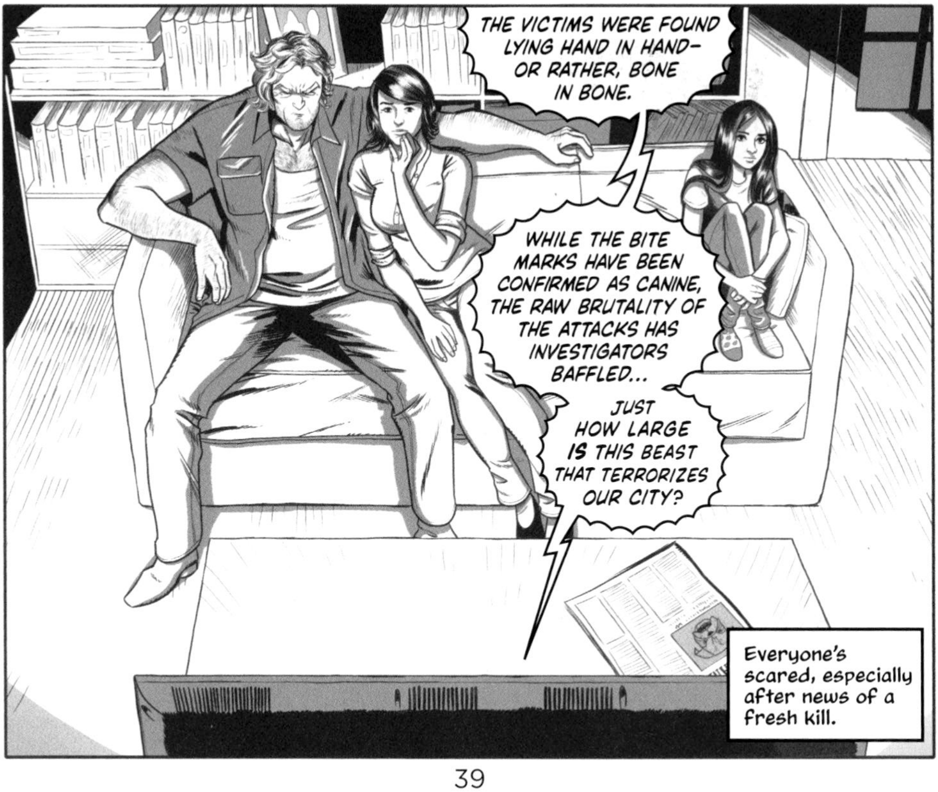
THE VICTIMS WERE FOUND LYING HAND IN HAND— OR RATHER, BONE IN BONE.
WHILE THE BITE MARKS HAVE BEEN CONFIRMED AS CANINE, THE RAW BRUTALITY OF THE ATTACKS HAS INVESTIGATORS BAFFLED...
JUST HOW LARGE *IS* THIS BEAST THAT TERRORIZES OUR CITY?
Everyone's scared, especially after news of a fresh kill.

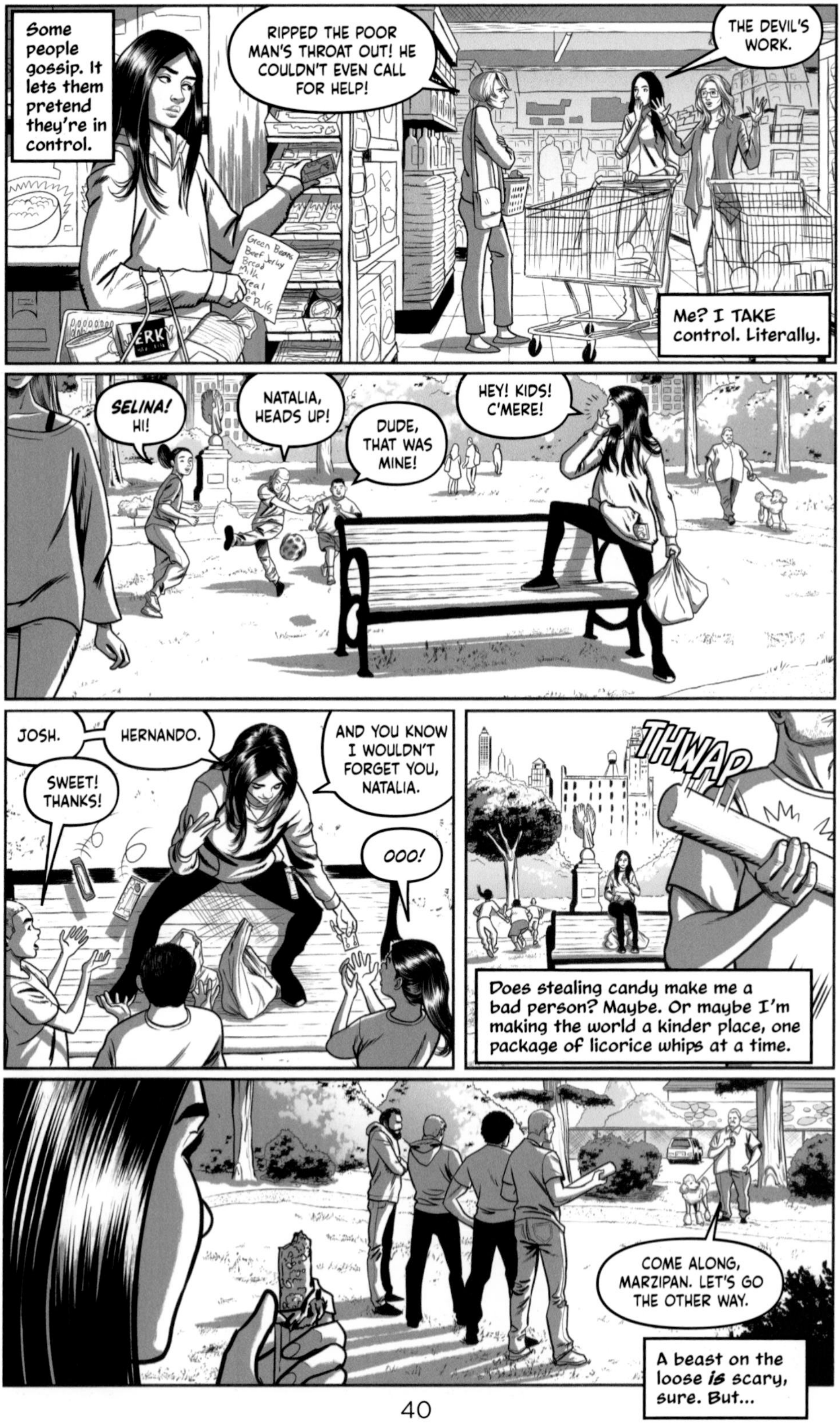
Some people gossip. It lets them pretend they're in control.
RIPPED THE POOR MAN'S THROAT OUT! HE COULDN'T EVEN CALL FOR HELP!
THE DEVIL'S WORK.
Green Beans
Beef Jerky
Bread
Milk
Me? I TAKE control. Literally.
SELINA! HI!
NATALIA, HEADS UP!
DUDE, THAT WAS MINE!
HEY! KIDS! C'MERE!
JOSH.
HERNANDO.
SWEET! THANKS!
AND YOU KNOW I WOULDN'T FORGET YOU, NATALIA.
OOO!
THWAP
Does stealing candy make me a bad person? Maybe. Or maybe I'm making the world a kinder place, one package of licorice whips at a time.
COME ALONG, MARZIPAN. LET'S GO THE OTHER WAY.
A beast on the loose *is* scary, sure. But...

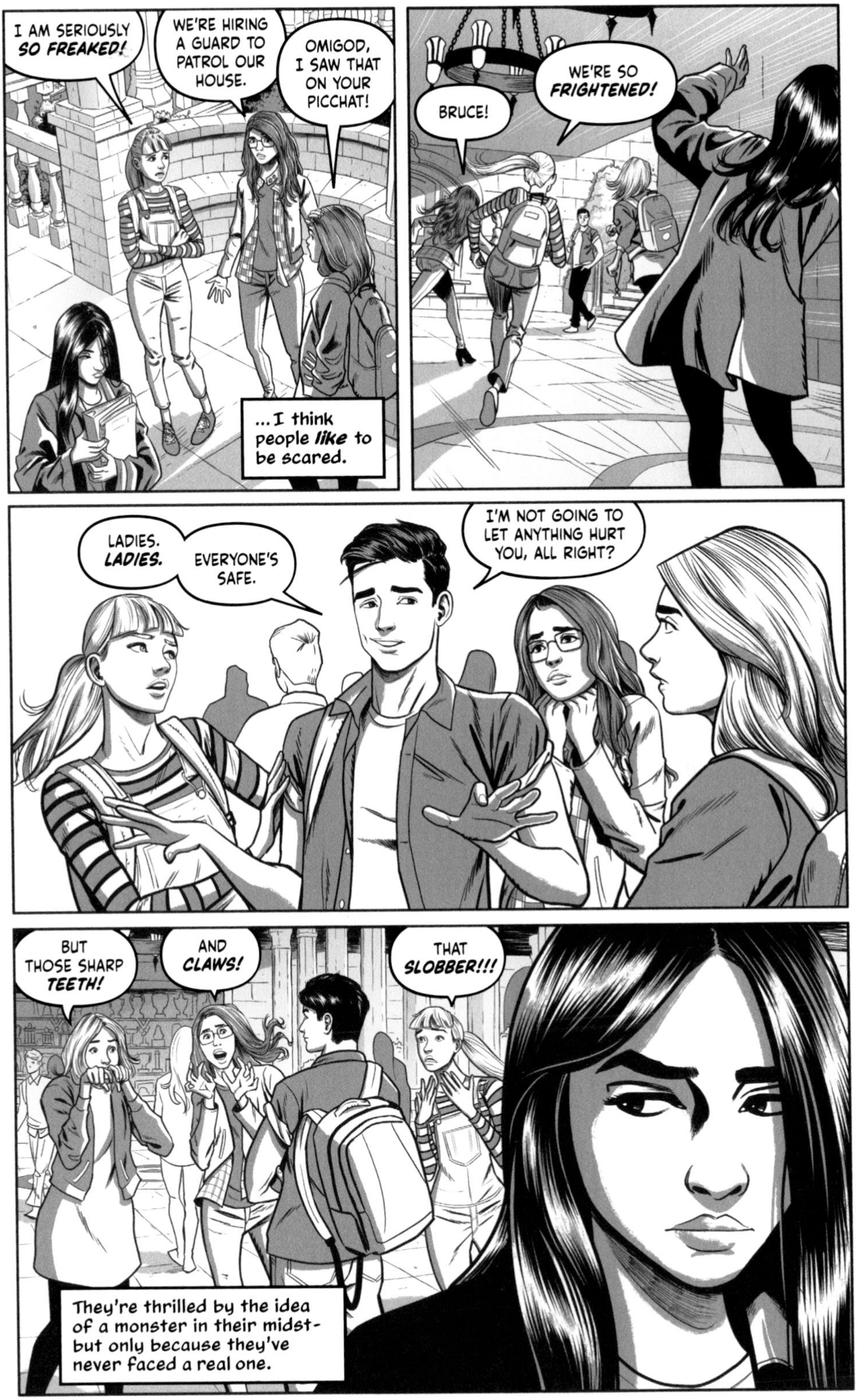
I AM SERIOUSLY SO FREAKED!
WE'RE HIRING A GUARD TO PATROL OUR HOUSE.
OMIGOD, I SAW THAT ON YOUR PICCHAT!
...I think people like to be scared.
BRUCE!
WE'RE SO FRIGHTENED!
LADIES. LADIES.
EVERYONE'S SAFE.
I'M NOT GOING TO LET ANYTHING HURT YOU, ALL RIGHT?
BUT THOSE SHARP TEETH!
AND CLAWS!
THAT SLOBBER!!!
They're thrilled by the idea of a monster in their midst-but only because they've never faced a real one.

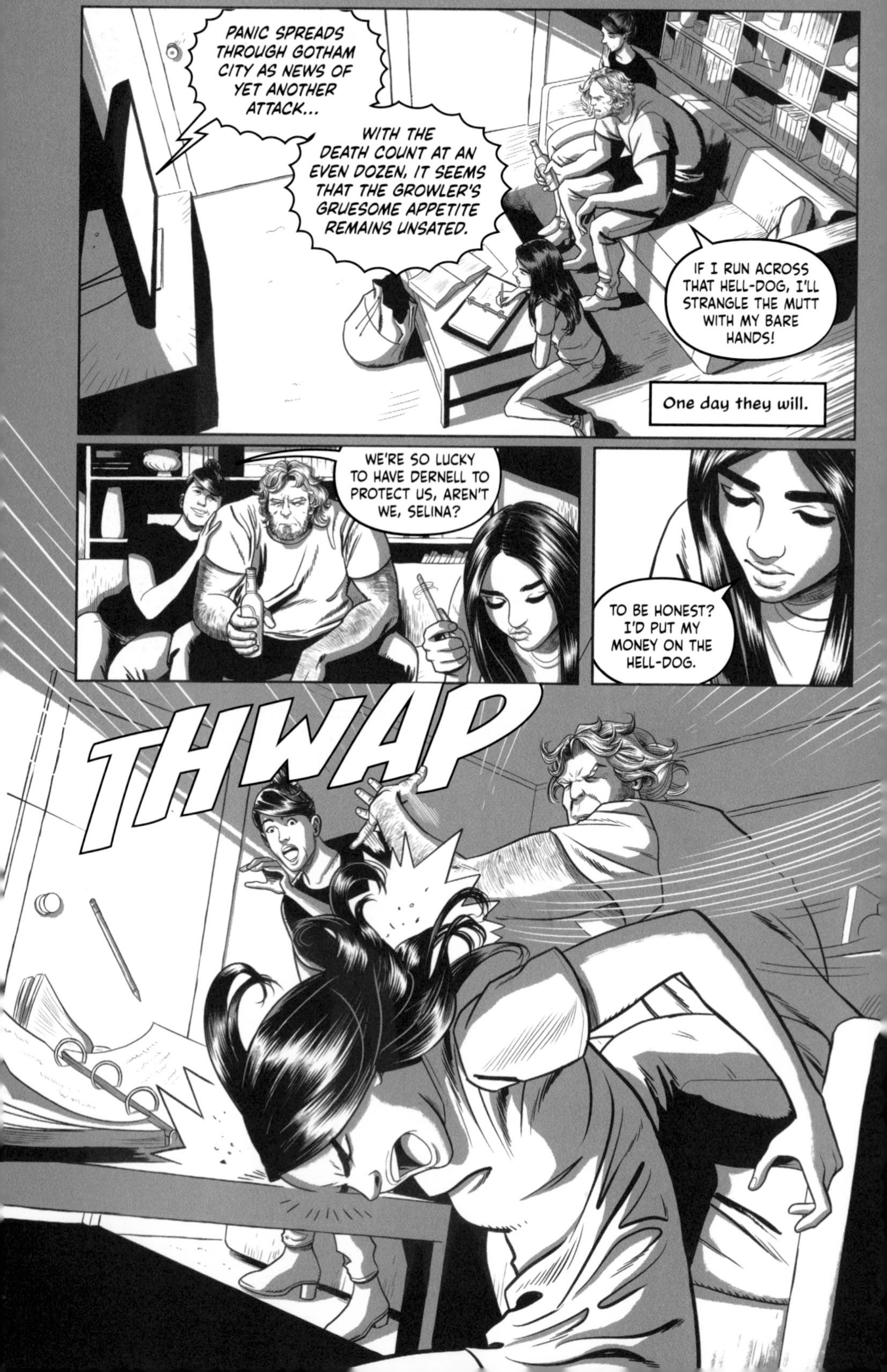
PANIC SPREADS THROUGH GOTHAM CITY AS NEWS OF YET ANOTHER ATTACK...
WITH THE DEATH COUNT AT AN EVEN DOZEN, IT SEEMS THAT THE GROWLER'S GRUESOME APPETITE REMAINS UNSATED.
IF I RUN ACROSS THAT HELL-DOG, I'LL STRANGLE THE MUTT WITH MY BARE HANDS!
One day they will.
WE'RE SO LUCKY TO HAVE DERNELL TO PROTECT US, AREN'T WE, SELINA?
TO BE HONEST? I'D PUT MY MONEY ON THE HELL-DOG.
THWAP

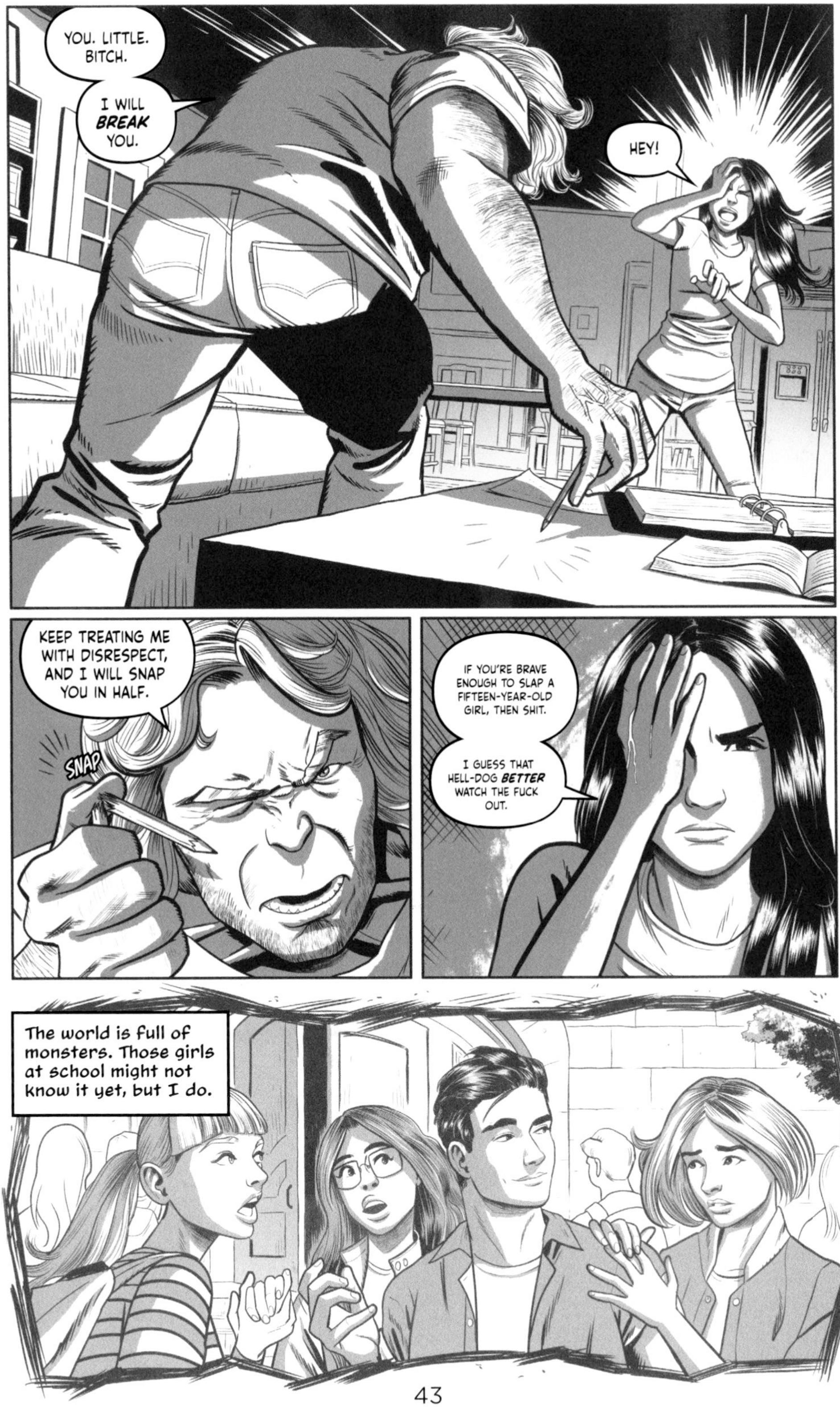
YOU. LITTLE. BITCH.
I WILL BREAK YOU.
HEY!
KEEP TREATING ME WITH DISRESPECT, AND I WILL SNAP YOU IN HALF.
SNAP
IF YOU'RE BRAVE ENOUGH TO SLAP A FIFTEEN-YEAR-OLD GIRL, THEN SHIT.
I GUESS THAT HELL-DOG BETTER WATCH THE FUCK OUT.
The world is full of monsters. Those girls at school might not know it yet, but I do.

ONE PURRRFECT MOMENT

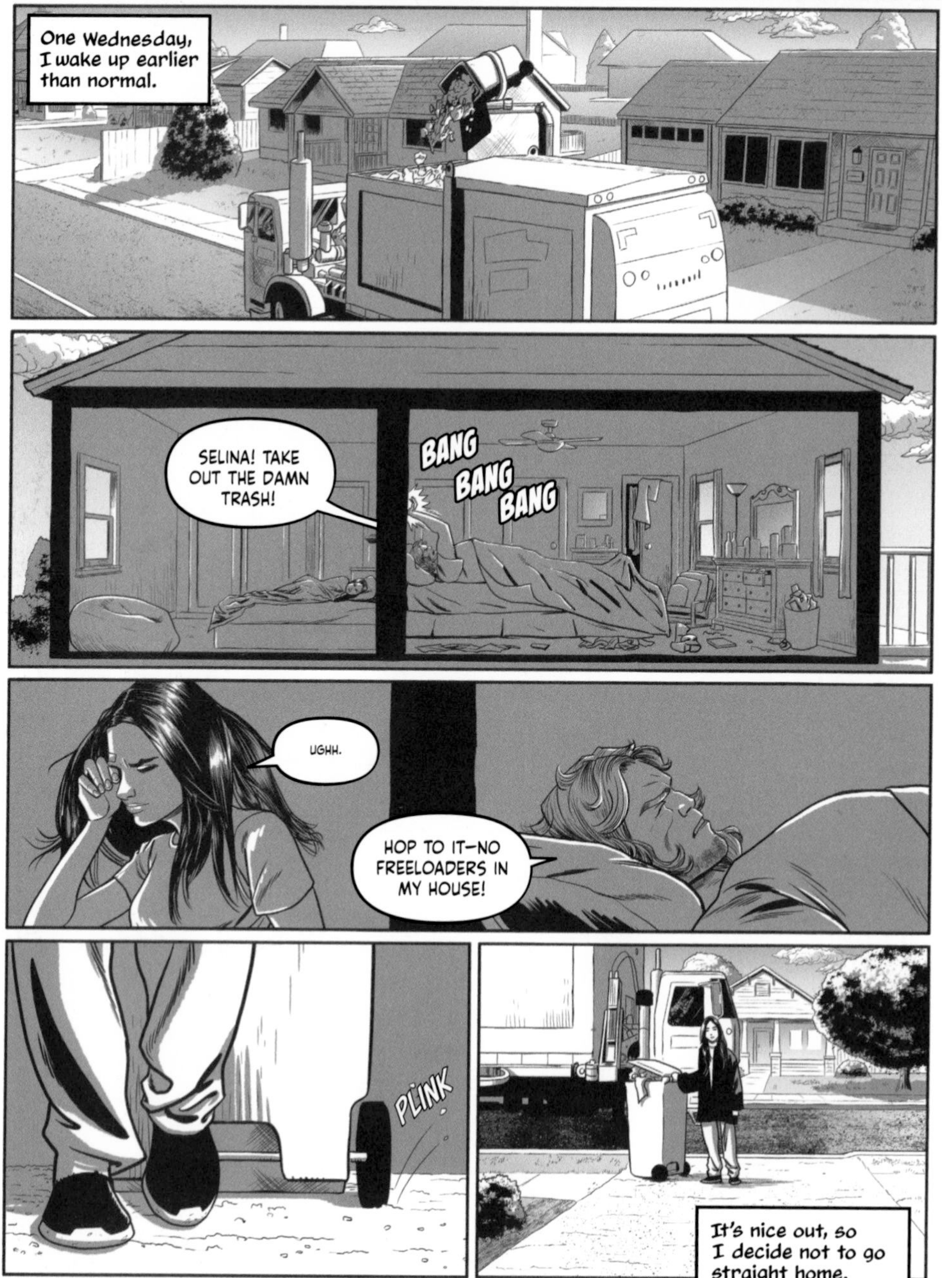

One Wednesday, I wake up earlier than normal.
SELINA! TAKE OUT THE DAMN TRASH!
BANG
BANG
BANG
UGHH.
HOP TO IT—NO FREELOADERS IN MY HOUSE!
PLINK
It's nice out, so I decide not to go straight home.

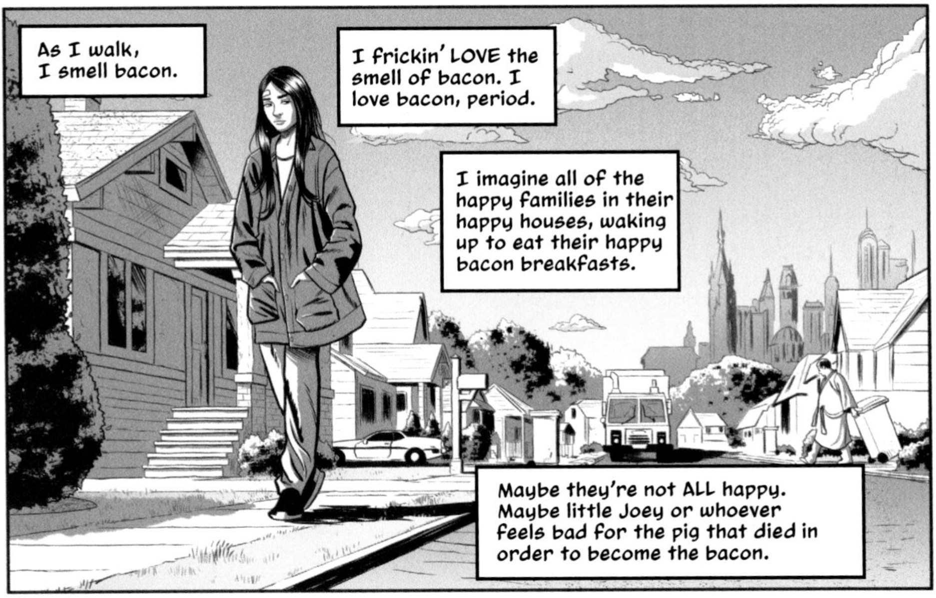
As I walk, I smell bacon.
I frickin' LOVE the smell of bacon. I love bacon, period.
I imagine all of the happy families in their happy houses, waking up to eat their happy bacon breakfasts.
Maybe they're not ALL happy. Maybe little Joey or whoever feels bad for the pig that died in order to become the bacon.
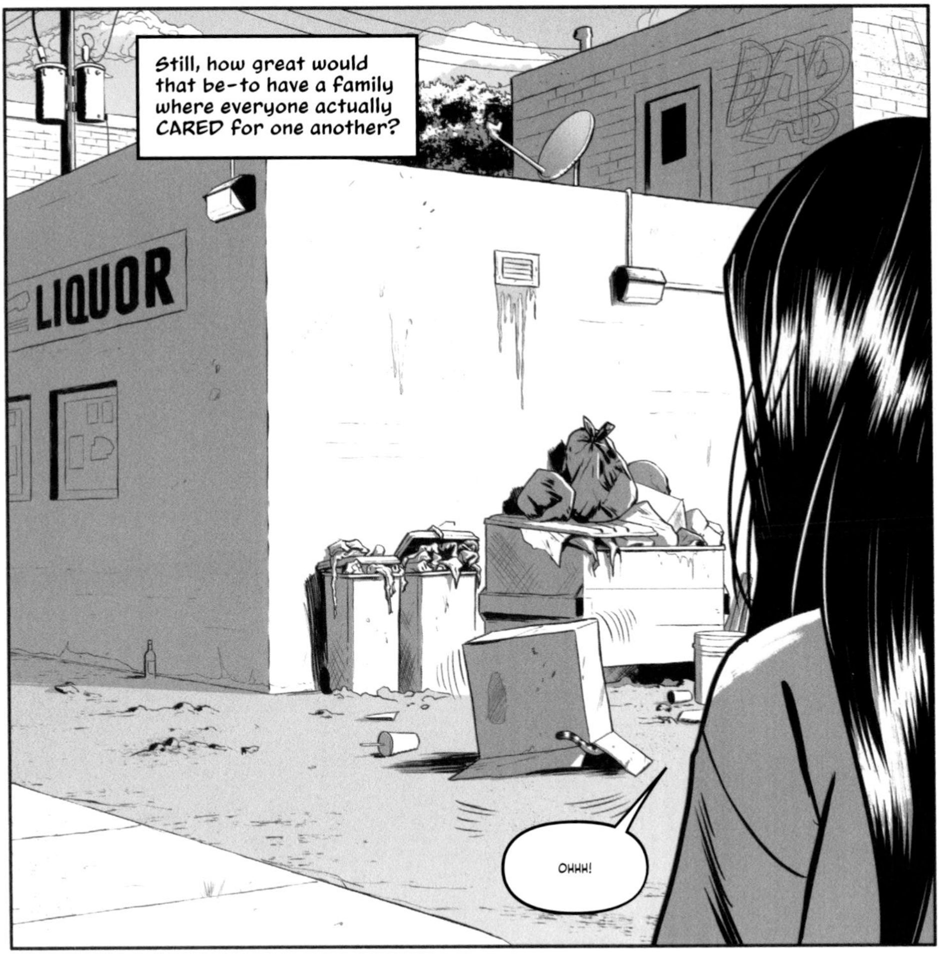
Still, how great would that be–to have a family where everyone actually CARED for one another?
LIQUOR
OHHH!

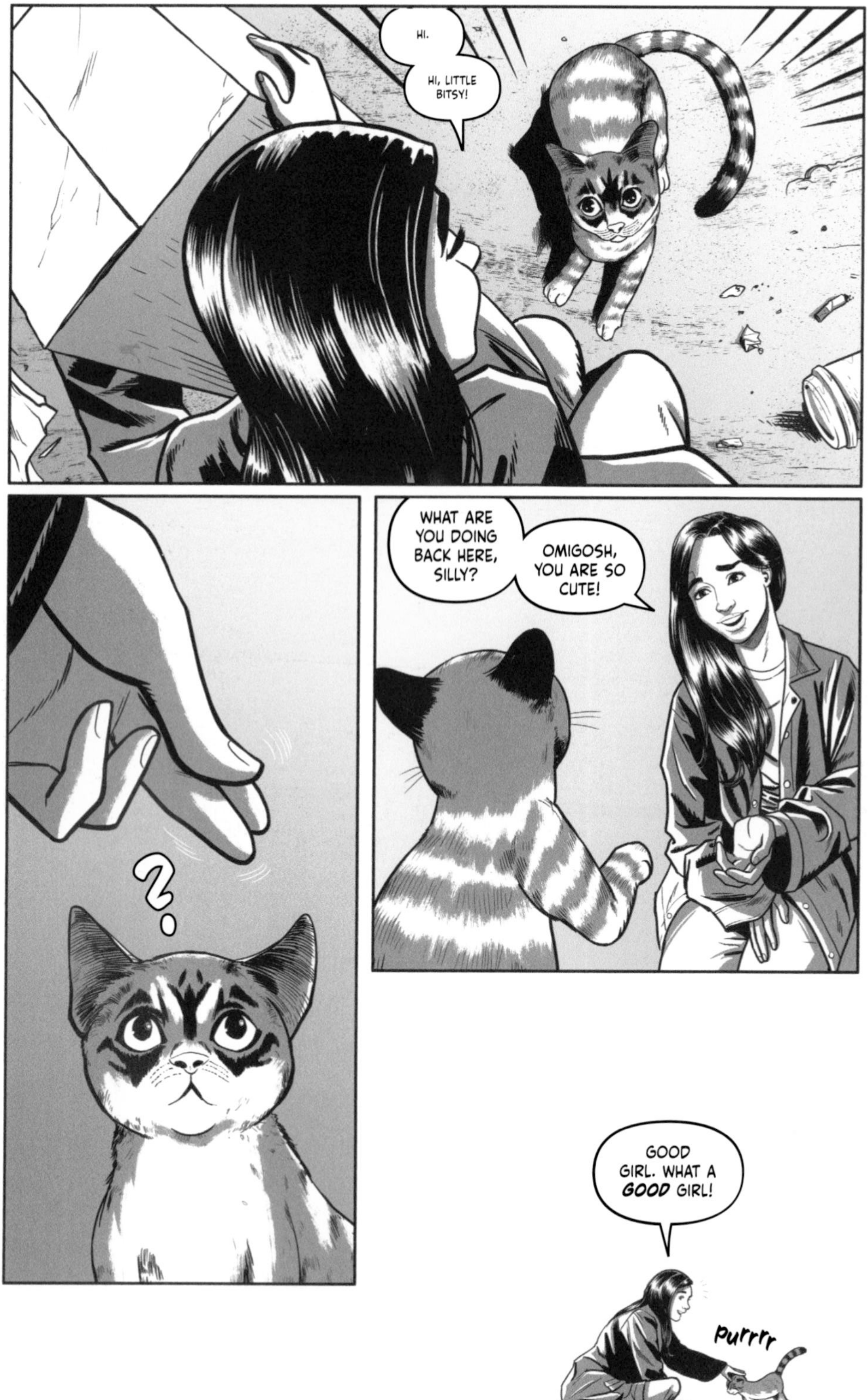
HI.
HI, LITTLE BITSY!
WHAT ARE YOU DOING BACK HERE, SILLY?
OMIGOSH, YOU ARE SO CUTE!
?
GOOD GIRL. WHAT A **GOOD** GIRL!
purrrr

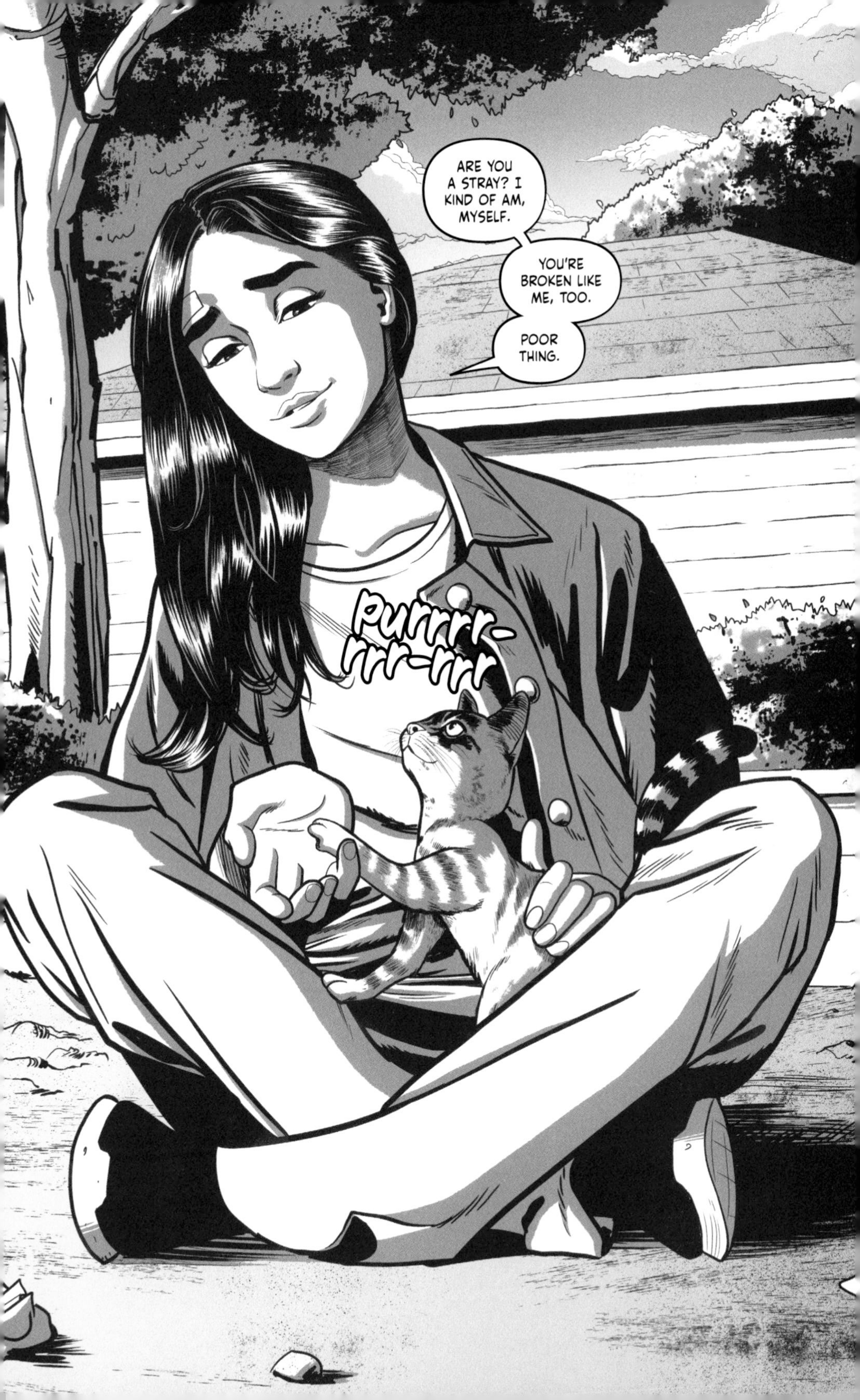
ARE YOU A STRAY? I KIND OF AM, MYSELF.
YOU'RE BROKEN LIKE ME, TOO.
POOR THING.
purrrr-rrr-rrr

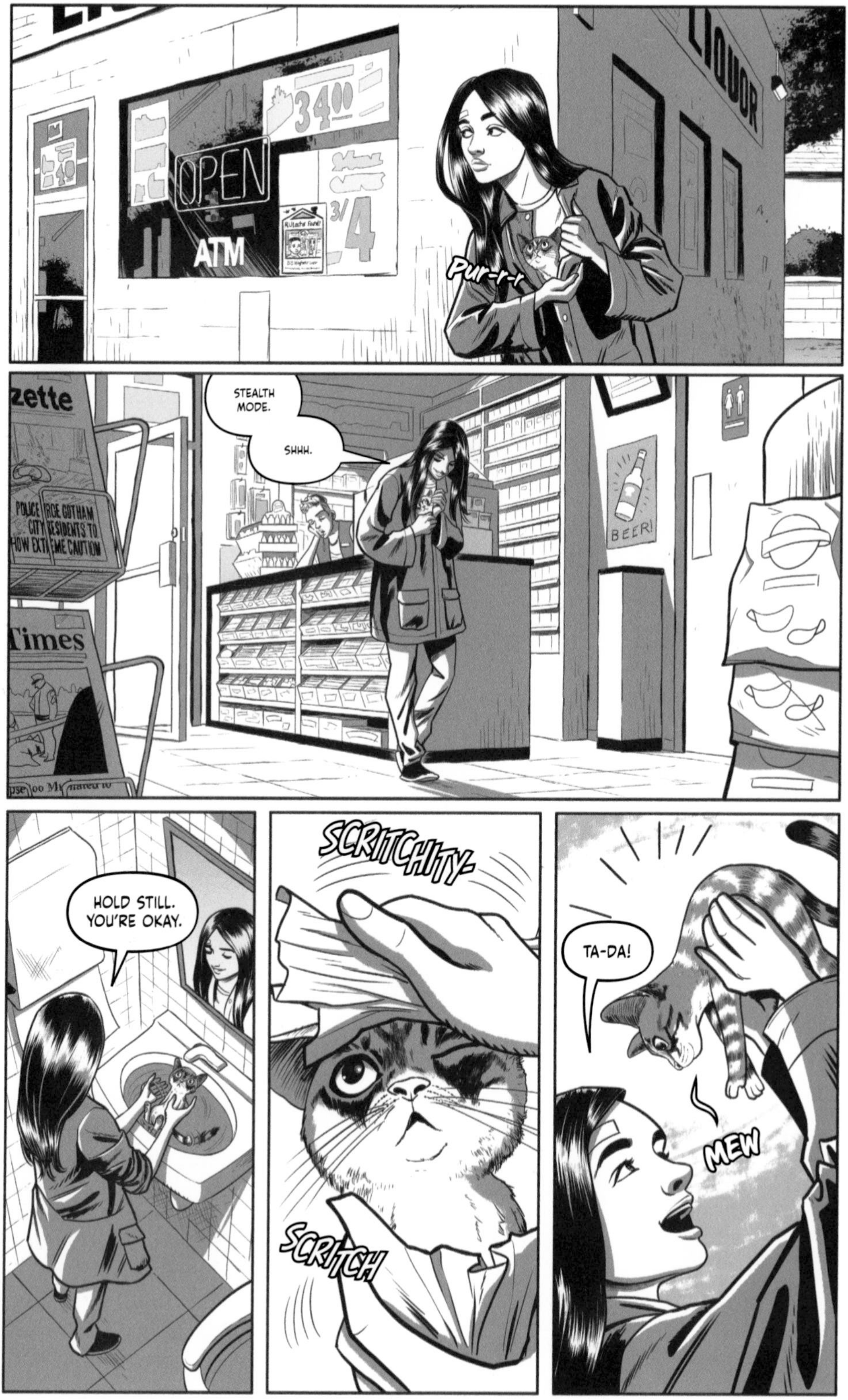
LIQUOR
OPEN
ATM
Pur-r-r
zette
Times
BEER!
STEALTH MODE.
SHHH.
HOLD STILL. YOU'RE OKAY.
SCRITCHITY-
SCRITCH
TA-DA!
MEW

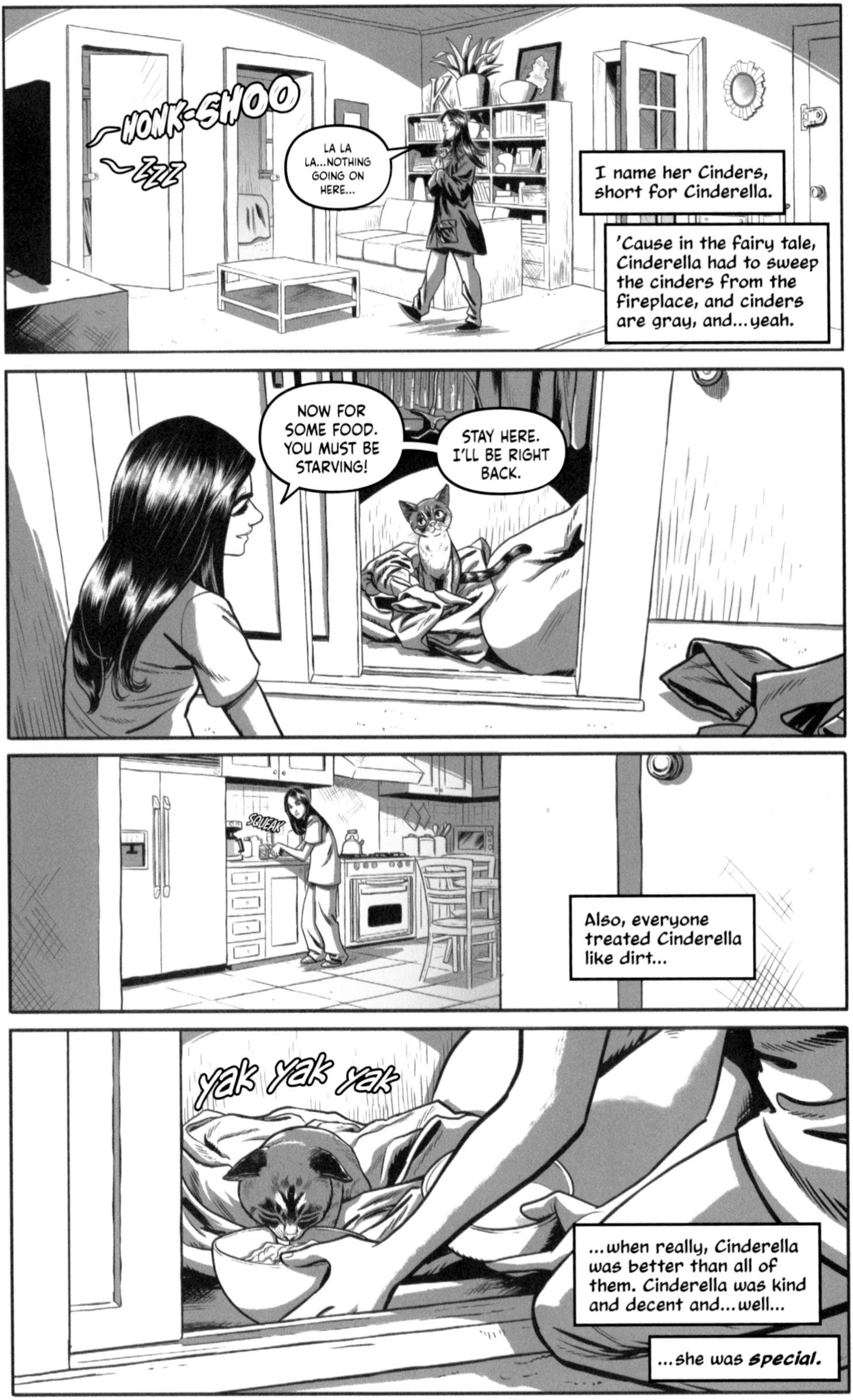
~HONK-SHOO
~ZZZ
LA LA LA...NOTHING GOING ON HERE...
I name her Cinders, short for Cinderella.
'Cause in the fairy tale, Cinderella had to sweep the cinders from the fireplace, and cinders are gray, and...yeah.
NOW FOR SOME FOOD. YOU MUST BE STARVING!
STAY HERE. I'LL BE RIGHT BACK.
SQUEAK
Also, everyone treated Cinderella like dirt...
yak yak yak
...when really, Cinderella was better than all of them. Cinderella was kind and decent and...well...
...she was *special.*

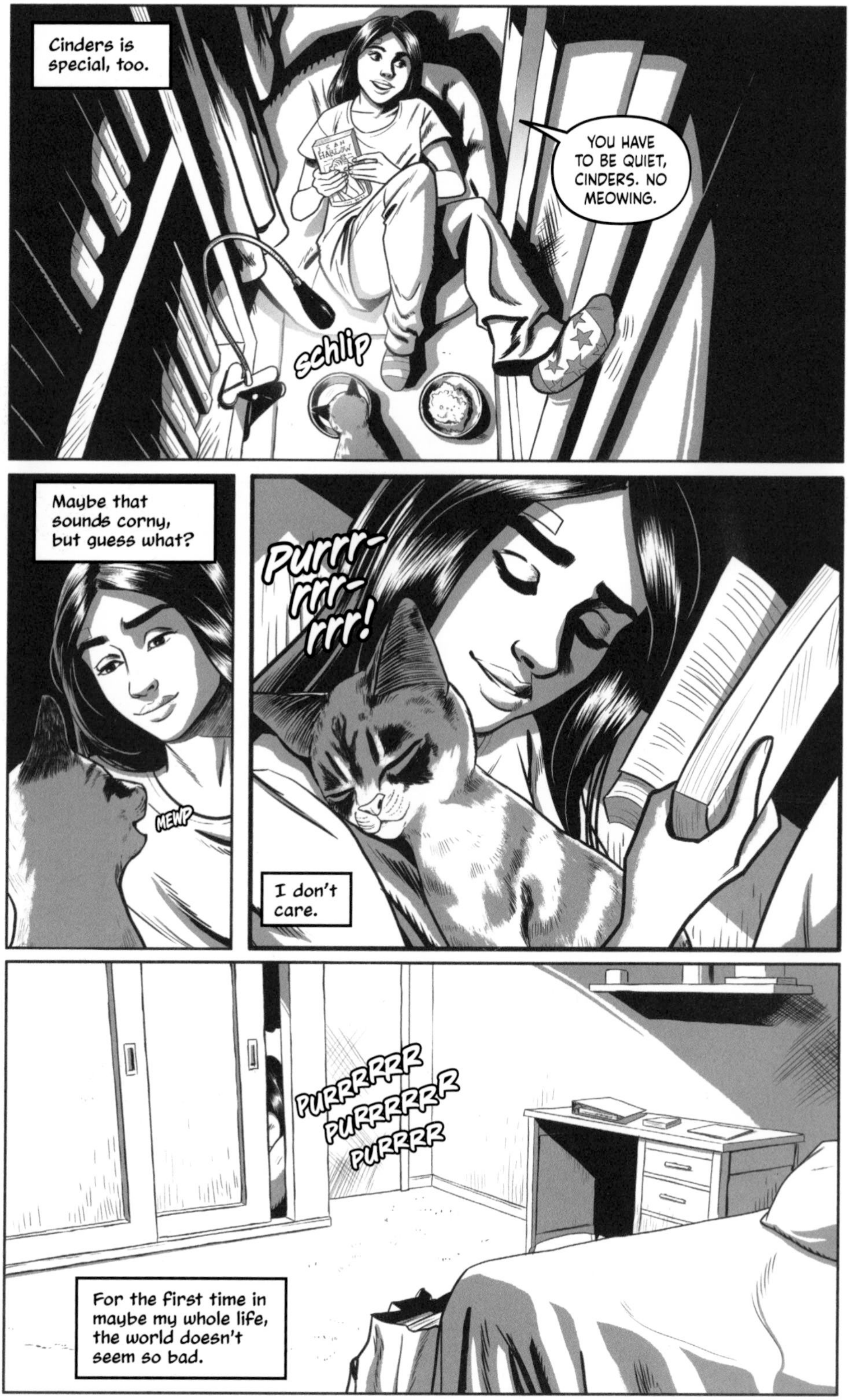
Cinders is special, too.
YOU HAVE TO BE QUIET, CINDERS. NO MEOWING.
schlip
Maybe that sounds corny, but guess what?
MEWP
Purrr-rrr-rrr!
I don't care.
PURRRRRR
PURRRRRR
PURRRR
For the first time in maybe my whole life, the world doesn't seem so bad.

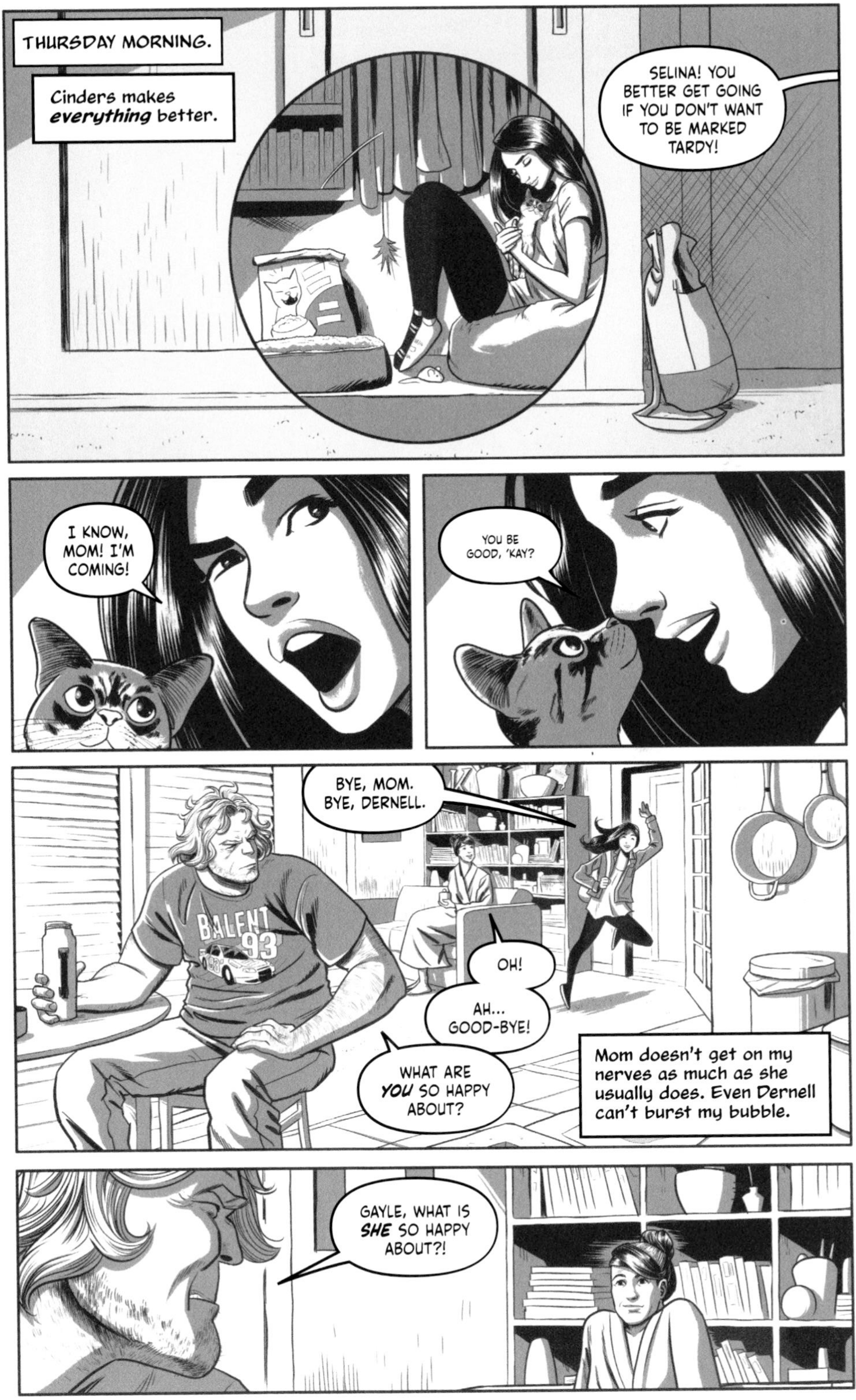
THURSDAY MORNING.
Cinders makes *everything* better.
SELINA! YOU BETTER GET GOING IF YOU DON'T WANT TO BE MARKED TARDY!
I KNOW, MOM! I'M COMING!
YOU BE GOOD, 'KAY?
BYE, MOM. BYE, DERNELL.
OH!
AH... GOOD-BYE!
WHAT ARE *YOU* SO HAPPY ABOUT?
Mom doesn't get on my nerves as much as she usually does. Even Dernell can't burst my bubble.
GAYLE, WHAT IS *SHE* SO HAPPY ABOUT?!

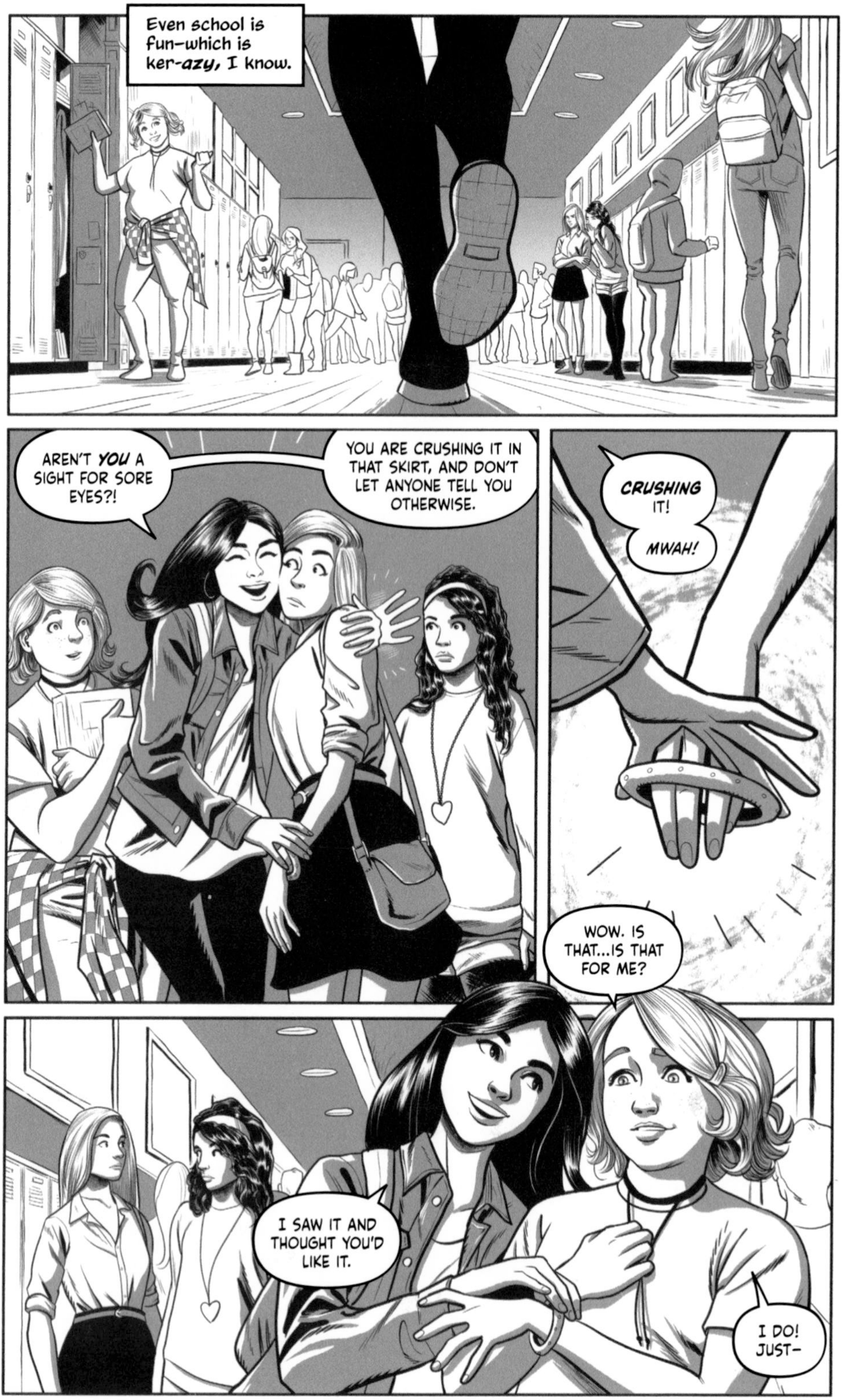
Even school is fun–which is ker-*azy,* I know.
AREN'T *YOU* A SIGHT FOR SORE EYES?!
YOU ARE CRUSHING IT IN THAT SKIRT, AND DON'T LET ANYONE TELL YOU OTHERWISE.
CRUSHING IT!
MWAH!
WOW. IS THAT...IS THAT FOR ME?
I SAW IT AND THOUGHT YOU'D LIKE IT.
I DO! JUST–

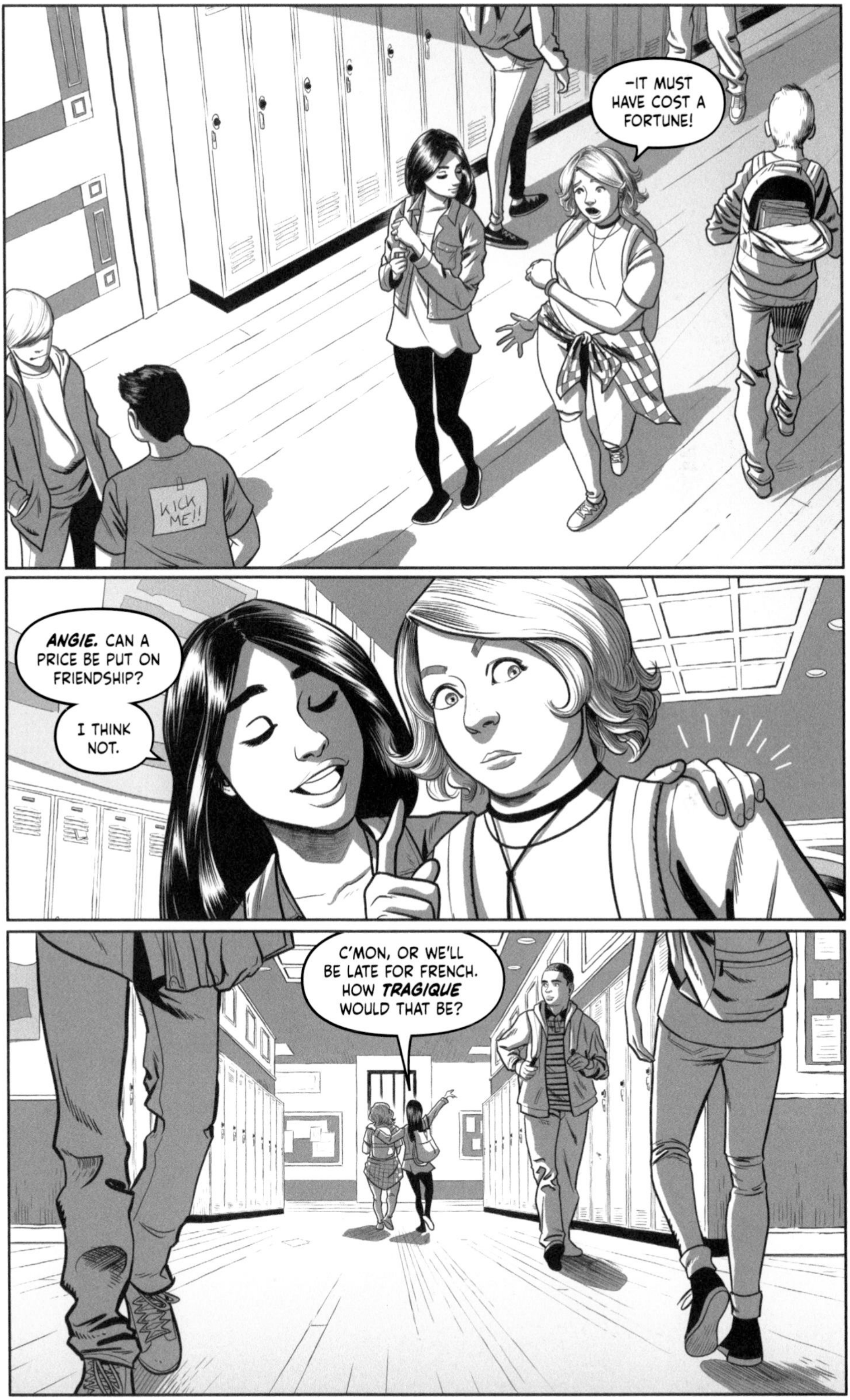

–IT MUST HAVE COST A FORTUNE!
KICK ME!!
ANGIE. CAN A PRICE BE PUT ON FRIENDSHIP?
I THINK NOT.
C'MON, OR WE'LL BE LATE FOR FRENCH. HOW TRAGIQUE WOULD THAT BE?

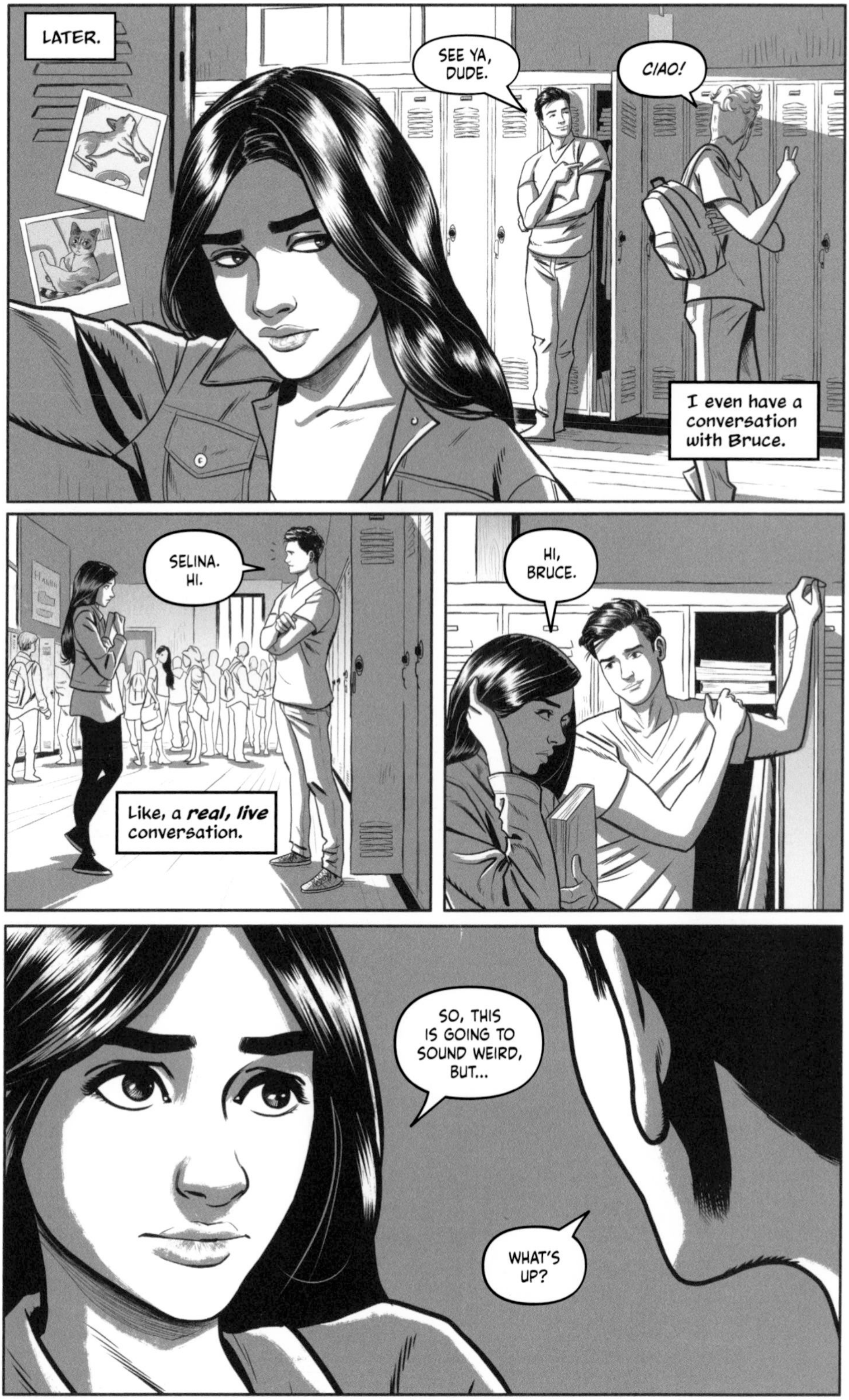
LATER.
SEE YA, DUDE.
CIAO!
I even have a conversation with Bruce.
SELINA. HI.
Like, a ***real, live*** conversation.
HI, BRUCE.
SO, THIS IS GOING TO SOUND WEIRD, BUT...
WHAT'S UP?

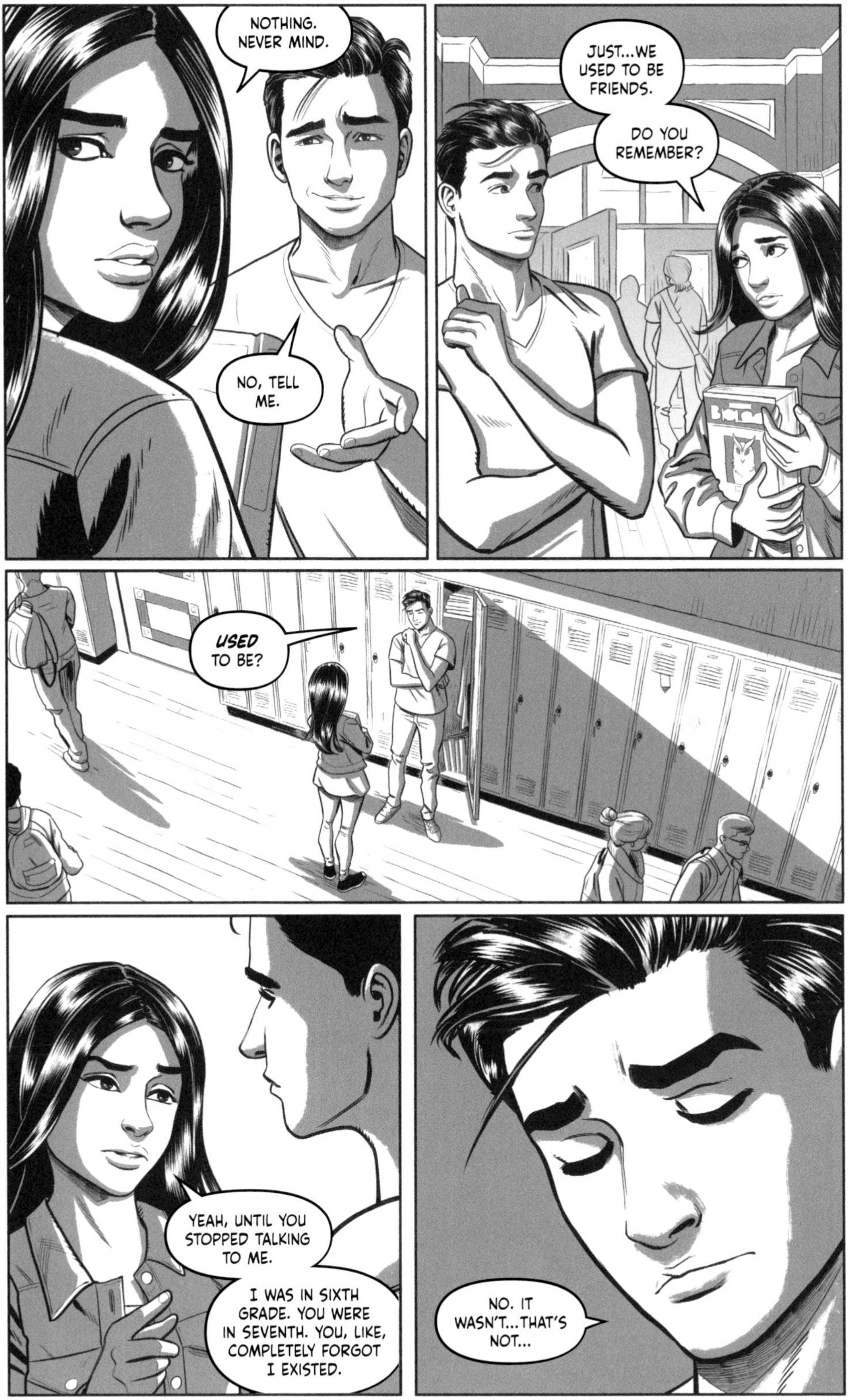
NOTHING. NEVER MIND.
NO, TELL ME.
JUST...WE USED TO BE FRIENDS.
DO YOU REMEMBER?
USED TO BE?
YEAH, UNTIL YOU STOPPED TALKING TO ME.
I WAS IN SIXTH GRADE. YOU WERE IN SEVENTH. YOU, LIKE, COMPLETELY FORGOT I EXISTED.
NO. IT WASN'T...THAT'S NOT...

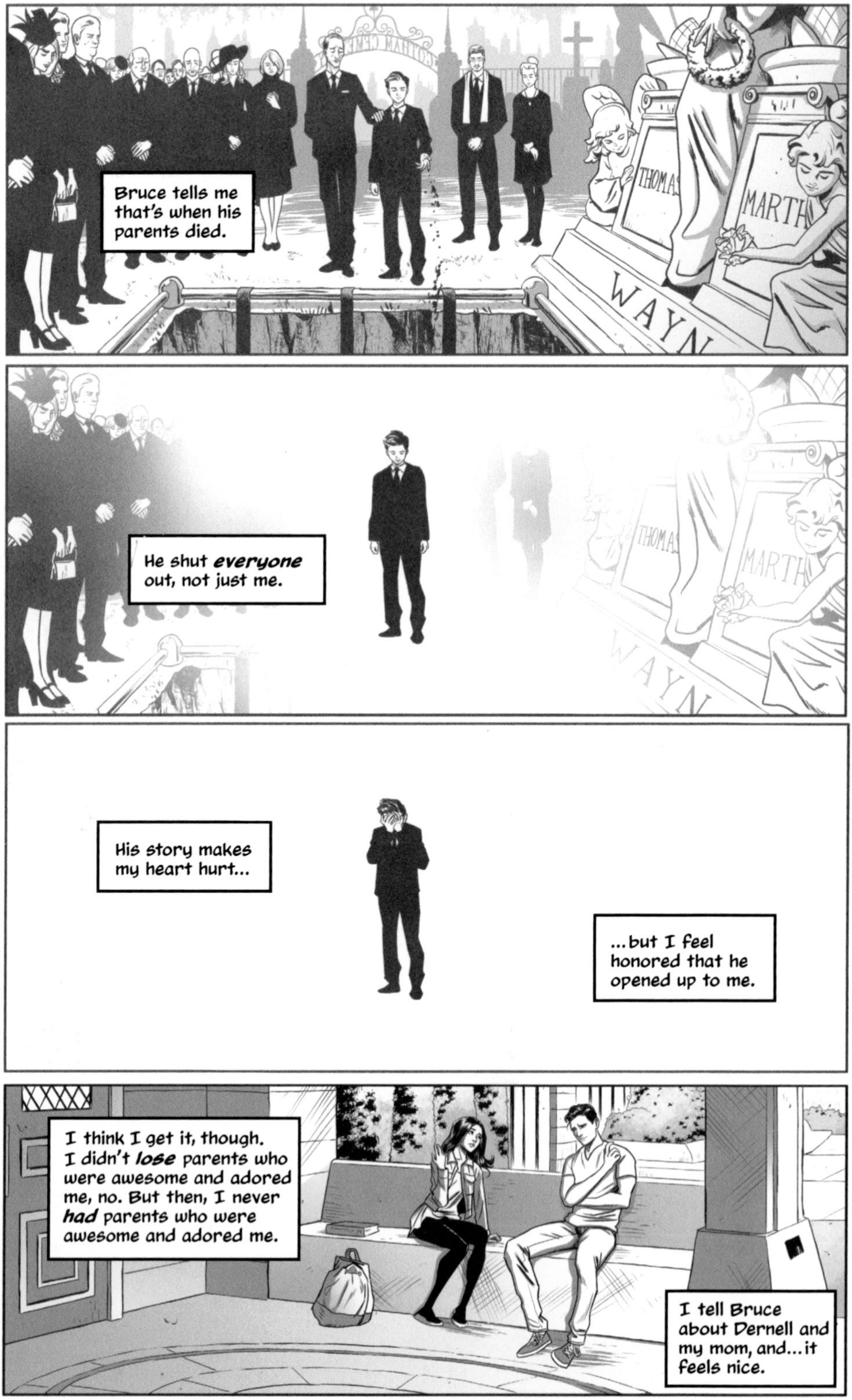

Bruce tells me that's when his parents died.
THOMAS
MARTH
WAYN
He shut *everyone* out, not just me.
His story makes my heart hurt...
...but I feel honored that he opened up to me.
I think I get it, though. I didn't *lose* parents who were awesome and adored me, no. But then, I never *had* parents who were awesome and adored me.
I tell Bruce about Dernell and my mom, and...it feels nice.

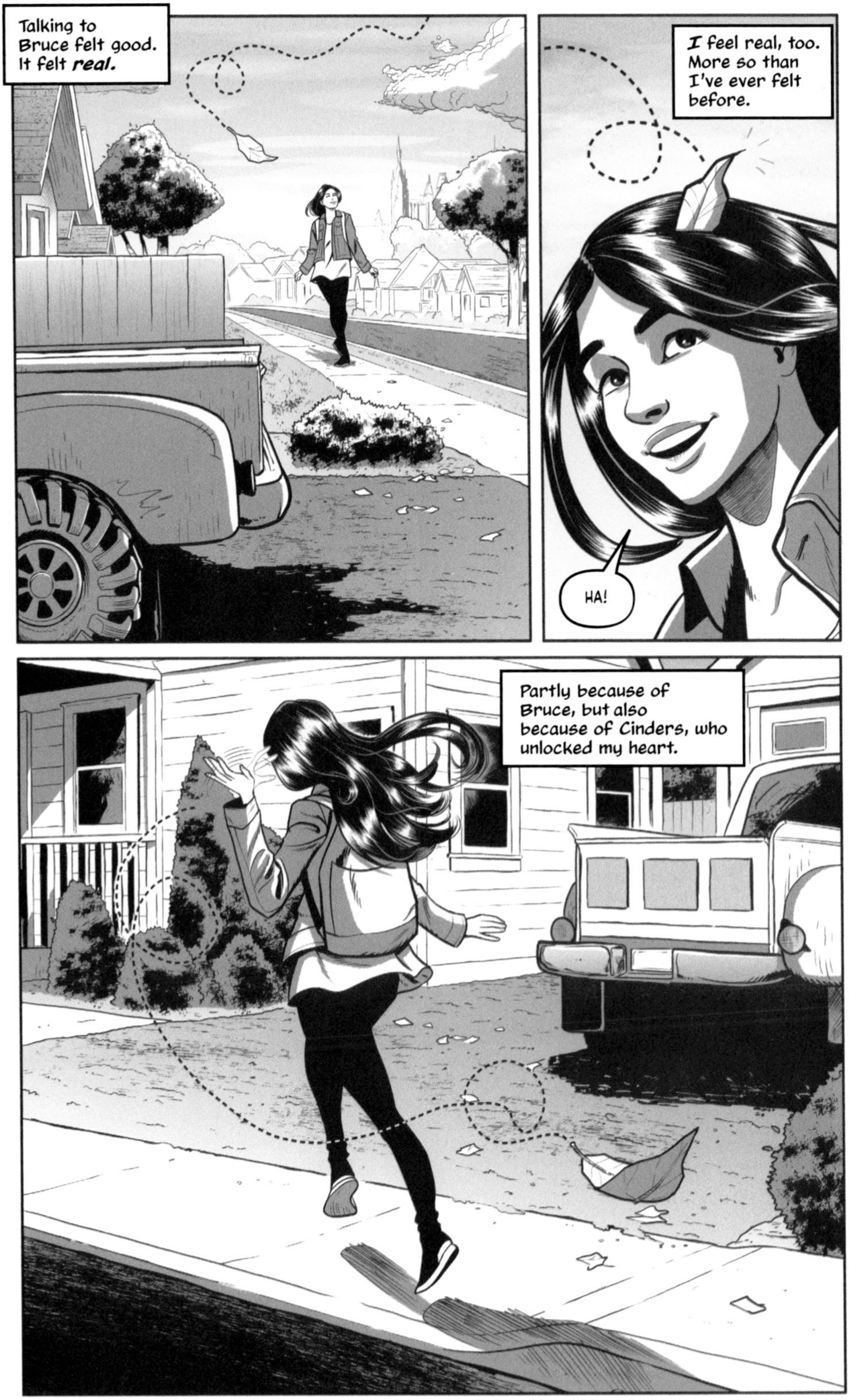
Talking to Bruce felt good. It felt *real.*
I feel real, too. More so than I've ever felt before.
HA!
Partly because of Bruce, but also because of Cinders, who unlocked my heart.

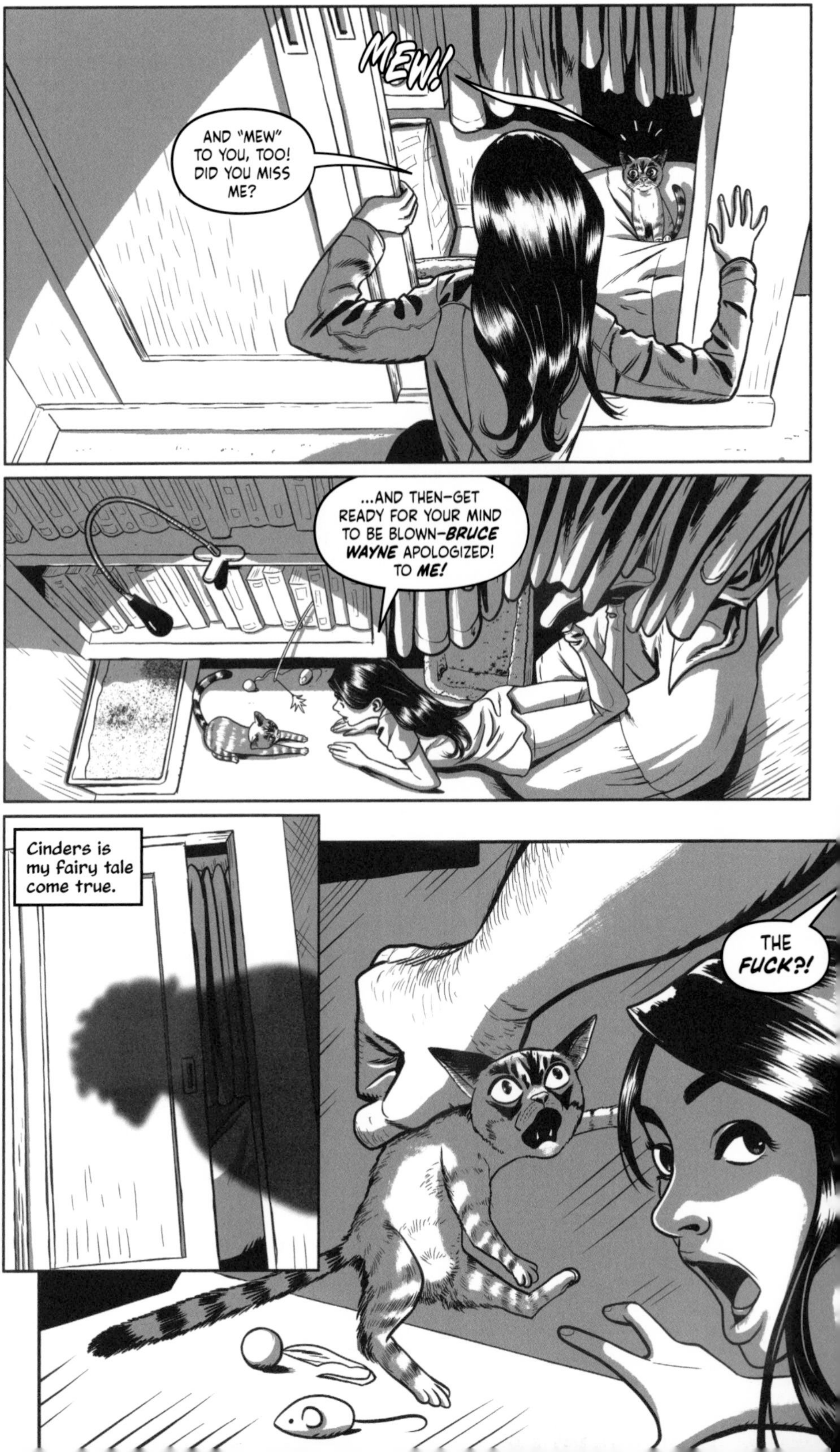
MEW!
AND "MEW" TO YOU, TOO! DID YOU MISS ME?
...AND THEN—GET READY FOR YOUR MIND TO BE BLOWN—BRUCE WAYNE APOLOGIZED! TO ME!
Cinders is my fairy tale come true.
THE FUCK?!

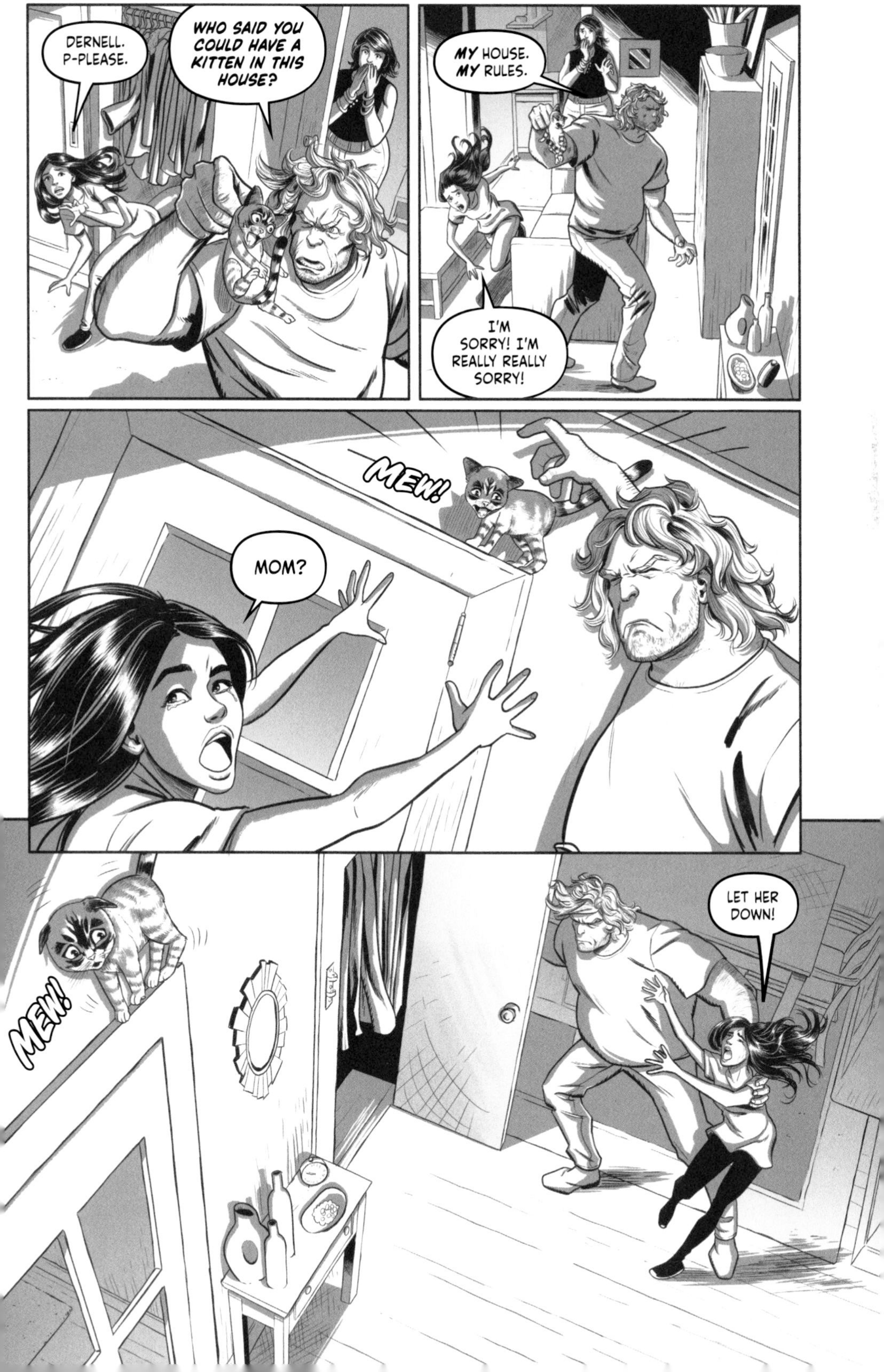
DERNELL. P-PLEASE.
WHO SAID YOU COULD HAVE A KITTEN IN THIS HOUSE?
MY HOUSE. MY RULES.
I'M SORRY! I'M REALLY REALLY SORRY!
MEW!
MOM?
MEW!
LET HER DOWN!

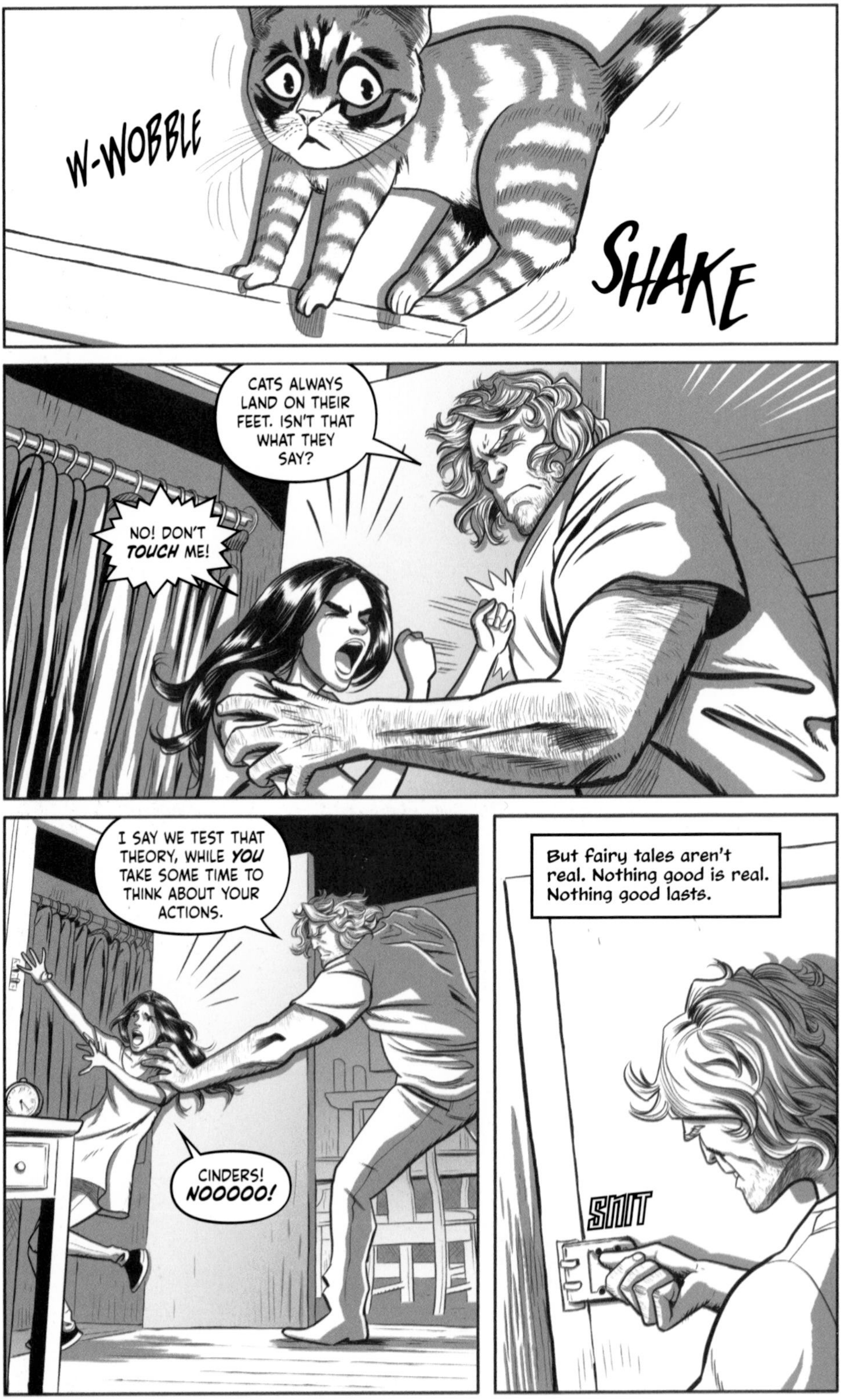
W-WOBBLE
SHAKE
CATS ALWAYS LAND ON THEIR FEET. ISN'T THAT WHAT THEY SAY?
NO! DON'T TOUCH ME!
I SAY WE TEST THAT THEORY, WHILE YOU TAKE SOME TIME TO THINK ABOUT YOUR ACTIONS.
CINDERS! NOOOOO!
But fairy tales aren't real. Nothing good is real. Nothing good lasts.
SNIT

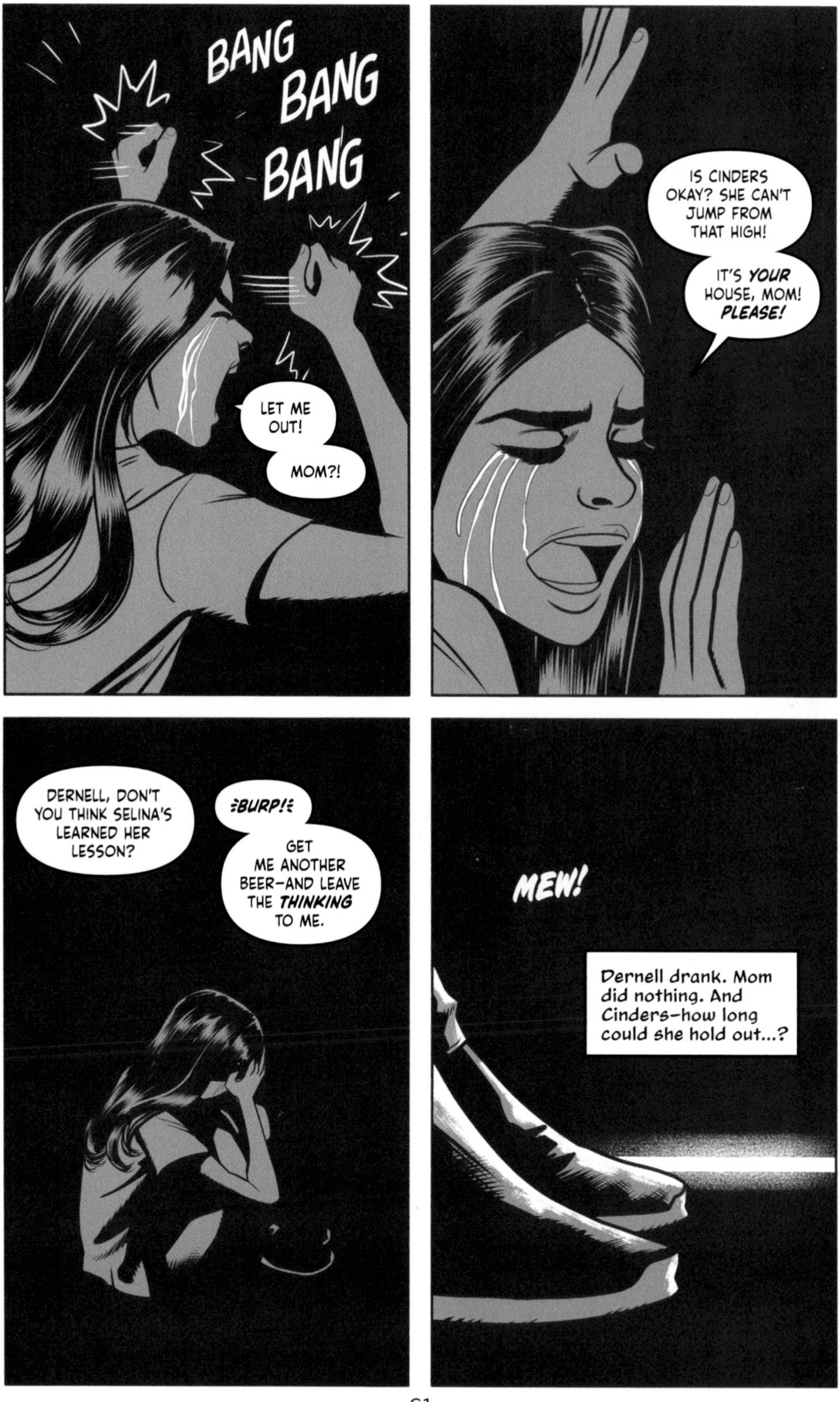
BANG BANG BANG
LET ME OUT!
MOM?!
IS CINDERS OKAY? SHE CAN'T JUMP FROM THAT HIGH!
IT'S *YOUR* HOUSE, MOM! *PLEASE!*
DERNELL, DON'T YOU THINK SELINA'S LEARNED HER LESSON?
BURP!
GET ME ANOTHER BEER—AND LEAVE THE *THINKING* TO ME.
MEW!
Dernell drank. Mom did nothing. And Cinders—how long could she hold out...?

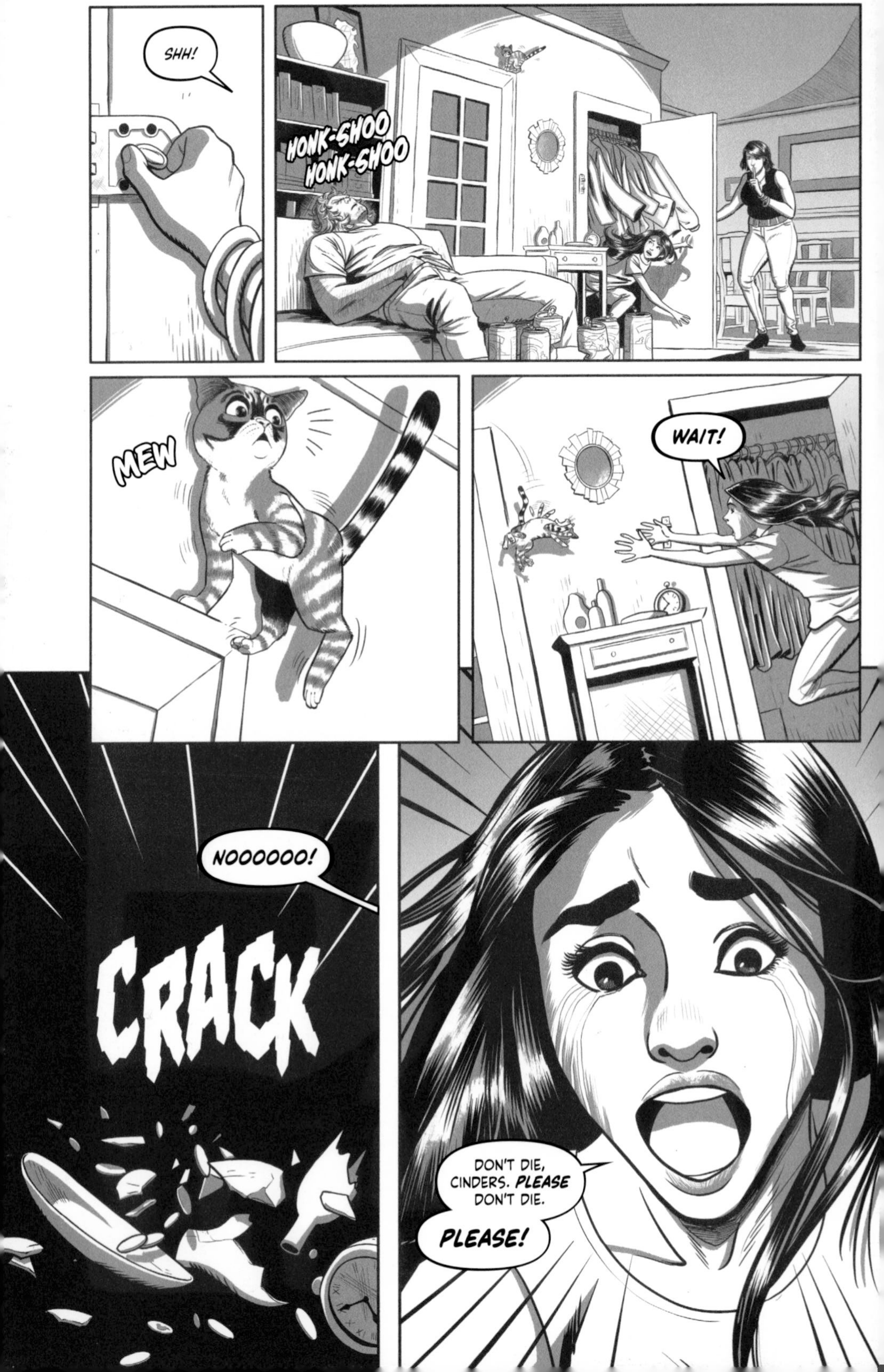
SHH!
HONK-SHOO
HONK-SHOO
MEW
WAIT!
NOOOOOO!
CRACK
DON'T DIE, CINDERS. *PLEASE* DON'T DIE.
PLEASE!

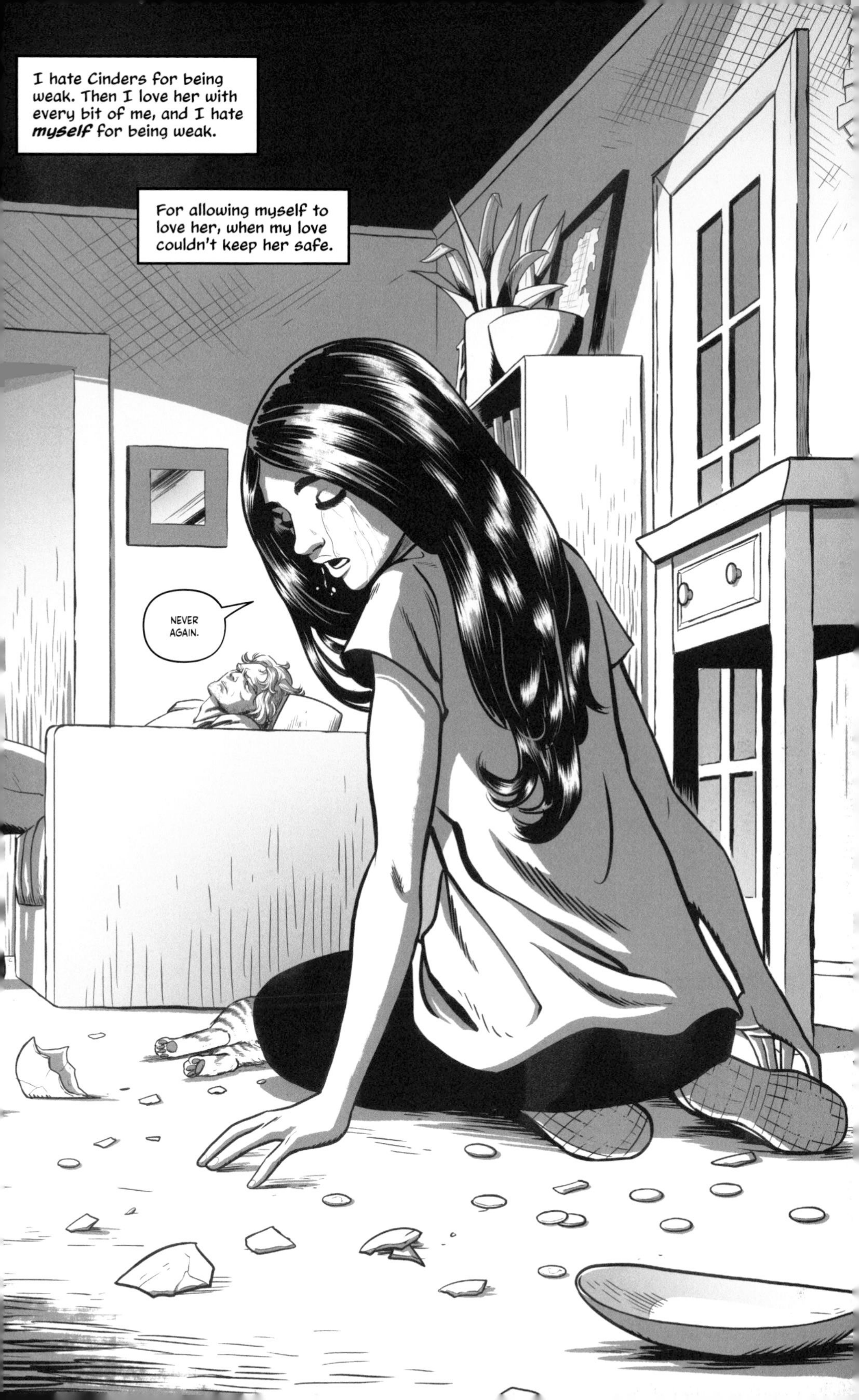
I hate Cinders for being weak. Then I love her with every bit of me, and I hate ***myself*** for being weak.
For allowing myself to love her, when my love couldn't keep her safe.
NEVER AGAIN.

THE LEAVING

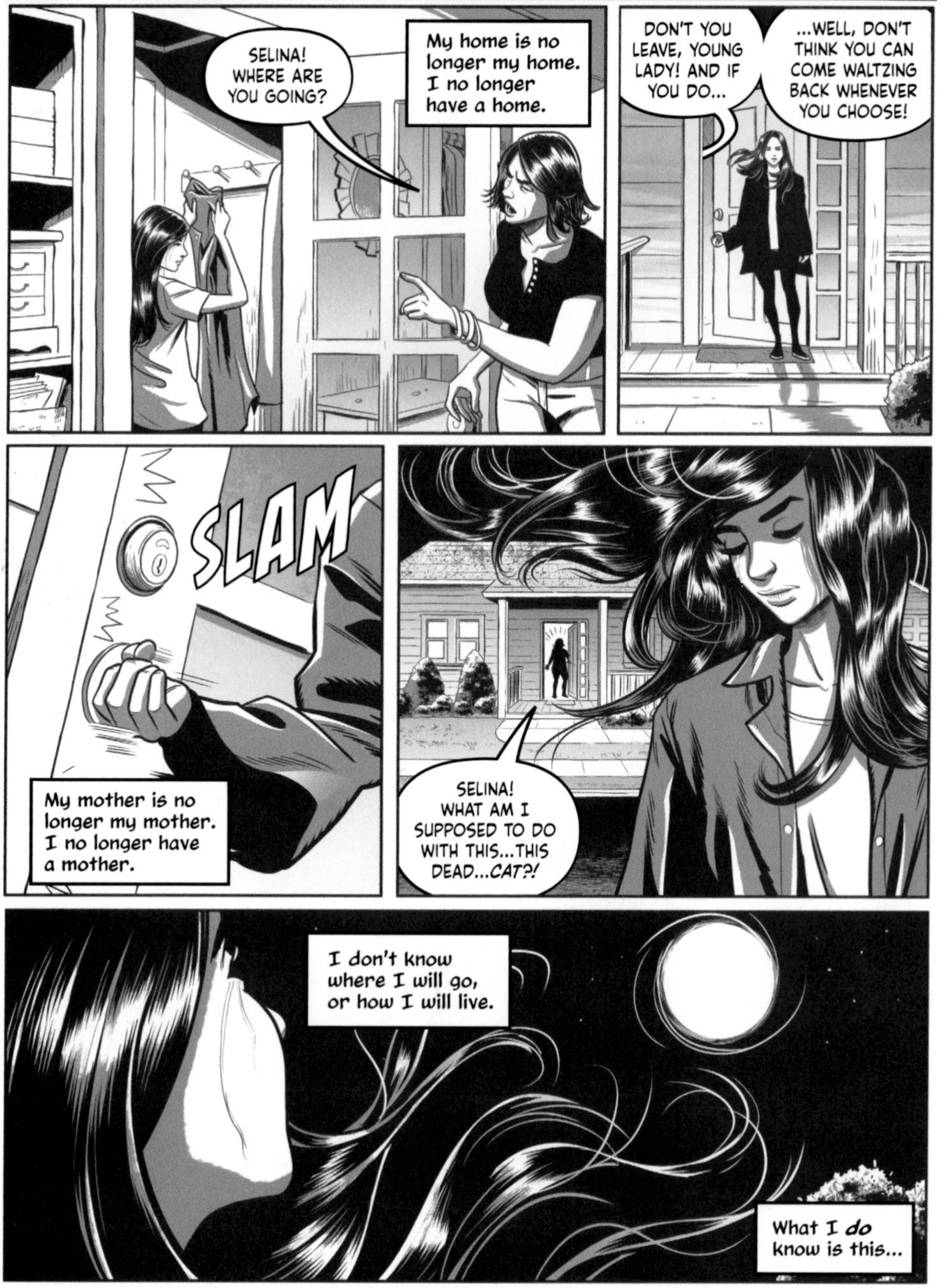
SELINA! WHERE ARE YOU GOING?
My home is no longer my home. I no longer have a home.
DON'T YOU LEAVE, YOUNG LADY! AND IF YOU DO...
...WELL, DON'T THINK YOU CAN COME WALTZING BACK WHENEVER YOU CHOOSE!
SLAM
My mother is no longer my mother. I no longer have a mother.
SELINA! WHAT AM I SUPPOSED TO DO WITH THIS...THIS DEAD...*CAT?!*
I don't know where I will go, or how I will live.
What I *do* know is this...

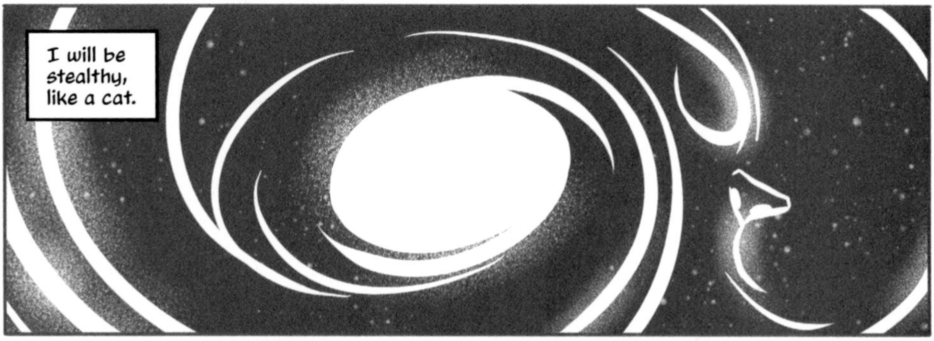
I will be stealthy, like a cat.

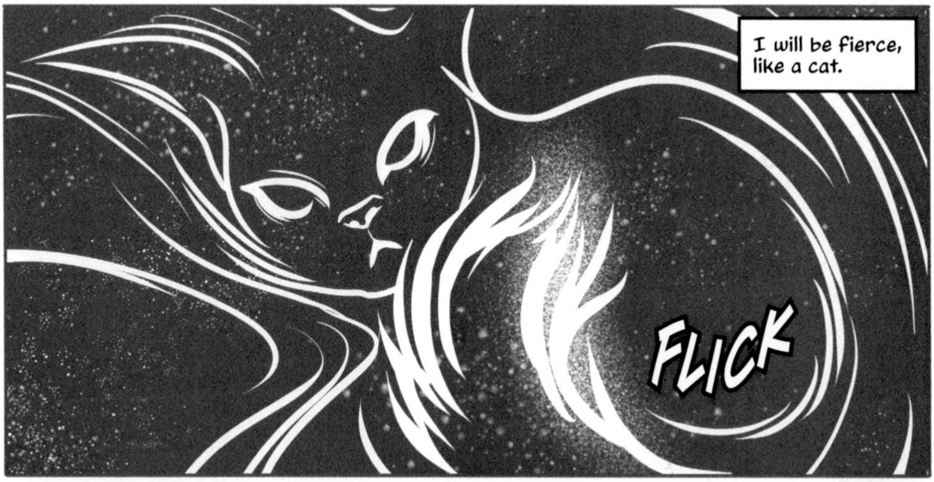
I will be fierce, like a cat.
FLICK

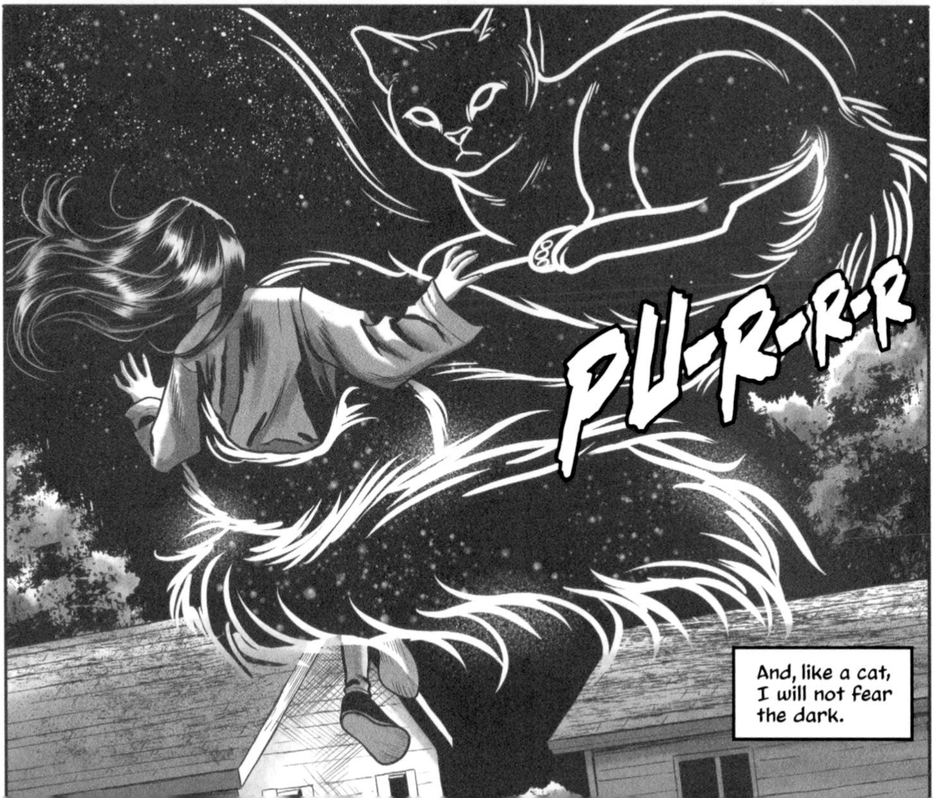
PU-R-R-R
And, like a cat, I will not fear the dark.

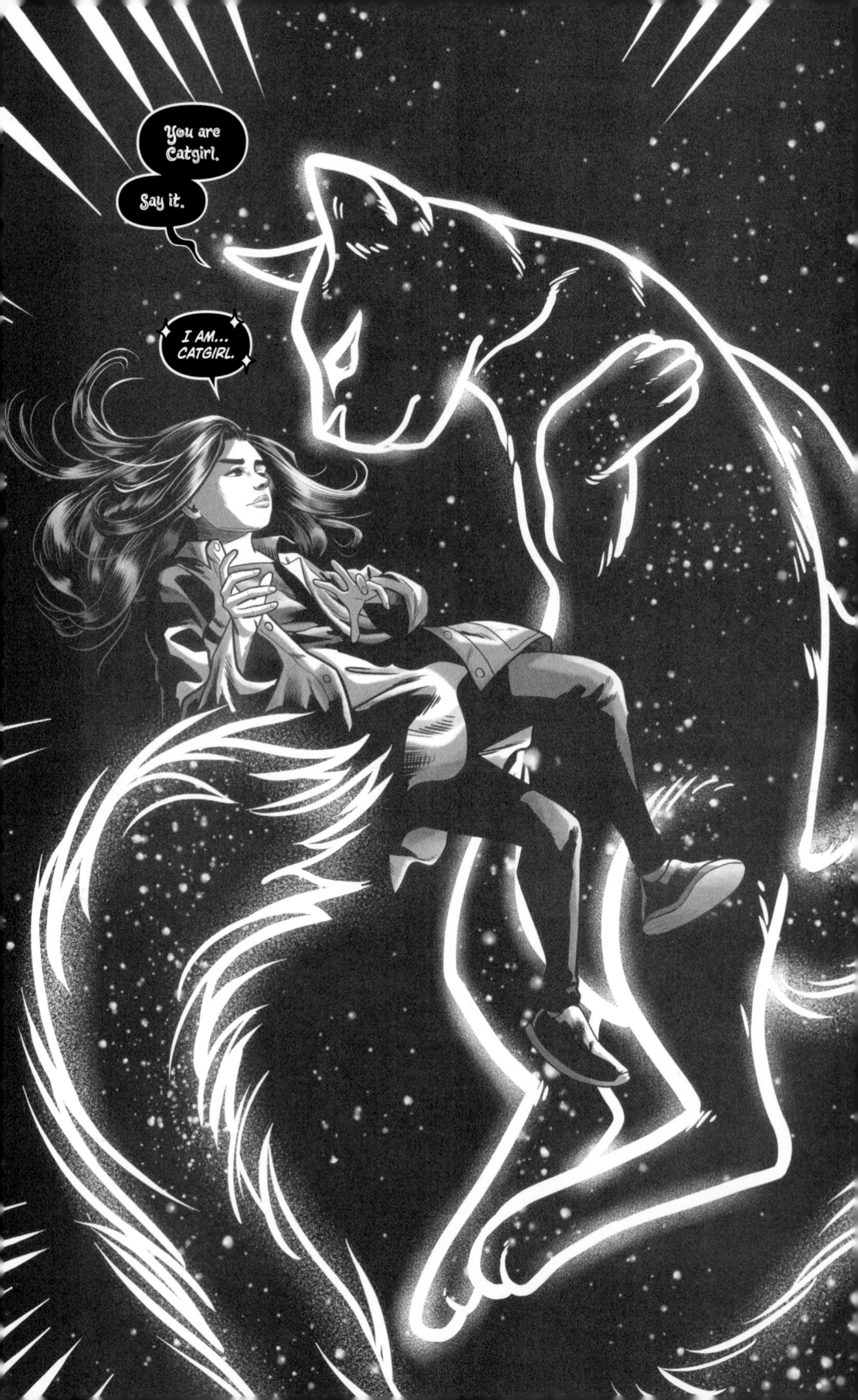
You are Catgirl.
Say it.
I AM... CATGIRL.

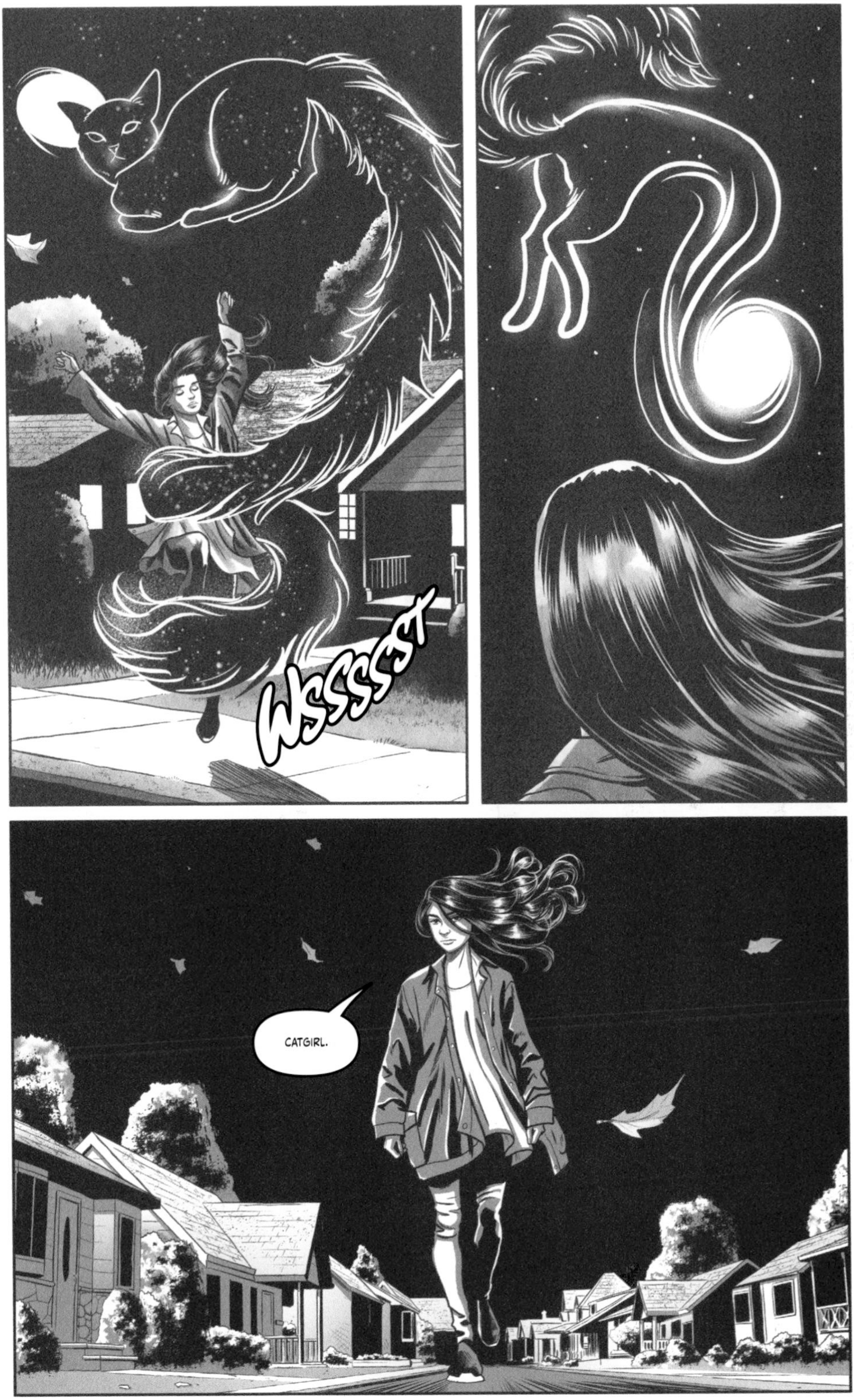
WSSSSST
CATGIRL.

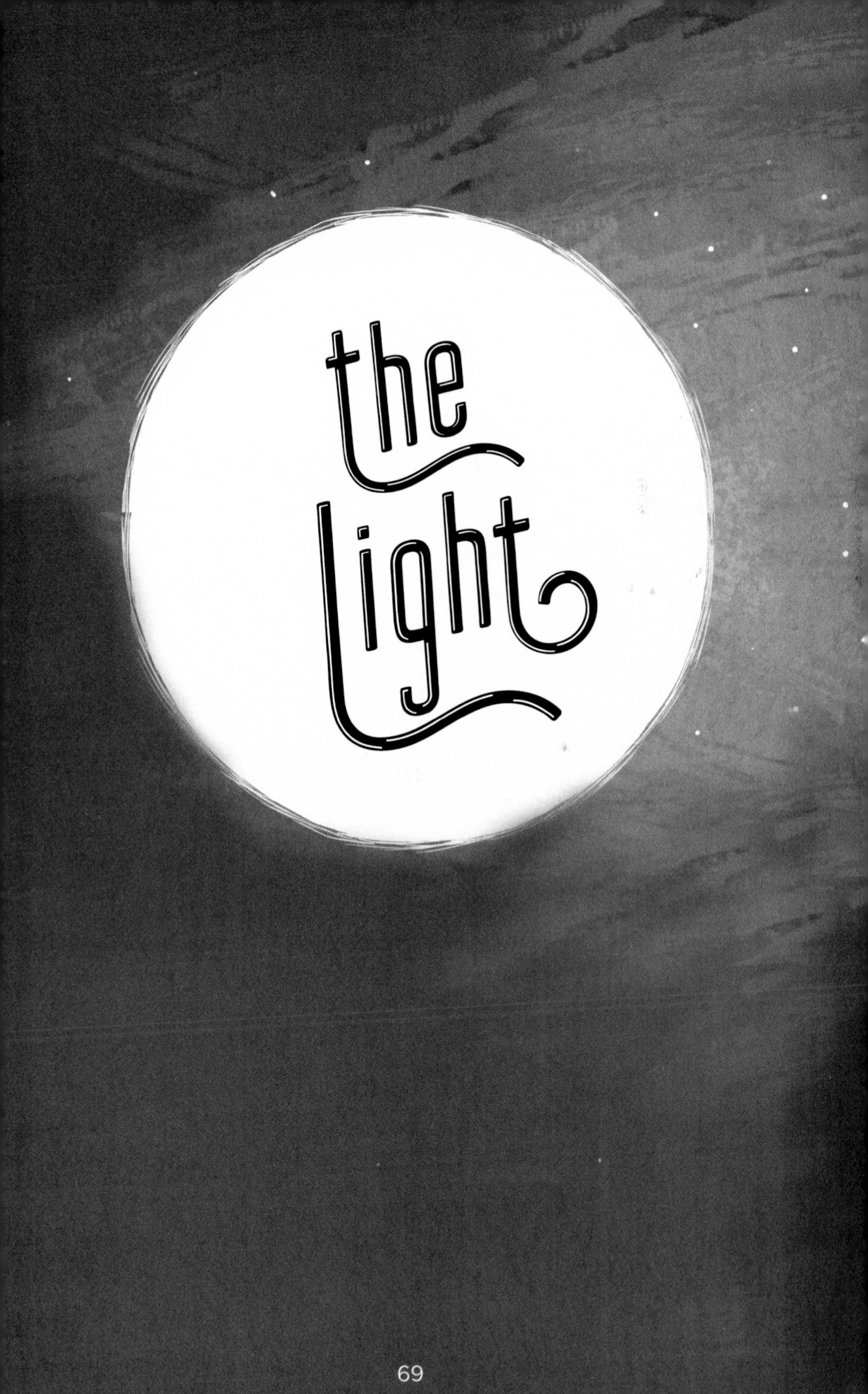
the Light

THE KNIFE

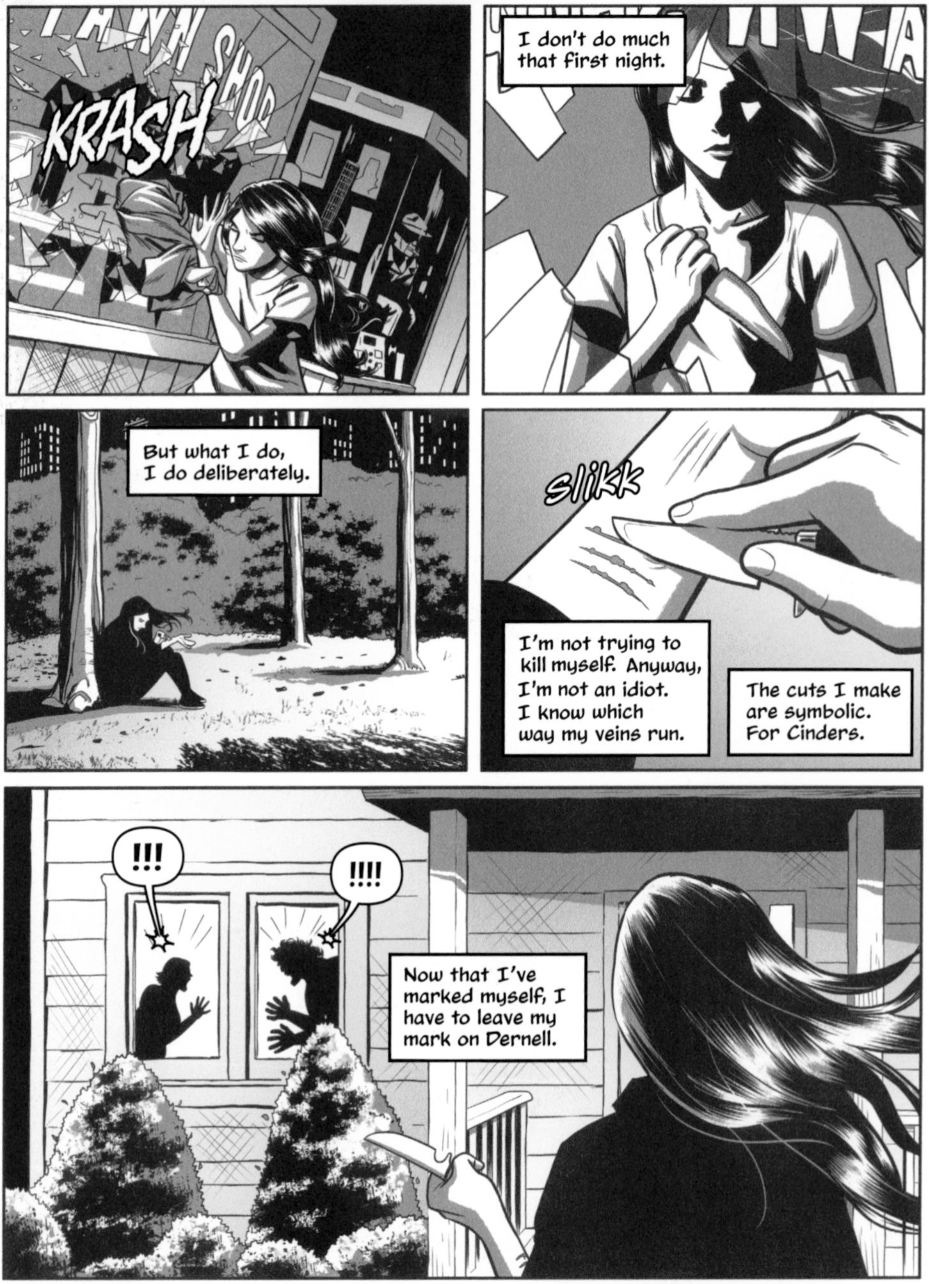
KRASH
I don't do much that first night.
But what I do, I do deliberately.
slikk
I'm not trying to kill myself. Anyway, I'm not an idiot. I know which way my veins run.
The cuts I make are symbolic. For Cinders.
!!!
!!!!
Now that I've marked myself, I have to leave my mark on Dernell.

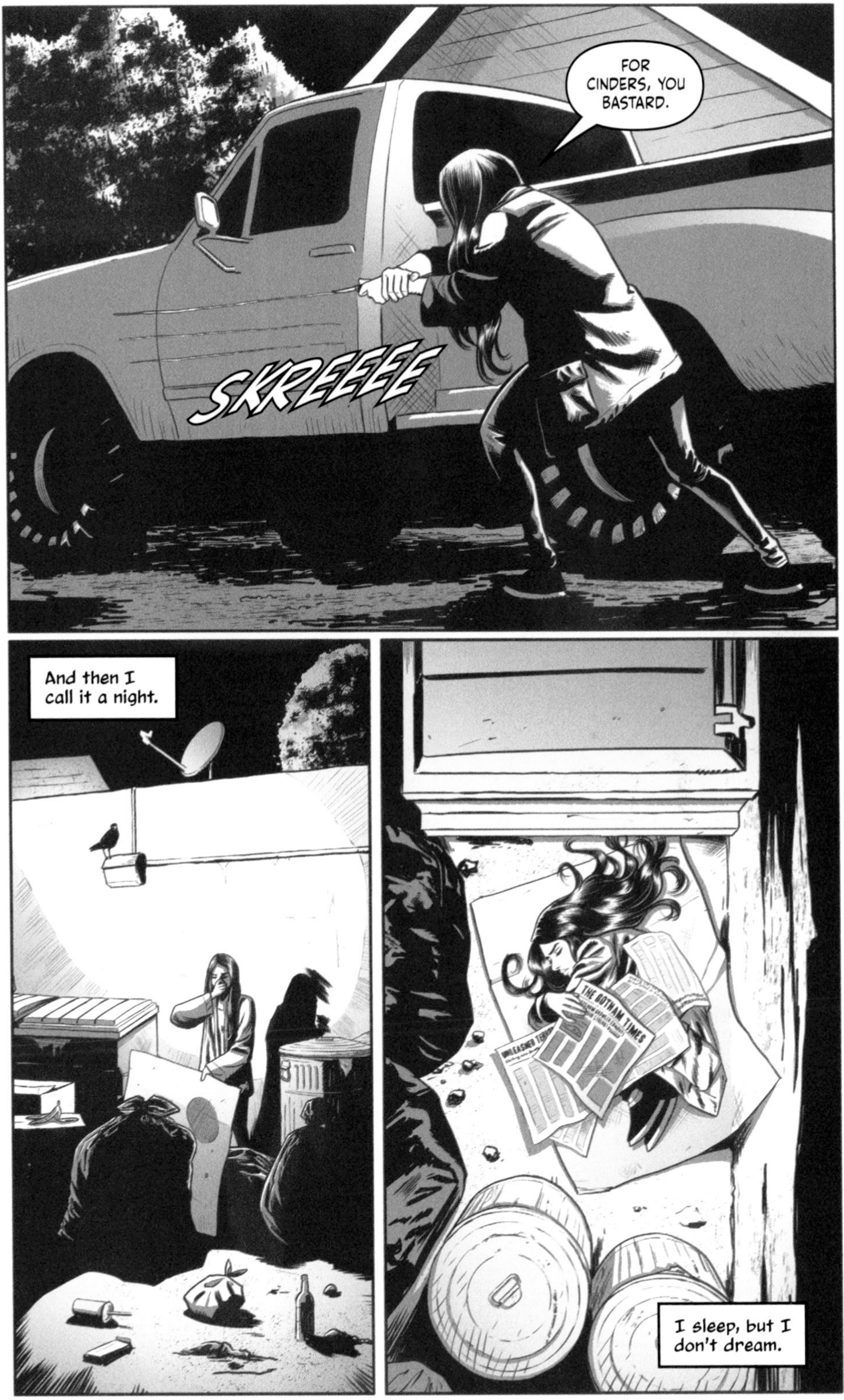
FOR CINDERS, YOU BASTARD.
SKREEEEE
And then I call it a night.
THE GOTHAM TIMES
I sleep, but I don't dream.

PARALLAX:

n. *The apparent displacement of an observed object due to a change in the position of the observer.*

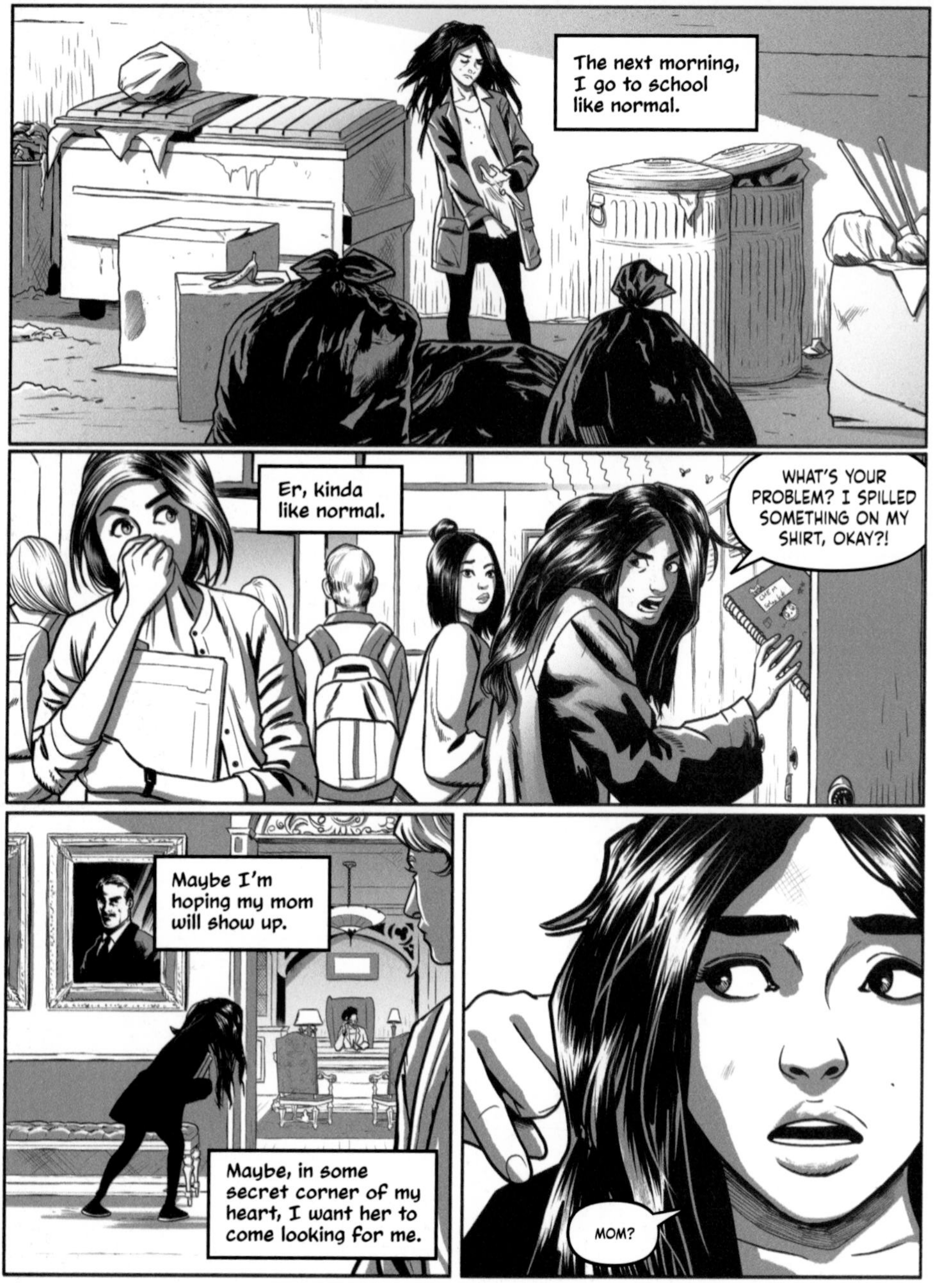

The next morning, I go to school like normal.
Er, kinda like normal.
WHAT'S YOUR PROBLEM? I SPILLED SOMETHING ON MY SHIRT, OKAY?!
Maybe I'm hoping my mom will show up.
Maybe, in some secret corner of my heart, I want her to come looking for me.
MOM?

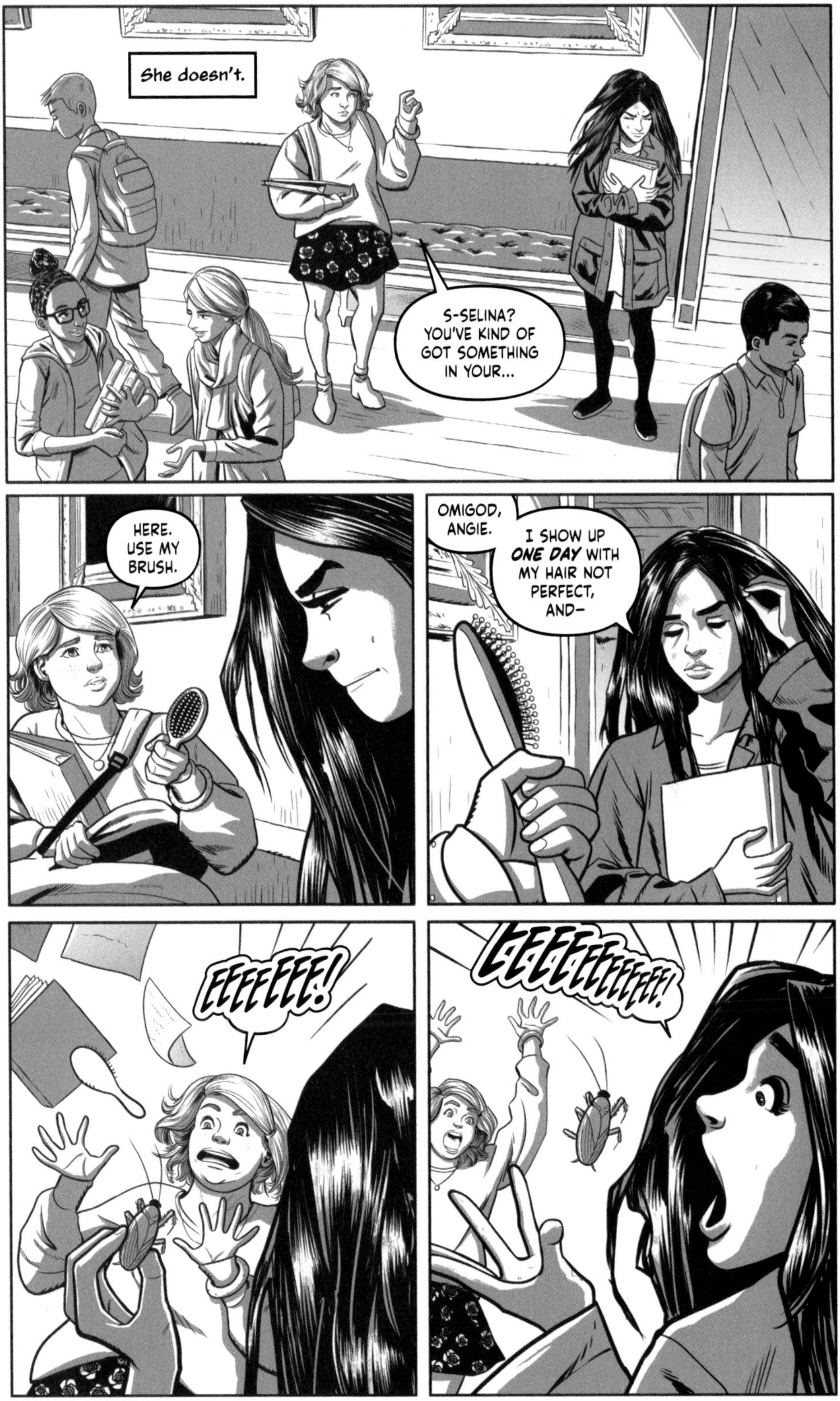
She doesn't.
S-SELINA? YOU'VE KIND OF GOT SOMETHING IN YOUR...
HERE. USE MY BRUSH.
OMIGOD, ANGIE.
I SHOW UP ONE DAY WITH MY HAIR NOT PERFECT, AND–
EEEEEEE!
EEEEEEEEEEEE!

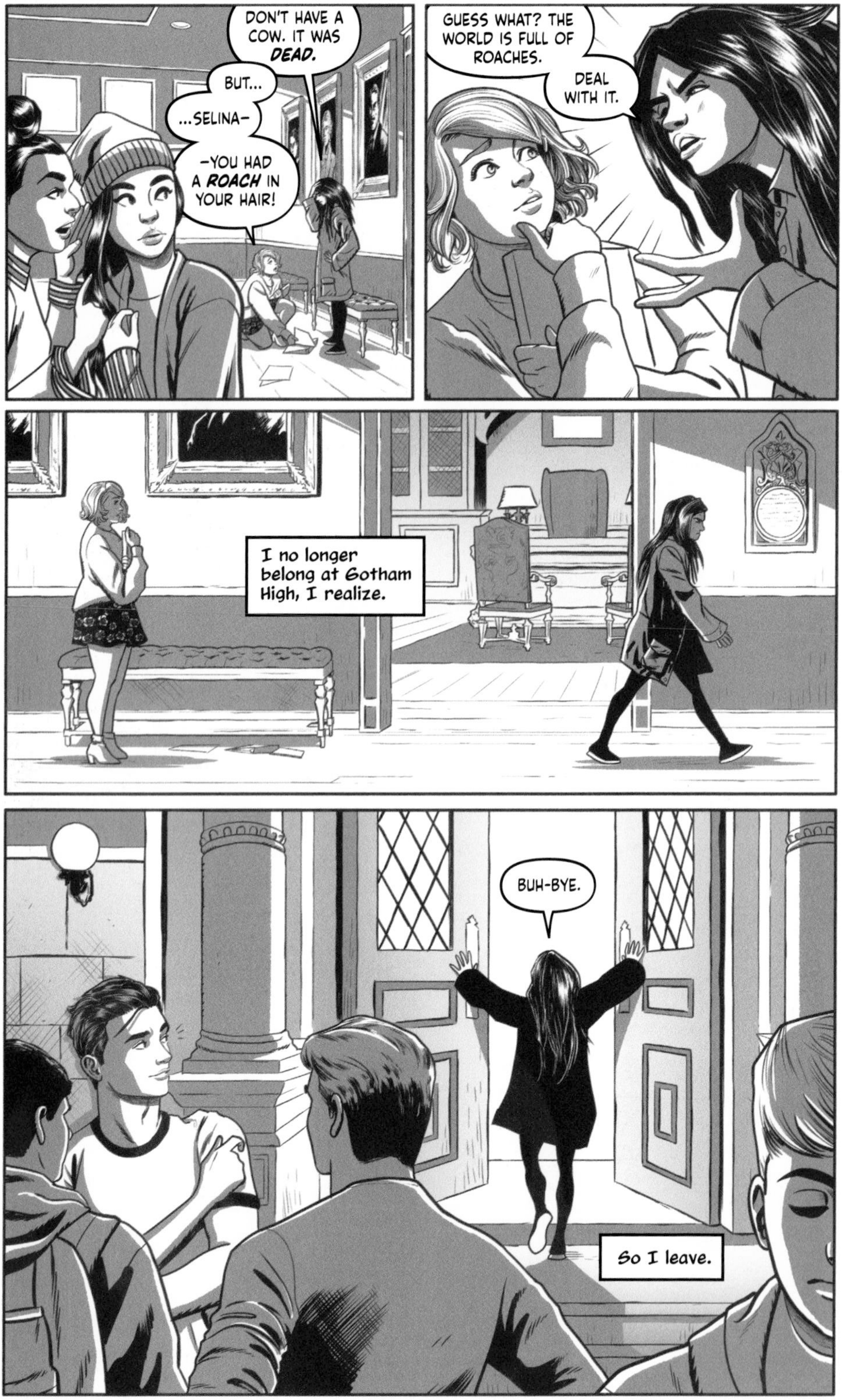
DON'T HAVE A COW. IT WAS DEAD.
BUT...
...SELINA–
–YOU HAD A ROACH IN YOUR HAIR!
GUESS WHAT? THE WORLD IS FULL OF ROACHES.
DEAL WITH IT.
I no longer belong at Gotham High, I realize.
BUH-BYE.
So I leave.

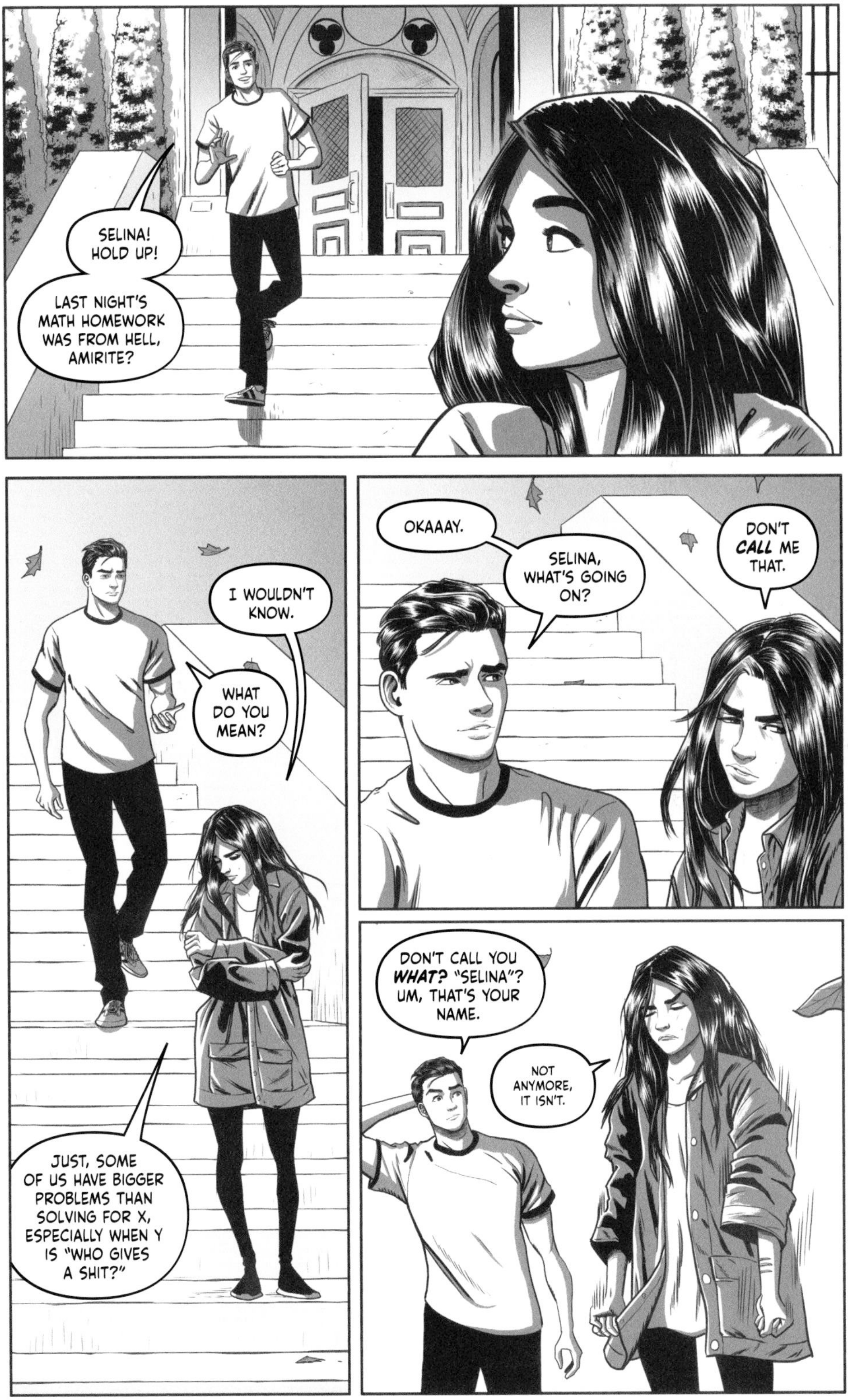
SELINA! HOLD UP!
LAST NIGHT'S MATH HOMEWORK WAS FROM HELL, AMIRITE?
I WOULDN'T KNOW.
WHAT DO YOU MEAN?
JUST, SOME OF US HAVE BIGGER PROBLEMS THAN SOLVING FOR X, ESPECIALLY WHEN Y IS "WHO GIVES A SHIT?"
OKAAAY.
SELINA, WHAT'S GOING ON?
DON'T CALL ME THAT.
DON'T CALL YOU WHAT? "SELINA"? UM, THAT'S YOUR NAME.
NOT ANYMORE, IT ISN'T.

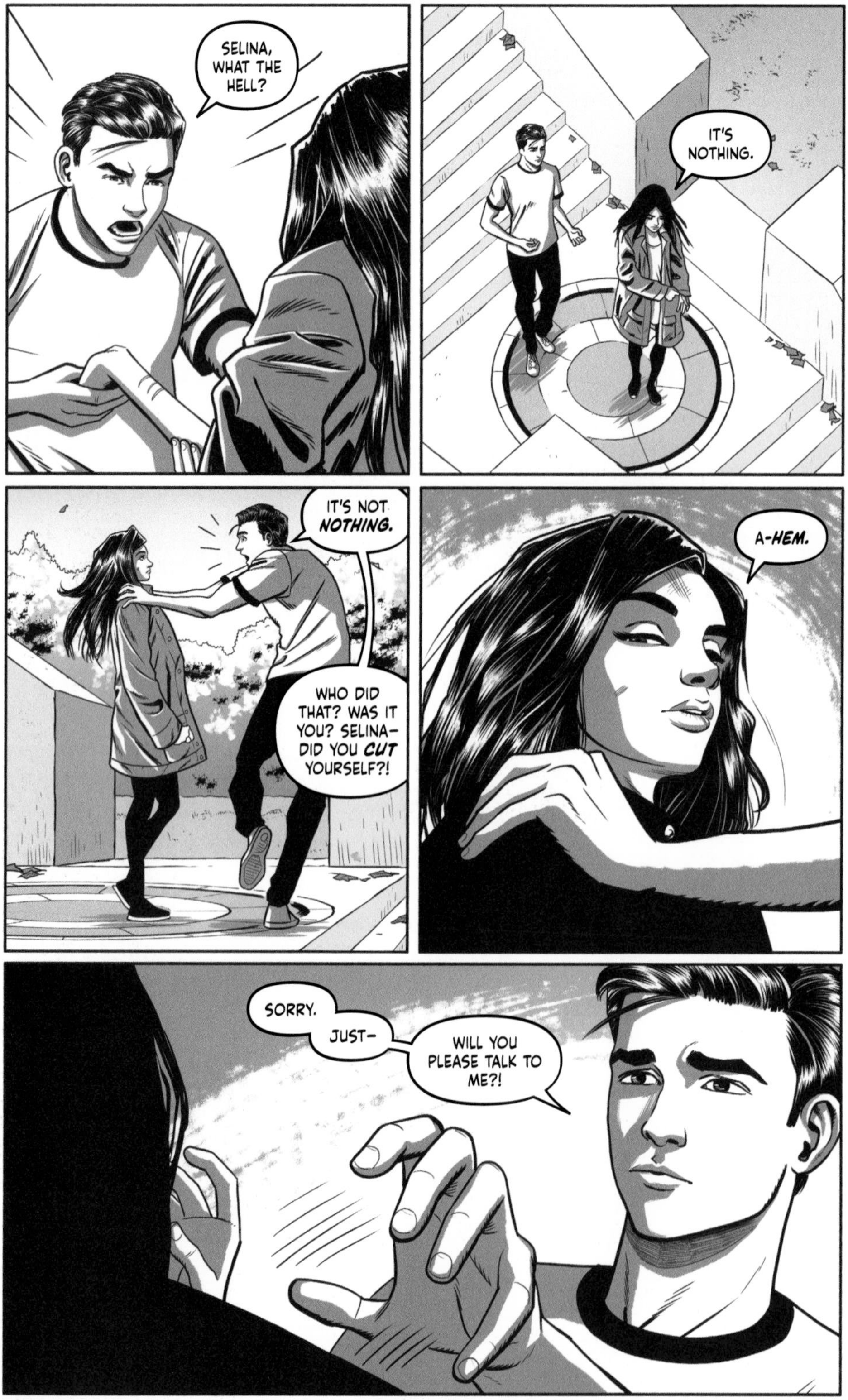
SELINA, WHAT THE HELL?
IT'S NOTHING.
IT'S NOT NOTHING.
WHO DID THAT? WAS IT YOU? SELINA- DID YOU CUT YOURSELF?!
A-HEM.
SORRY.
JUST-
WILL YOU PLEASE TALK TO ME?!

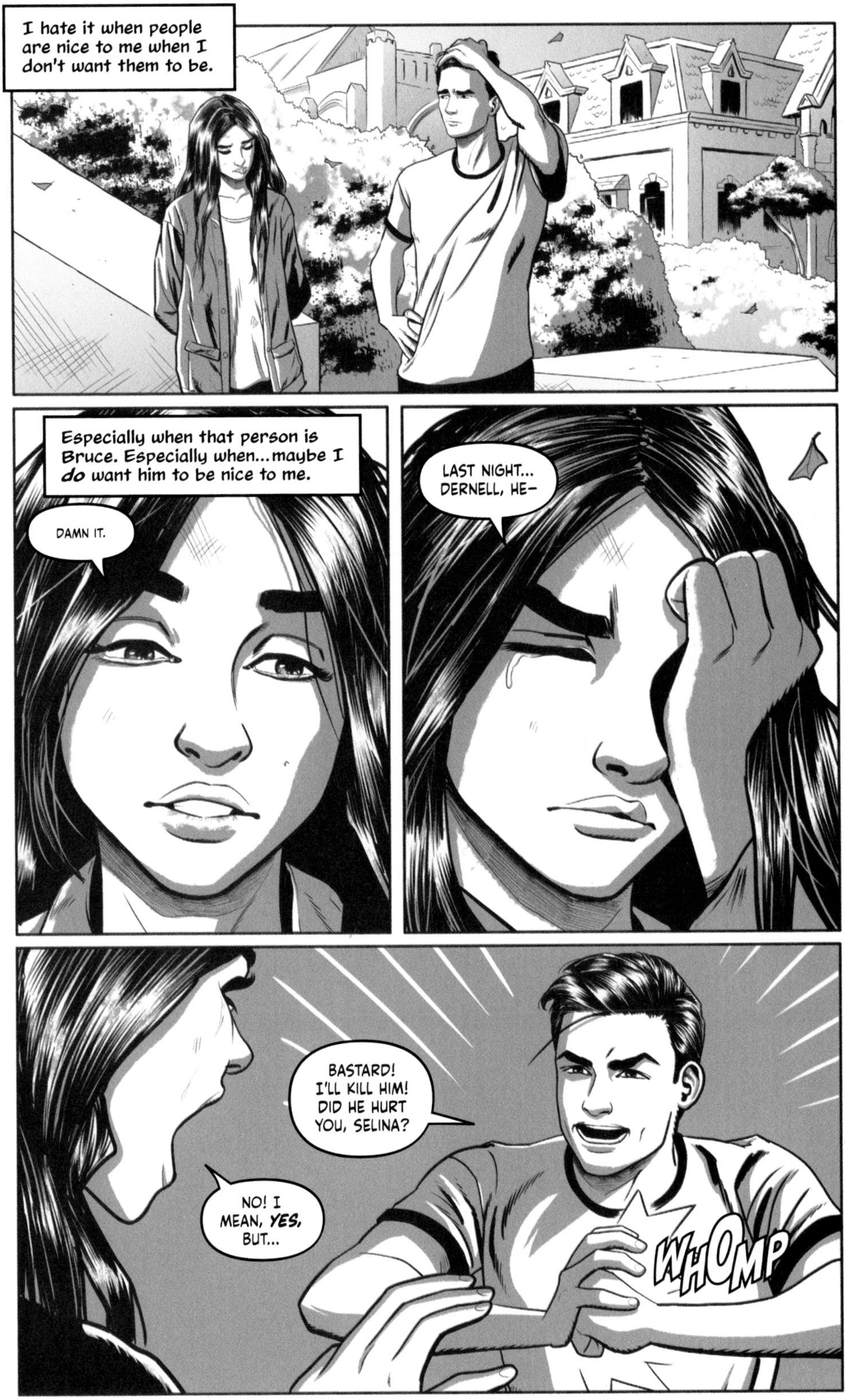
I hate it when people are nice to me when I don't want them to be.
Especially when that person is Bruce. Especially when...maybe I *do* want him to be nice to me.
DAMN IT.
LAST NIGHT... DERNELL, HE—
BASTARD! I'LL KILL HIM! DID HE HURT YOU, SELINA?
NO! I MEAN, *YES,* BUT...
WHOMP

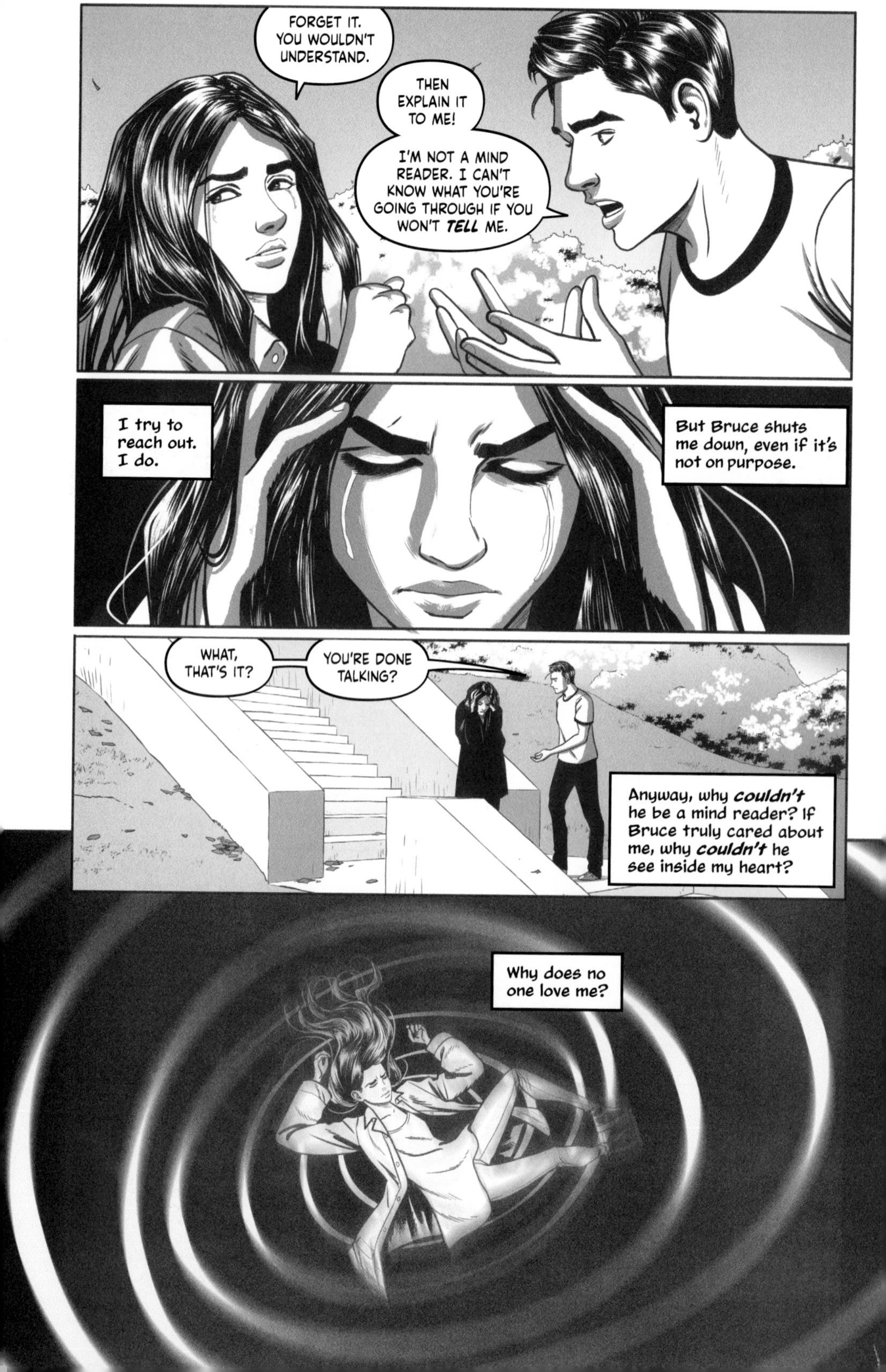
FORGET IT. YOU WOULDN'T UNDERSTAND.
THEN EXPLAIN IT TO ME!
I'M NOT A MIND READER. I CAN'T KNOW WHAT YOU'RE GOING THROUGH IF YOU WON'T ***TELL*** ME.
I try to reach out. I do.
But Bruce shuts me down, even if it's not on purpose.
WHAT, THAT'S IT?
YOU'RE DONE TALKING?
Anyway, why ***couldn't*** he be a mind reader? If Bruce truly cared about me, why ***couldn't*** he see inside my heart?
Why does no one love me?

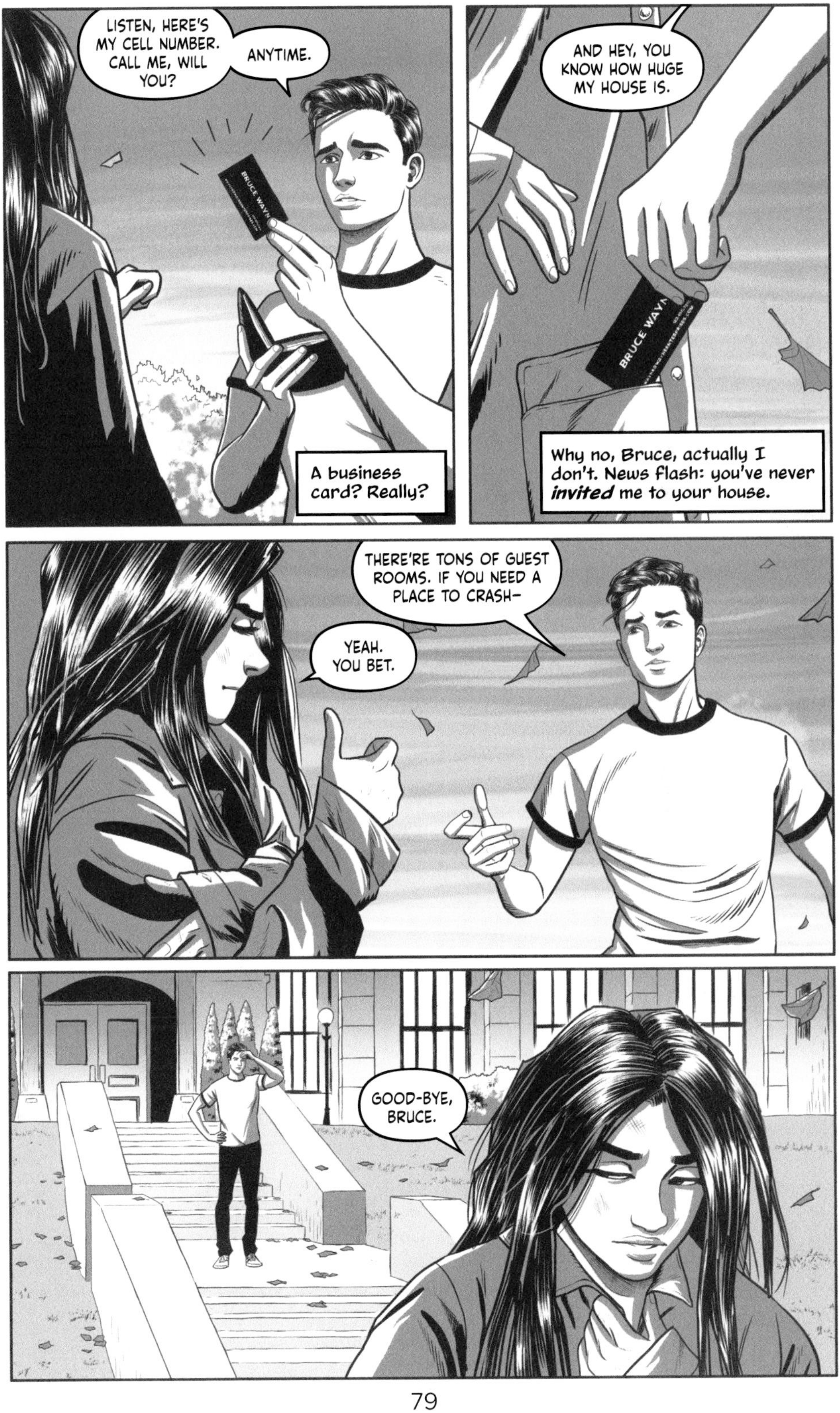
LISTEN, HERE'S MY CELL NUMBER. CALL ME, WILL YOU?
ANYTIME.
BRUCE WAYNE
A business card? Really?
AND HEY, YOU KNOW HOW HUGE MY HOUSE IS.
Why no, Bruce, actually I don't. News flash: you've never *invited* me to your house.
THERE'RE TONS OF GUEST ROOMS. IF YOU NEED A PLACE TO CRASH–
YEAH. YOU BET.
GOOD-BYE, BRUCE.

LICKING MY WOUNDS

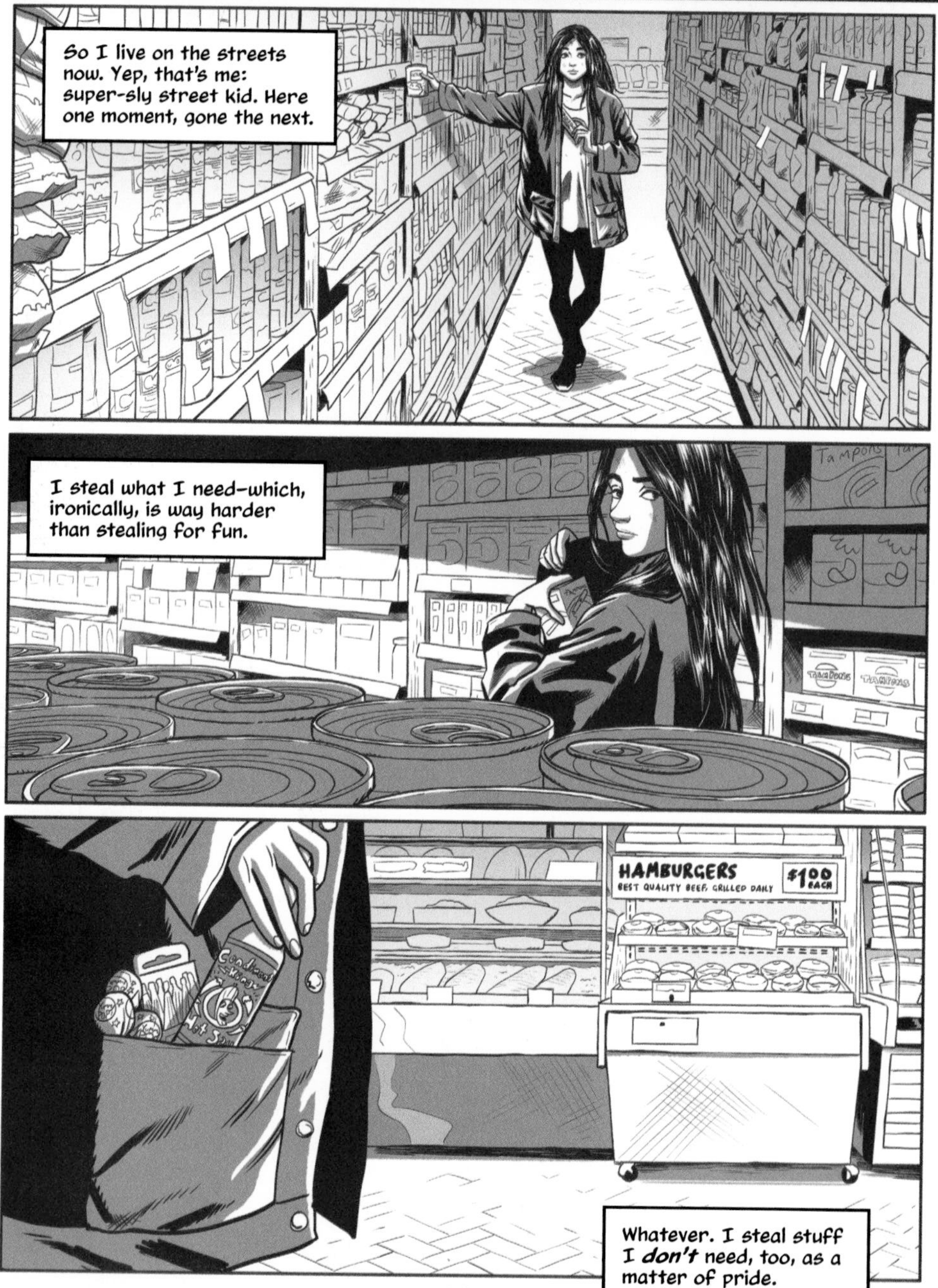
So I live on the streets now. Yep, that's me: super-sly street kid. Here one moment, gone the next.
I steal what I need–which, ironically, is way harder than stealing for fun.
HAMBURGERS
BEST QUALITY BEEF, GRILLED DAILY
$1.00 EACH
Whatever. I steal stuff I *don't* need, too, as a matter of pride.

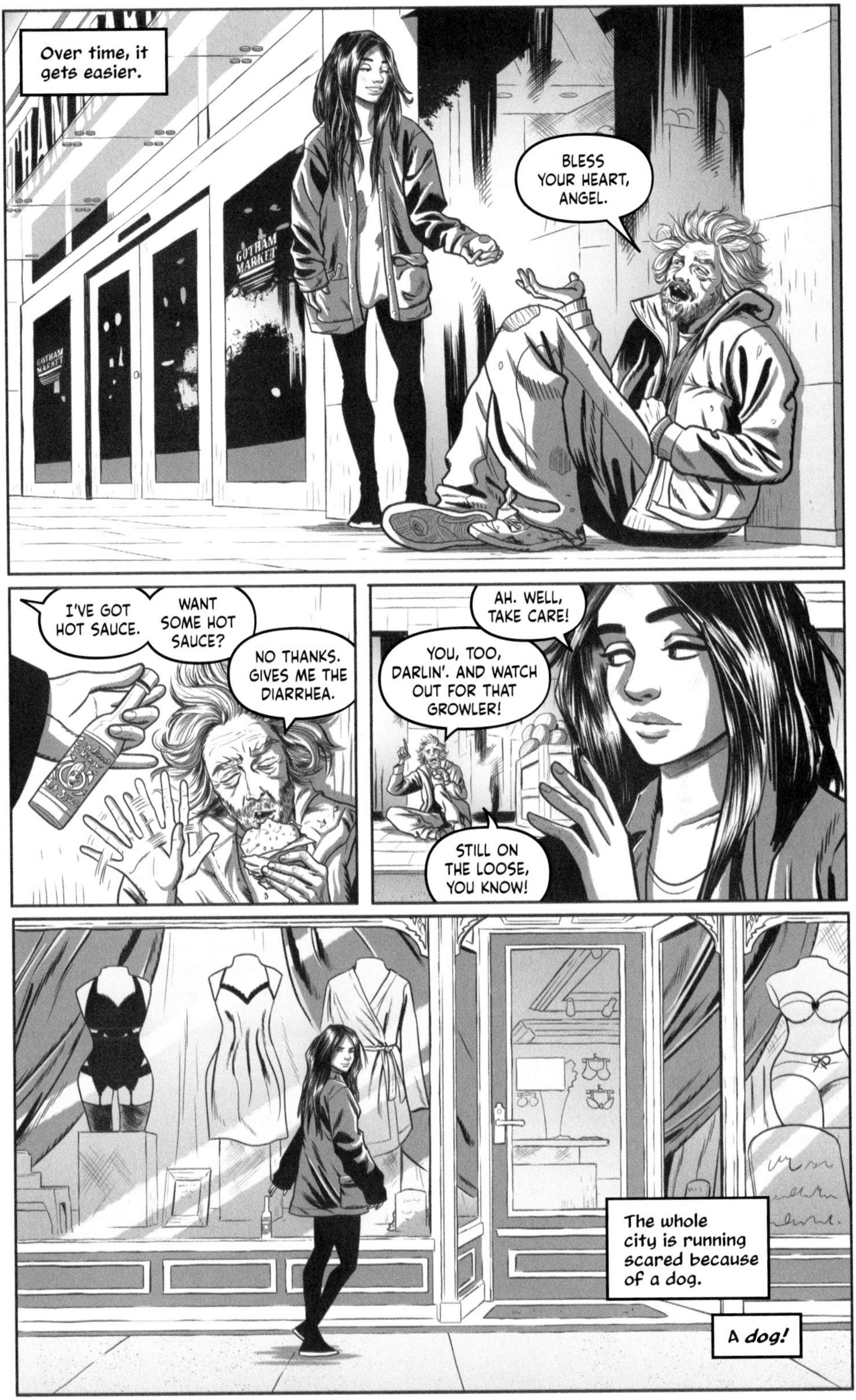
Over time, it gets easier.
BLESS YOUR HEART, ANGEL.
I'VE GOT HOT SAUCE.
WANT SOME HOT SAUCE?
NO THANKS. GIVES ME THE DIARRHEA.
AH. WELL, TAKE CARE!
YOU, TOO, DARLIN'. AND WATCH OUT FOR THAT GROWLER!
STILL ON THE LOOSE, YOU KNOW!
The whole city is running scared because of a dog.
A *dog!*

I don't bother with laundry.

My way is far easier.

R-R-RIP

THAT SHADE IS DIVINE.

ISN'T IT, THOUGH?

And I solve the "eau de dumpster" problem when I discover that the ritzier stores have "ladies lounges" instead of normal bathrooms.

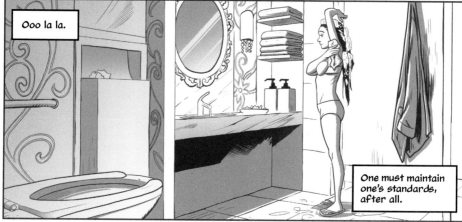

Ooo la la.

One must maintain one's standards, after all.

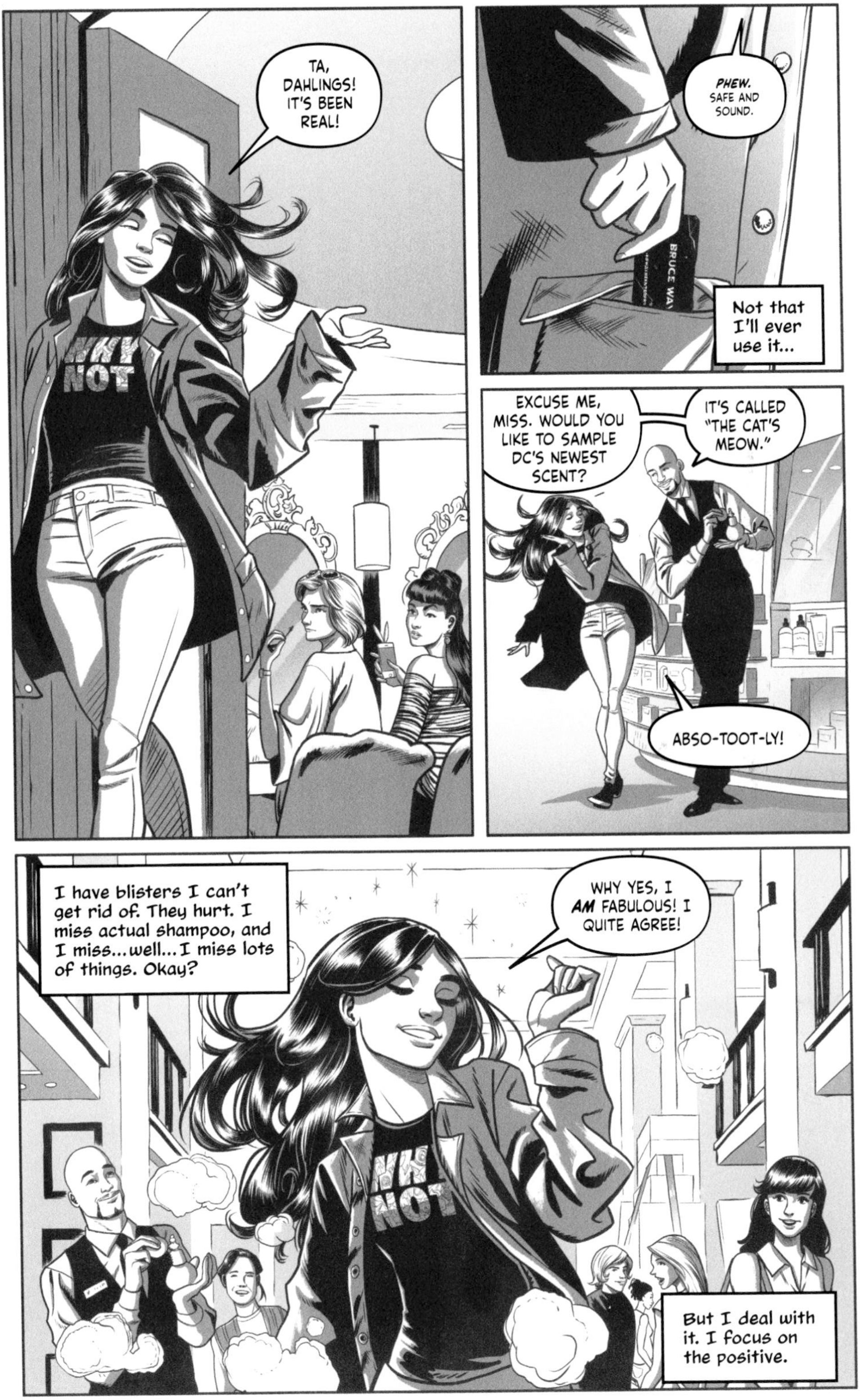
TA, DAHLINGS! IT'S BEEN REAL!
PHEW. SAFE AND SOUND.
BRUCE WA
Not that I'll ever use it...
EXCUSE ME, MISS. WOULD YOU LIKE TO SAMPLE DC'S NEWEST SCENT?
IT'S CALLED "THE CAT'S MEOW."
ABSO-TOOT-LY!
I have blisters I can't get rid of. They hurt. I miss actual shampoo, and I miss...well...I miss lots of things. Okay?
WHY YES, I *AM* FABULOUS! I QUITE AGREE!
WHY NOT
But I deal with it. I focus on the positive.

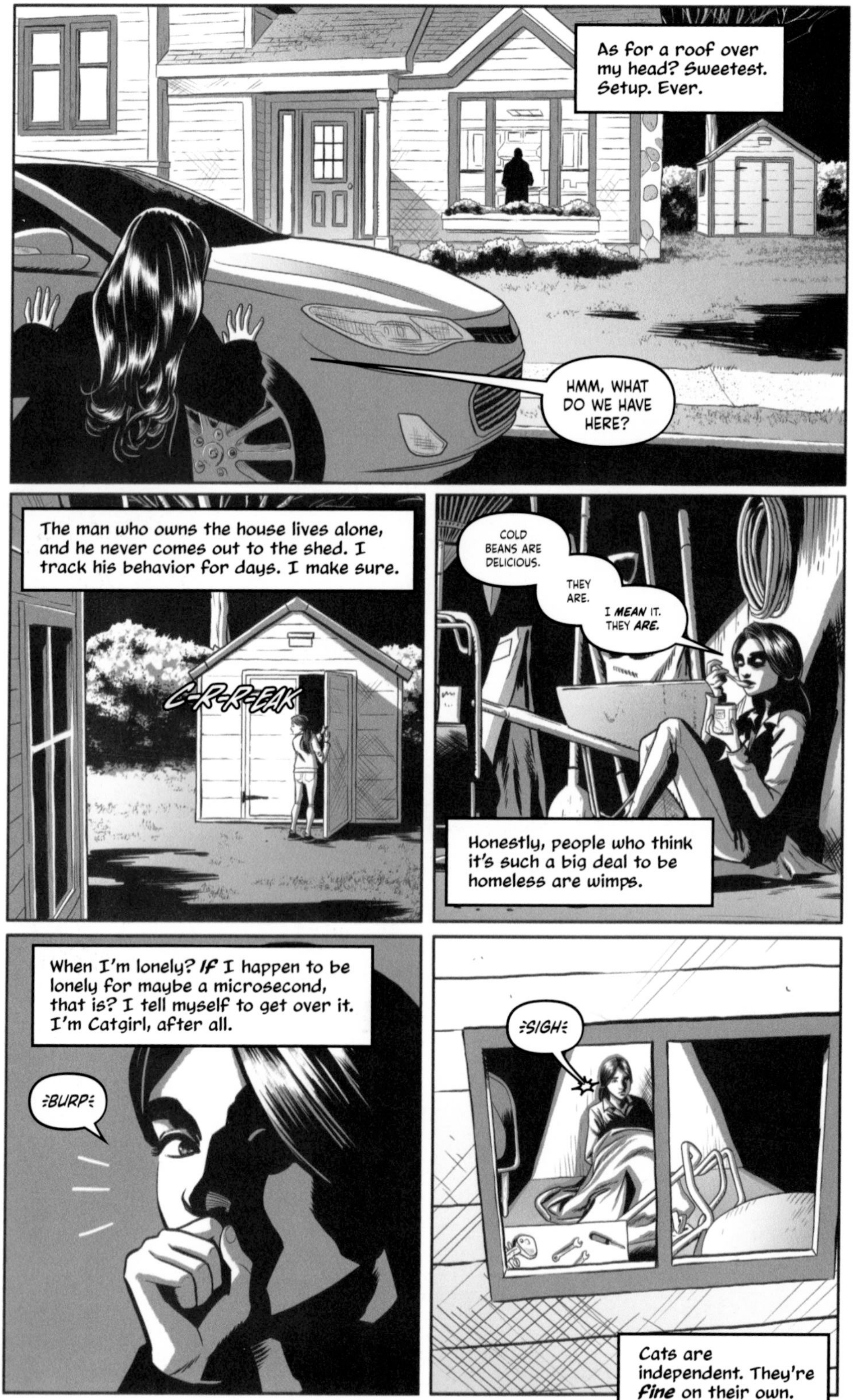
As for a roof over my head? Sweetest. Setup. Ever.
HMM, WHAT DO WE HAVE HERE?
The man who owns the house lives alone, and he never comes out to the shed. I track his behavior for days. I make sure.
C-R-R-EAK
COLD BEANS ARE DELICIOUS.
THEY ARE.
I MEAN IT. THEY ARE.
Honestly, people who think it's such a big deal to be homeless are wimps.
When I'm lonely? If I happen to be lonely for maybe a microsecond, that is? I tell myself to get over it. I'm Catgirl, after all.
BURP
SIGH
Cats are independent. They're fine on their own.

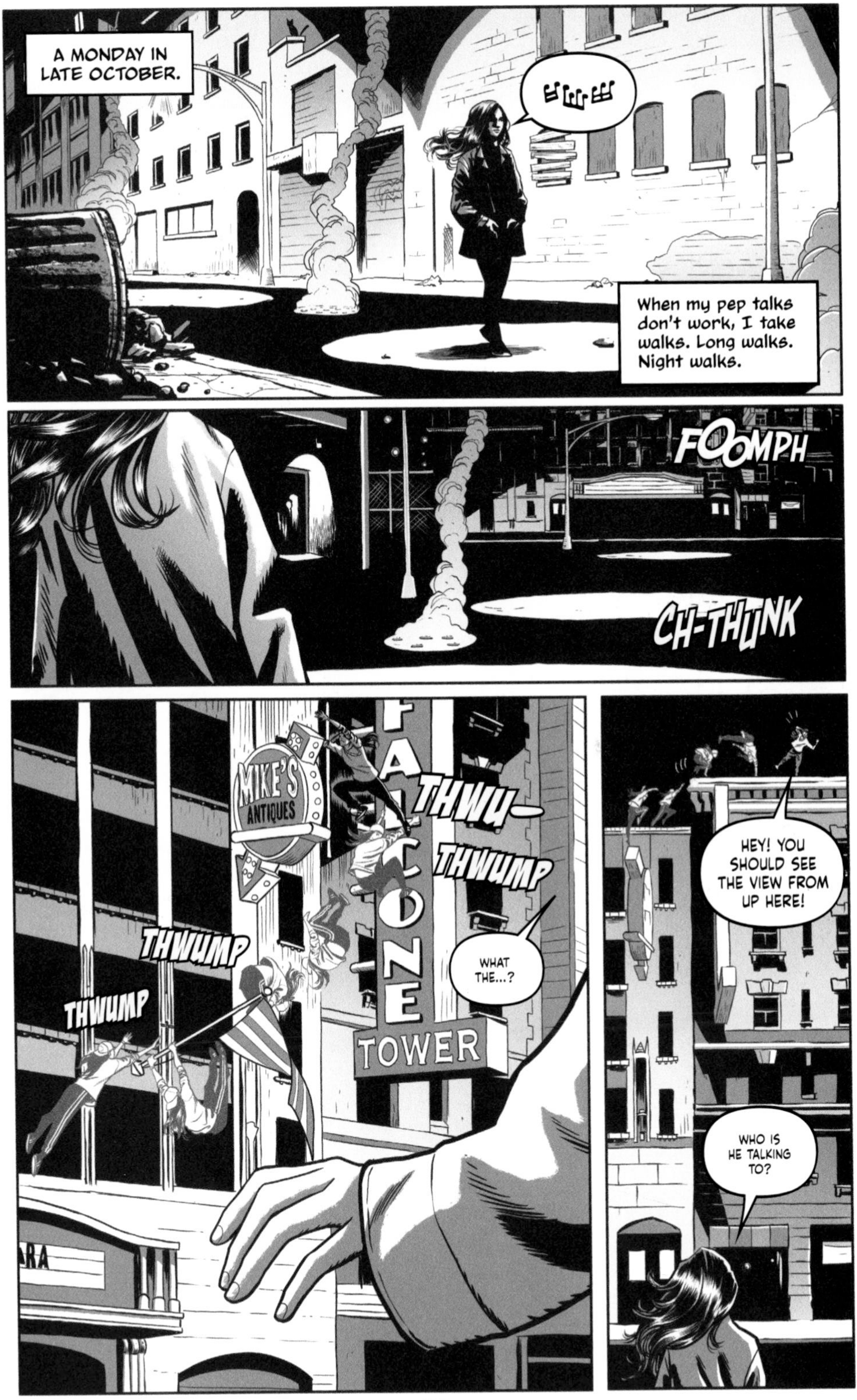
A MONDAY IN LATE OCTOBER.
When my pep talks don't work, I take walks. Long walks. Night walks.
FOOMPH
CH-THUNK
MIKE'S ANTIQUES
THWU-
THWUMP
THWUMP
THWUMP
TOWER
WHAT THE...?
HEY! YOU SHOULD SEE THE VIEW FROM UP HERE!
WHO IS HE TALKING TO?

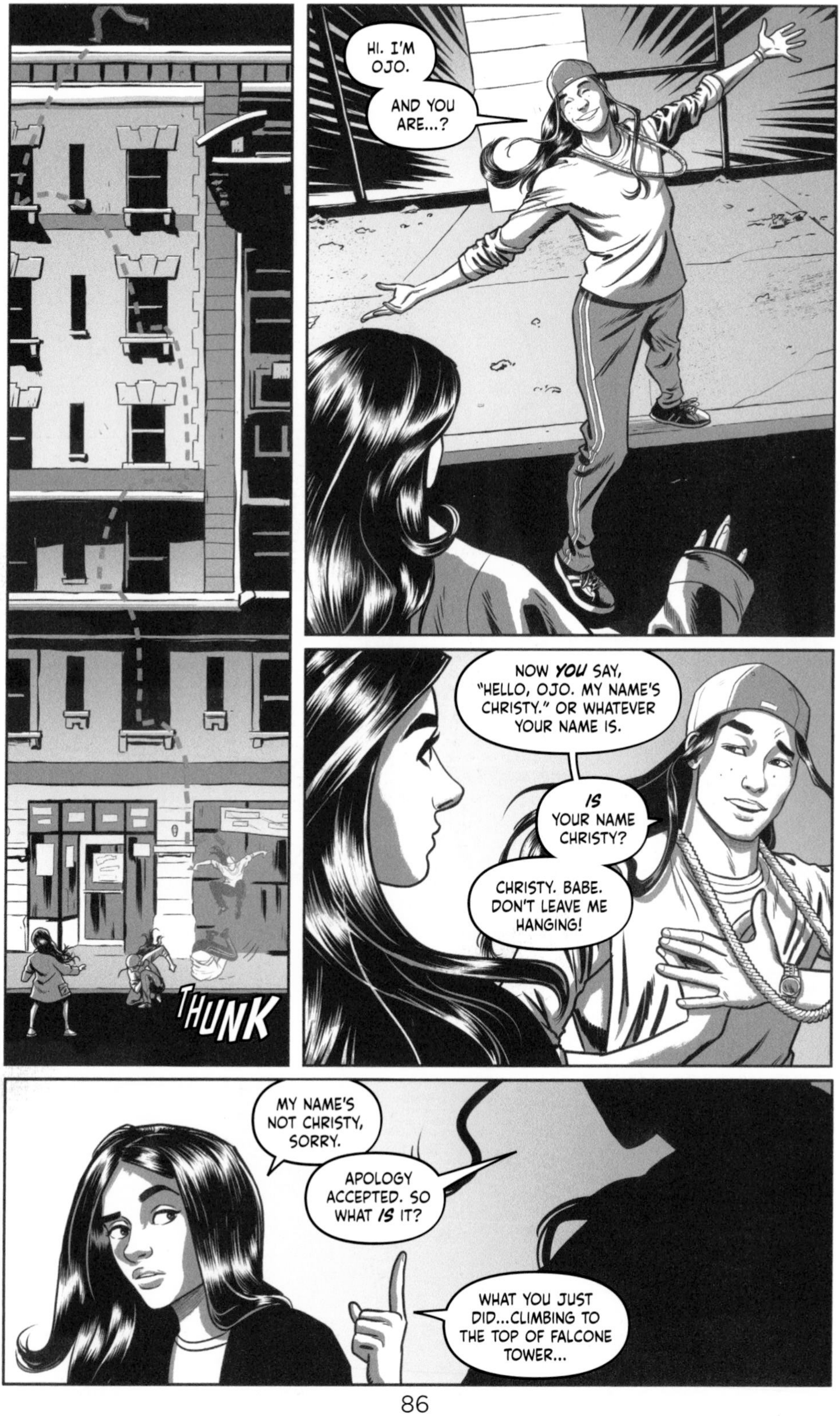
THUNK
HI. I'M OJO.
AND YOU ARE...?
NOW YOU SAY, "HELLO, OJO. MY NAME'S CHRISTY." OR WHATEVER YOUR NAME IS.
IS YOUR NAME CHRISTY?
CHRISTY. BABE. DON'T LEAVE ME HANGING!
MY NAME'S NOT CHRISTY, SORRY.
APOLOGY ACCEPTED. SO WHAT IS IT?
WHAT YOU JUST DID...CLIMBING TO THE TOP OF FALCONE TOWER...

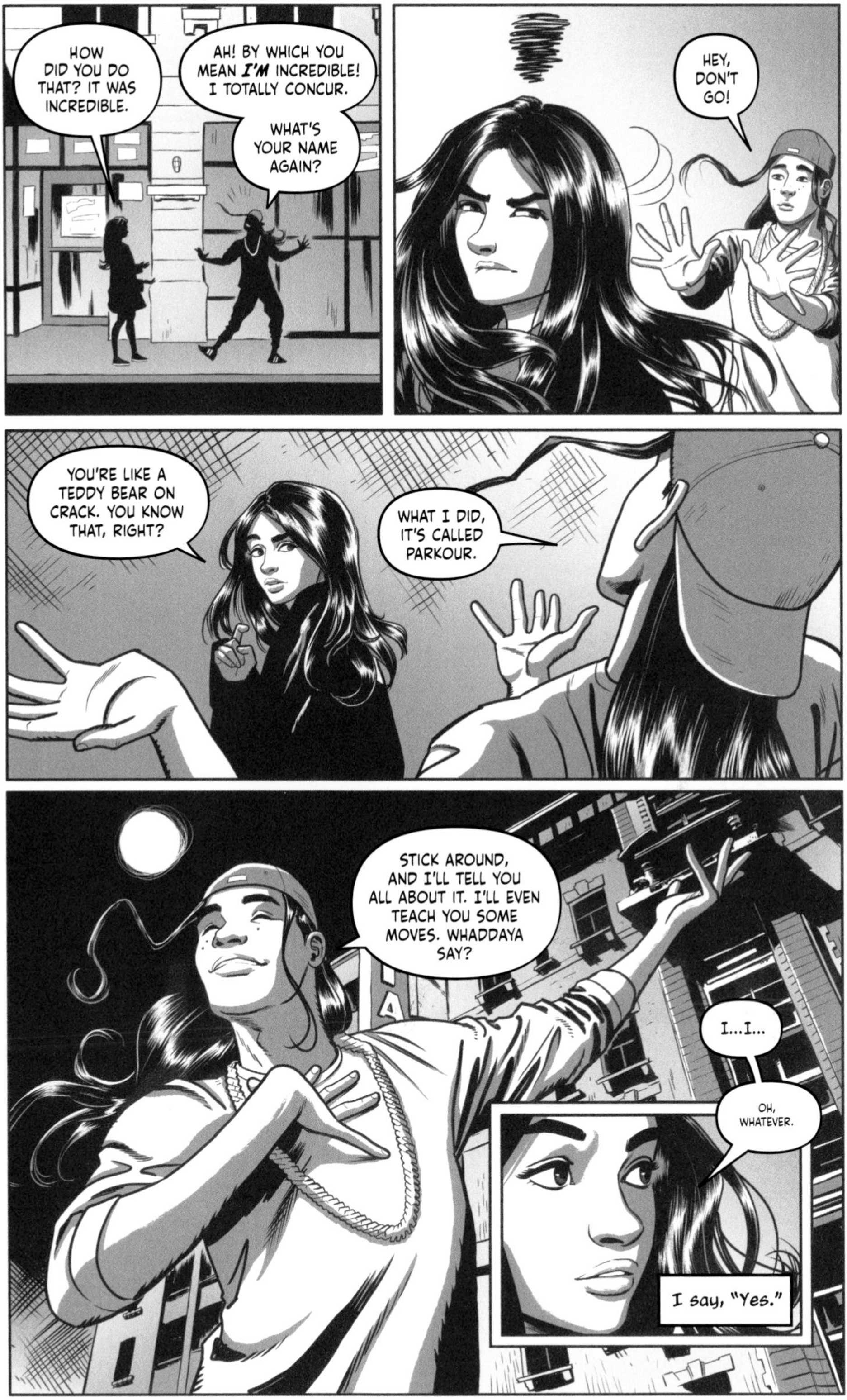
HOW DID YOU DO THAT? IT WAS INCREDIBLE.
AH! BY WHICH YOU MEAN ***I'M*** INCREDIBLE! I TOTALLY CONCUR.
WHAT'S YOUR NAME AGAIN?
HEY, DON'T GO!
YOU'RE LIKE A TEDDY BEAR ON CRACK. YOU KNOW THAT, RIGHT?
WHAT I DID, IT'S CALLED PARKOUR.
STICK AROUND, AND I'LL TELL YOU ALL ABOUT IT. I'LL EVEN TEACH YOU SOME MOVES. WHADDAYA SAY?
I...I...
OH, WHATEVER.
I say, "Yes."

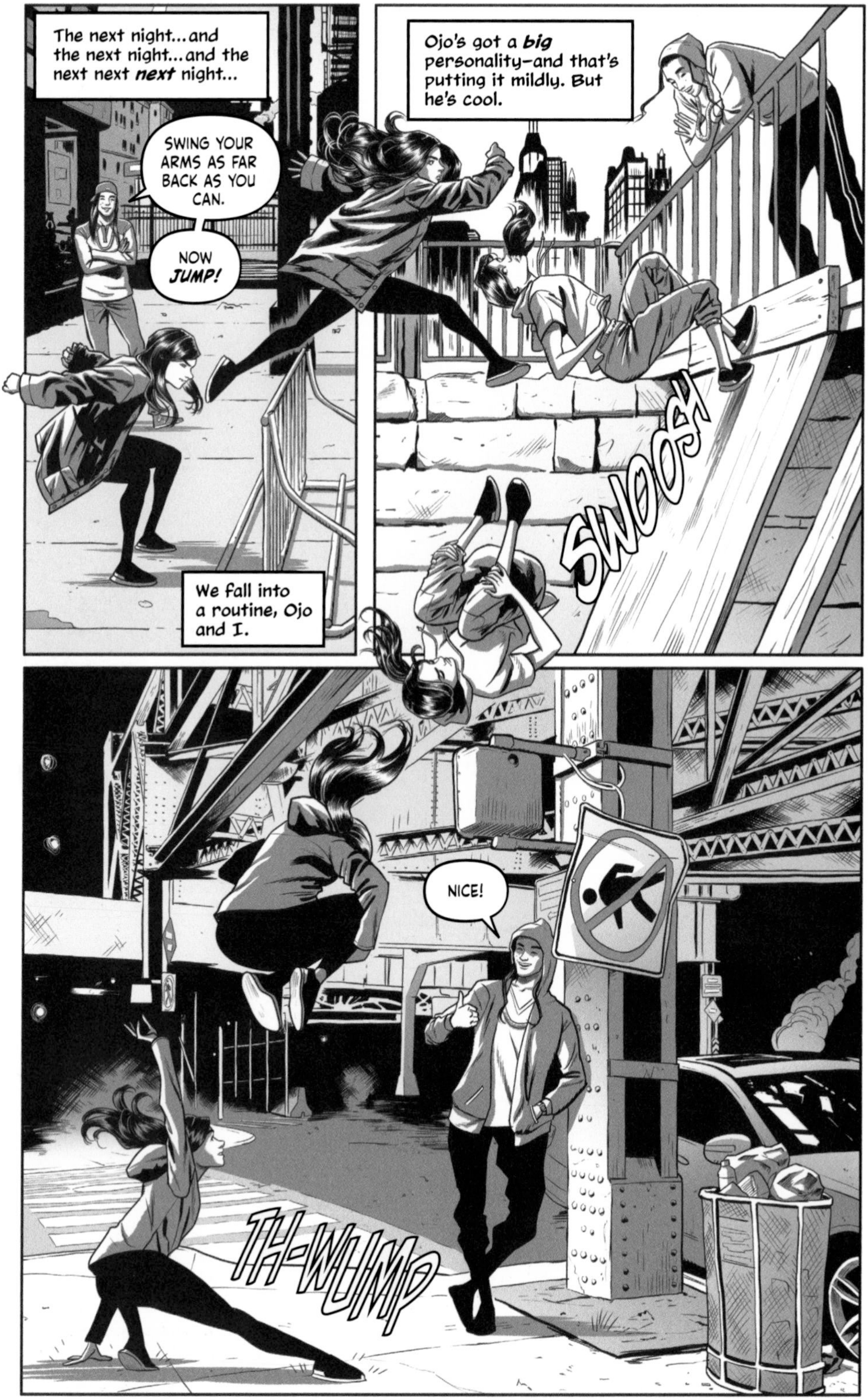
The next night...and the next night...and the next next *next* night...
SWING YOUR ARMS AS FAR BACK AS YOU CAN.
NOW *JUMP!*
We fall into a routine, Ojo and I.
Ojo's got a *big* personality—and that's putting it mildly. But he's cool.
SWOOSH
NICE!
TH-WUMP

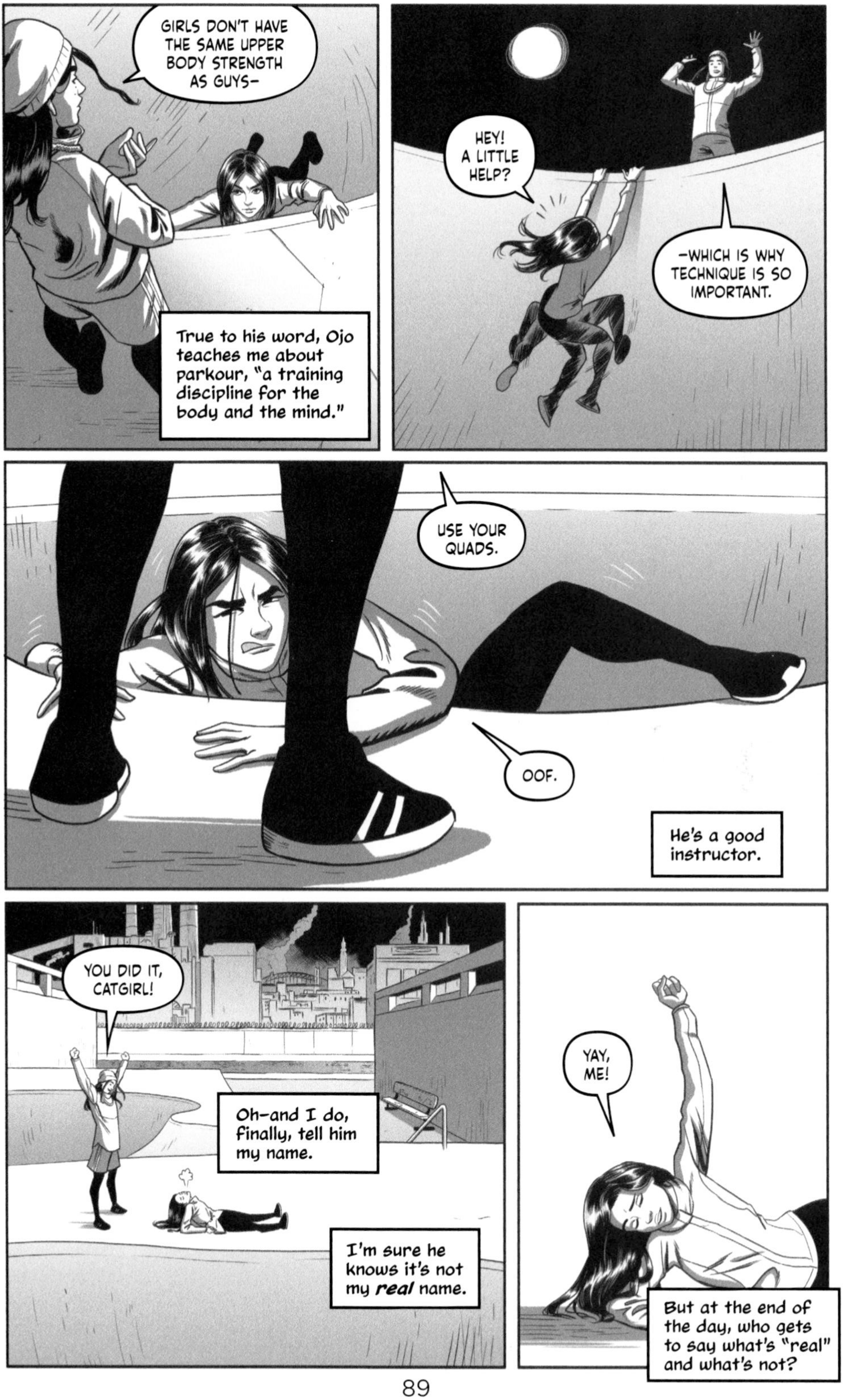
GIRLS DON'T HAVE THE SAME UPPER BODY STRENGTH AS GUYS—
True to his word, Ojo teaches me about parkour, "a training discipline for the body and the mind."
HEY! A LITTLE HELP?
—WHICH IS WHY TECHNIQUE IS SO IMPORTANT.
USE YOUR QUADS.
OOF.
He's a good instructor.
YOU DID IT, CATGIRL!
Oh—and I do, finally, tell him my name.
I'm sure he knows it's not my *real* name.
YAY, ME!
But at the end of the day, who gets to say what's "real" and what's not?

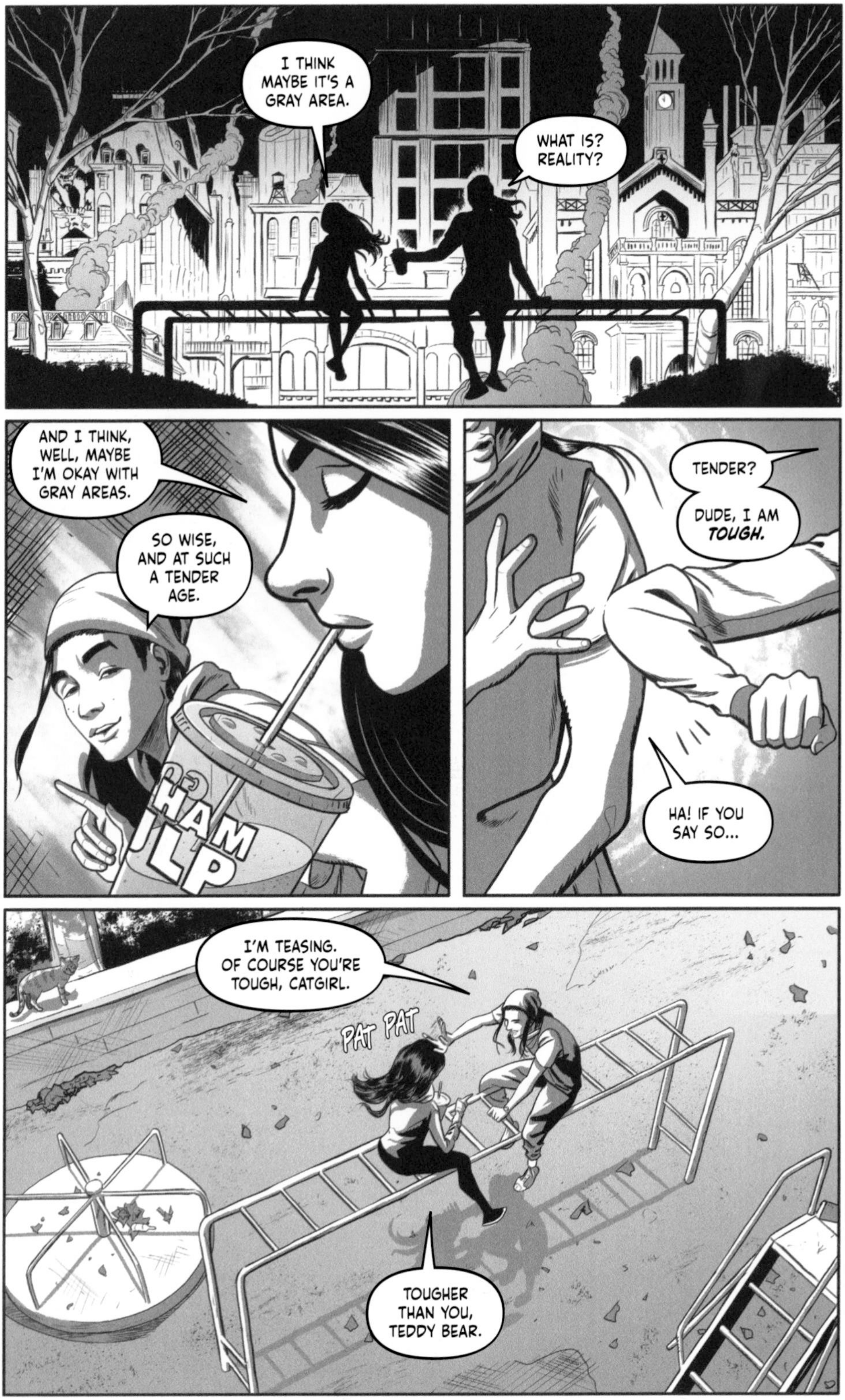
I THINK MAYBE IT'S A GRAY AREA.
WHAT IS? REALITY?
AND I THINK, WELL, MAYBE I'M OKAY WITH GRAY AREAS.
SO WISE, AND AT SUCH A TENDER AGE.
HAM
LP
TENDER?
DUDE, I AM *TOUGH.*
HA! IF YOU SAY SO...
I'M TEASING. OF COURSE YOU'RE TOUGH, CATGIRL.
PAT PAT
TOUGHER THAN YOU, TEDDY BEAR.

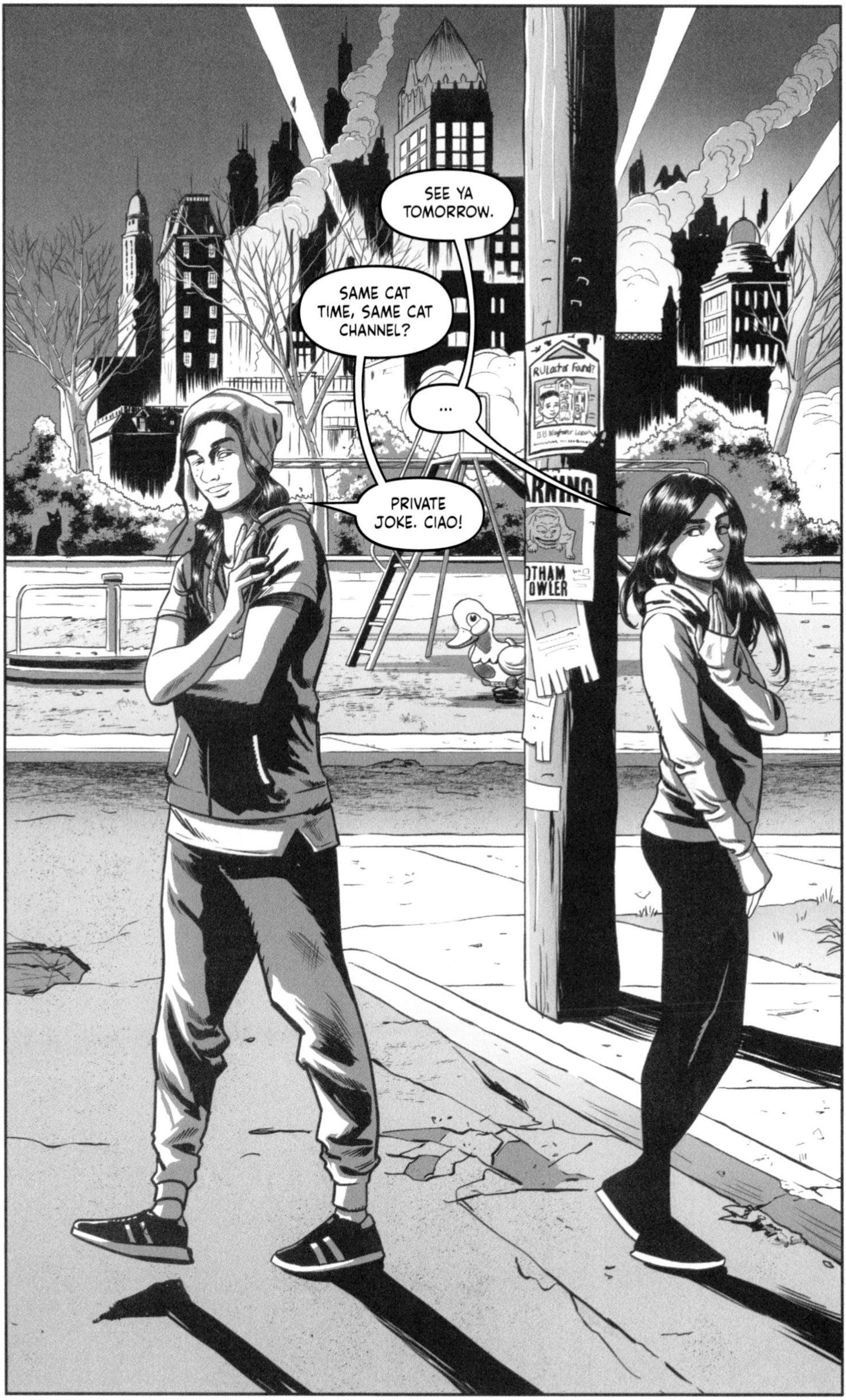
SEE YA TOMORROW.
SAME CAT TIME, SAME CAT CHANNEL?
...
PRIVATE JOKE. CIAO!

UNSHEATHED

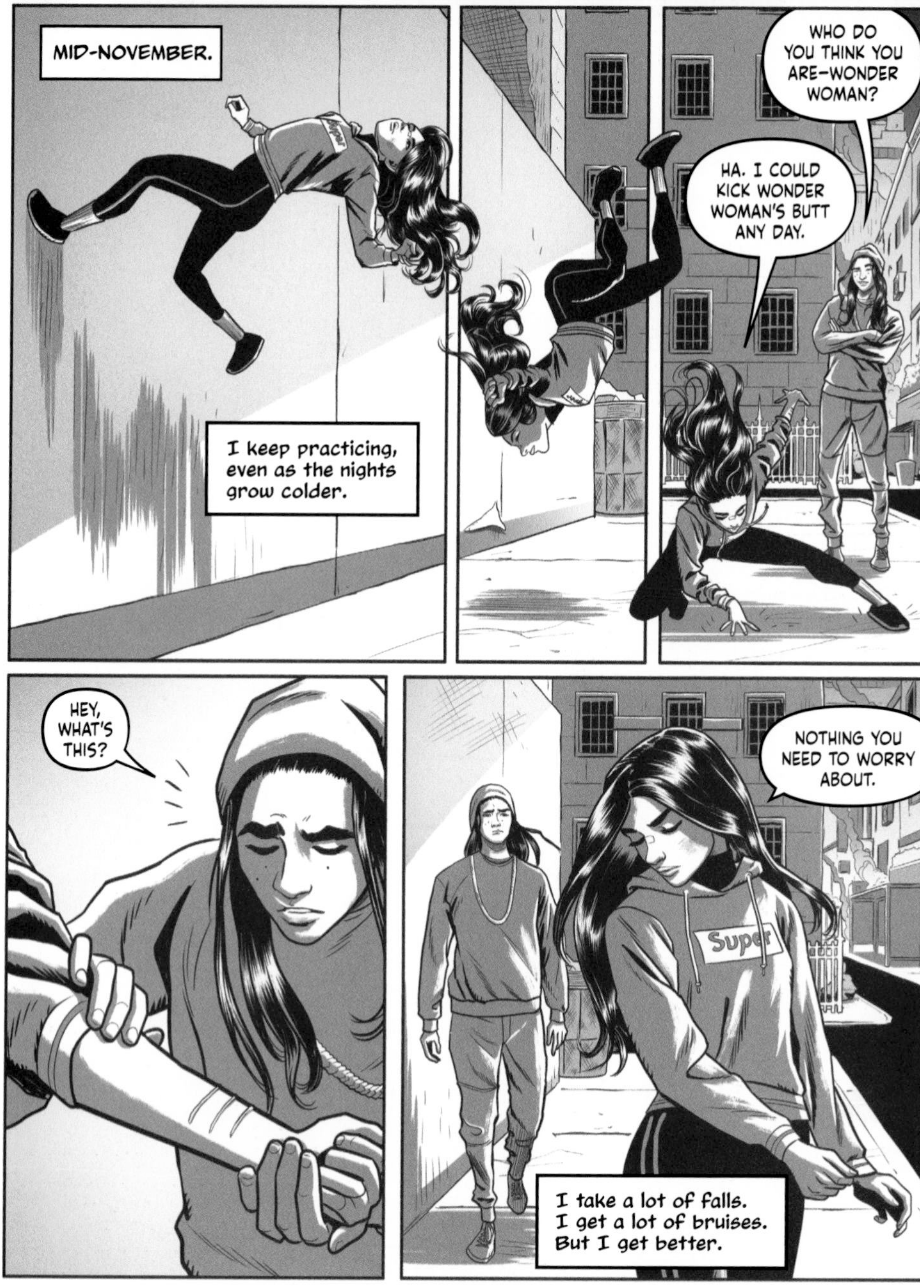

MID-NOVEMBER.
I keep practicing, even as the nights grow colder.
WHO DO YOU THINK YOU ARE—WONDER WOMAN?
HA. I COULD KICK WONDER WOMAN'S BUTT ANY DAY.
HEY, WHAT'S THIS?
NOTHING YOU NEED TO WORRY ABOUT.
Super
I take a lot of falls. I get a lot of bruises. But I get better.

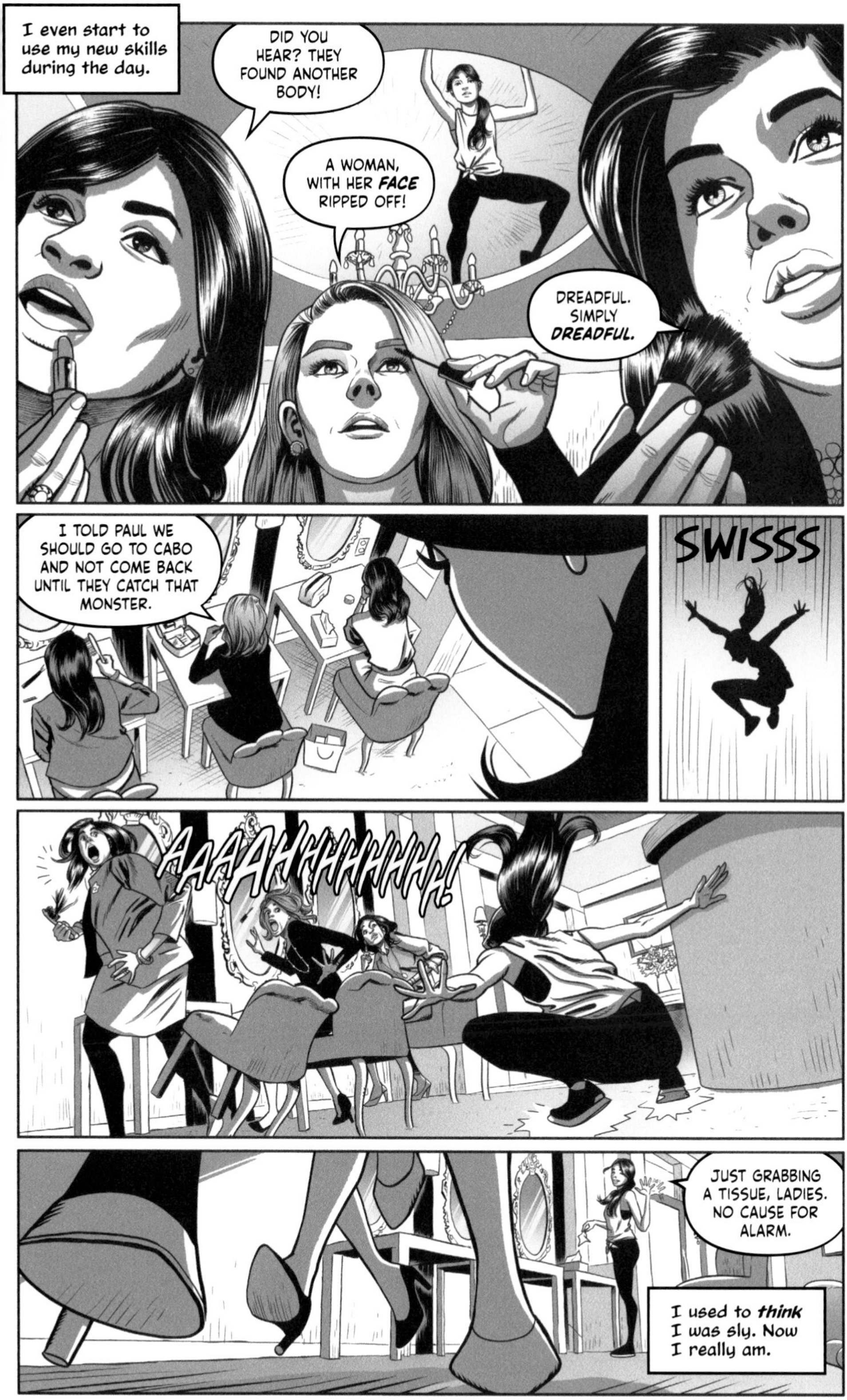
I even start to use my new skills during the day.
DID YOU HEAR? THEY FOUND ANOTHER BODY!
A WOMAN, WITH HER *FACE* RIPPED OFF!
DREADFUL. SIMPLY ***DREADFUL.***
I TOLD PAUL WE SHOULD GO TO CABO AND NOT COME BACK UNTIL THEY CATCH THAT MONSTER.
SWISSS
AAAAHHHHHHHH!
JUST GRABBING A TISSUE, LADIES. NO CAUSE FOR ALARM.
I used to ***think*** I was sly. Now I really am.

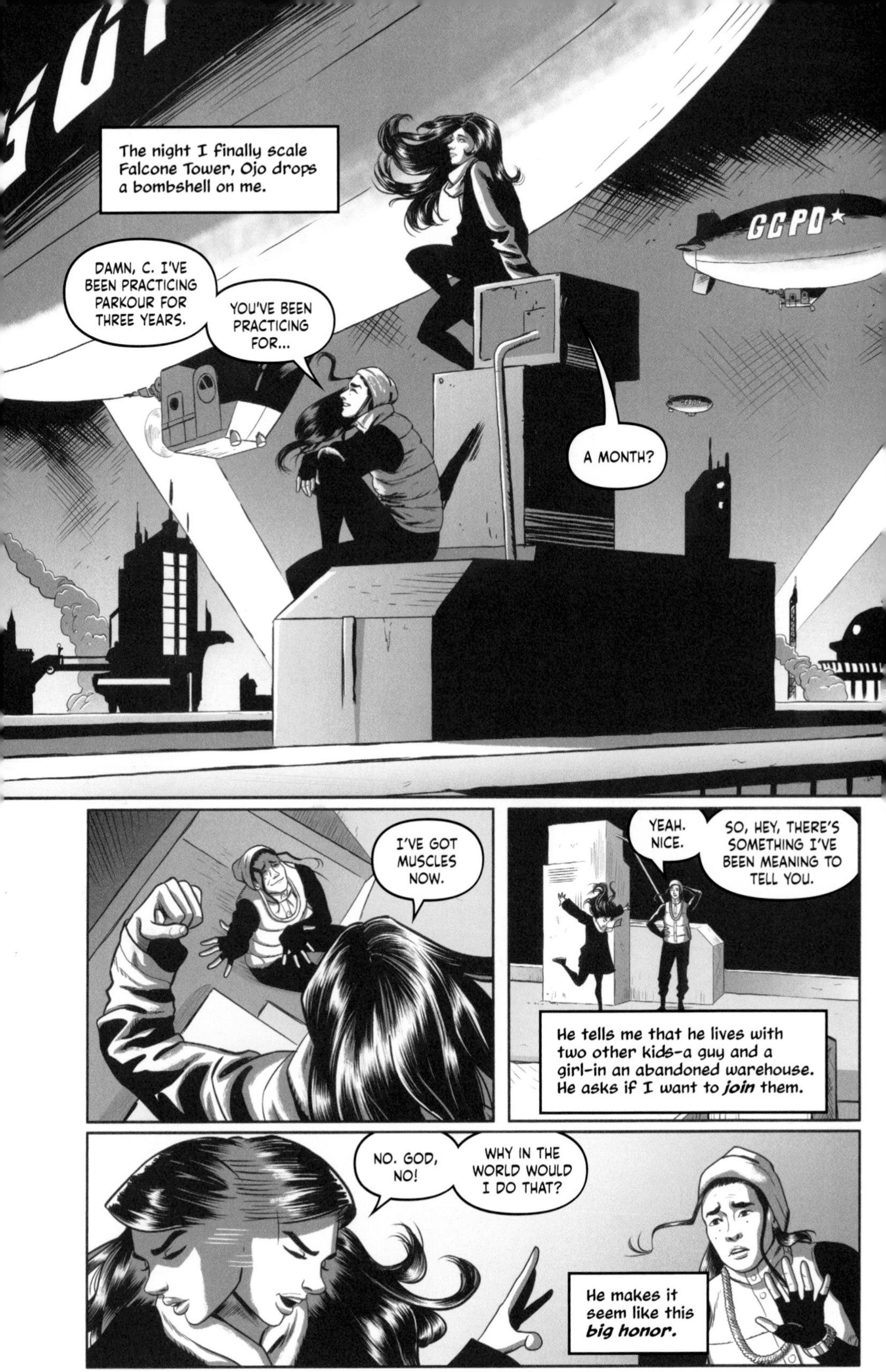
GCPD
The night I finally scale Falcone Tower, Ojo drops a bombshell on me.
DAMN, C. I'VE BEEN PRACTICING PARKOUR FOR THREE YEARS.
YOU'VE BEEN PRACTICING FOR...
A MONTH?
I'VE GOT MUSCLES NOW.
YEAH. NICE.
SO, HEY, THERE'S SOMETHING I'VE BEEN MEANING TO TELL YOU.
He tells me that he lives with two other kids–a guy and a girl–in an abandoned warehouse. He asks if I want to ***join*** them.
NO. GOD, NO!
WHY IN THE WORLD WOULD I DO THAT?
He makes it seem like this ***big honor.***

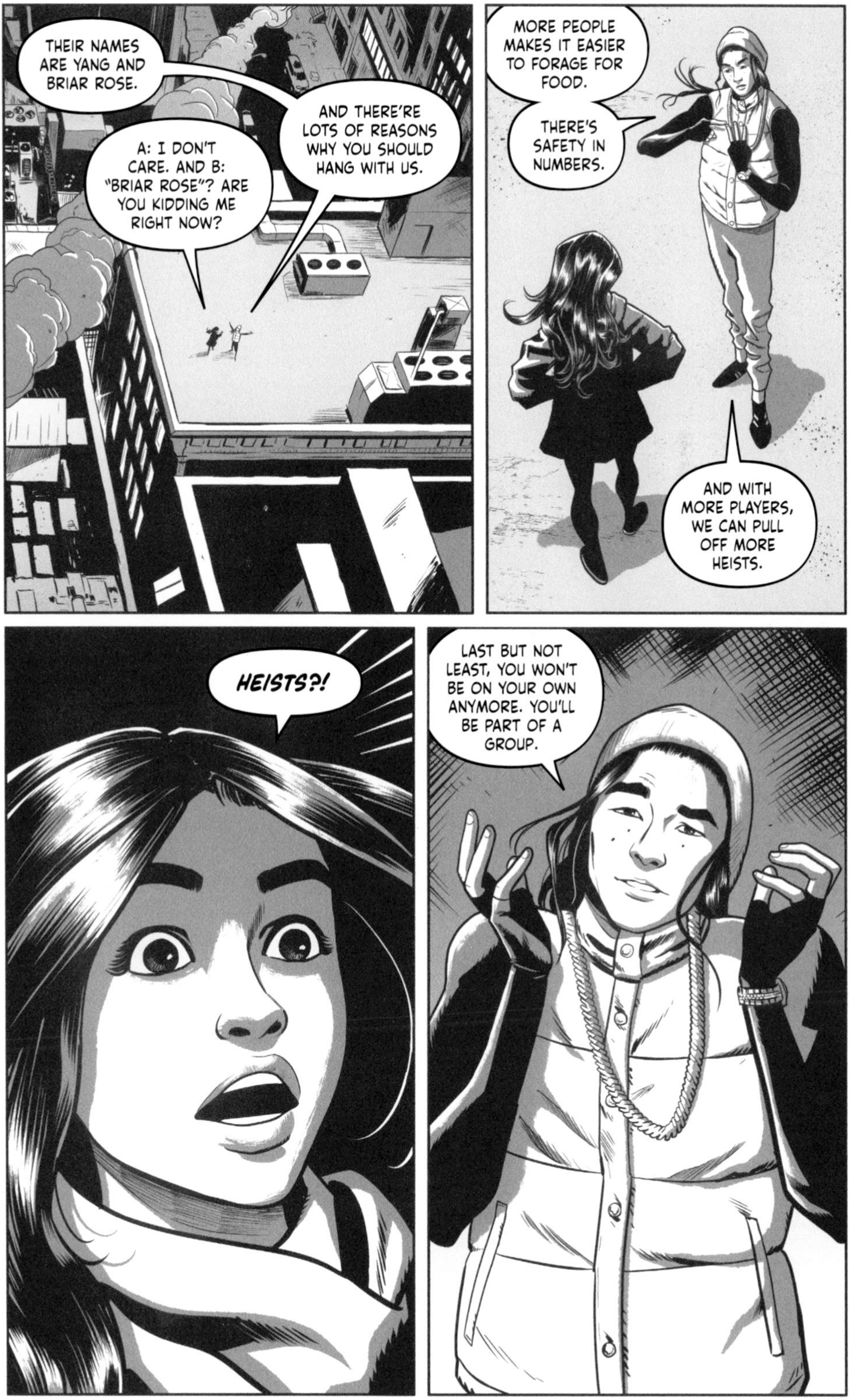
THEIR NAMES ARE YANG AND BRIAR ROSE.
AND THERE'RE LOTS OF REASONS WHY YOU SHOULD HANG WITH US.
A: I DON'T CARE. AND B: "BRIAR ROSE"? ARE YOU KIDDING ME RIGHT NOW?
MORE PEOPLE MAKES IT EASIER TO FORAGE FOR FOOD.
THERE'S SAFETY IN NUMBERS.
AND WITH MORE PLAYERS, WE CAN PULL OFF MORE HEISTS.
HEISTS?!
LAST BUT NOT LEAST, YOU WON'T BE ON YOUR OWN ANYMORE. YOU'LL BE PART OF A GROUP.

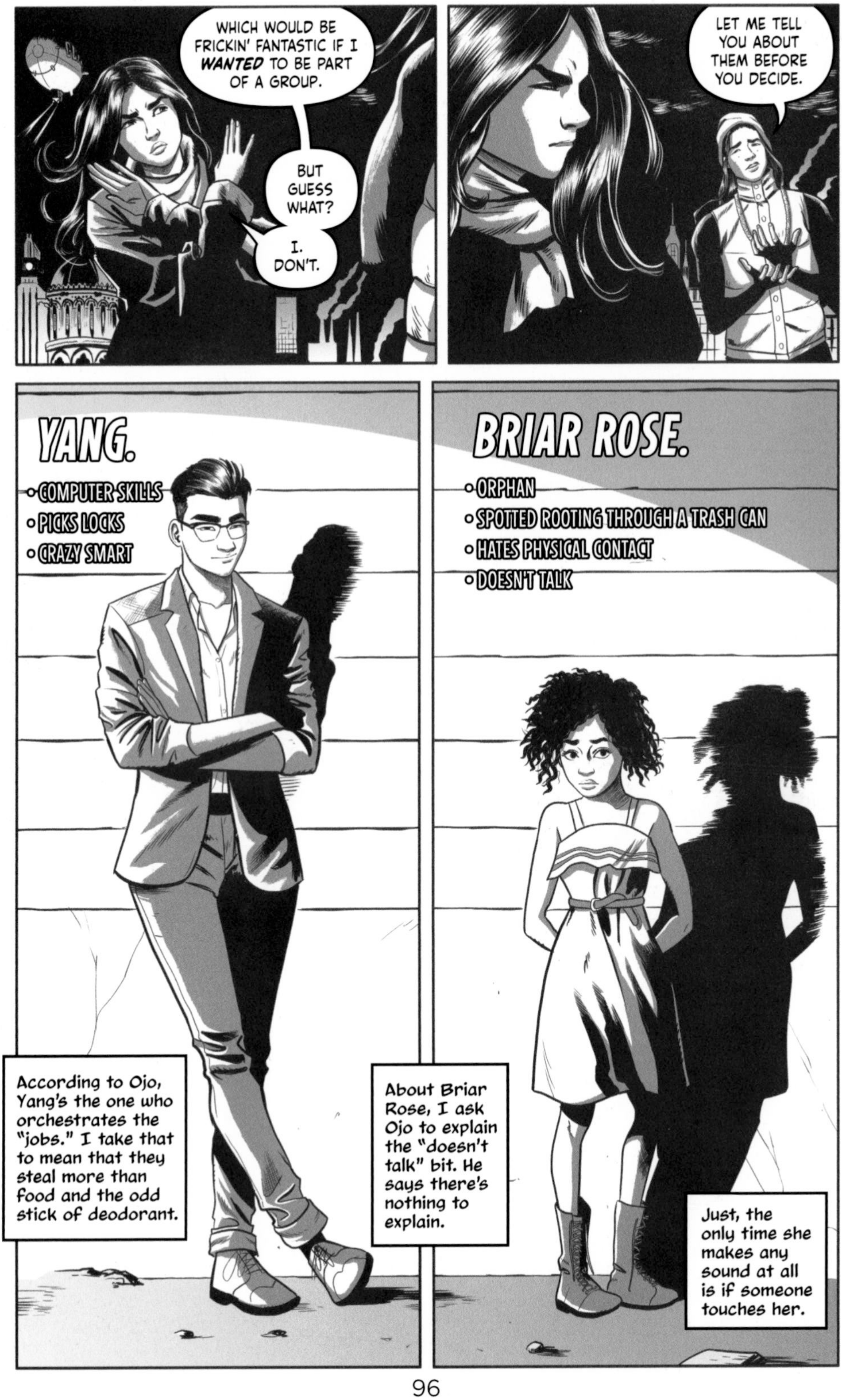
WHICH WOULD BE FRICKIN' FANTASTIC IF I *WANTED* TO BE PART OF A GROUP.
BUT GUESS WHAT?
I. DON'T.
LET ME TELL YOU ABOUT THEM BEFORE YOU DECIDE.
YANG.
• COMPUTER SKILLS
• PICKS LOCKS
• CRAZY SMART
According to Ojo, Yang's the one who orchestrates the "jobs." I take that to mean that they steal more than food and the odd stick of deodorant.
BRIAR ROSE.
• ORPHAN
• SPOTTED ROOTING THROUGH A TRASH CAN
• HATES PHYSICAL CONTACT
• DOESN'T TALK
About Briar Rose, I ask Ojo to explain the "doesn't talk" bit. He says there's nothing to explain.
Just, the only time she makes any sound at all is if someone touches her.

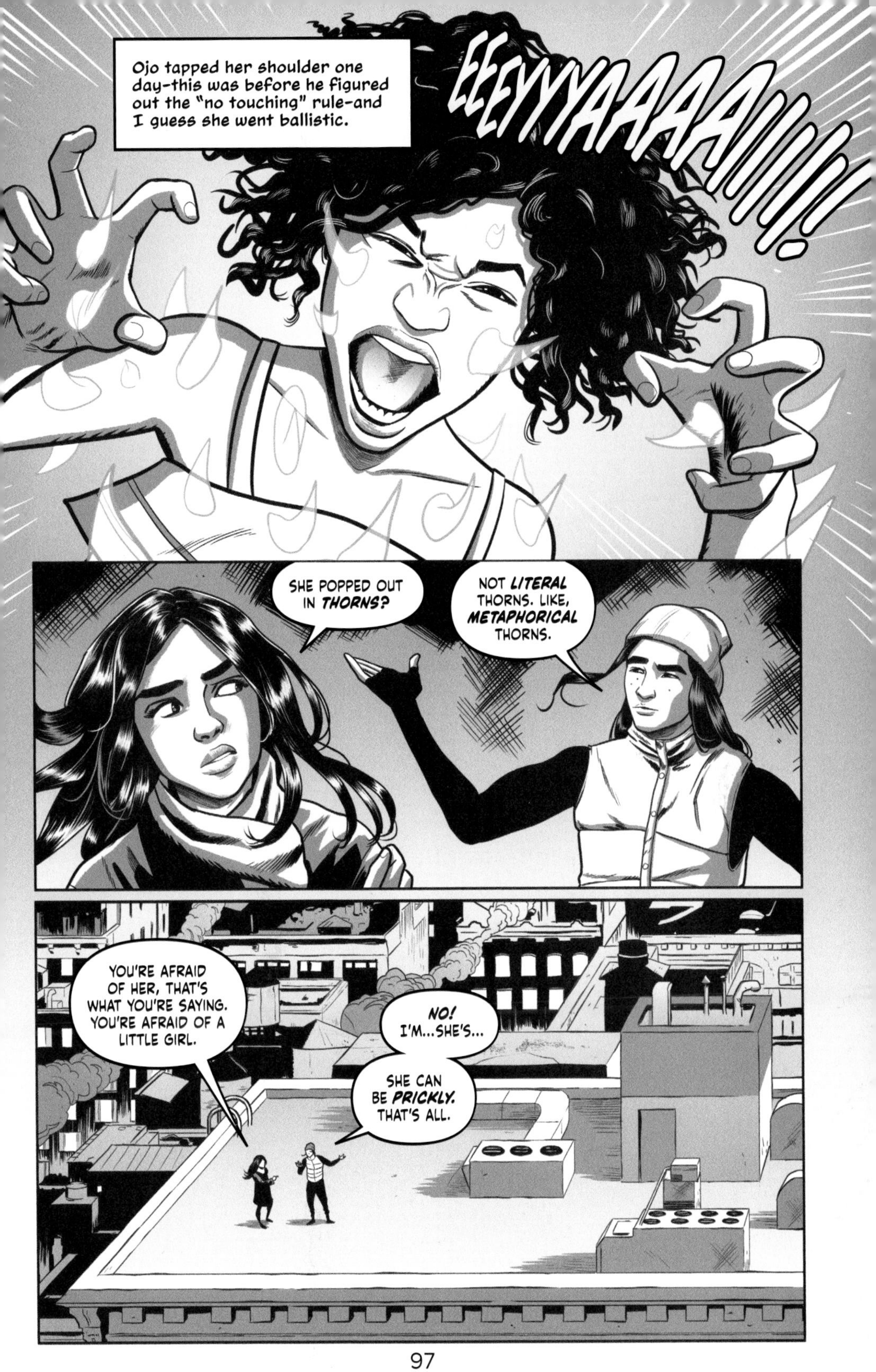
Ojo tapped her shoulder one day-this was before he figured out the "no touching" rule-and I guess she went ballistic.
EEEYYYAAAAA!!!!!!
SHE POPPED OUT IN THORNS?
NOT LITERAL THORNS. LIKE, METAPHORICAL THORNS.
YOU'RE AFRAID OF HER, THAT'S WHAT YOU'RE SAYING. YOU'RE AFRAID OF A LITTLE GIRL.
NO! I'M...SHE'S...
SHE CAN BE PRICKLY. THAT'S ALL.

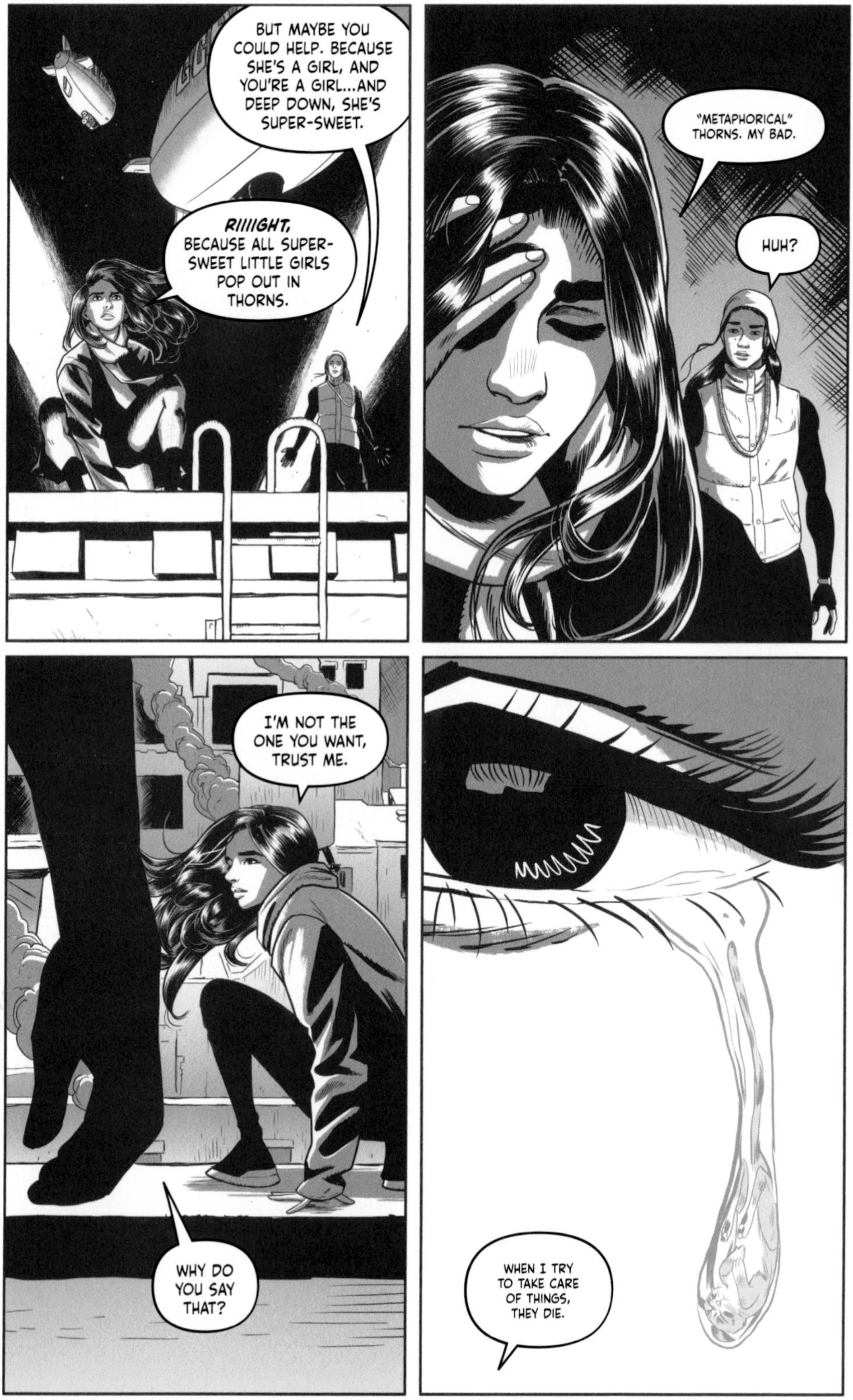
BUT MAYBE YOU COULD HELP. BECAUSE SHE'S A GIRL, AND YOU'RE A GIRL...AND DEEP DOWN, SHE'S SUPER-SWEET.
RIIIIGHT, BECAUSE ALL SUPER-SWEET LITTLE GIRLS POP OUT IN THORNS.
"METAPHORICAL" THORNS. MY BAD.
HUH?
I'M NOT THE ONE YOU WANT, TRUST ME.
WHY DO YOU SAY THAT?
WHEN I TRY TO TAKE CARE OF THINGS, THEY DIE.

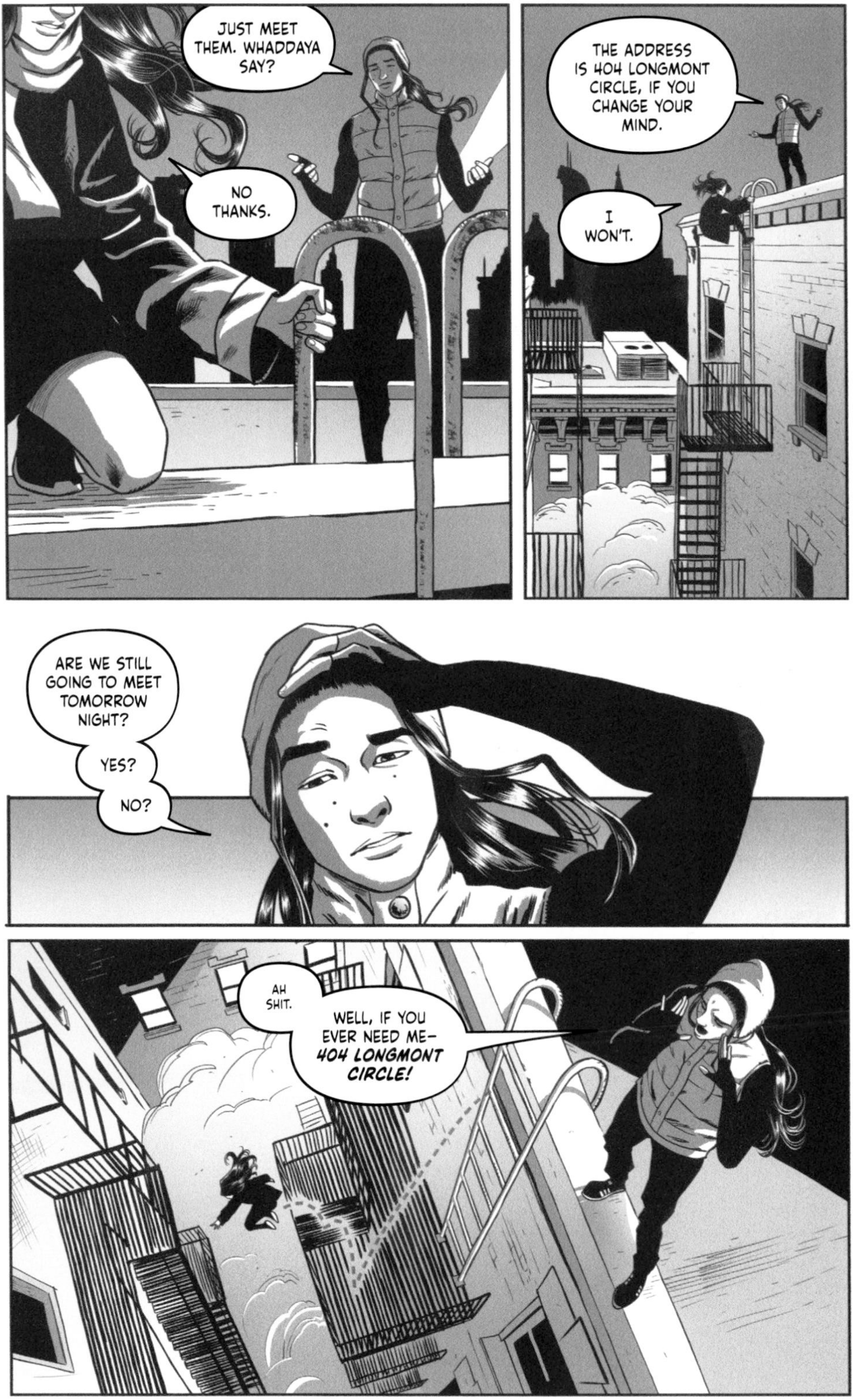
JUST MEET THEM. WHADDAYA SAY?
NO THANKS.
THE ADDRESS IS 404 LONGMONT CIRCLE, IF YOU CHANGE YOUR MIND.
I WON'T.
ARE WE STILL GOING TO MEET TOMORROW NIGHT?
YES?
NO?
AH SHIT.
WELL, IF YOU EVER NEED ME– **404 LONGMONT CIRCLE!**

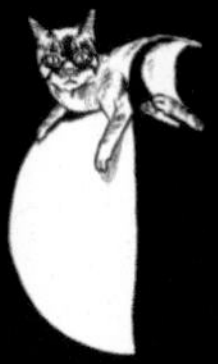

DECLAWED

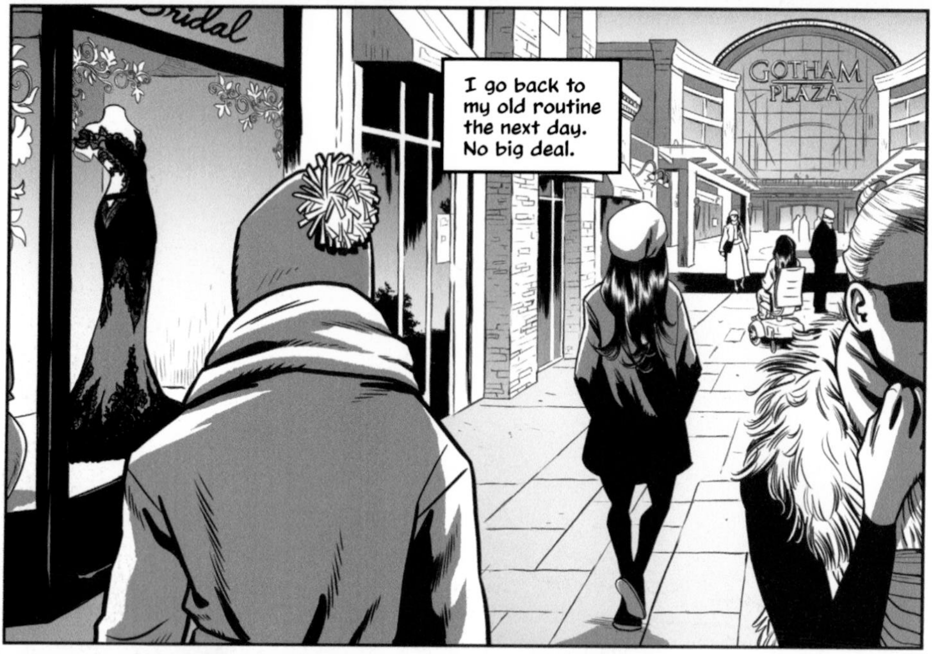
GOTHAM PLAZA
I go back to my old routine the next day. No big deal.

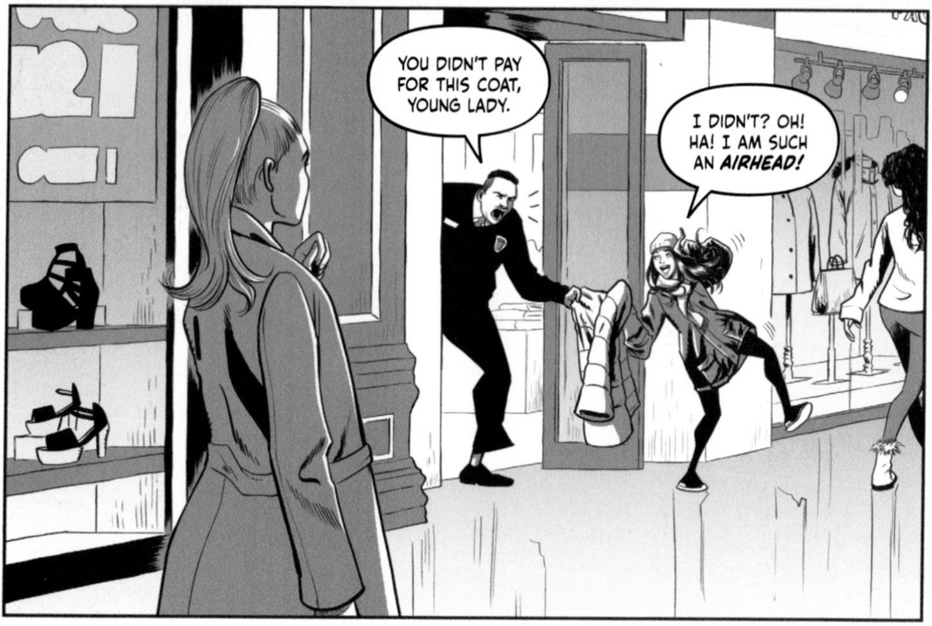
YOU DIDN'T PAY FOR THIS COAT, YOUNG LADY.
I DIDN'T? OH! HA! I AM SUCH AN *AIRHEAD!*

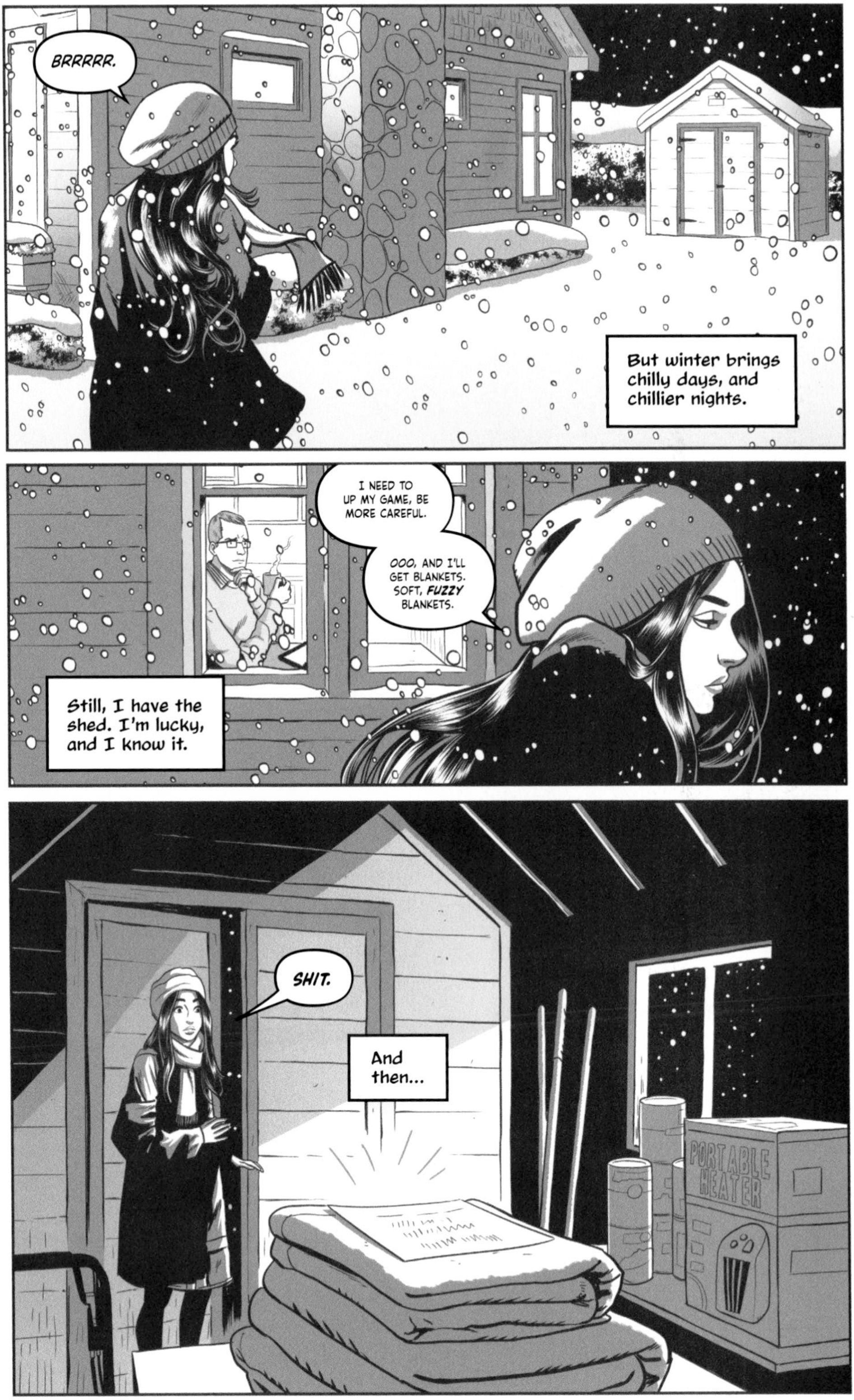
BRRRRR.
But winter brings chilly days, and chillier nights.
I NEED TO UP MY GAME, BE MORE CAREFUL.
OOO, AND I'LL GET BLANKETS. SOFT, FUZZY BLANKETS.
Still, I have the shed. I'm lucky, and I know it.
SHIT.
And then...
PORTABLE HEATER

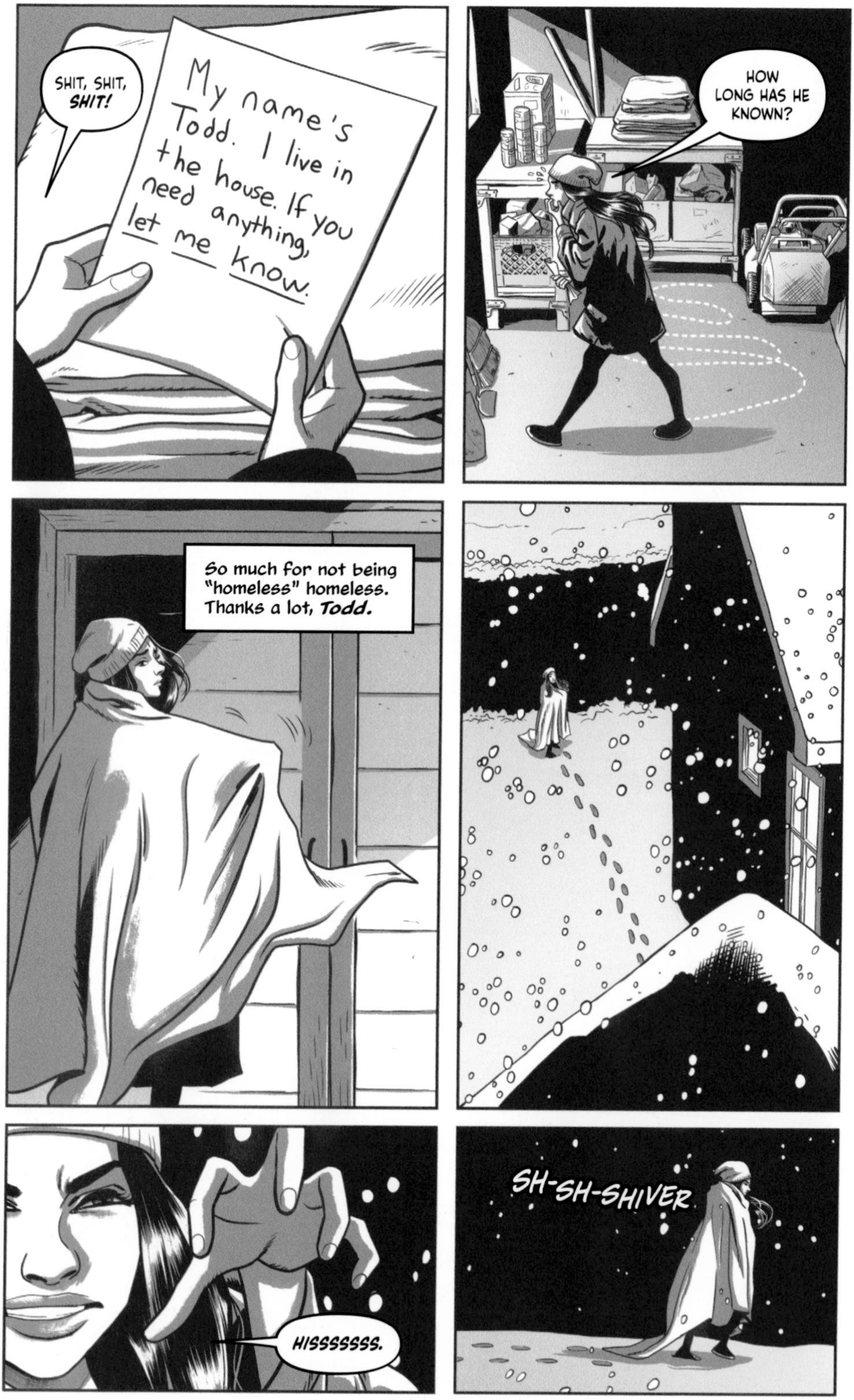
SHIT, SHIT, SHIT!
My name's Todd. I live in the house. If you need anything, let me know.
HOW LONG HAS HE KNOWN?
So much for not being "homeless" homeless. Thanks a lot, Todd.
HISSSSSSS.
SH-SH-SHIVER

WHY HUMANS SHOULD HAVE FUR

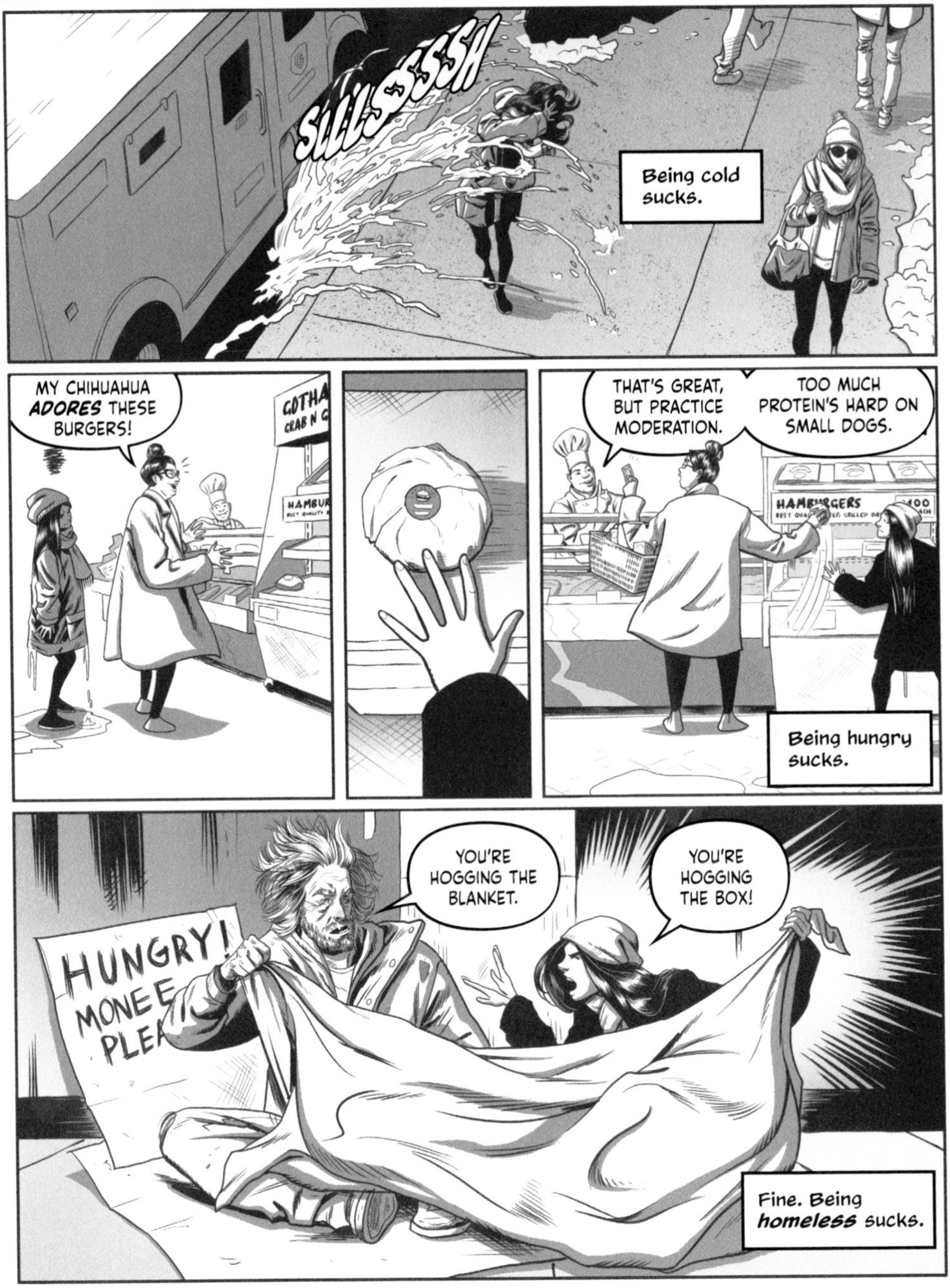

SLLLSSSSH
Being cold sucks.
MY CHIHUAHUA *ADORES* THESE BURGERS!
GOTHA
CRAB N G
THAT'S GREAT, BUT PRACTICE MODERATION.
TOO MUCH PROTEIN'S HARD ON SMALL DOGS.
HAMBURGERS
Being hungry sucks.
YOU'RE HOGGING THE BLANKET.
YOU'RE HOGGING THE BOX!
HUNGRY!
MONEE
PLEA
Fine. Being *homeless* sucks.

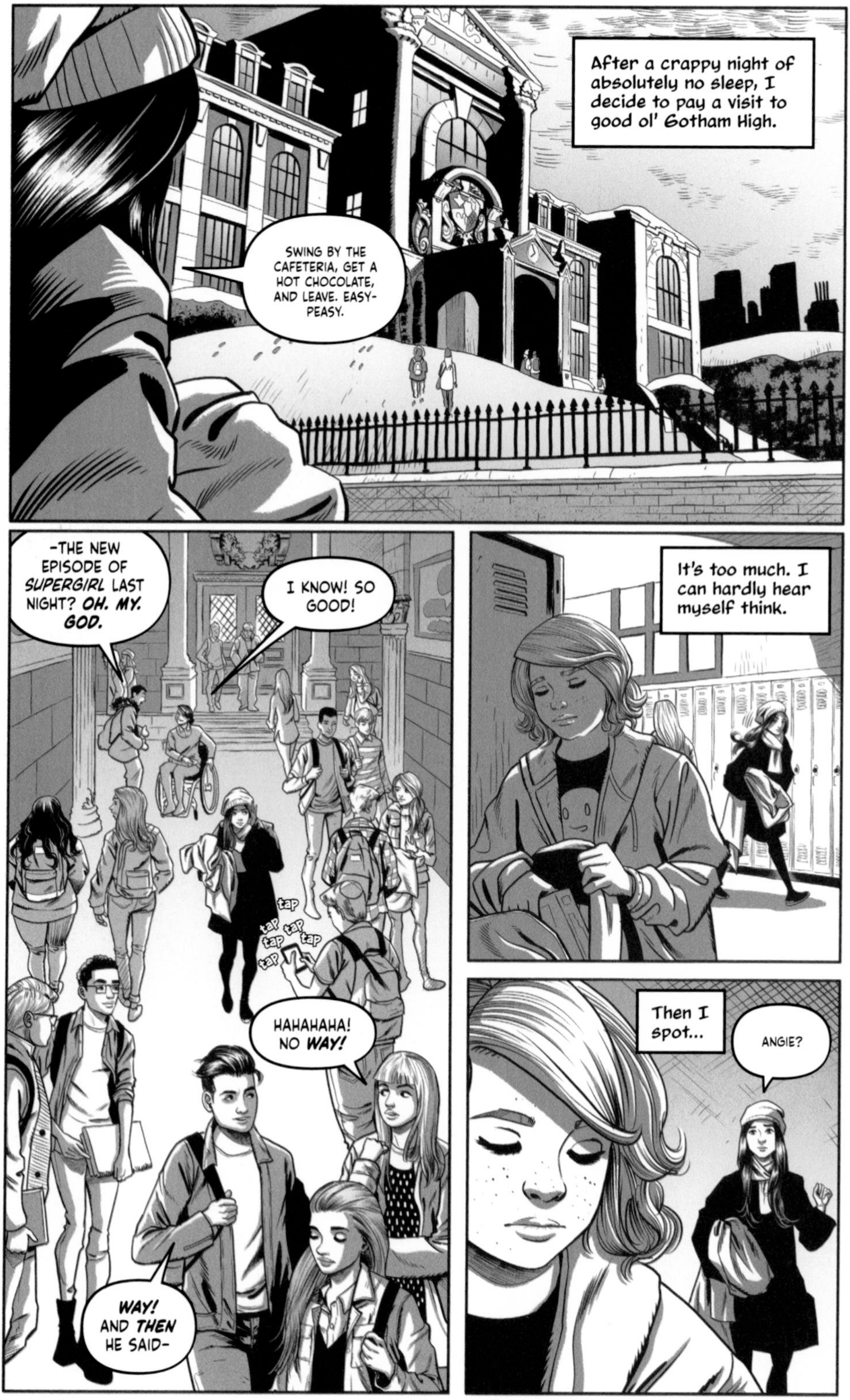
After a crappy night of absolutely no sleep, I decide to pay a visit to good ol' Gotham High.
SWING BY THE CAFETERIA, GET A HOT CHOCOLATE, AND LEAVE. EASY-PEASY.
-THE NEW EPISODE OF SUPERGIRL LAST NIGHT? OH. MY. GOD.
I KNOW! SO GOOD!
tap tap tap tap tap
HAHAHAHA! NO WAY!
WAY! AND THEN HE SAID-
It's too much. I can hardly hear myself think.
Then I spot...
ANGIE?

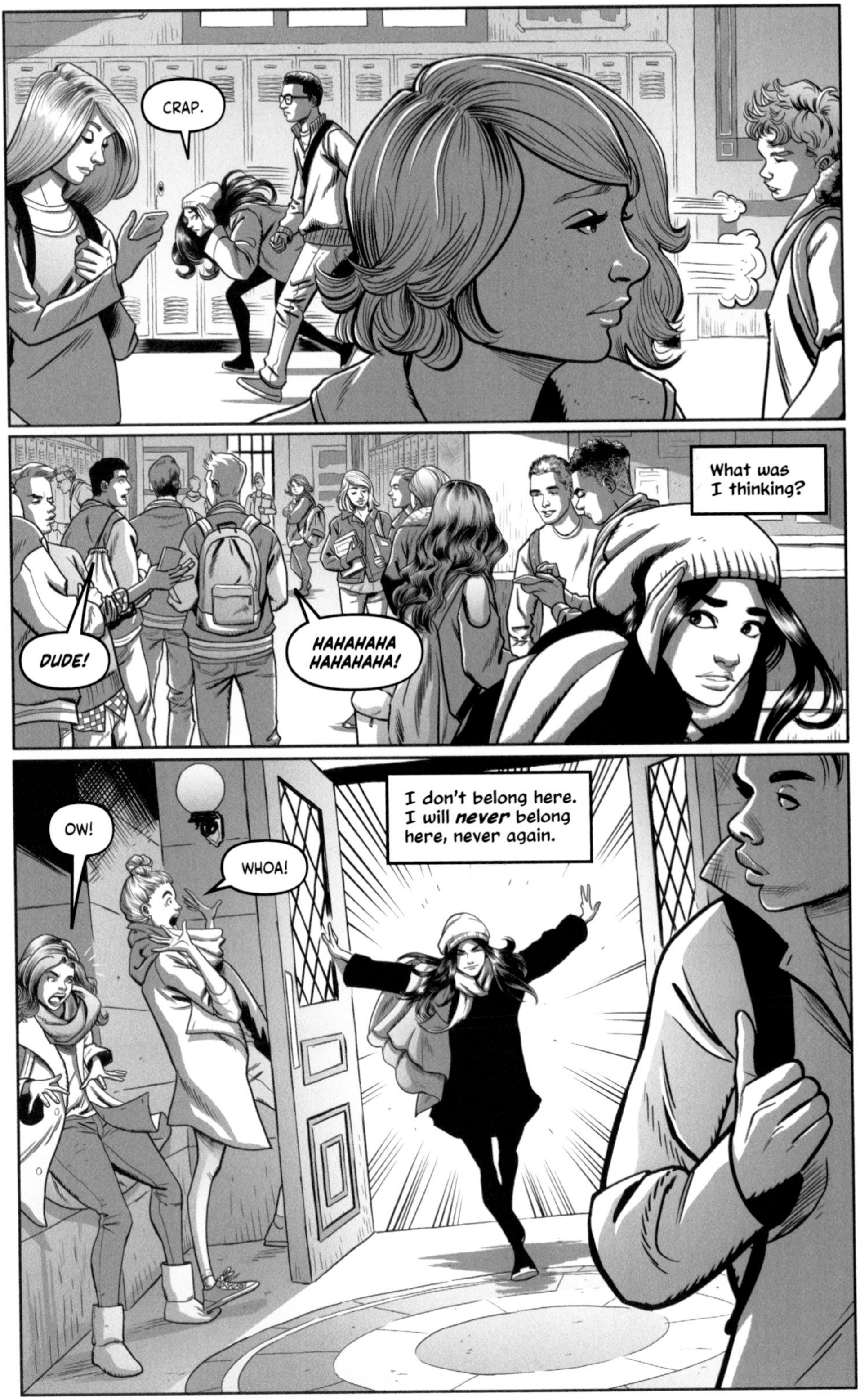
CRAP.
What was I thinking?
DUDE!
HAHAHAHA HAHAHAHA!
I don't belong here. I will *never* belong here, never again.
OW!
WHOA!

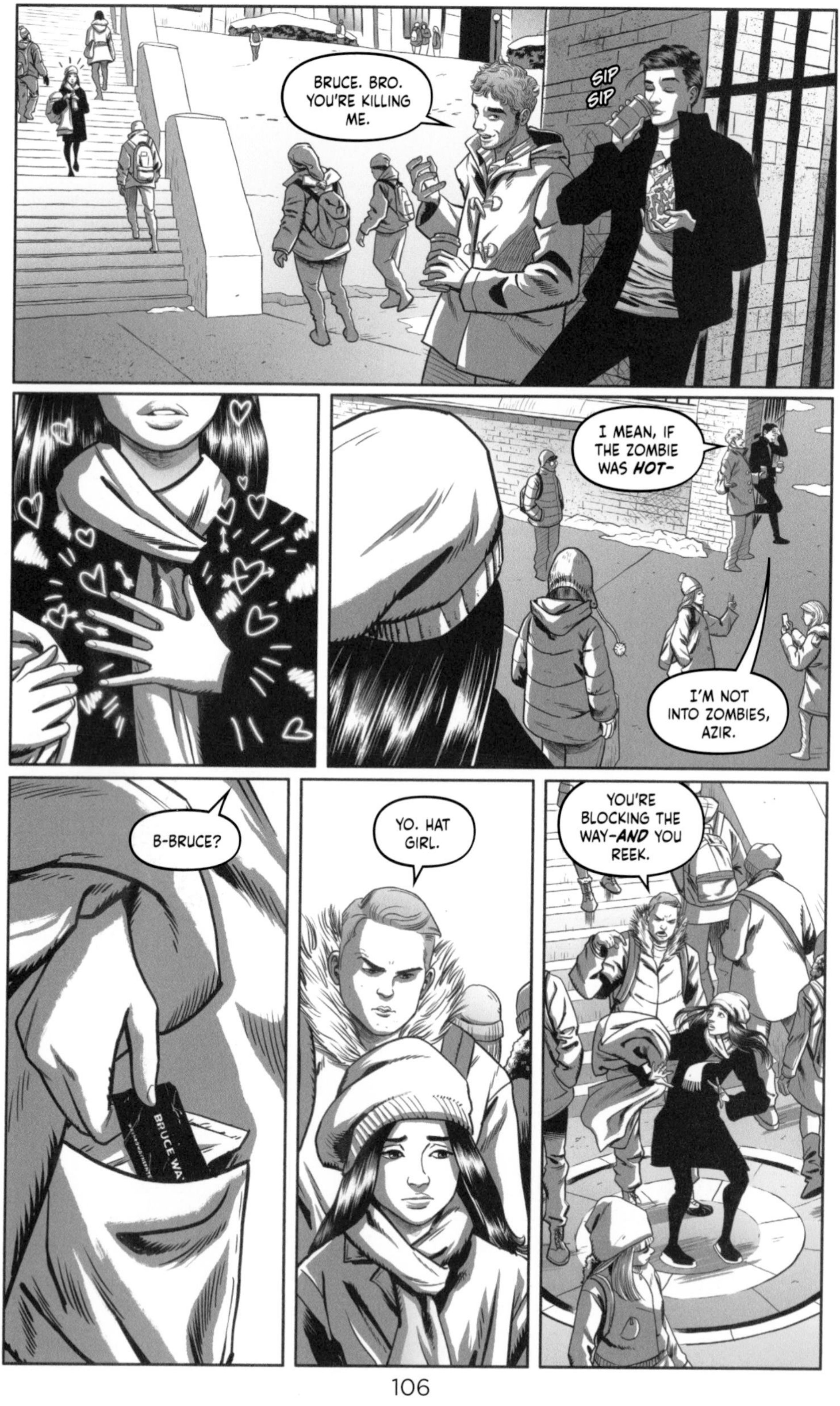

BRUCE. BRO. YOU'RE KILLING ME.
SIP SIP
I MEAN, IF THE ZOMBIE WAS ***HOT***-
I'M NOT INTO ZOMBIES, AZIR.
B-BRUCE?
BRUCE WA
YO. HAT GIRL.
YOU'RE BLOCKING THE WAY-***AND*** YOU REEK.

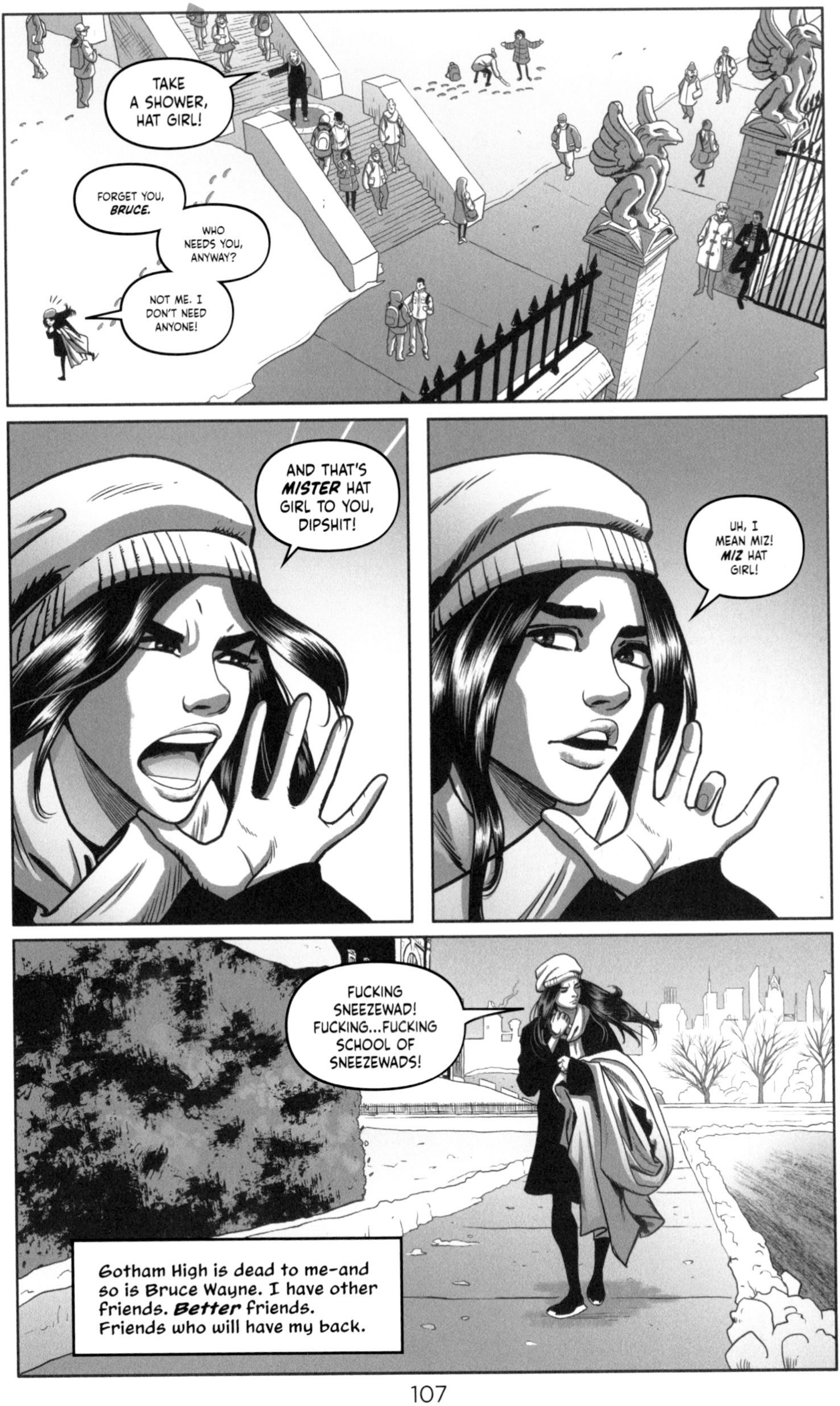
TAKE A SHOWER, HAT GIRL!
FORGET YOU, ***BRUCE.***
WHO NEEDS YOU, ANYWAY?
NOT ME. I DON'T NEED ANYONE!
AND THAT'S ***MISTER*** HAT GIRL TO YOU, DIPSHIT!
UH, I MEAN MIZ! ***MIZ*** HAT GIRL!
FUCKING SNEEZEWAD! FUCKING...FUCKING SCHOOL OF SNEEZEWADS!
Gotham High is dead to me–and so is Bruce Wayne. I have other friends. ***Better*** friends. Friends who will have my back.

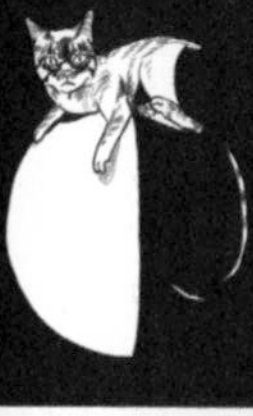

SCAREDY CAT

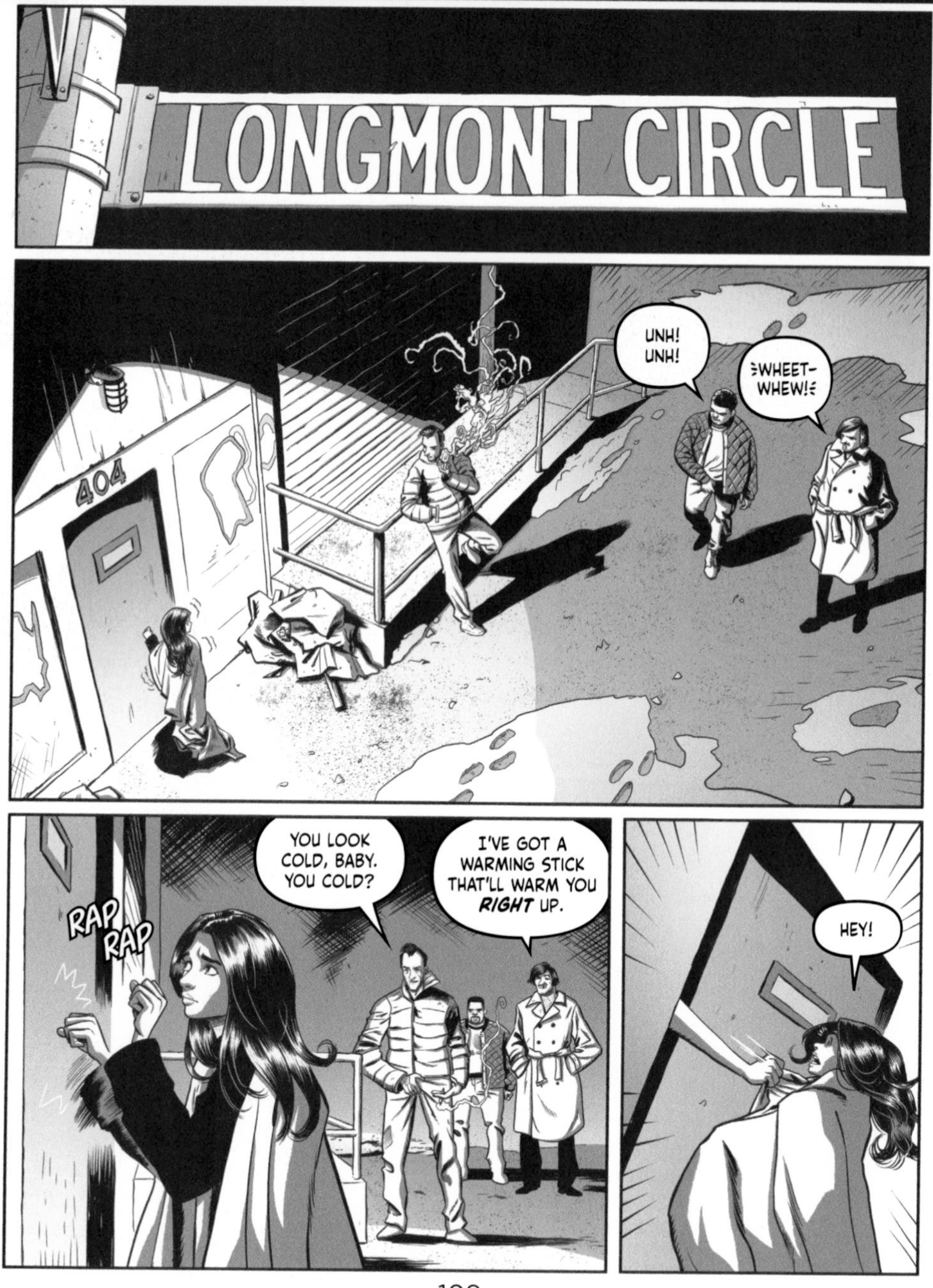

LONGMONT CIRCLE
404
UNH! UNH!
WHEET-WHEW!
RAP RAP
YOU LOOK COLD, BABY. YOU COLD?
I'VE GOT A WARMING STICK THAT'LL WARM YOU *RIGHT* UP.
HEY!

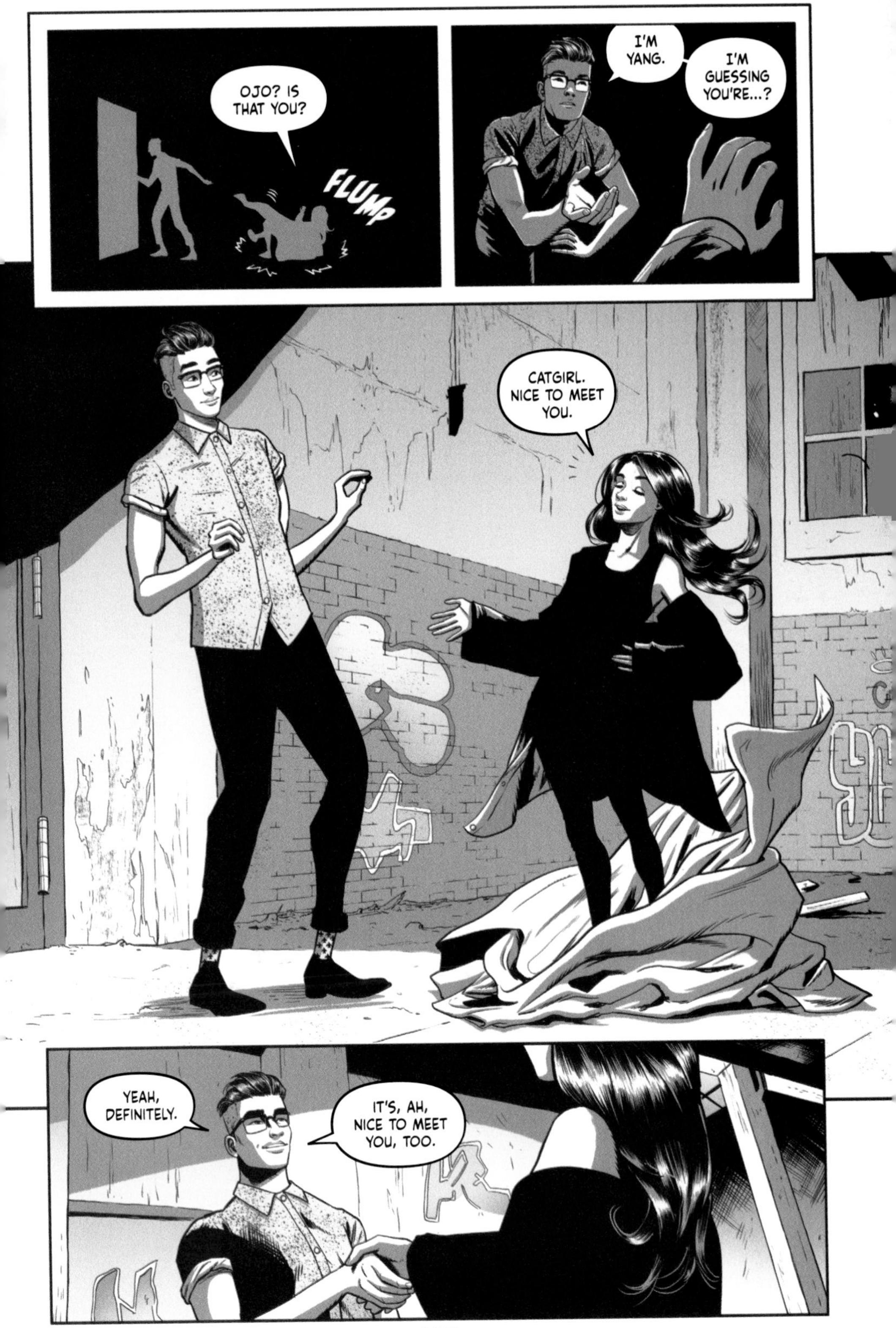
OJO? IS THAT YOU?
FLUMP
I'M YANG.
I'M GUESSING YOU'RE...?
CATGIRL. NICE TO MEET YOU.
YEAH, DEFINITELY.
IT'S, AH, NICE TO MEET YOU, TOO.

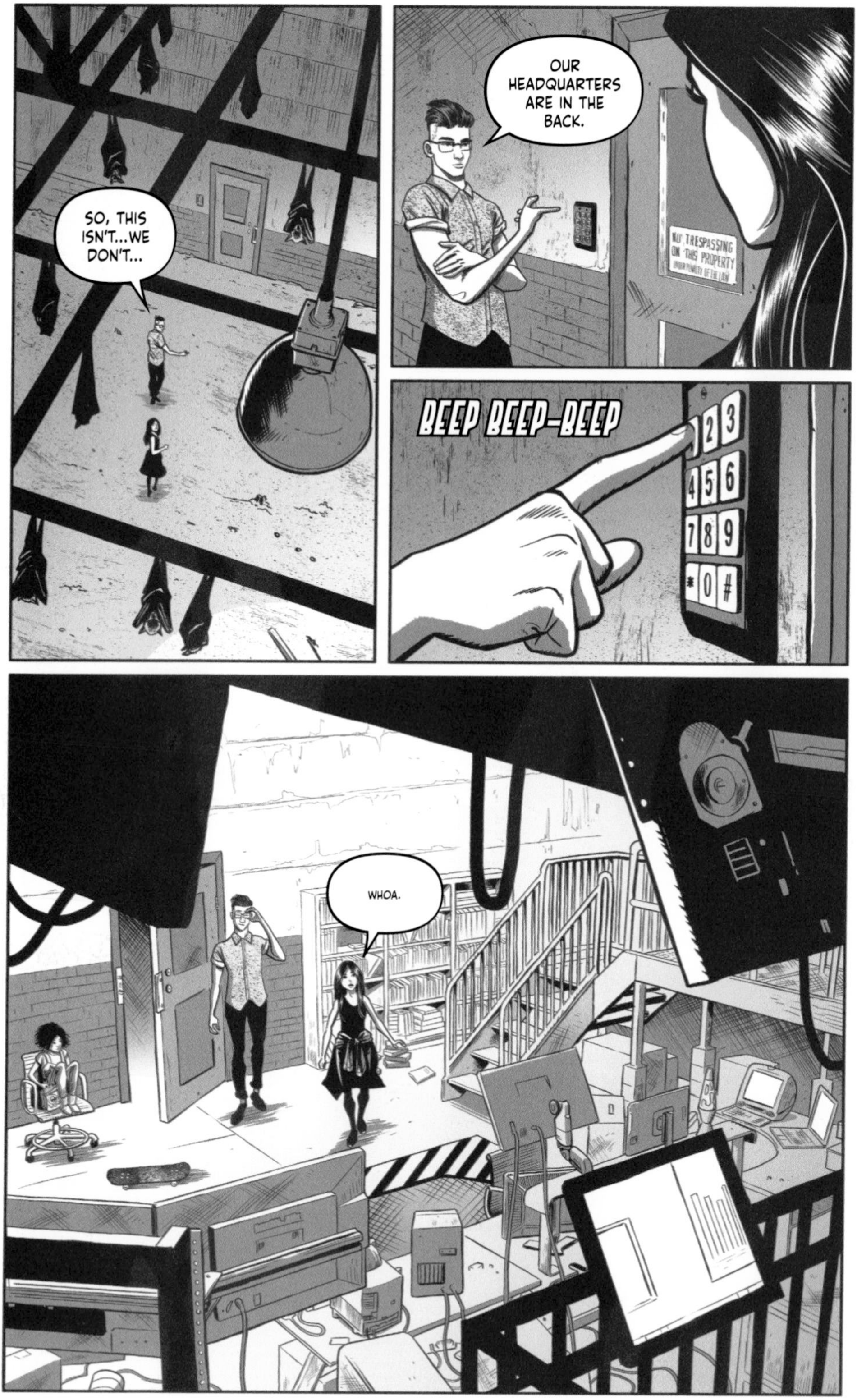
SO, THIS ISN'T...WE DON'T...
OUR HEADQUARTERS ARE IN THE BACK.
NO TRESPASSING ON THIS PROPERTY
BEEP BEEP-BEEP
WHOA.

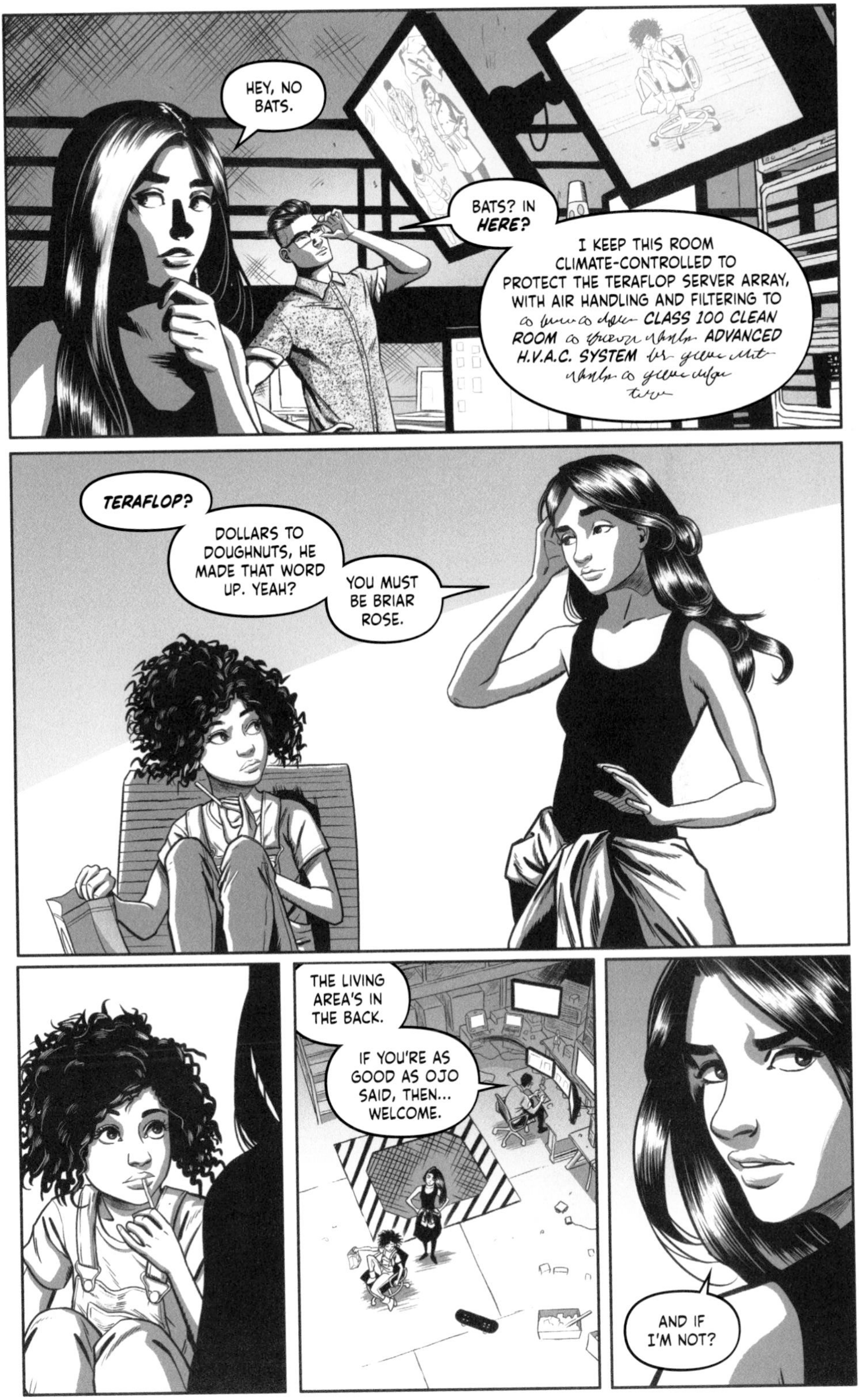
HEY, NO BATS.
BATS? IN *HERE?*
I KEEP THIS ROOM CLIMATE-CONTROLLED TO PROTECT THE TERAFLOP SERVER ARRAY, WITH AIR HANDLING AND FILTERING TO *CLASS 100 CLEAN ROOM* *ADVANCED H.V.A.C. SYSTEM*
TERAFLOP?
DOLLARS TO DOUGHNUTS, HE MADE THAT WORD UP. YEAH?
YOU MUST BE BRIAR ROSE.
THE LIVING AREA'S IN THE BACK.
IF YOU'RE AS GOOD AS OJO SAID, THEN... WELCOME.
AND IF I'M NOT?

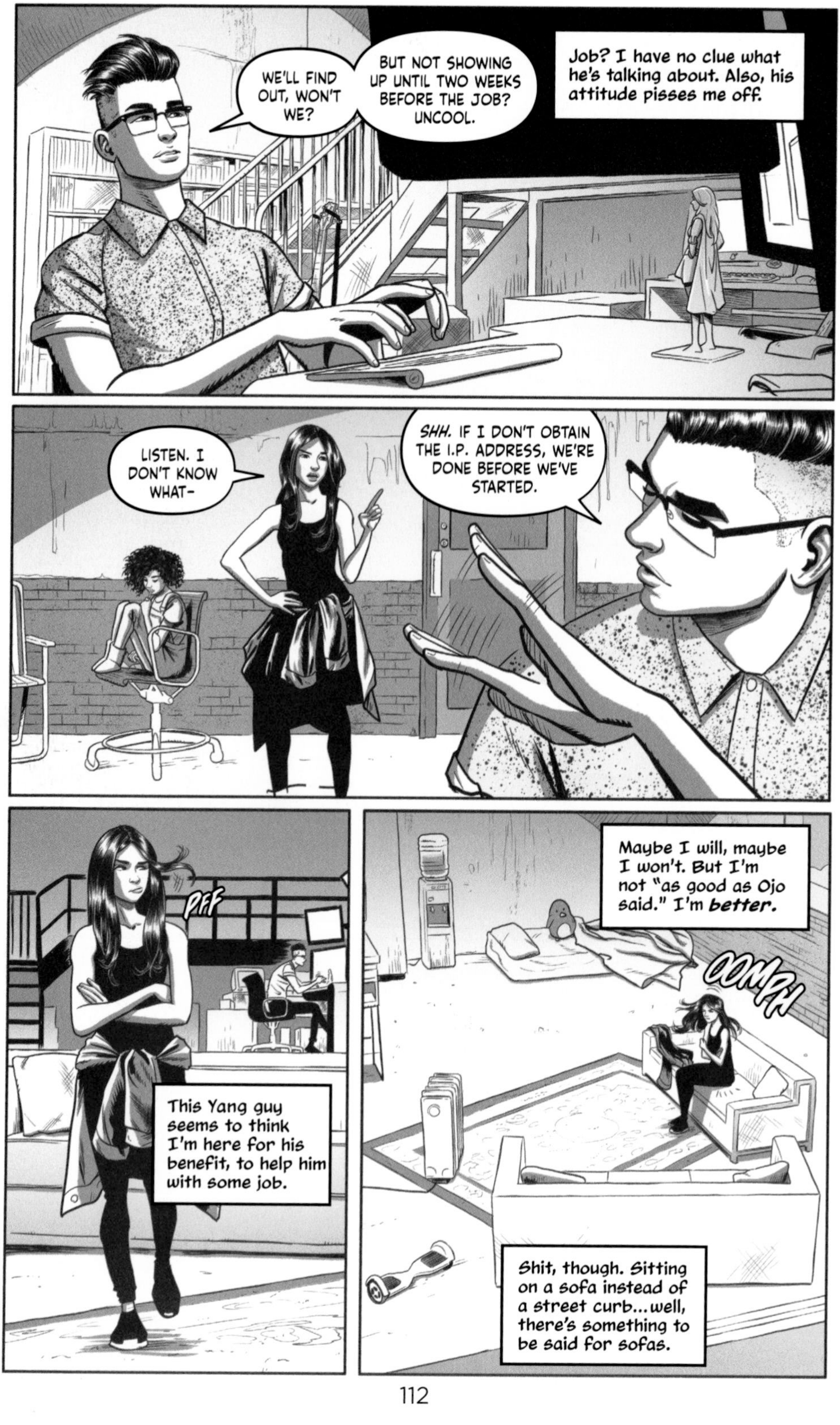
WE'LL FIND OUT, WON'T WE?
BUT NOT SHOWING UP UNTIL TWO WEEKS BEFORE THE JOB? UNCOOL.
Job? I have no clue what he's talking about. Also, his attitude pisses me off.
LISTEN. I DON'T KNOW WHAT-
SHH. IF I DON'T OBTAIN THE I.P. ADDRESS, WE'RE DONE BEFORE WE'VE STARTED.
PFF
This Yang guy seems to think I'm here for his benefit, to help him with some job.
Maybe I will, maybe I won't. But I'm not "as good as Ojo said." I'm better.
OOMPH
Shit, though. Sitting on a sofa instead of a street curb...well, there's something to be said for sofas.

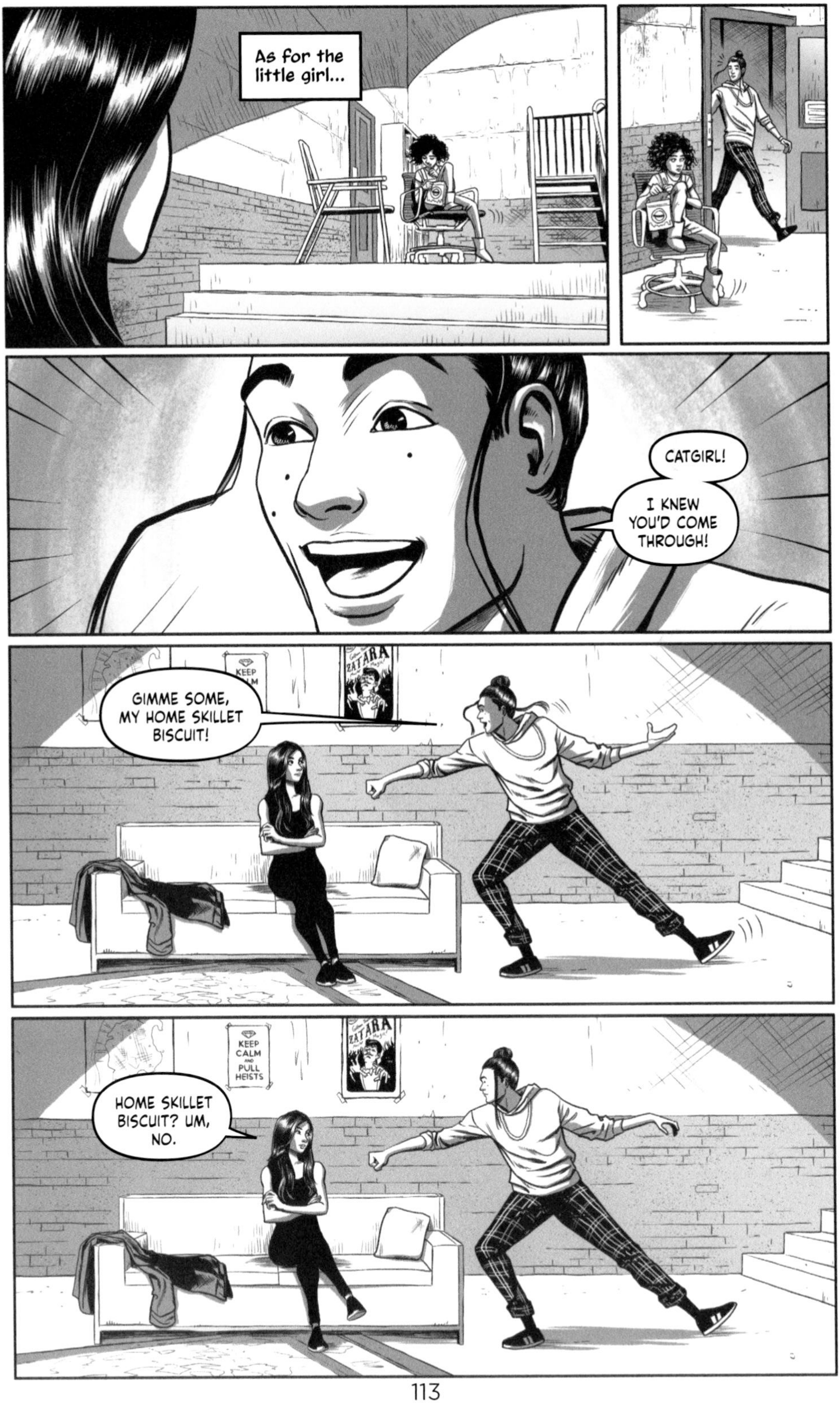
As for the little girl...
CATGIRL!
I KNEW YOU'D COME THROUGH!
GIMME SOME, MY HOME SKILLET BISCUIT!
KEEP CALM AND PULL HEISTS
ZATARA
HOME SKILLET BISCUIT? UM, NO.

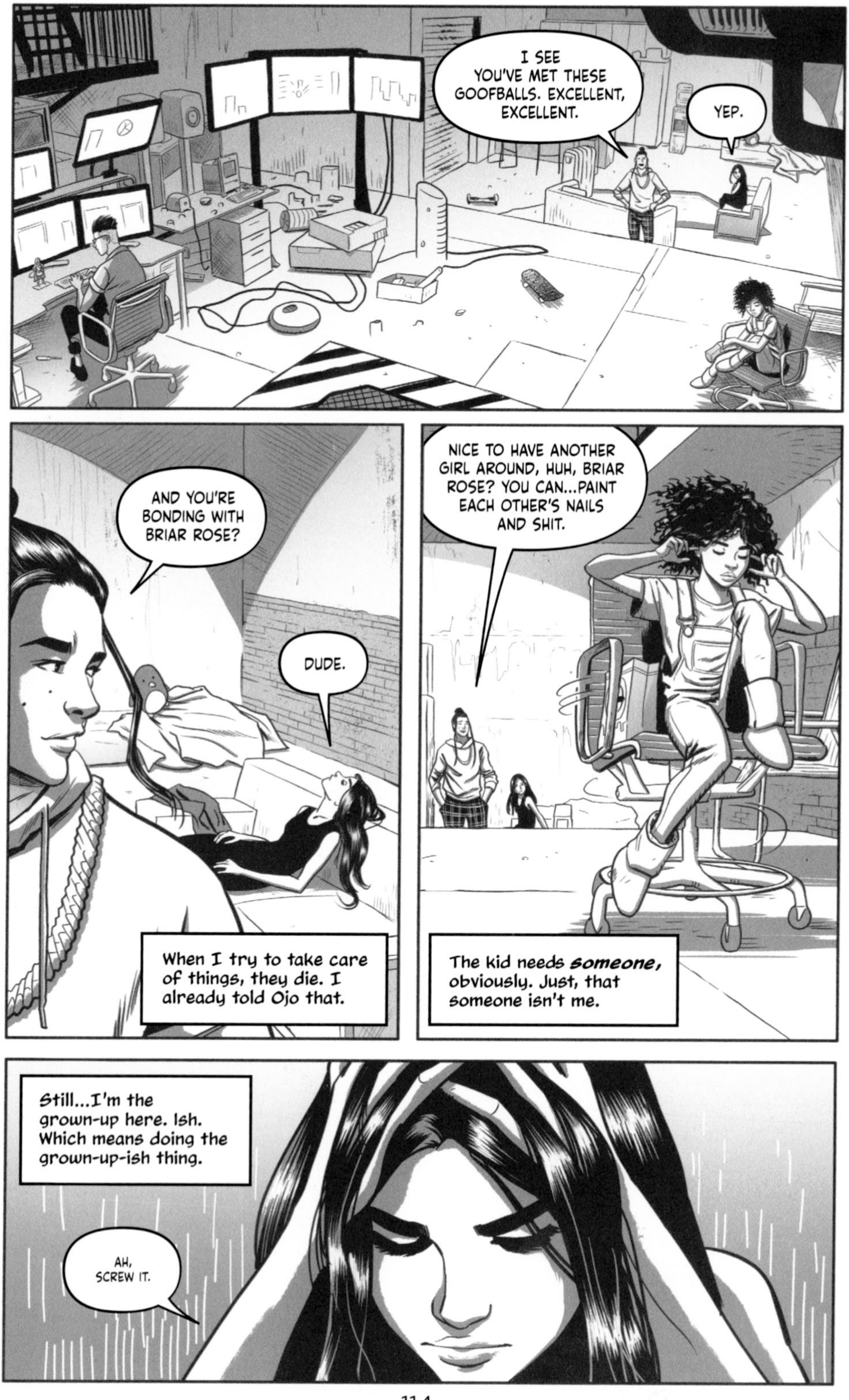
I SEE YOU'VE MET THESE GOOFBALLS. EXCELLENT, EXCELLENT.
YEP.
AND YOU'RE BONDING WITH BRIAR ROSE?
DUDE.
When I try to take care of things, they die. I already told Ojo that.
NICE TO HAVE ANOTHER GIRL AROUND, HUH, BRIAR ROSE? YOU CAN...PAINT EACH OTHER'S NAILS AND SHIT.
The kid needs *someone,* obviously. Just, that someone isn't me.
Still...I'm the grown-up here. Ish. Which means doing the grown-up-ish thing.
AH, SCREW IT.

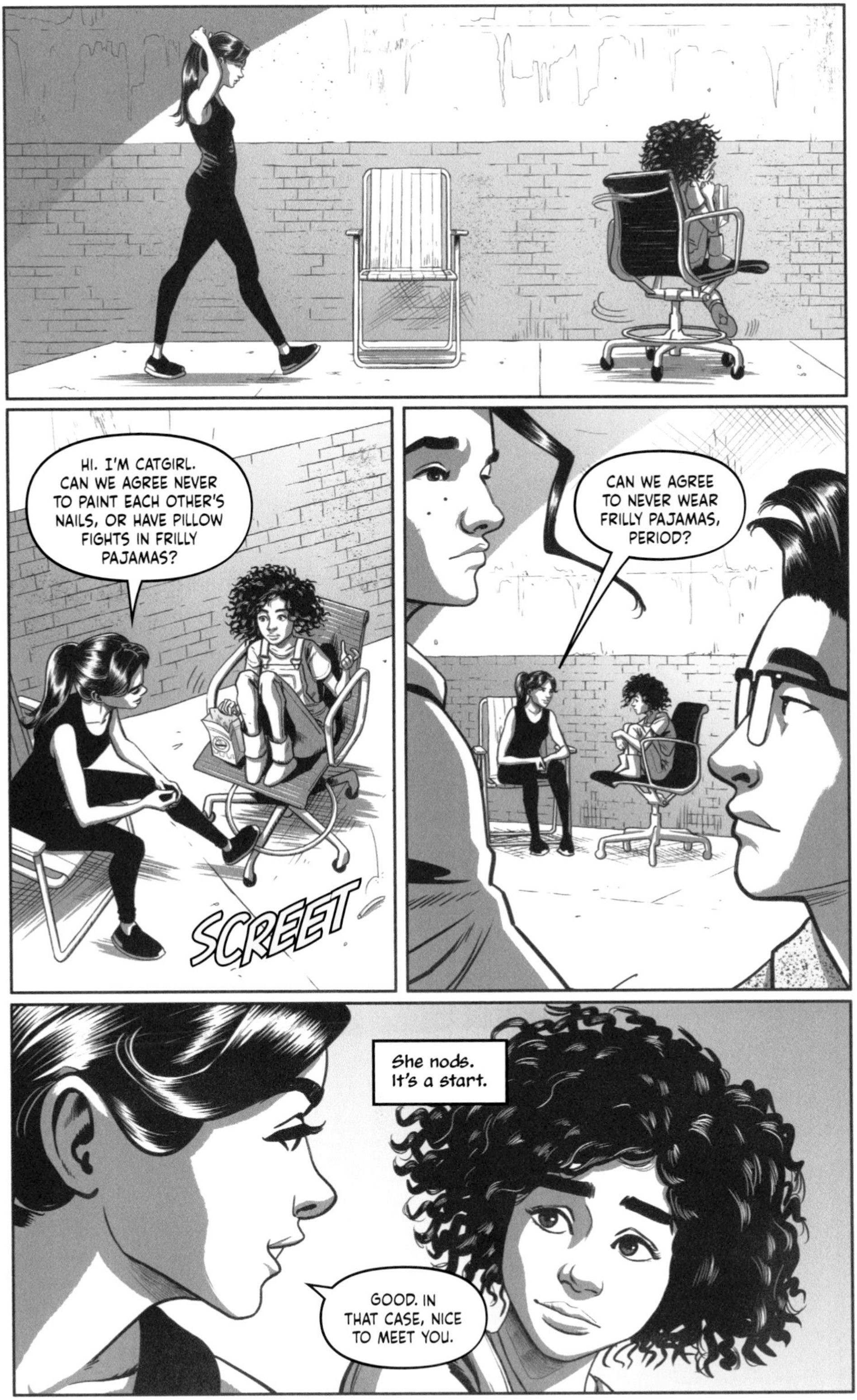
HI. I'M CATGIRL. CAN WE AGREE NEVER TO PAINT EACH OTHER'S NAILS, OR HAVE PILLOW FIGHTS IN FRILLY PAJAMAS?
SCREEET
CAN WE AGREE TO NEVER WEAR FRILLY PAJAMAS, PERIOD?
She nods. It's a start.
GOOD. IN THAT CASE, NICE TO MEET YOU.

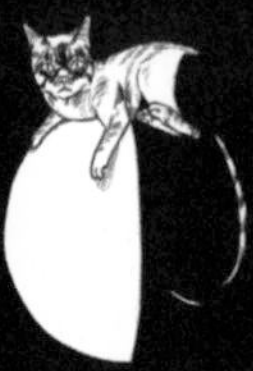

LIFE IN A PACT

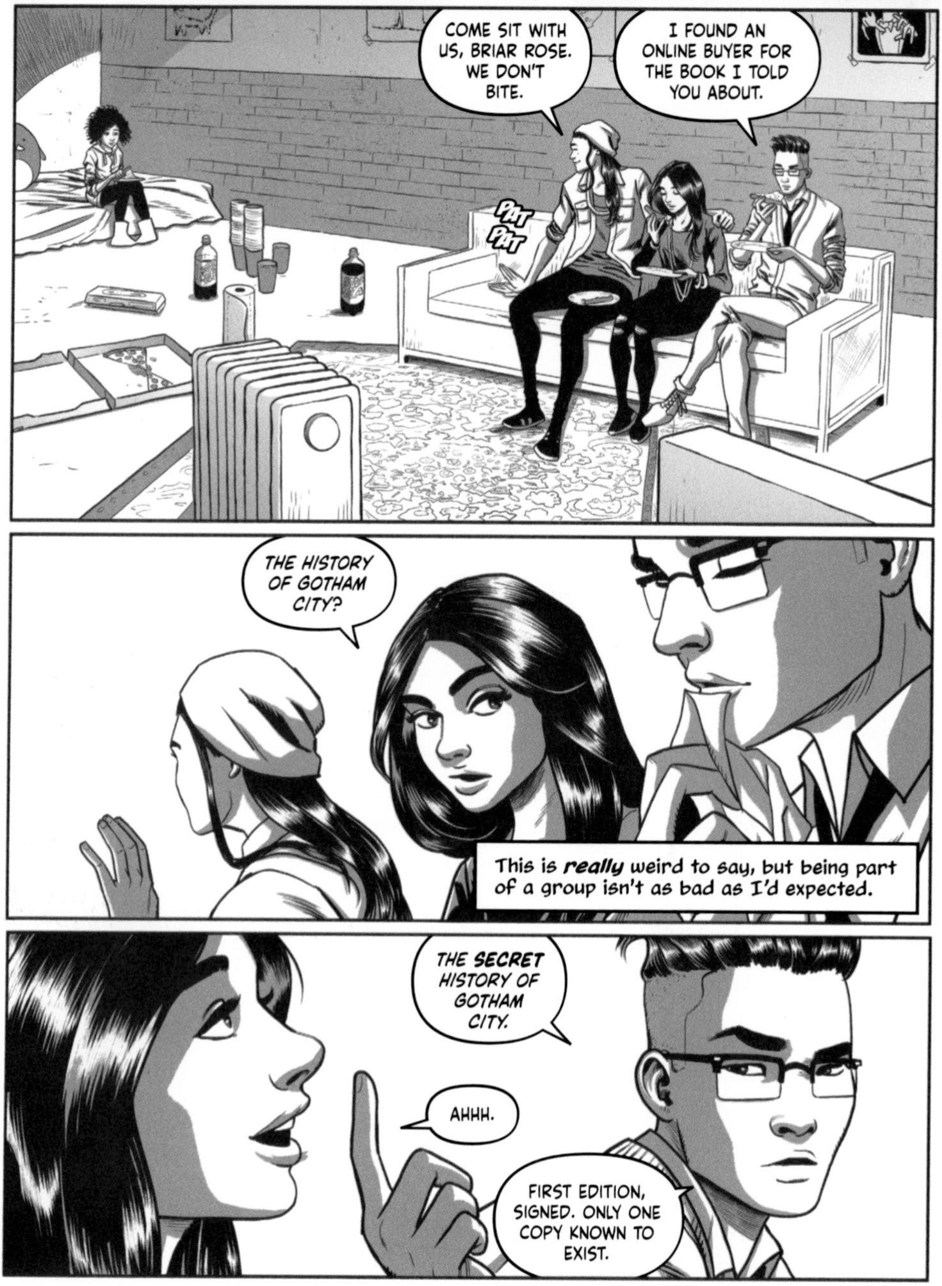
COME SIT WITH US, BRIAR ROSE. WE DON'T BITE.
I FOUND AN ONLINE BUYER FOR THE BOOK I TOLD YOU ABOUT.
PAT PAT
THE HISTORY OF GOTHAM CITY?
This is *really* weird to say, but being part of a group isn't as bad as I'd expected.
THE **SECRET** HISTORY OF GOTHAM CITY.
AHHH.
FIRST EDITION, SIGNED. ONLY ONE COPY KNOWN TO EXIST.

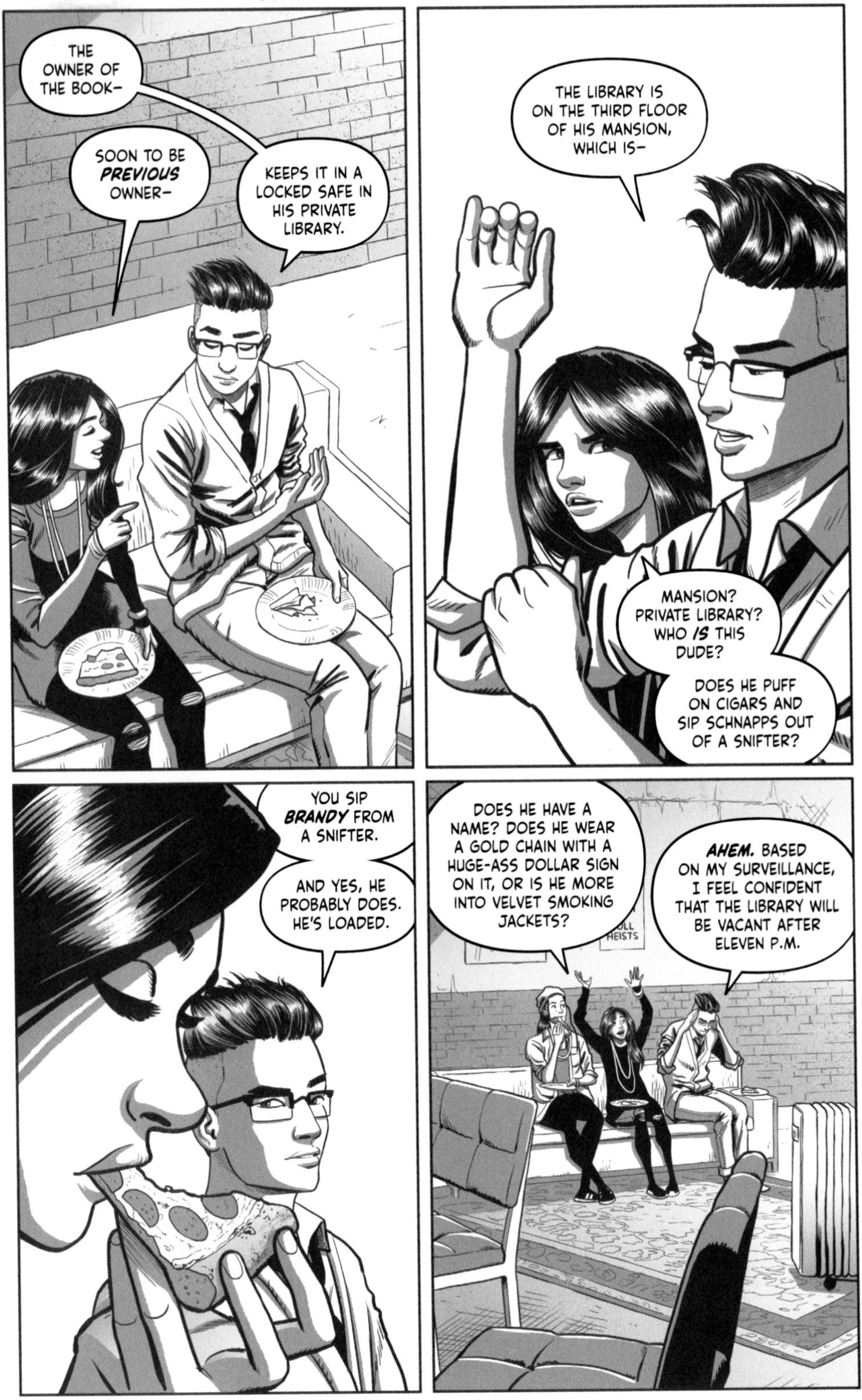
THE OWNER OF THE BOOK–
SOON TO BE **PREVIOUS** OWNER–
KEEPS IT IN A LOCKED SAFE IN HIS PRIVATE LIBRARY.
THE LIBRARY IS ON THE THIRD FLOOR OF HIS MANSION, WHICH IS–
MANSION? PRIVATE LIBRARY? WHO *IS* THIS DUDE?
DOES HE PUFF ON CIGARS AND SIP SCHNAPPS OUT OF A SNIFTER?
YOU SIP **BRANDY** FROM A SNIFTER.
AND YES, HE PROBABLY DOES. HE'S LOADED.
DOES HE HAVE A NAME? DOES HE WEAR A GOLD CHAIN WITH A HUGE-ASS DOLLAR SIGN ON IT, OR IS HE MORE INTO VELVET SMOKING JACKETS?
AHEM. BASED ON MY SURVEILLANCE, I FEEL CONFIDENT THAT THE LIBRARY WILL BE VACANT AFTER ELEVEN P.M.

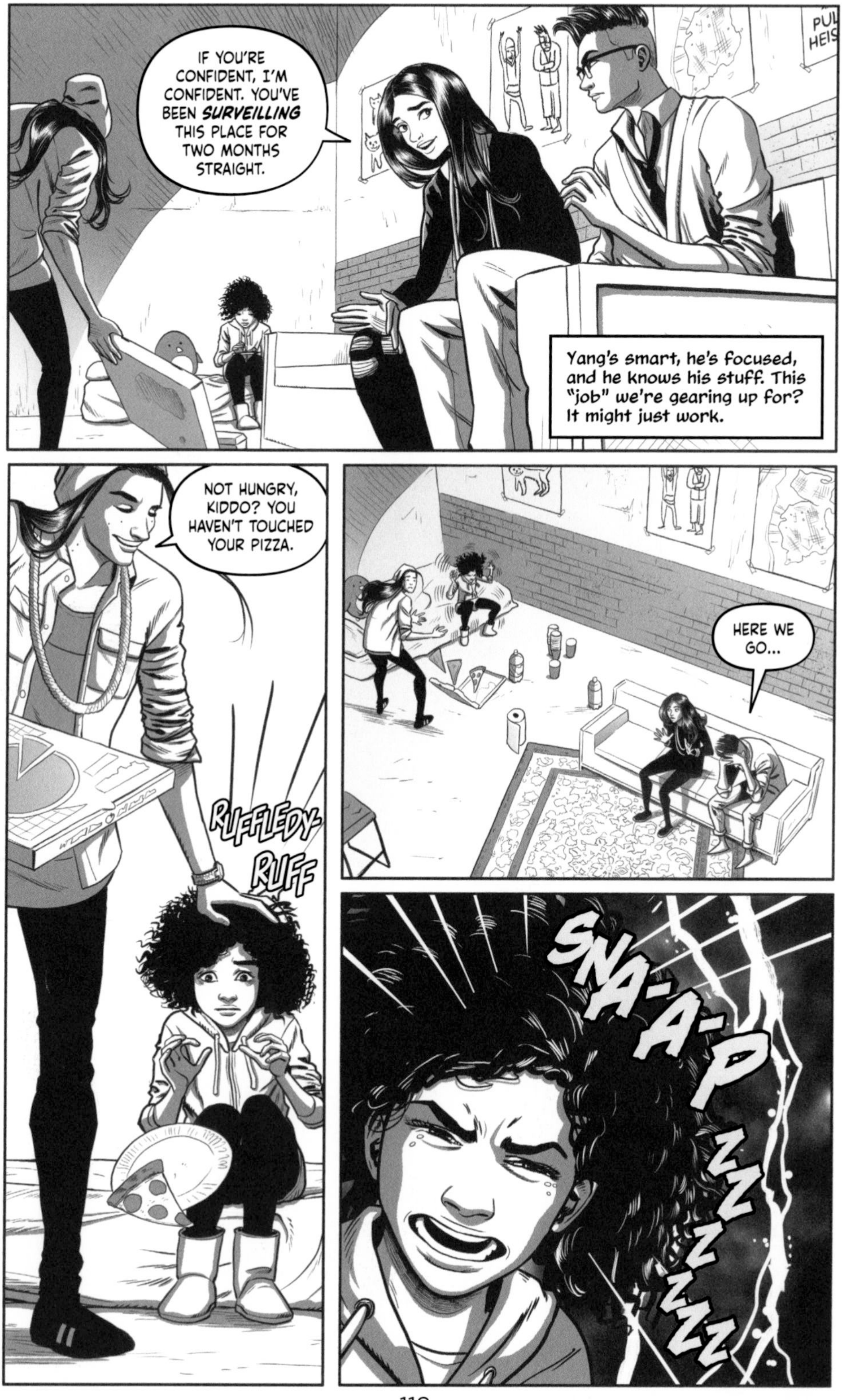
PUL
HEIS
IF YOU'RE CONFIDENT, I'M CONFIDENT. YOU'VE BEEN ***SURVEILLING*** THIS PLACE FOR TWO MONTHS STRAIGHT.
Yang's smart, he's focused, and he knows his stuff. This "job" we're gearing up for? It might just work.
NOT HUNGRY, KIDDO? YOU HAVEN'T TOUCHED YOUR PIZZA.
RUFFLEDY-RUFF
HERE WE GO...
SNA-A-P
ZZZZZZ

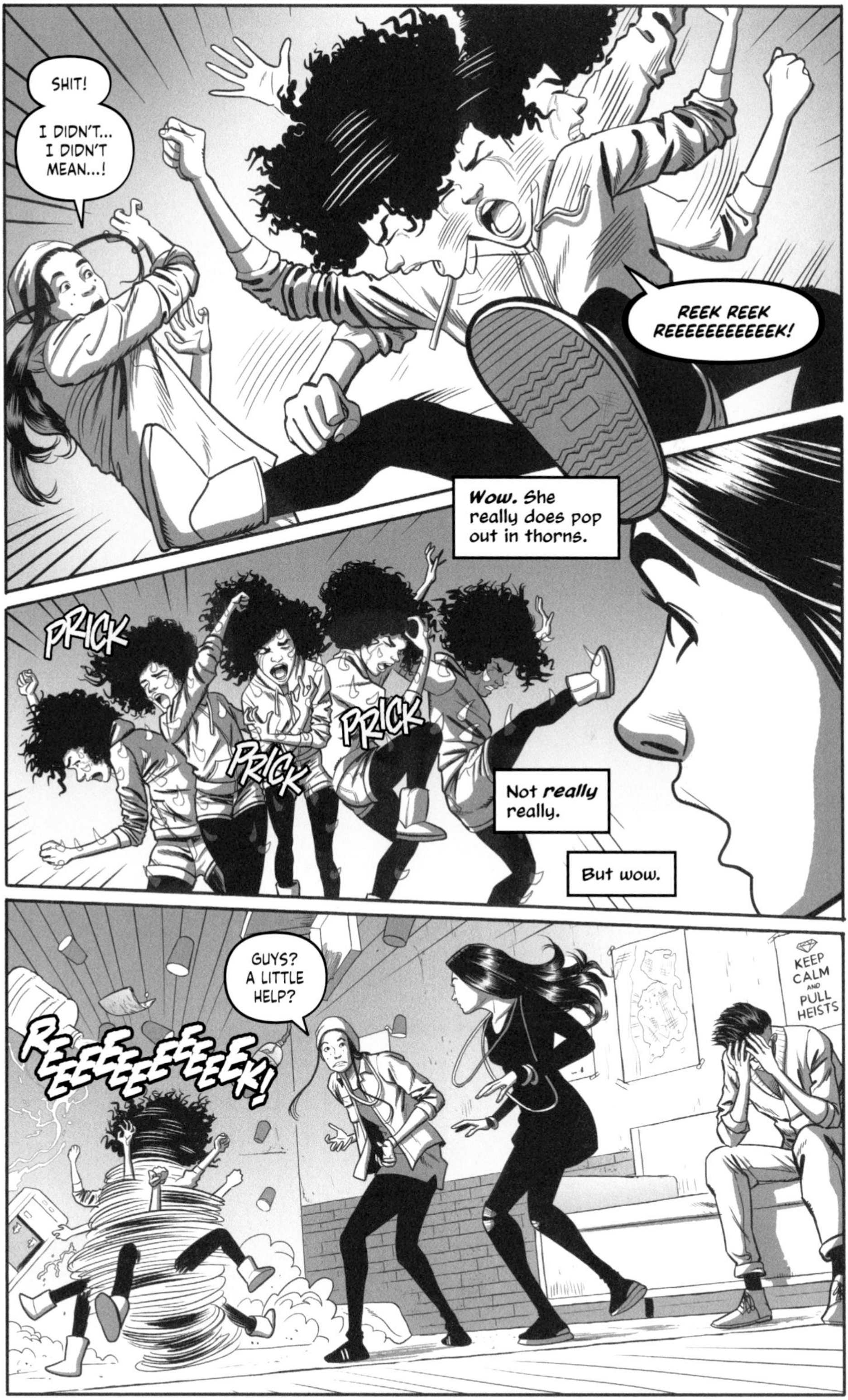
SHIT!
I DIDN'T... I DIDN'T MEAN...!
REEK REEK REEEEEEEEEEEK!
Wow. She really does pop out in thorns.
PRICK
PRICK
PRICK
Not really really.
But wow.
GUYS? A LITTLE HELP?
REEEEEEEEEEEEK!
KEEP CALM AND PULL HEISTS

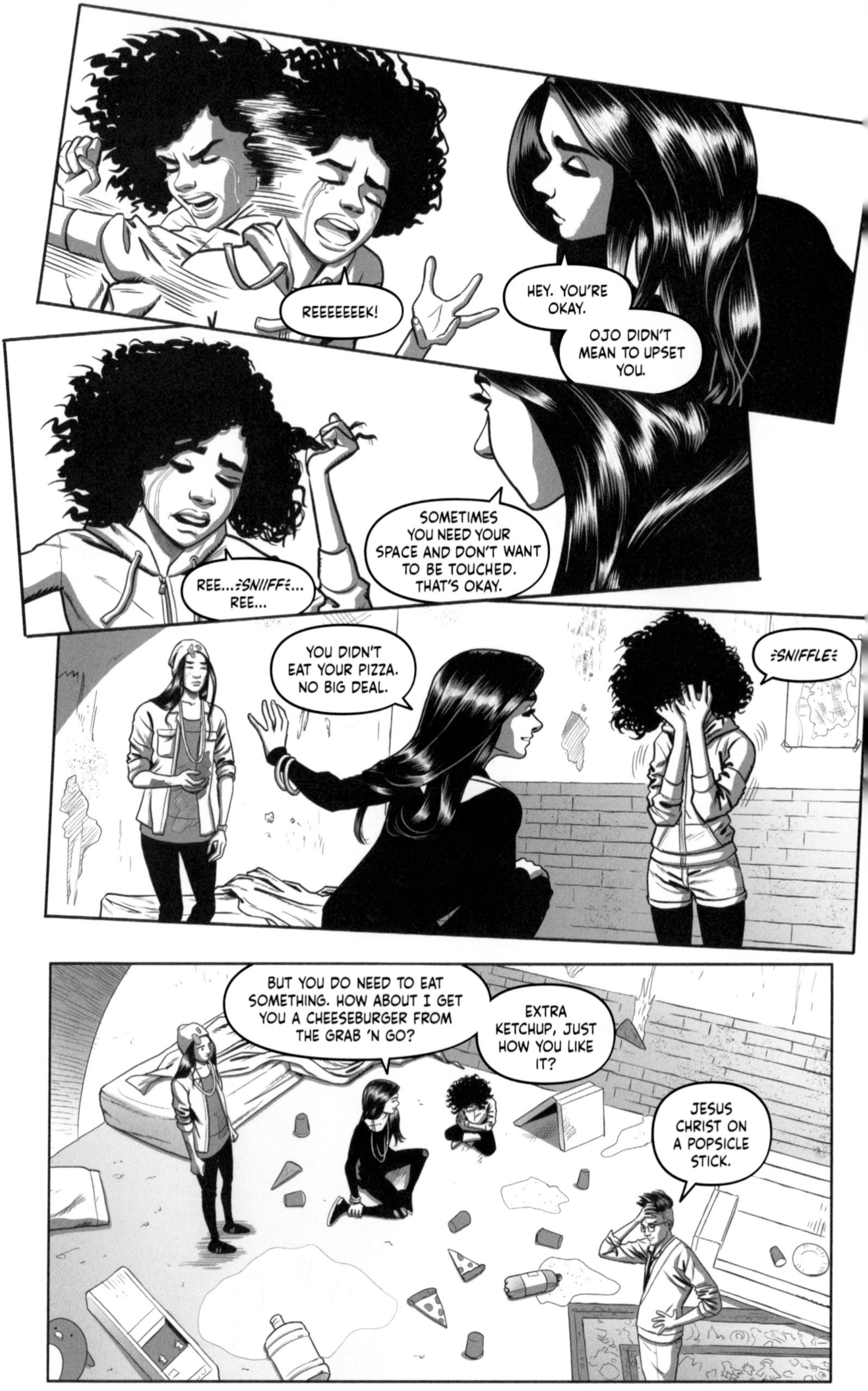
REEEEEEEK!
HEY. YOU'RE OKAY.
OJO DIDN'T MEAN TO UPSET YOU.
REE... SNIIFF... REE...
SOMETIMES YOU NEED YOUR SPACE AND DON'T WANT TO BE TOUCHED. THAT'S OKAY.
YOU DIDN'T EAT YOUR PIZZA. NO BIG DEAL.
SNIFFLE
BUT YOU DO NEED TO EAT SOMETHING. HOW ABOUT I GET YOU A CHEESEBURGER FROM THE GRAB 'N GO?
EXTRA KETCHUP, JUST HOW YOU LIKE IT?
JESUS CHRIST ON A POPSICLE STICK.

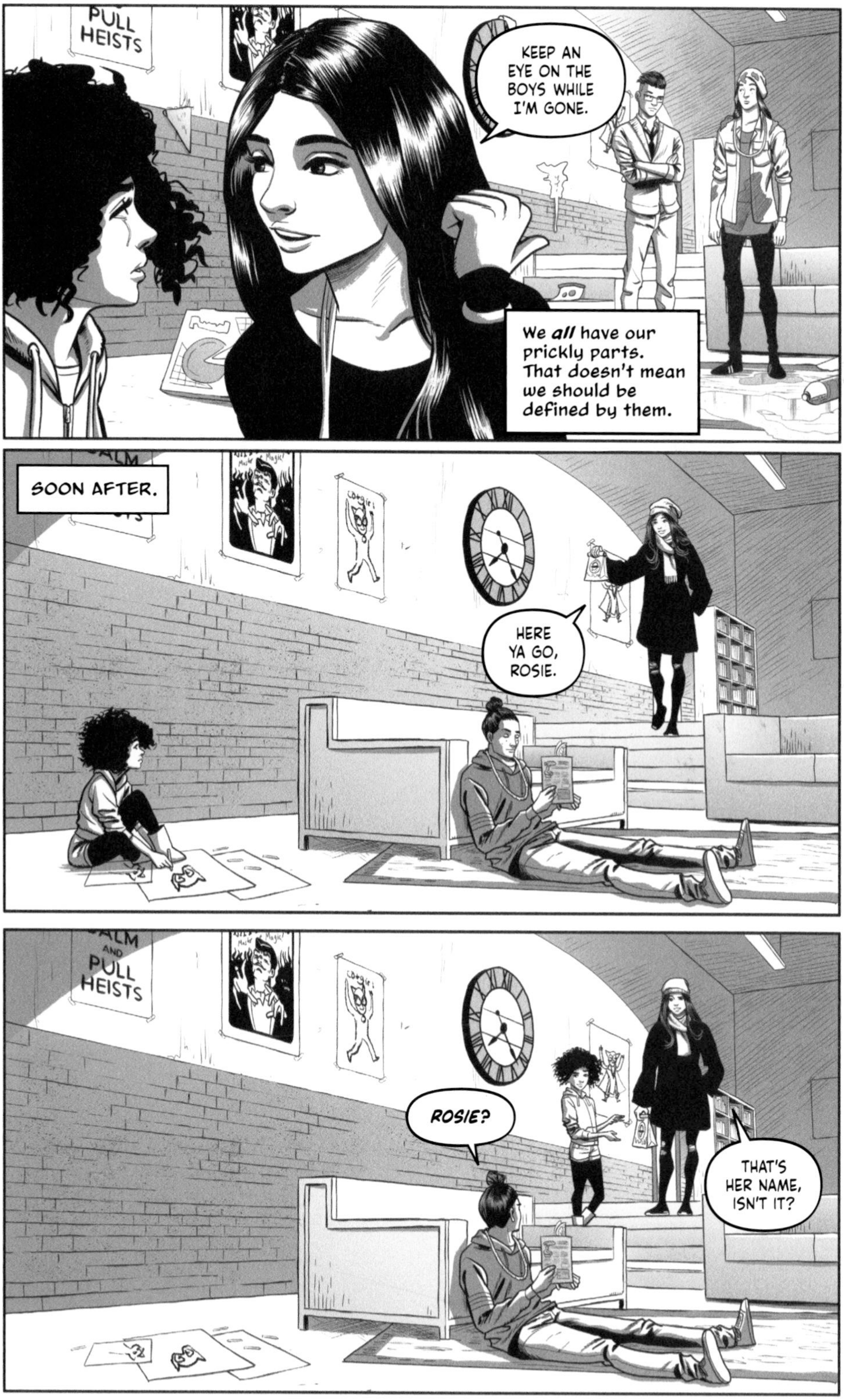
PULL HEISTS
KEEP AN EYE ON THE BOYS WHILE I'M GONE.
We *all* have our prickly parts. That doesn't mean we should be defined by them.
SOON AFTER.
HERE YA GO, ROSIE.
PULL HEISTS
ROSIE?
THAT'S HER NAME, ISN'T IT?

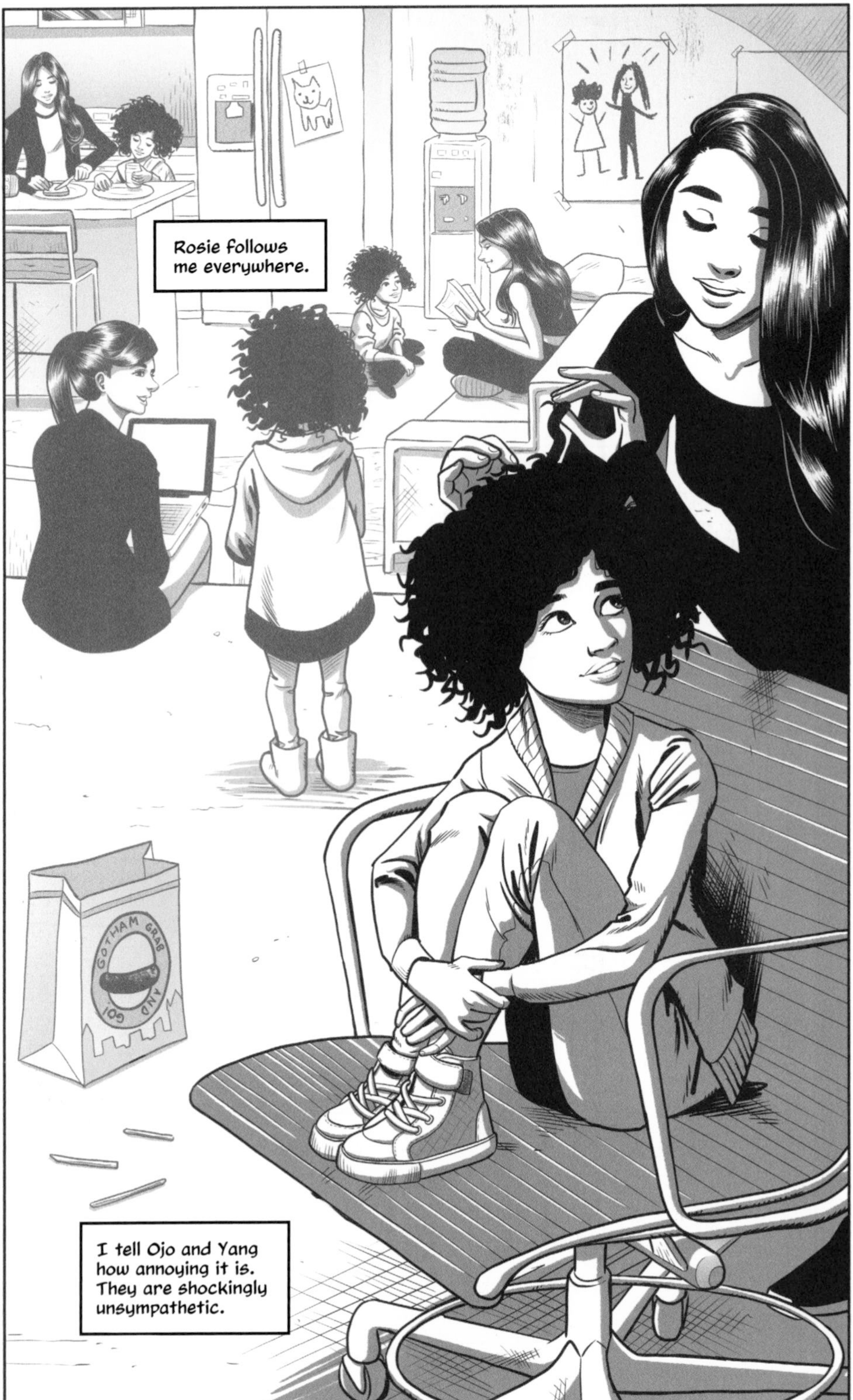
Rosie follows me everywhere.
GOTHAM GRAB AND GO!
I tell Ojo and Yang how annoying it is. They are shockingly unsympathetic.

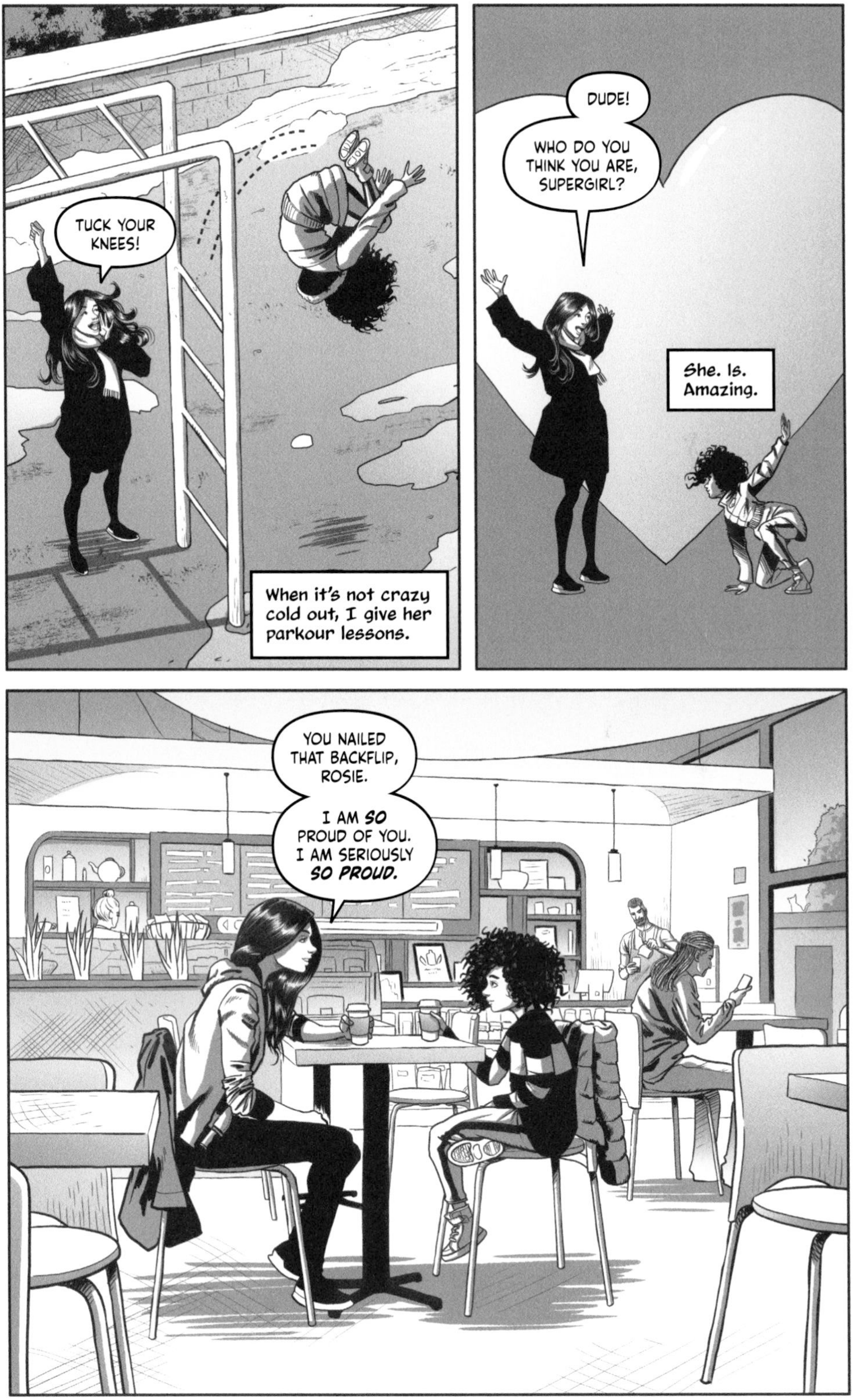
TUCK YOUR KNEES!
When it's not crazy cold out, I give her parkour lessons.
DUDE!
WHO DO YOU THINK YOU ARE, SUPERGIRL?
She. Is. Amazing.
YOU NAILED THAT BACKFLIP, ROSIE.
I AM ***SO*** PROUD OF YOU. I AM SERIOUSLY ***SO PROUD.***

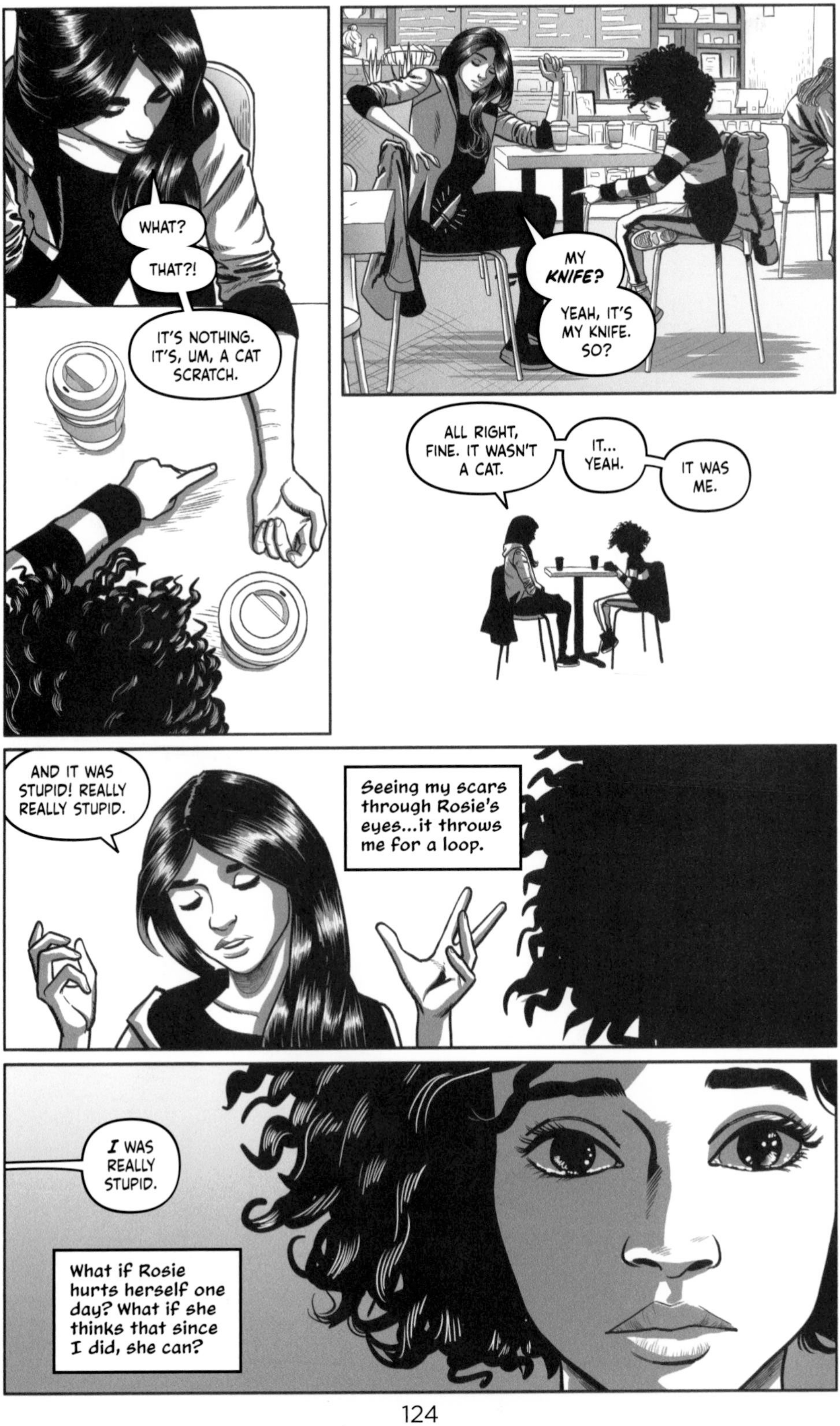
WHAT?
THAT?!
IT'S NOTHING. IT'S, UM, A CAT SCRATCH.
MY KNIFE?
YEAH, IT'S MY KNIFE. SO?
ALL RIGHT, FINE. IT WASN'T A CAT.
IT... YEAH.
IT WAS ME.
AND IT WAS STUPID! REALLY REALLY STUPID.
Seeing my scars through Rosie's eyes...it throws me for a loop.
I WAS REALLY STUPID.
What if Rosie hurts herself one day? What if she thinks that since I did, she can?

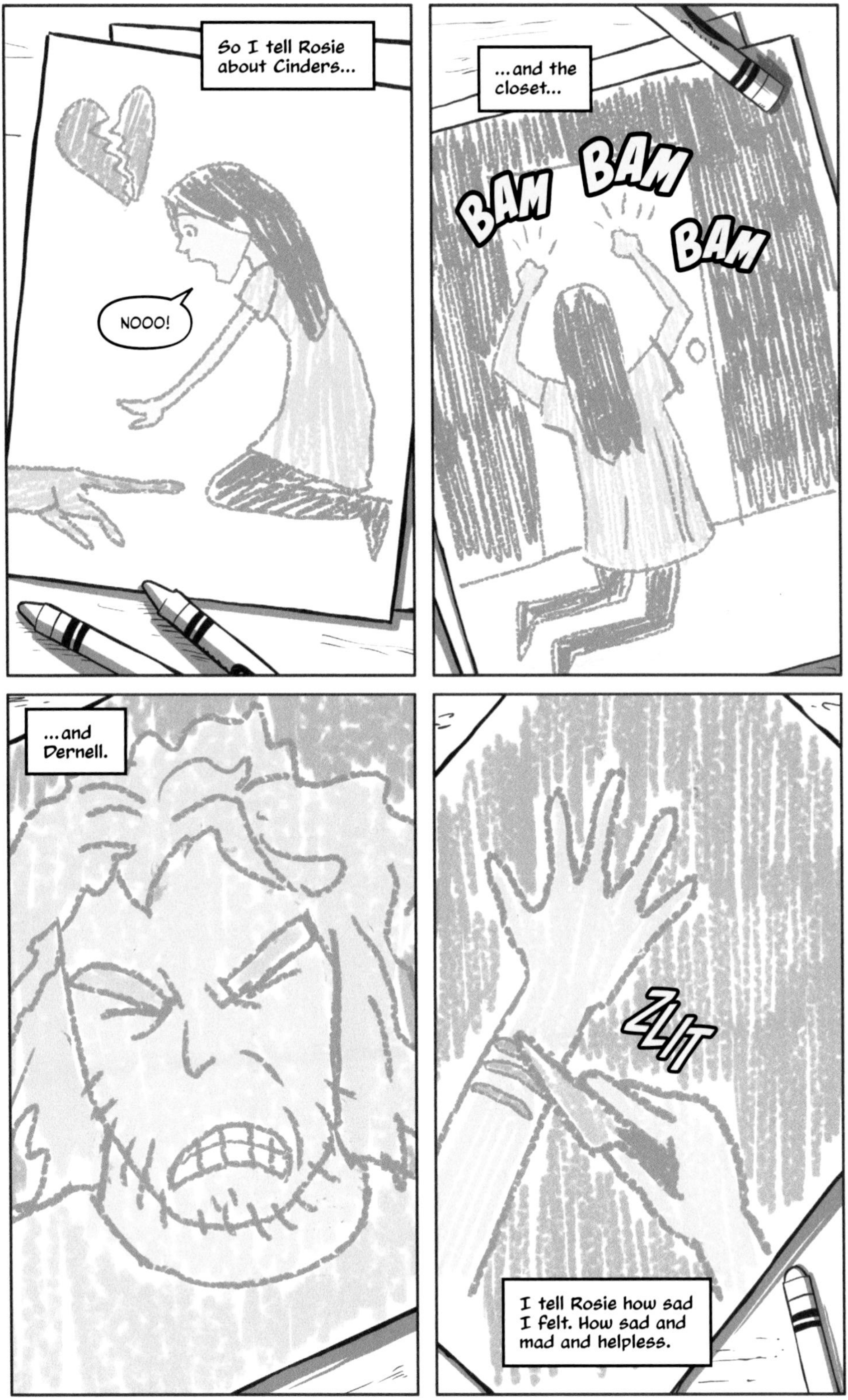
So I tell Rosie about Cinders...
NOOO!
...and the closet...
BAM
BAM
BAM
...and Dernell.
ZLIT
I tell Rosie how sad I felt. How sad and mad and helpless.

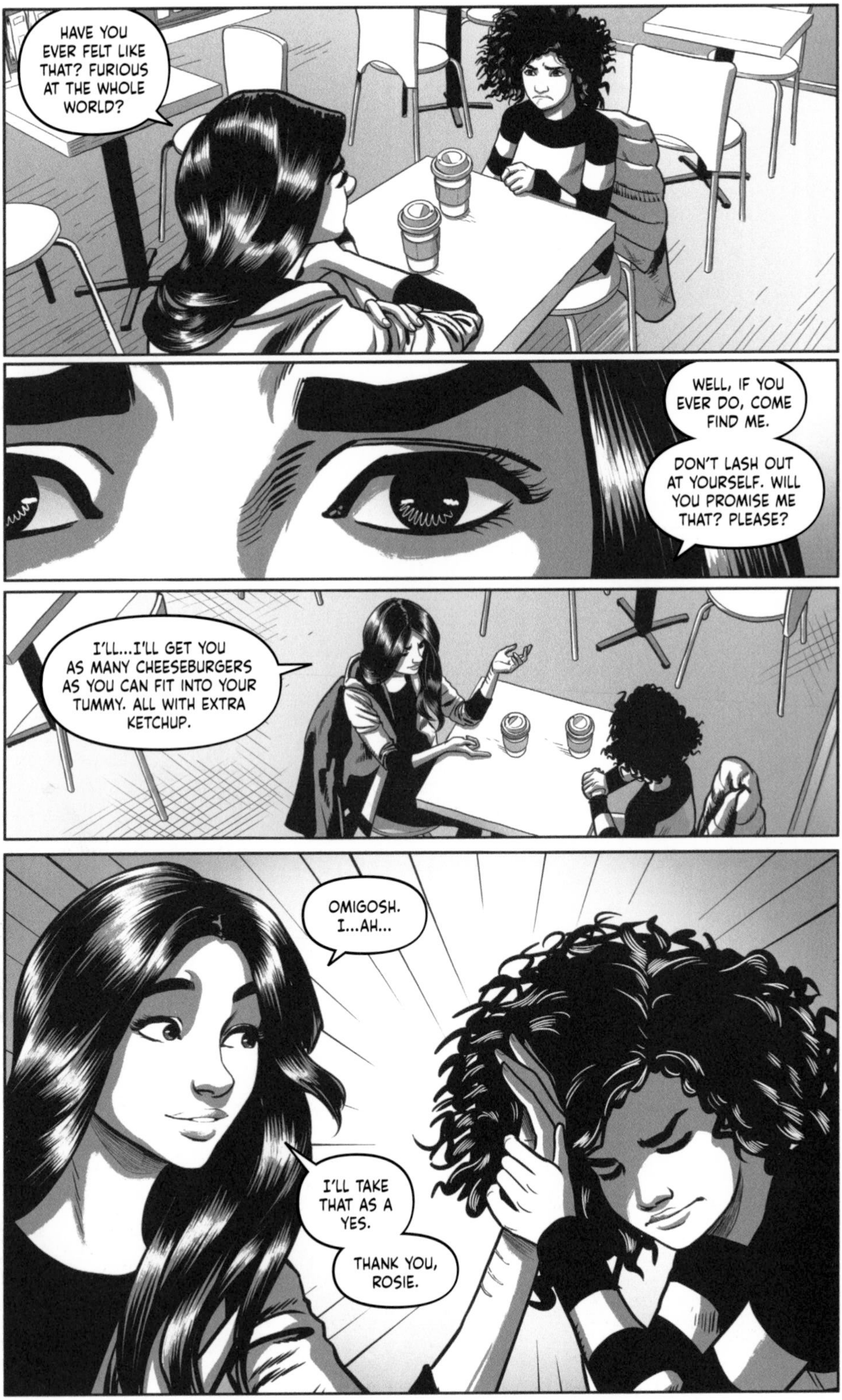
HAVE YOU EVER FELT LIKE THAT? FURIOUS AT THE WHOLE WORLD?
WELL, IF YOU EVER DO, COME FIND ME.
DON'T LASH OUT AT YOURSELF. WILL YOU PROMISE ME THAT? PLEASE?
I'LL...I'LL GET YOU AS MANY CHEESEBURGERS AS YOU CAN FIT INTO YOUR TUMMY. ALL WITH EXTRA KETCHUP.
OMIGOSH. I...AH...
I'LL TAKE THAT AS A YES.
THANK YOU, ROSIE.

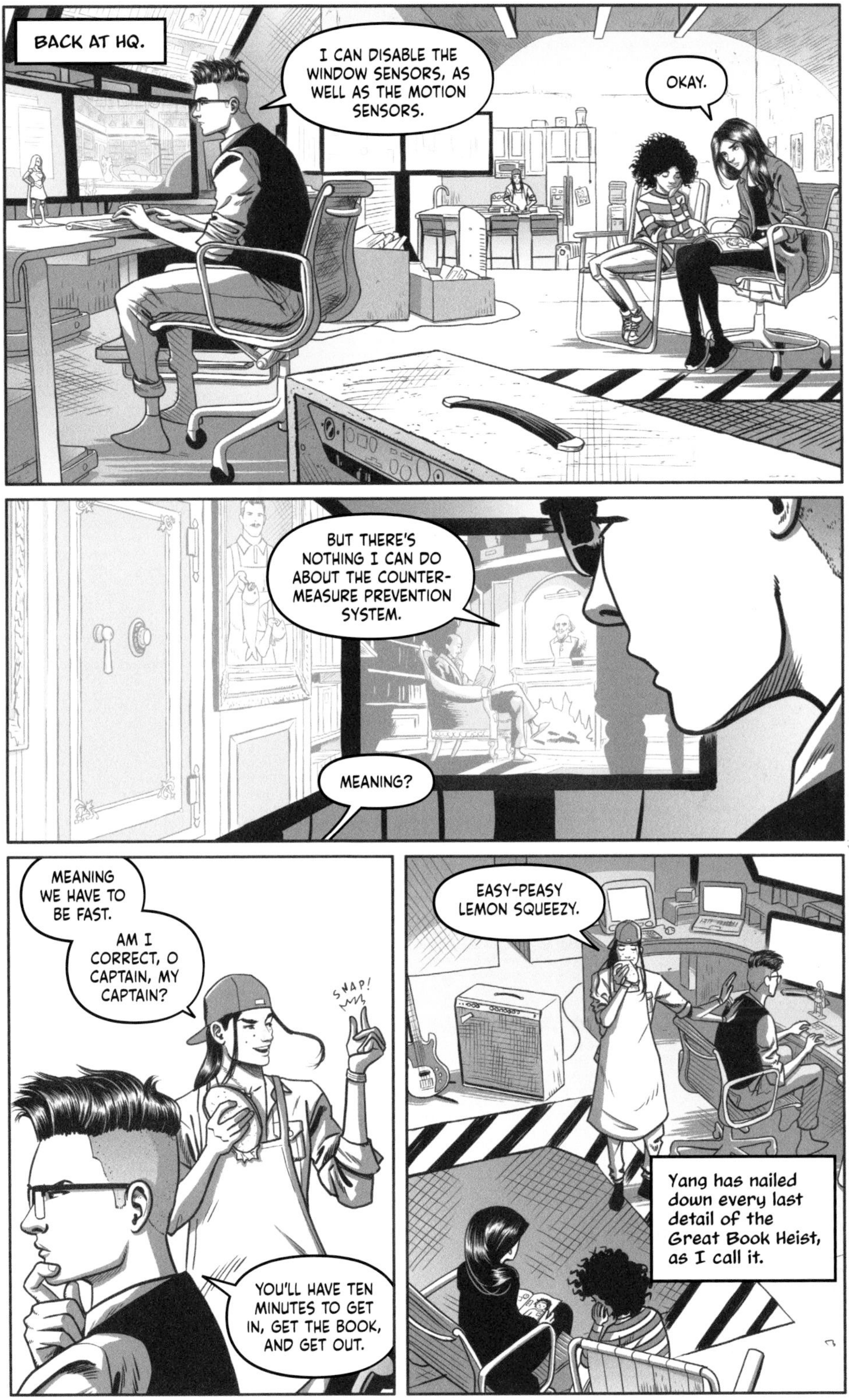
BACK AT HQ.
I CAN DISABLE THE WINDOW SENSORS, AS WELL AS THE MOTION SENSORS.
OKAY.
BUT THERE'S NOTHING I CAN DO ABOUT THE COUNTER-MEASURE PREVENTION SYSTEM.
MEANING?
MEANING WE HAVE TO BE FAST.
AM I CORRECT, O CAPTAIN, MY CAPTAIN?
SNAP!
YOU'LL HAVE TEN MINUTES TO GET IN, GET THE BOOK, AND GET OUT.
EASY-PEASY LEMON SQUEEZY.
Yang has nailed down every last detail of the Great Book Heist, as I call it.

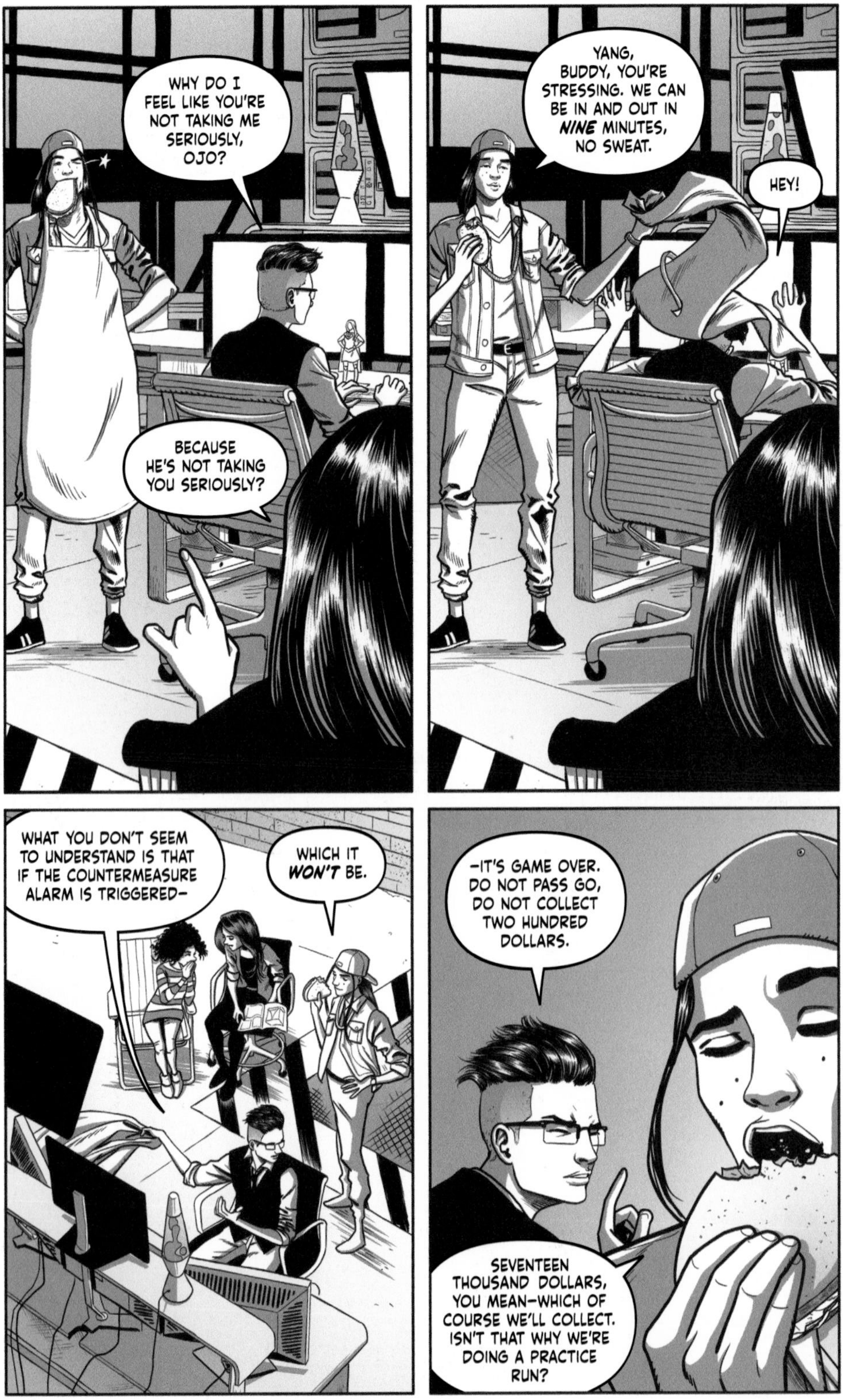
WHY DO I FEEL LIKE YOU'RE NOT TAKING ME SERIOUSLY, OJO?
BECAUSE HE'S NOT TAKING YOU SERIOUSLY?
YANG, BUDDY, YOU'RE STRESSING. WE CAN BE IN AND OUT IN *NINE* MINUTES, NO SWEAT.
HEY!
WHAT YOU DON'T SEEM TO UNDERSTAND IS THAT IF THE COUNTERMEASURE ALARM IS TRIGGERED—
WHICH IT *WON'T* BE.
—IT'S GAME OVER. DO NOT PASS GO, DO NOT COLLECT TWO HUNDRED DOLLARS.
SEVENTEEN THOUSAND DOLLARS, YOU MEAN—WHICH OF COURSE WE'LL COLLECT. ISN'T THAT WHY WE'RE DOING A PRACTICE RUN?

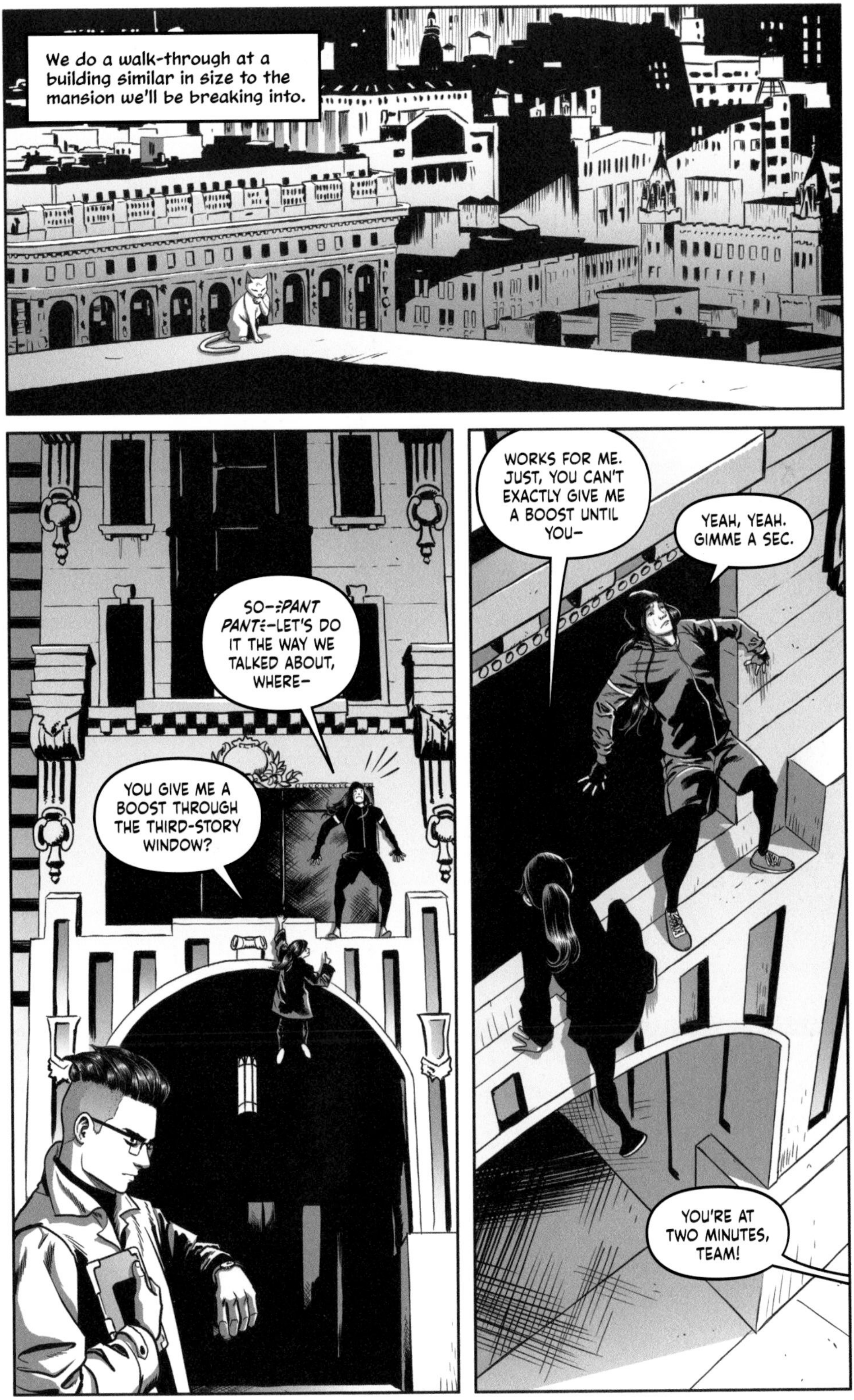
We do a walk-through at a building similar in size to the mansion we'll be breaking into.
SO-*PANT PANT*-LET'S DO IT THE WAY WE TALKED ABOUT, WHERE-
YOU GIVE ME A BOOST THROUGH THE THIRD-STORY WINDOW?
WORKS FOR ME. JUST, YOU CAN'T EXACTLY GIVE ME A BOOST UNTIL YOU-
YEAH, YEAH. GIMME A SEC.
YOU'RE AT TWO MINUTES, TEAM!

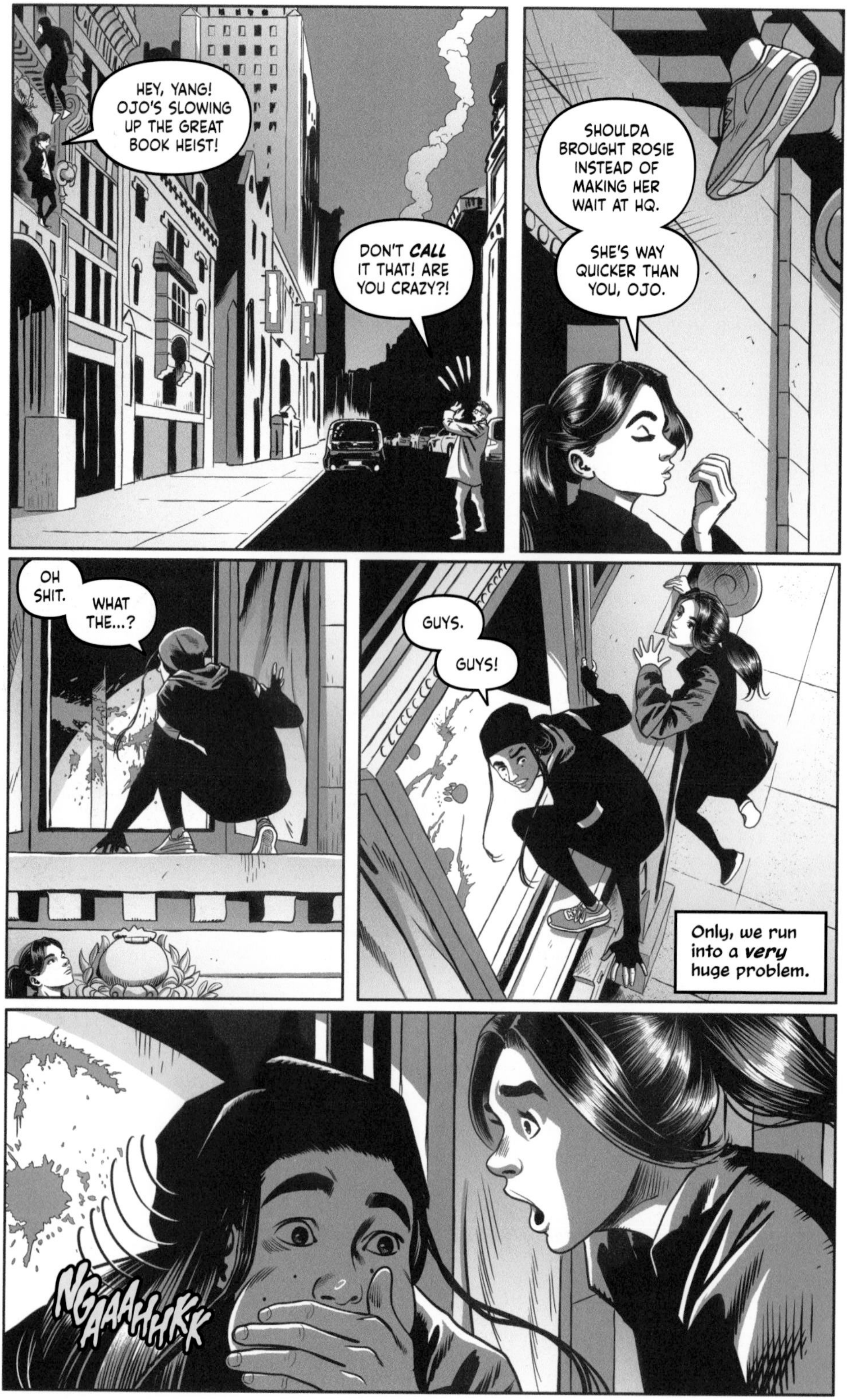
HEY, YANG! OJO'S SLOWING UP THE GREAT BOOK HEIST!
DON'T **CALL** IT THAT! ARE YOU CRAZY?!
SHOULDA BROUGHT ROSIE INSTEAD OF MAKING HER WAIT AT HQ.
SHE'S WAY QUICKER THAN YOU, OJO.
OH SHIT.
WHAT THE...?
GUYS.
GUYS!
Only, we run into a ***very*** huge problem.
NGAAAHHKK

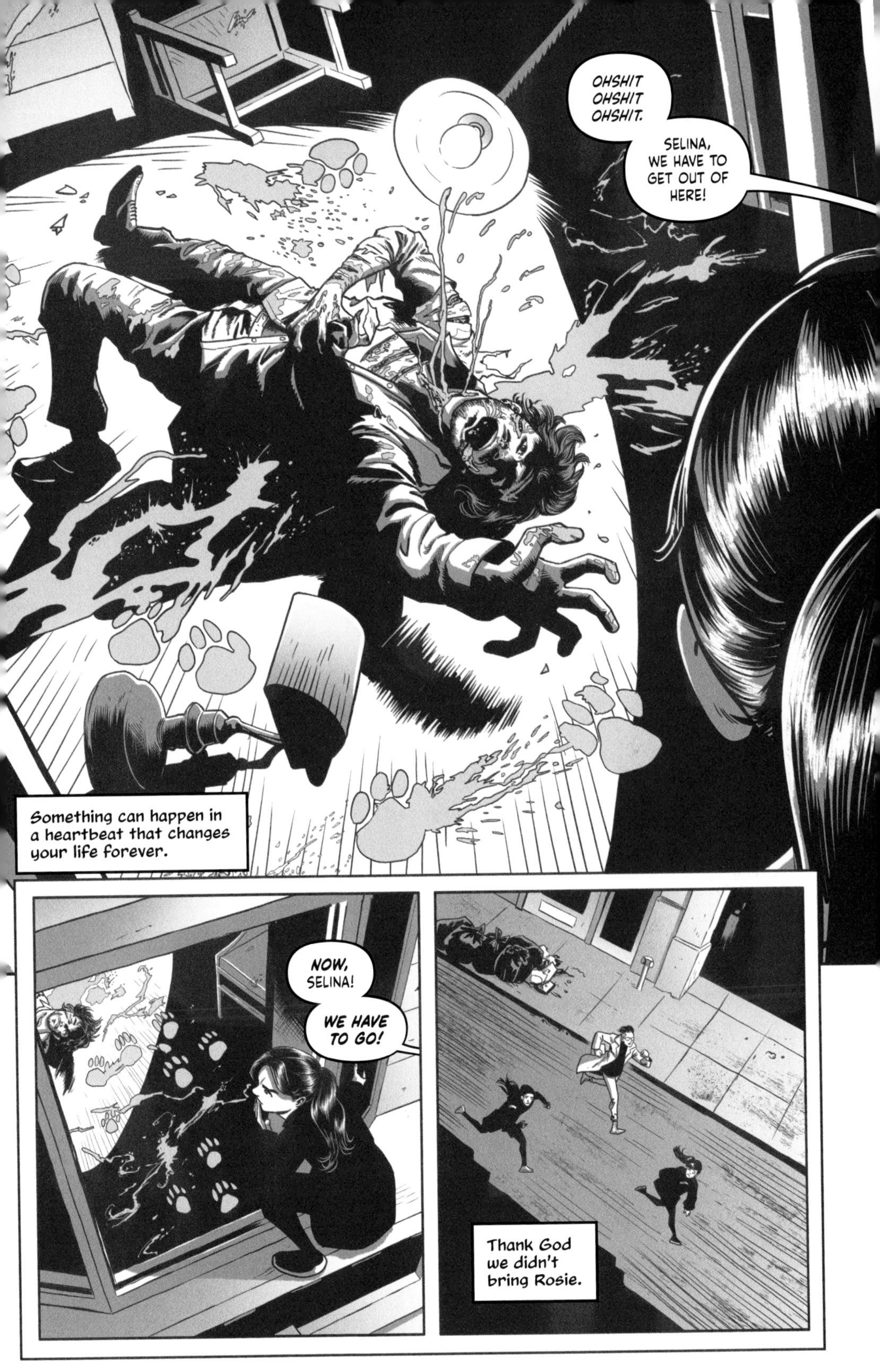
OHSHIT
OHSHIT
OHSHIT.
SELINA, WE HAVE TO GET OUT OF HERE!
Something can happen in a heartbeat that changes your life forever.
NOW, SELINA!
WE HAVE TO GO!
Thank God we didn't bring Rosie.

HELL-DOG

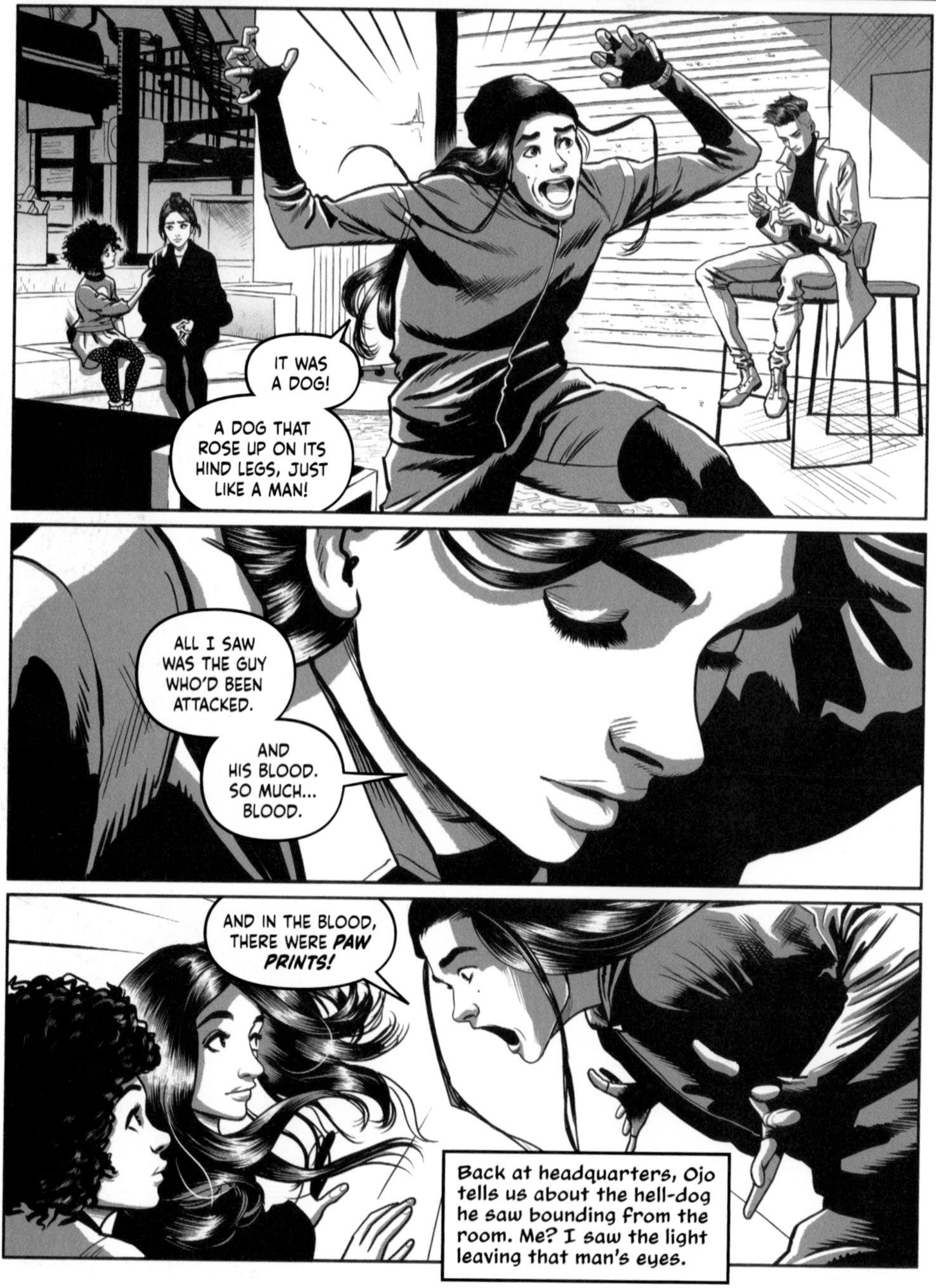
IT WAS A DOG!
A DOG THAT ROSE UP ON ITS HIND LEGS, JUST LIKE A MAN!
ALL I SAW WAS THE GUY WHO'D BEEN ATTACKED.
AND HIS BLOOD. SO MUCH... BLOOD.
AND IN THE BLOOD, THERE WERE *PAW PRINTS!*
Back at headquarters, Ojo tells us about the hell-dog he saw bounding from the room. Me? I saw the light leaving that man's eyes.

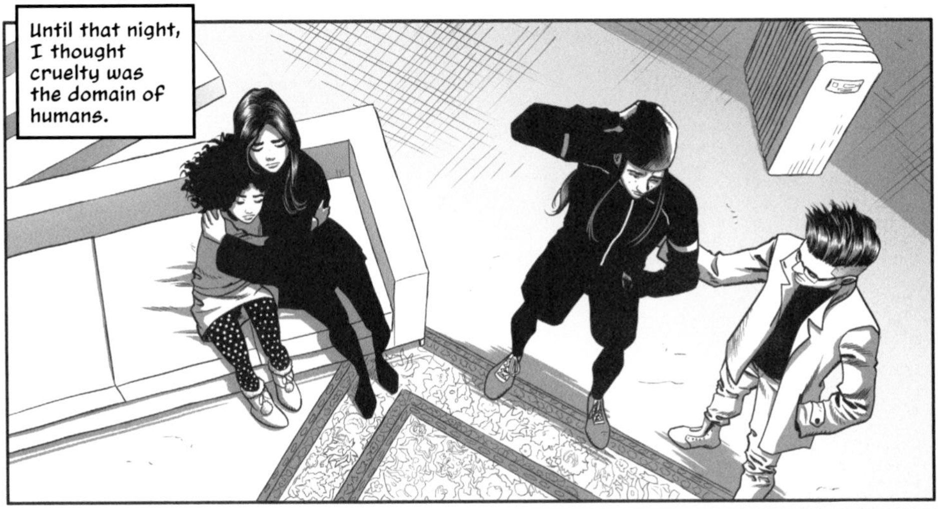
Until that night, I thought cruelty was the domain of humans.

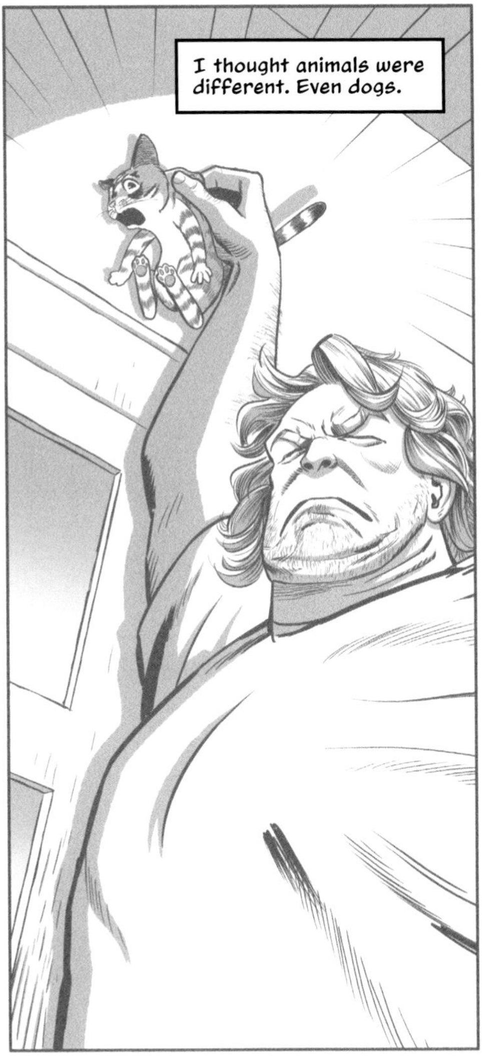
I thought animals were different. Even dogs.

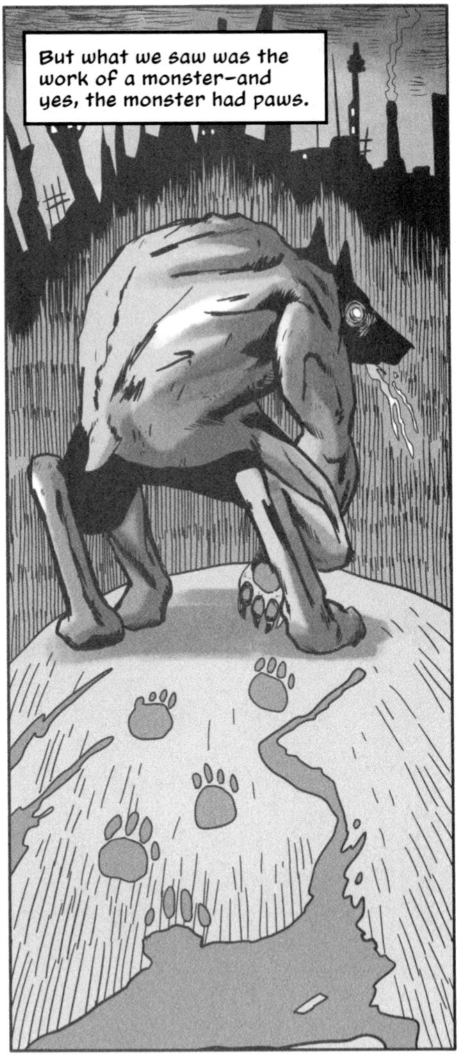
But what we saw was the work of a monster—and yes, the monster had paws.

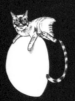

BAD TO THE BONE

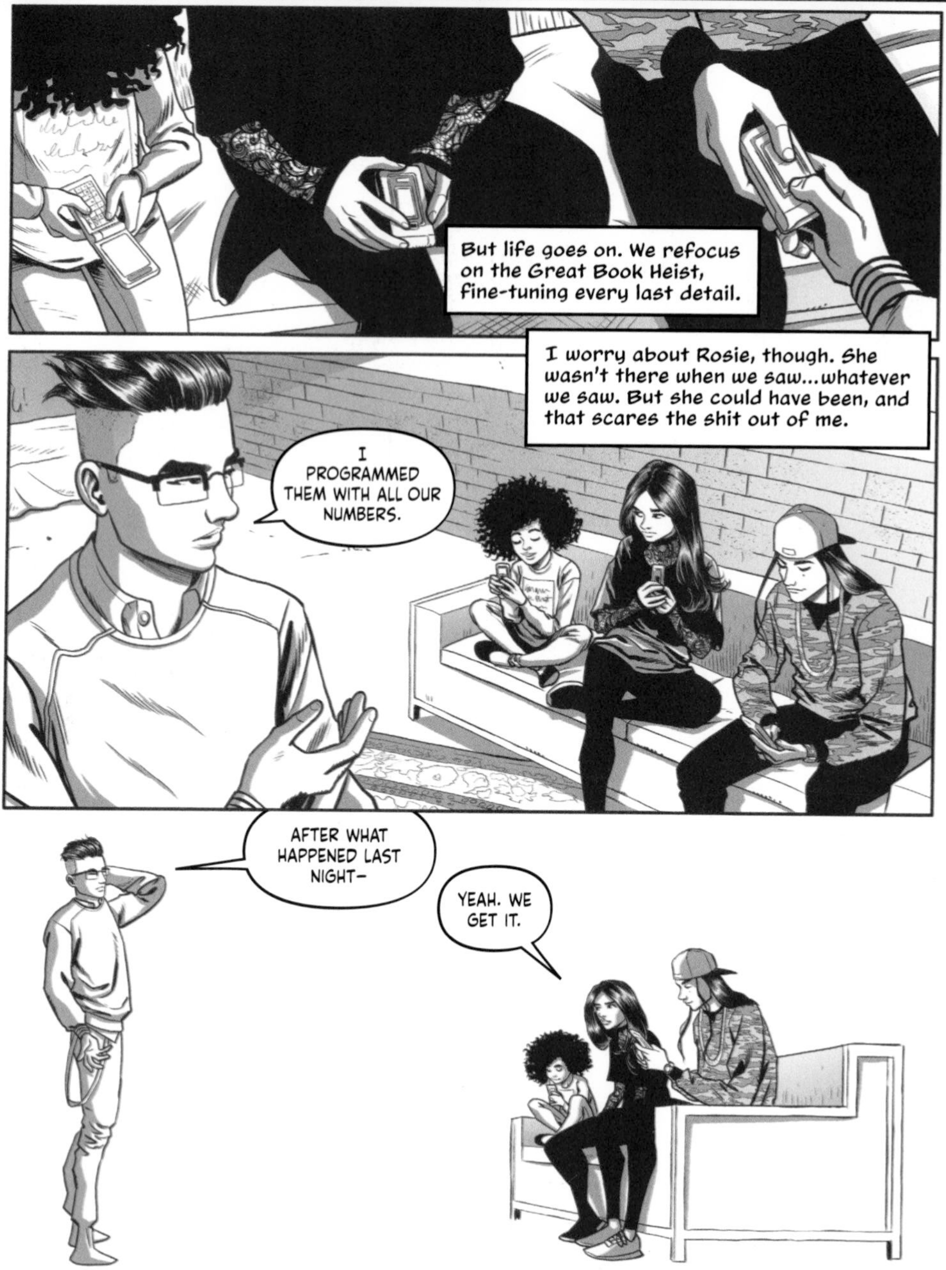

But life goes on. We refocus on the Great Book Heist, fine-tuning every last detail.
I worry about Rosie, though. She wasn't there when we saw...whatever we saw. But she could have been, and that scares the shit out of me.
I PROGRAMMED THEM WITH ALL OUR NUMBERS.
AFTER WHAT HAPPENED LAST NIGHT–
YEAH. WE GET IT.

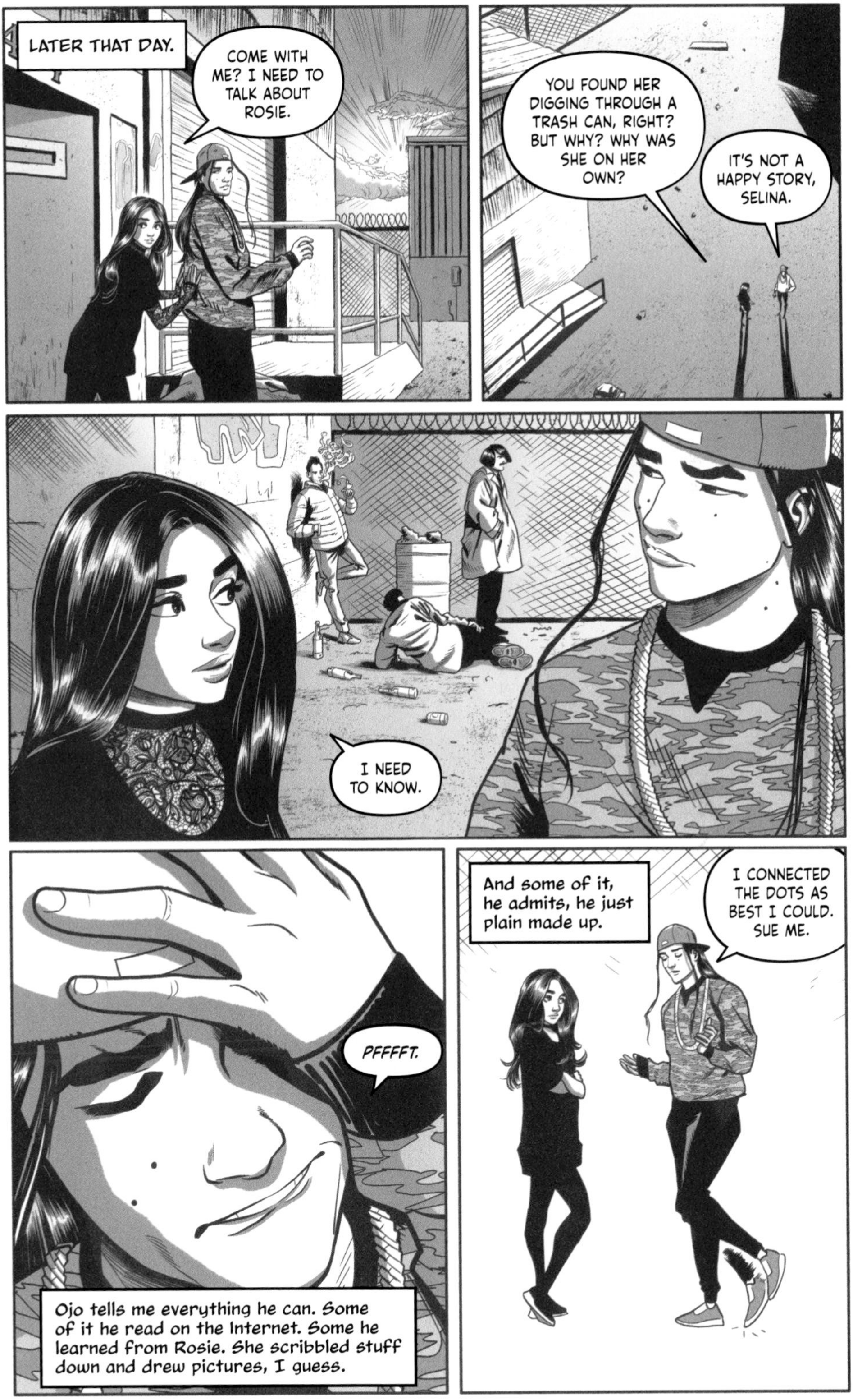
LATER THAT DAY.
COME WITH ME? I NEED TO TALK ABOUT ROSIE.
YOU FOUND HER DIGGING THROUGH A TRASH CAN, RIGHT? BUT WHY? WHY WAS SHE ON HER OWN?
IT'S NOT A HAPPY STORY, SELINA.
I NEED TO KNOW.
PFFFFT.
Ojo tells me everything he can. Some of it he read on the Internet. Some he learned from Rosie. She scribbled stuff down and drew pictures, I guess.
And some of it, he admits, he just plain made up.
I CONNECTED THE DOTS AS BEST I COULD. SUE ME.

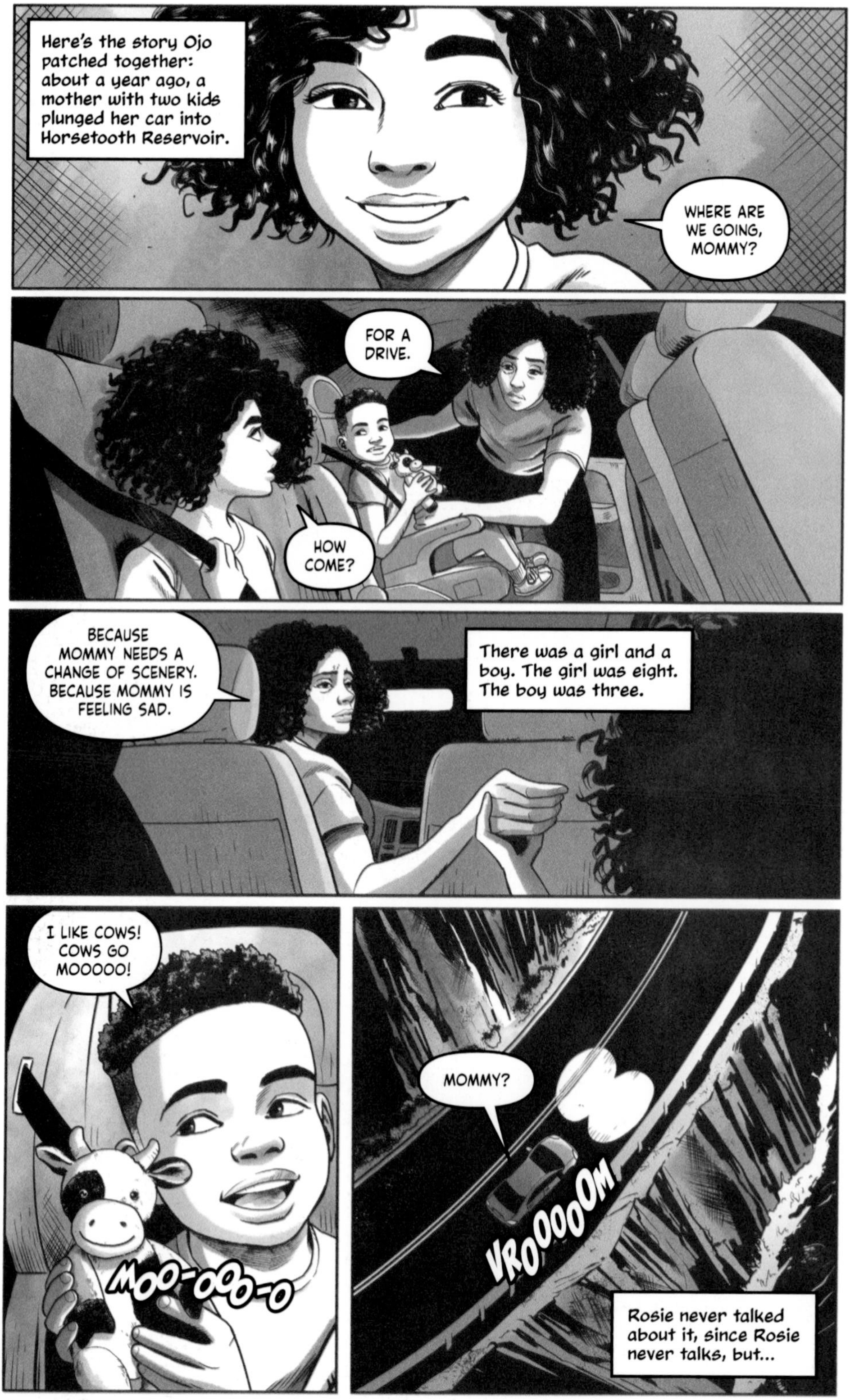

Here's the story Ojo patched together: about a year ago, a mother with two kids plunged her car into Horsetooth Reservoir.
WHERE ARE WE GOING, MOMMY?
FOR A DRIVE.
HOW COME?
BECAUSE MOMMY NEEDS A CHANGE OF SCENERY. BECAUSE MOMMY IS FEELING SAD.
There was a girl and a boy. The girl was eight. The boy was three.
I LIKE COWS! COWS GO MOOOOO!
MOO-OOO-O
MOMMY?
VROOOOOM
Rosie never talked about it, since Rosie never talks, but...

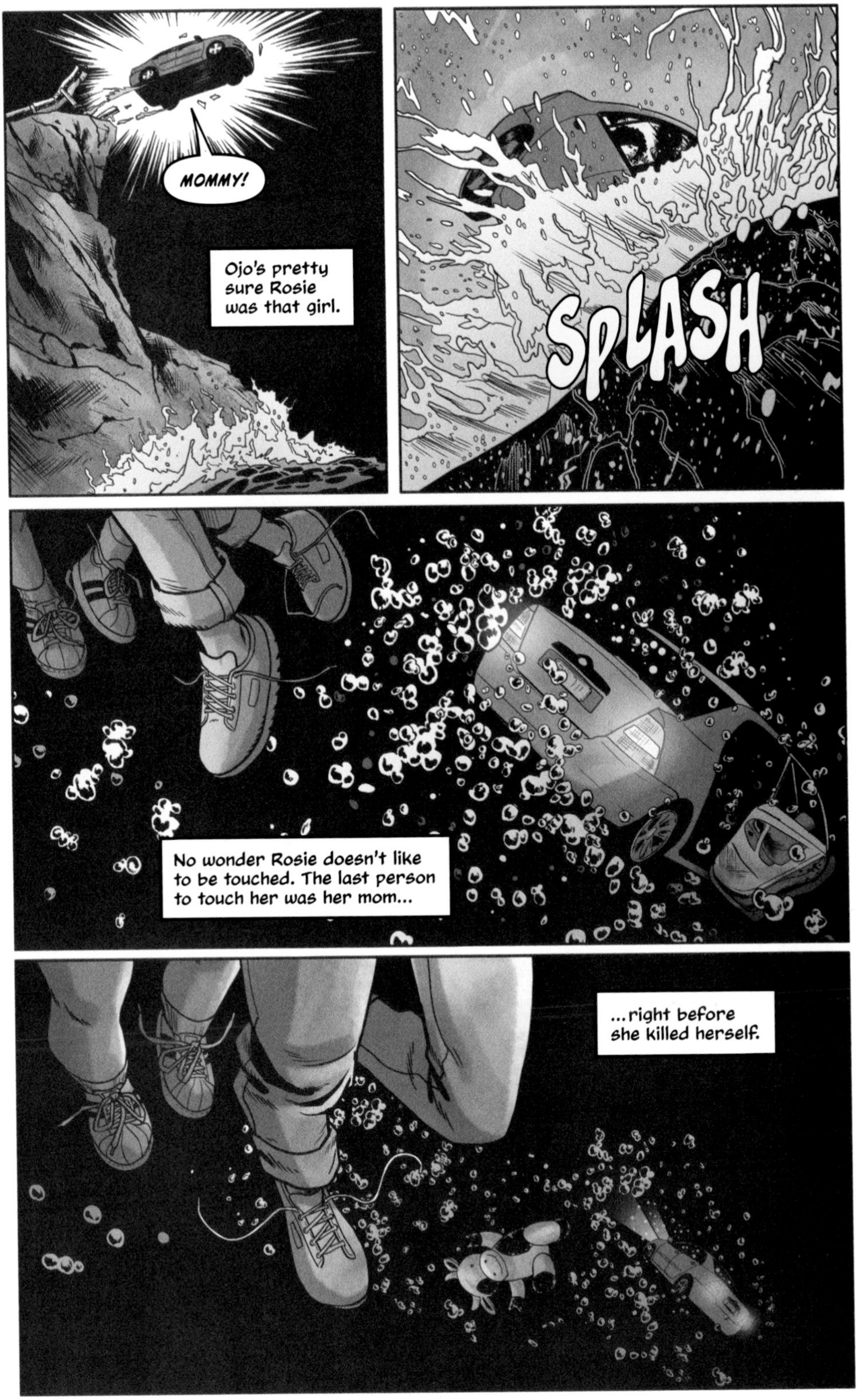
MOMMY!
Ojo's pretty sure Rosie was that girl.
SPLASH
No wonder Rosie doesn't like to be touched. The last person to touch her was her mom...
...right before she killed herself.

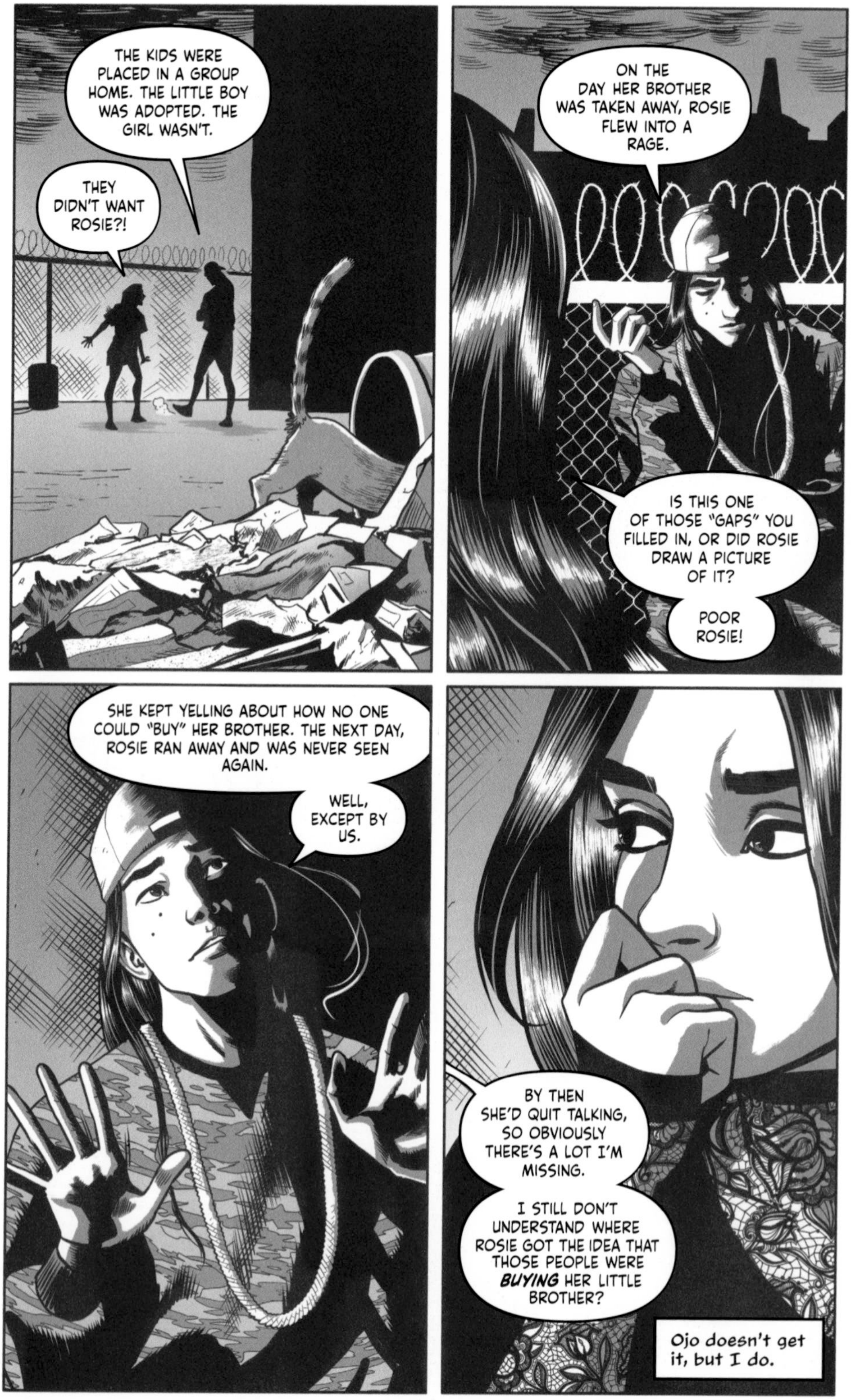
THE KIDS WERE PLACED IN A GROUP HOME. THE LITTLE BOY WAS ADOPTED. THE GIRL WASN'T.
THEY DIDN'T WANT ROSIE?!
ON THE DAY HER BROTHER WAS TAKEN AWAY, ROSIE FLEW INTO A RAGE.
IS THIS ONE OF THOSE "GAPS" YOU FILLED IN, OR DID ROSIE DRAW A PICTURE OF IT?
POOR ROSIE!
SHE KEPT YELLING ABOUT HOW NO ONE COULD "BUY" HER BROTHER. THE NEXT DAY, ROSIE RAN AWAY AND WAS NEVER SEEN AGAIN.
WELL, EXCEPT BY US.
BY THEN SHE'D QUIT TALKING, SO OBVIOUSLY THERE'S A LOT I'M MISSING.
I STILL DON'T UNDERSTAND WHERE ROSIE GOT THE IDEA THAT THOSE PEOPLE WERE ***BUYING*** HER LITTLE BROTHER?
Ojo doesn't get it, but I do.

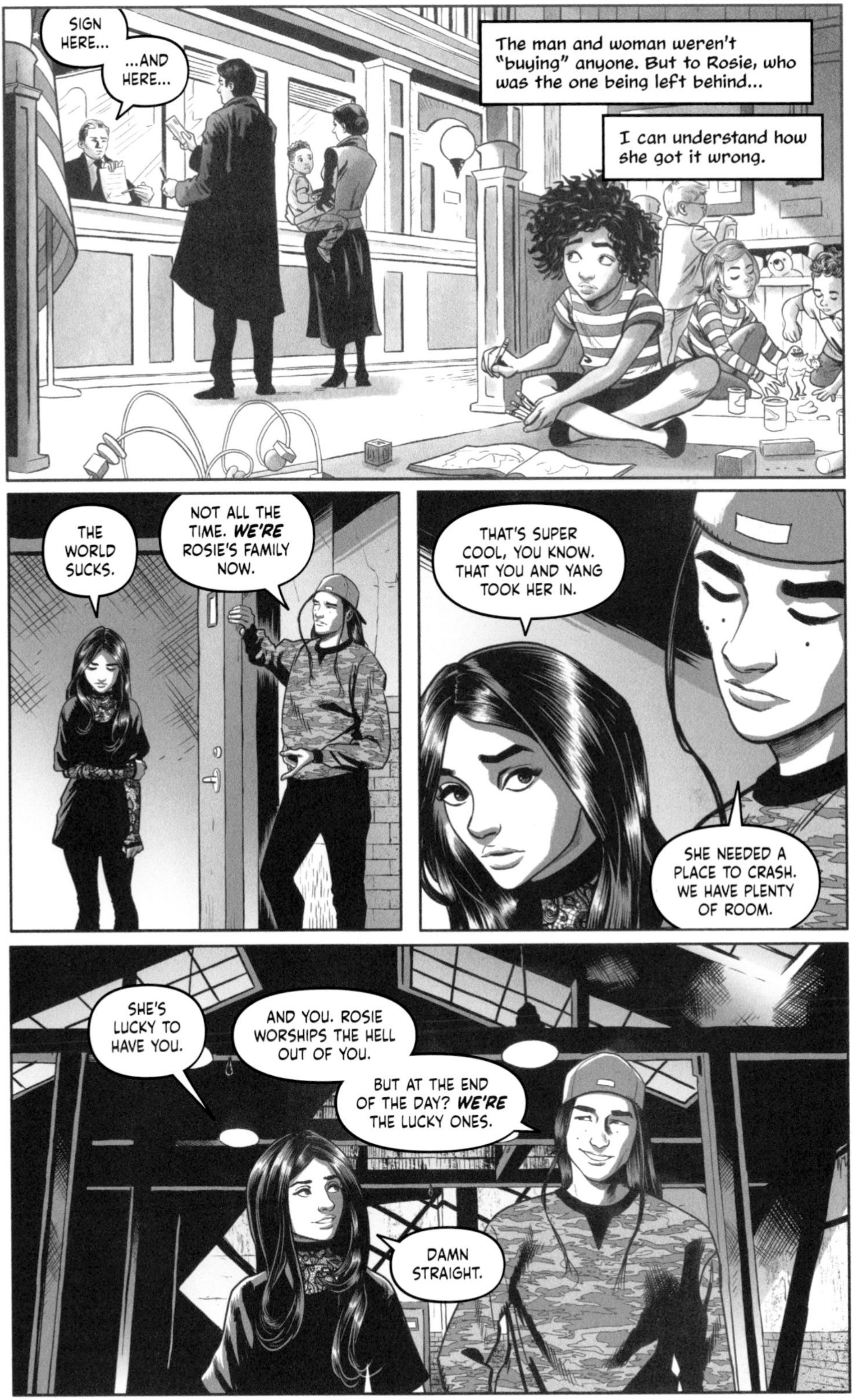

SIGN HERE...
...AND HERE...
The man and woman weren't "buying" anyone. But to Rosie, who was the one being left behind...
I can understand how she got it wrong.
THE WORLD SUCKS.
NOT ALL THE TIME. WE'RE ROSIE'S FAMILY NOW.
THAT'S SUPER COOL, YOU KNOW. THAT YOU AND YANG TOOK HER IN.
SHE NEEDED A PLACE TO CRASH. WE HAVE PLENTY OF ROOM.
SHE'S LUCKY TO HAVE YOU.
AND YOU. ROSIE WORSHIPS THE HELL OUT OF YOU.
BUT AT THE END OF THE DAY? WE'RE THE LUCKY ONES.
DAMN STRAIGHT.

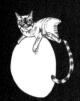

THE BIG DAY

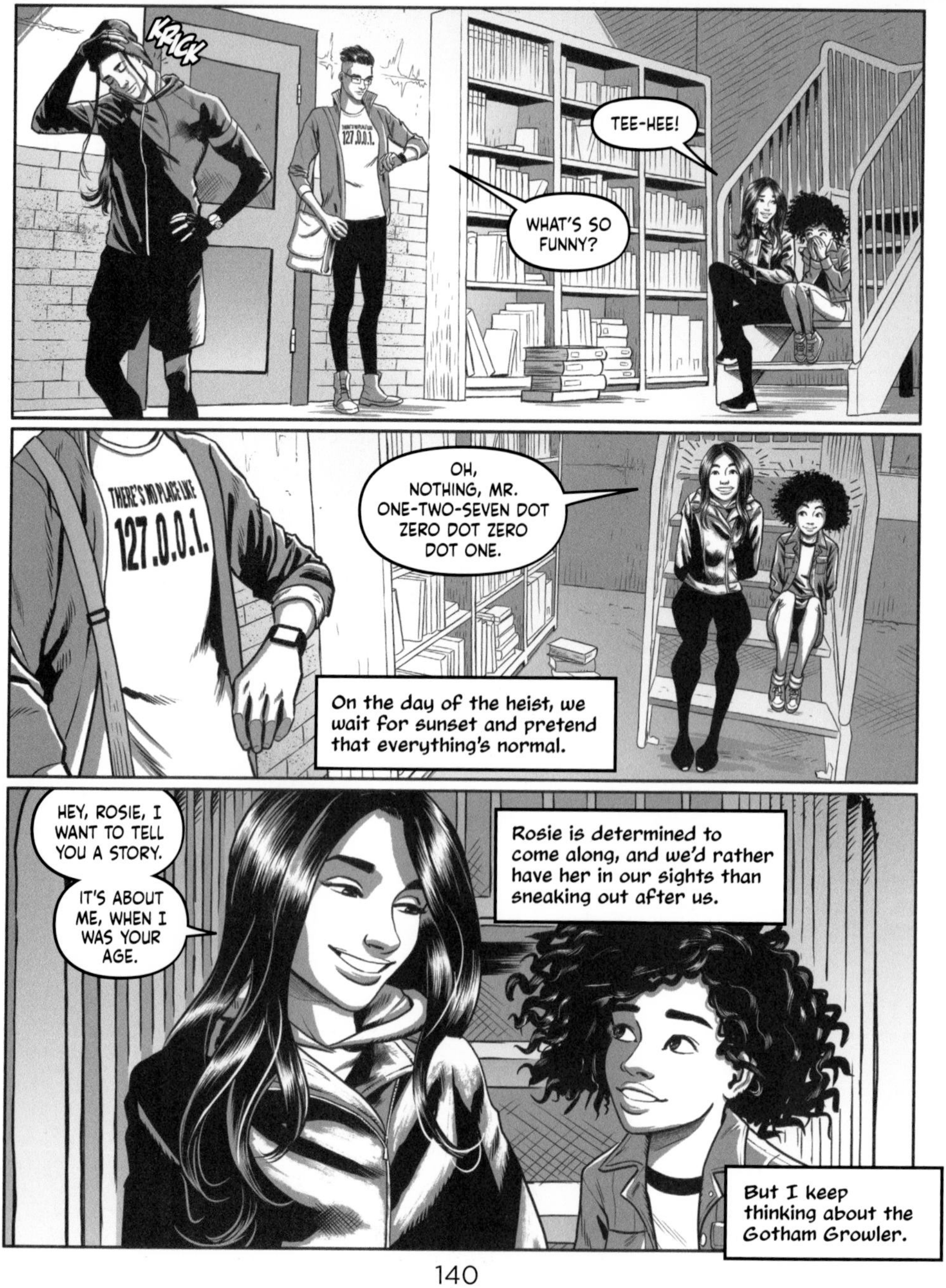

KRACK
THERE'S NO PLACE LIKE 127.0.0.1.
TEE-HEE!
WHAT'S SO FUNNY?
THERE'S NO PLACE LIKE 127.0.0.1.
OH, NOTHING, MR. ONE-TWO-SEVEN DOT ZERO DOT ZERO DOT ONE.
On the day of the heist, we wait for sunset and pretend that everything's normal.
HEY, ROSIE, I WANT TO TELL YOU A STORY.
IT'S ABOUT ME, WHEN I WAS YOUR AGE.
Rosie is determined to come along, and we'd rather have her in our sights than sneaking out after us.
But I keep thinking about the Gotham Growler.

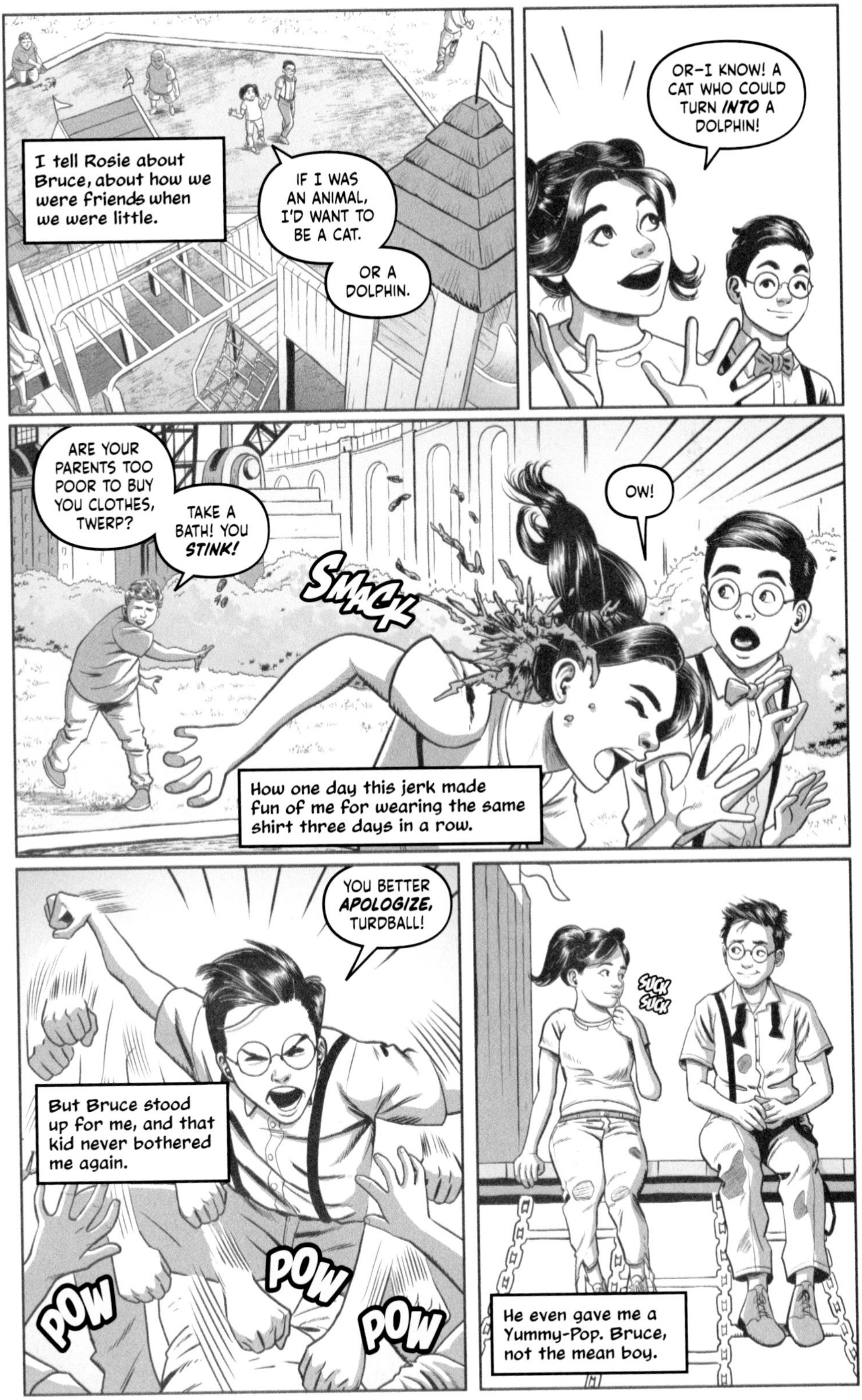
I tell Rosie about Bruce, about how we were friends when we were little.
IF I WAS AN ANIMAL, I'D WANT TO BE A CAT.
OR A DOLPHIN.
OR—I KNOW! A CAT WHO COULD TURN *INTO* A DOLPHIN!
ARE YOUR PARENTS TOO POOR TO BUY YOU CLOTHES, TWERP?
TAKE A BATH! YOU *STINK!*
SMACK
OW!
How one day this jerk made fun of me for wearing the same shirt three days in a row.
YOU BETTER *APOLOGIZE,* TURDBALL!
But Bruce stood up for me, and that kid never bothered me again.
POW
POW
POW
SUCK SUCK
He even gave me a Yummy-Pop. Bruce, not the mean boy.

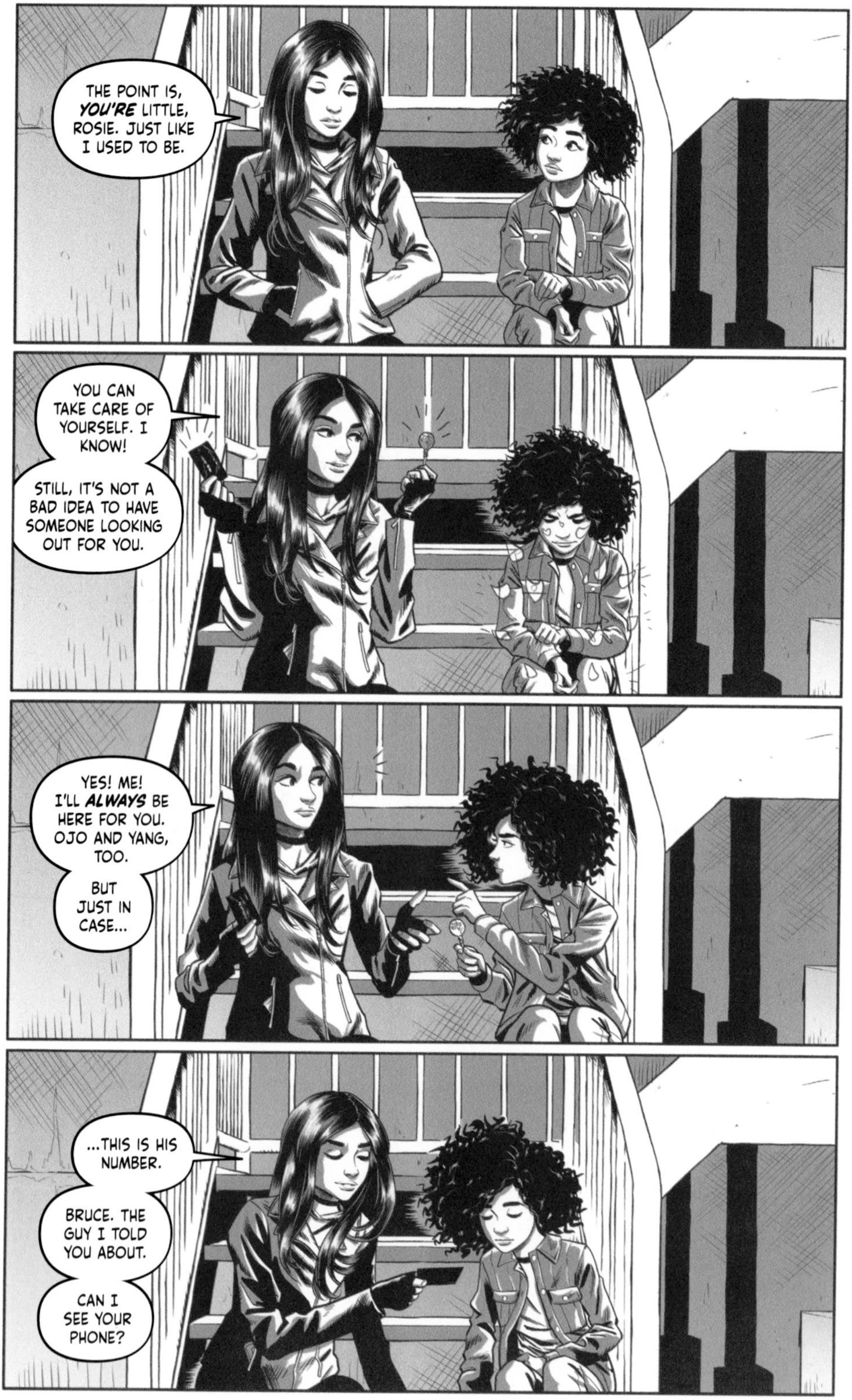
THE POINT IS, ***YOU'RE*** LITTLE, ROSIE. JUST LIKE I USED TO BE.
YOU CAN TAKE CARE OF YOURSELF. I KNOW!
STILL, IT'S NOT A BAD IDEA TO HAVE SOMEONE LOOKING OUT FOR YOU.
YES! ME! I'LL ***ALWAYS*** BE HERE FOR YOU. OJO AND YANG, TOO.
BUT JUST IN CASE...
...THIS IS HIS NUMBER.
BRUCE. THE GUY I TOLD YOU ABOUT.
CAN I SEE YOUR PHONE?

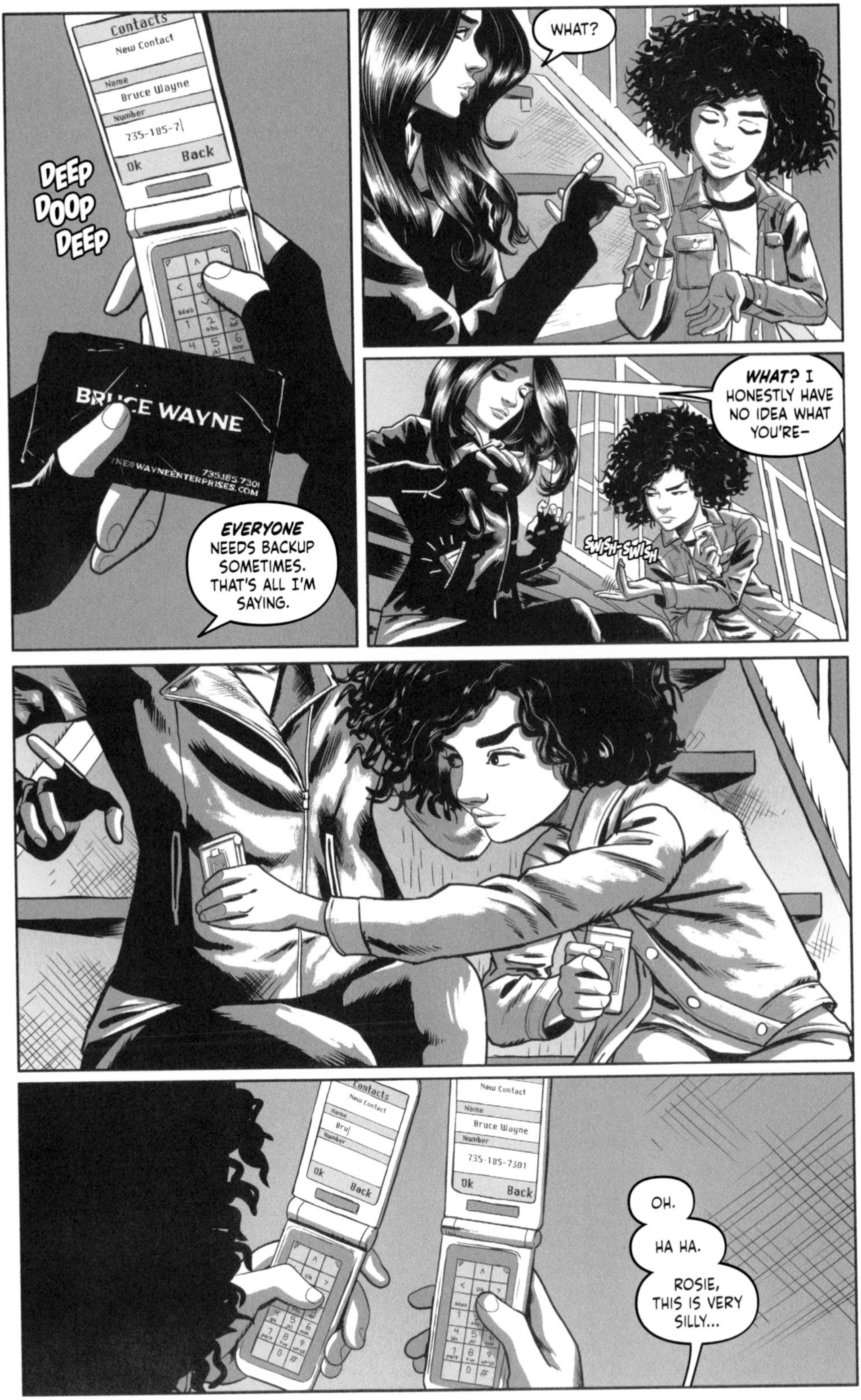
Contacts
New Contact
Name
Bruce Wayne
Number
735-185-7
Ok
Back
DEEP
DOOP
DEEP
BRUCE WAYNE
735.185.7301
WAYNEENTERPRISES.COM
EVERYONE NEEDS BACKUP SOMETIMES. THAT'S ALL I'M SAYING.
WHAT?
WHAT? I HONESTLY HAVE NO IDEA WHAT YOU'RE–
SWISH-SWISH
Contacts
New Contact
Name
Bru
Number
Ok
Back
New Contact
Name
Bruce Wayne
Number
735-185-7301
Ok
Back
OH.
HA HA.
ROSIE, THIS IS VERY SILLY...

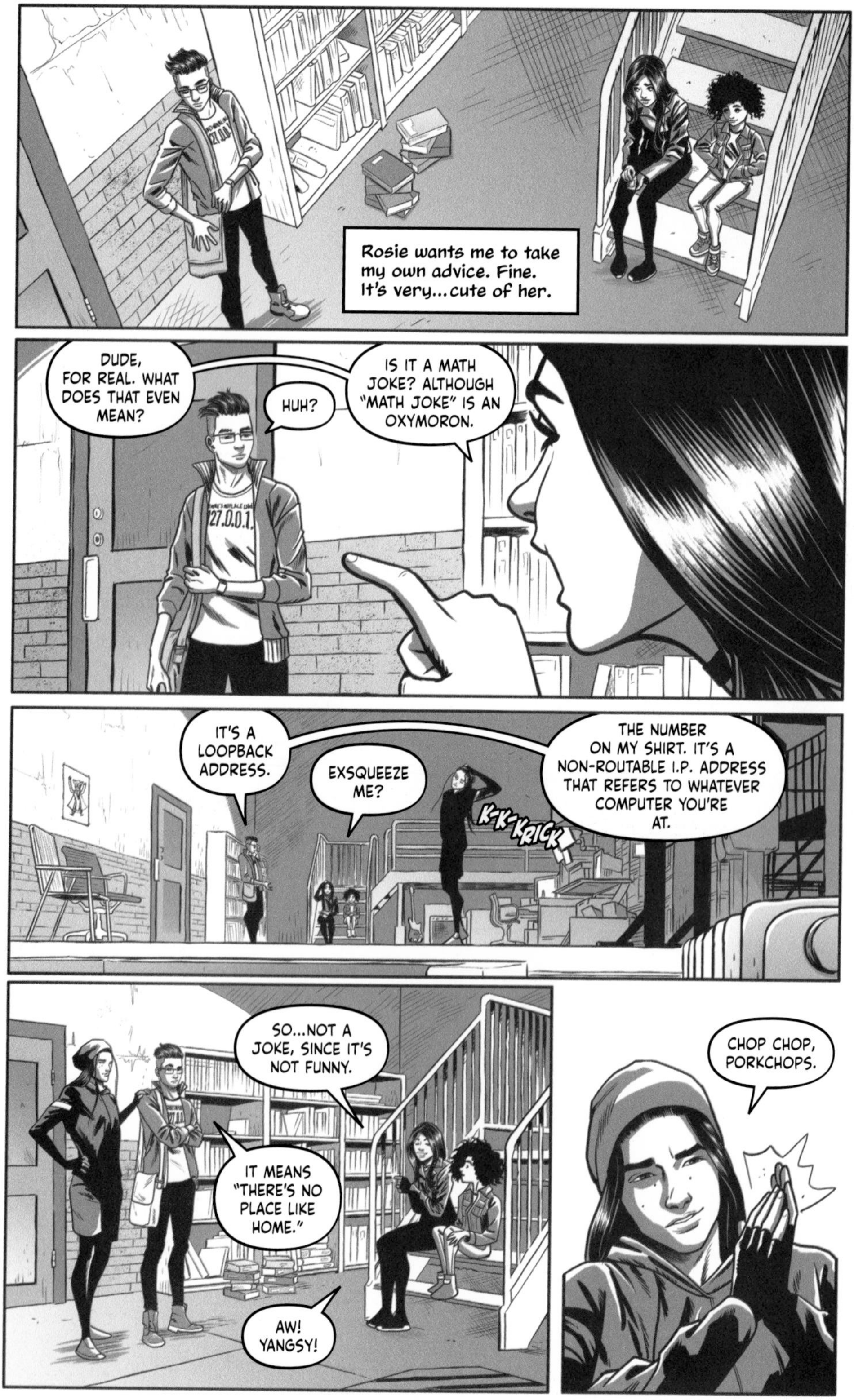
Rosie wants me to take my own advice. Fine. It's very...cute of her.
DUDE, FOR REAL. WHAT DOES THAT EVEN MEAN?
HUH?
IS IT A MATH JOKE? ALTHOUGH "MATH JOKE" IS AN OXYMORON.
127.0.0.1
IT'S A LOOPBACK ADDRESS.
EXSQUEEZE ME?
THE NUMBER ON MY SHIRT. IT'S A NON-ROUTABLE I.P. ADDRESS THAT REFERS TO WHATEVER COMPUTER YOU'RE AT.
K-K-KRICK
SO...NOT A JOKE, SINCE IT'S NOT FUNNY.
IT MEANS "THERE'S NO PLACE LIKE HOME."
AW! YANGSY!
CHOP CHOP, PORKCHOPS.

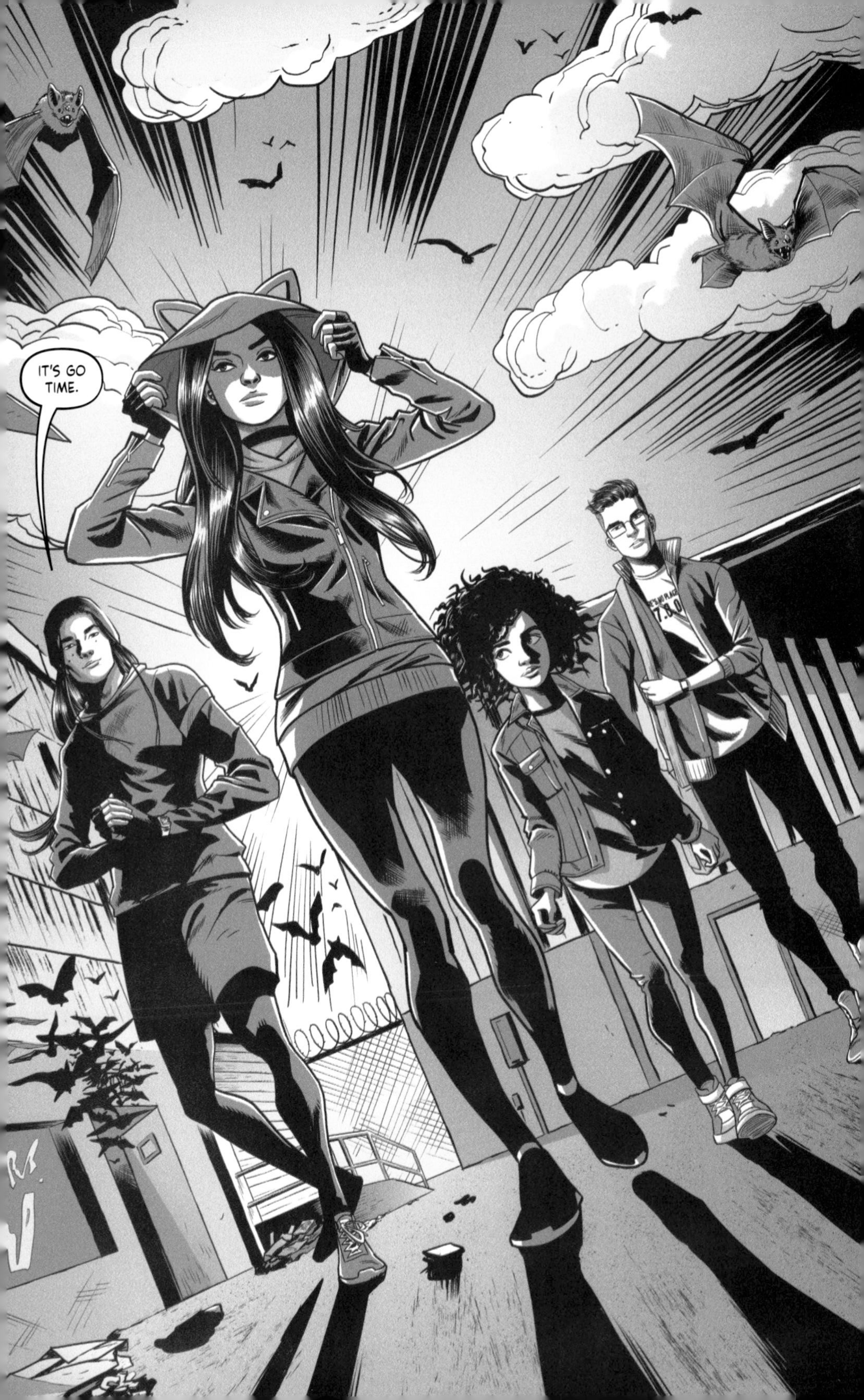
IT'S GO TIME.

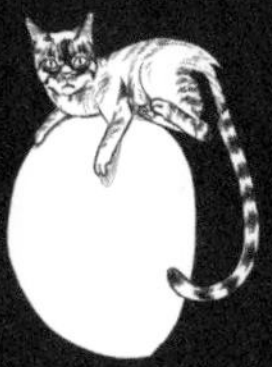

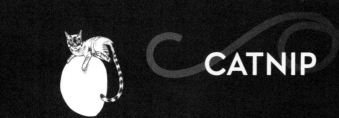

CATNIP

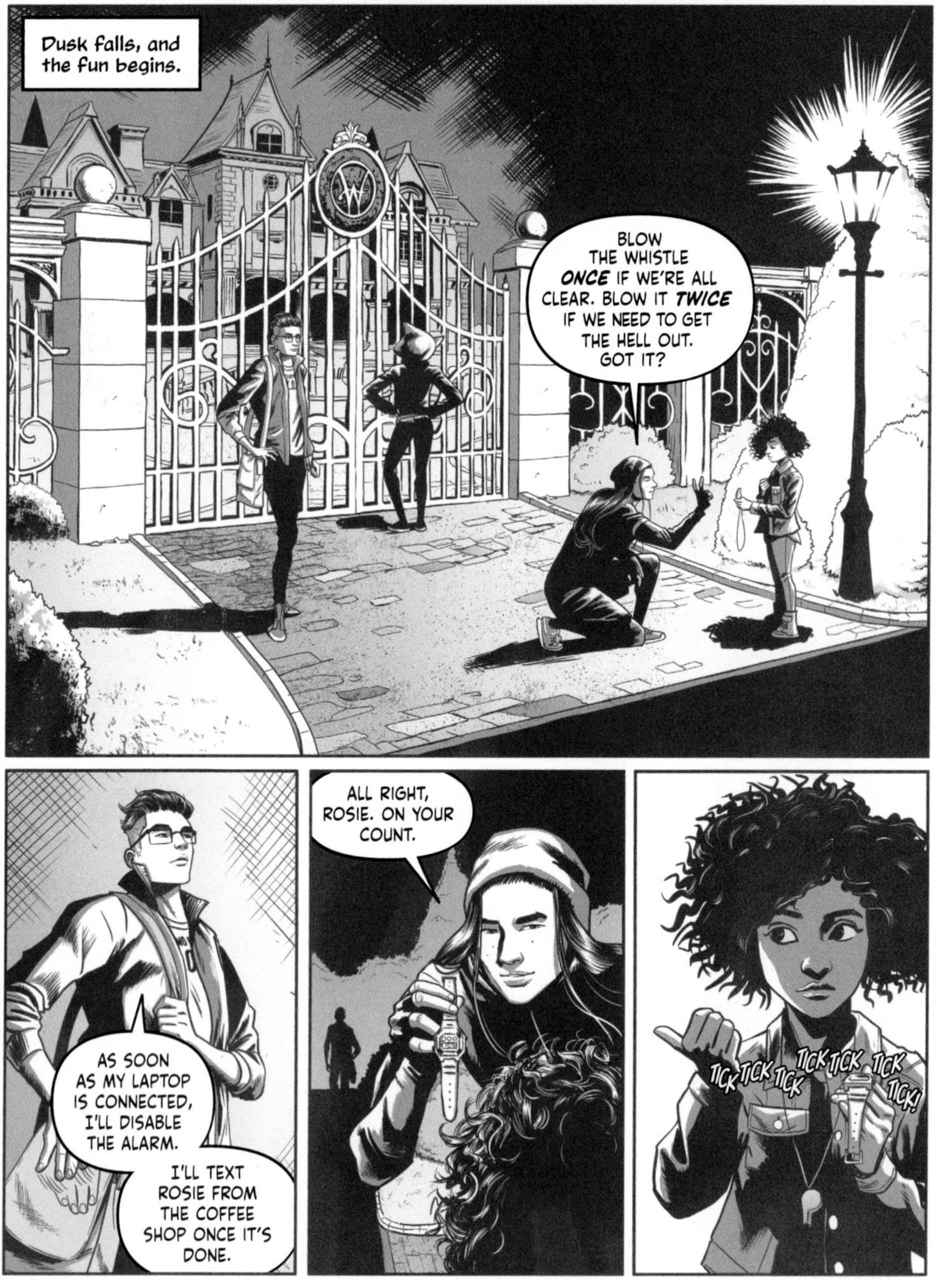
Dusk falls, and the fun begins.
BLOW THE WHISTLE ONCE IF WE'RE ALL CLEAR. BLOW IT TWICE IF WE NEED TO GET THE HELL OUT. GOT IT?
AS SOON AS MY LAPTOP IS CONNECTED, I'LL DISABLE THE ALARM.
I'LL TEXT ROSIE FROM THE COFFEE SHOP ONCE IT'S DONE.
ALL RIGHT, ROSIE. ON YOUR COUNT.
TICK TICK TICK TICK TICK TICK TICK!

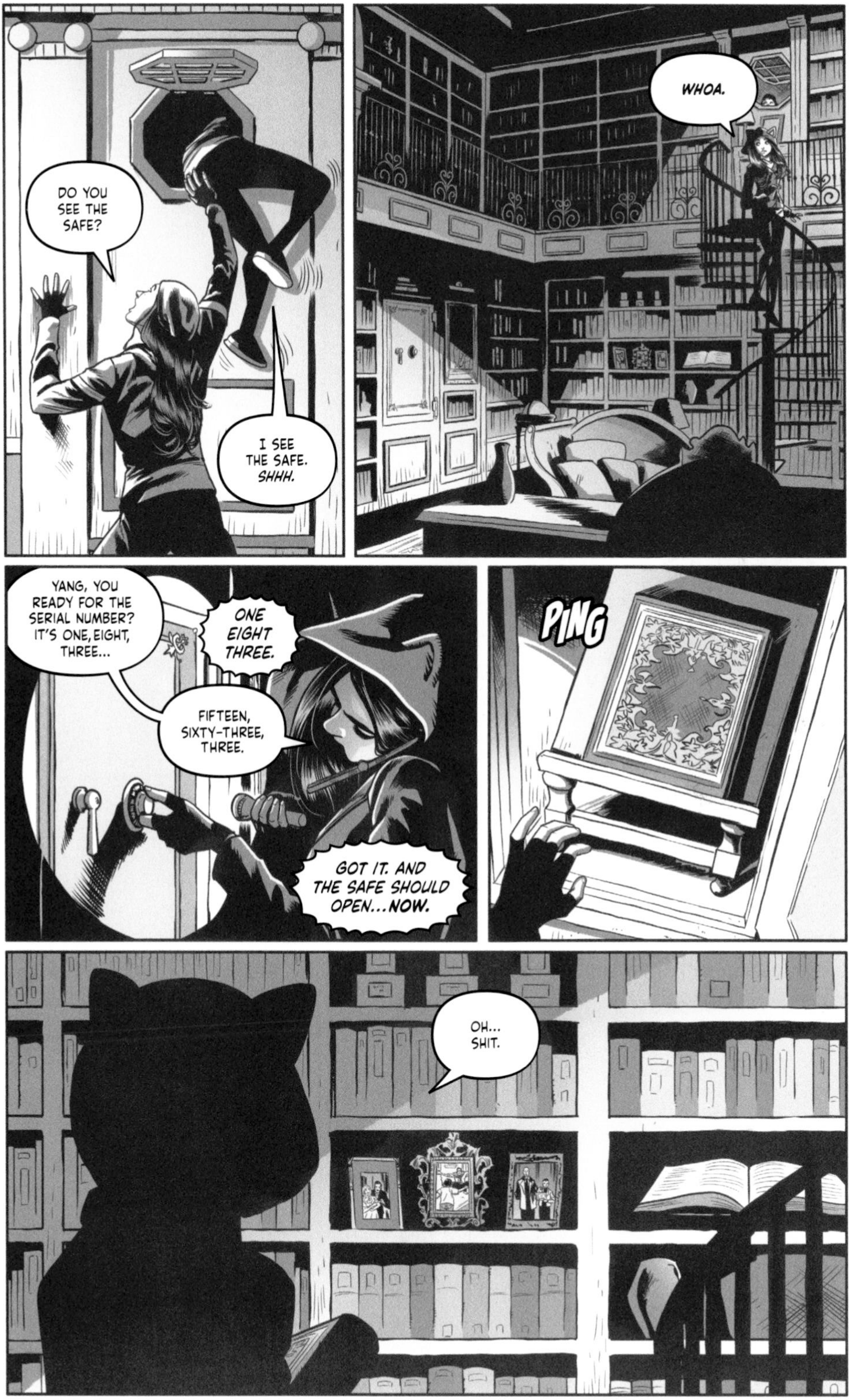
DO YOU SEE THE SAFE?
I SEE THE SAFE. SHHH.
WHOA.
YANG, YOU READY FOR THE SERIAL NUMBER? IT'S ONE, EIGHT, THREE...
ONE EIGHT THREE.
FIFTEEN, SIXTY-THREE, THREE.
GOT IT. AND THE SAFE SHOULD OPEN...NOW.
PING
OH... SHIT.

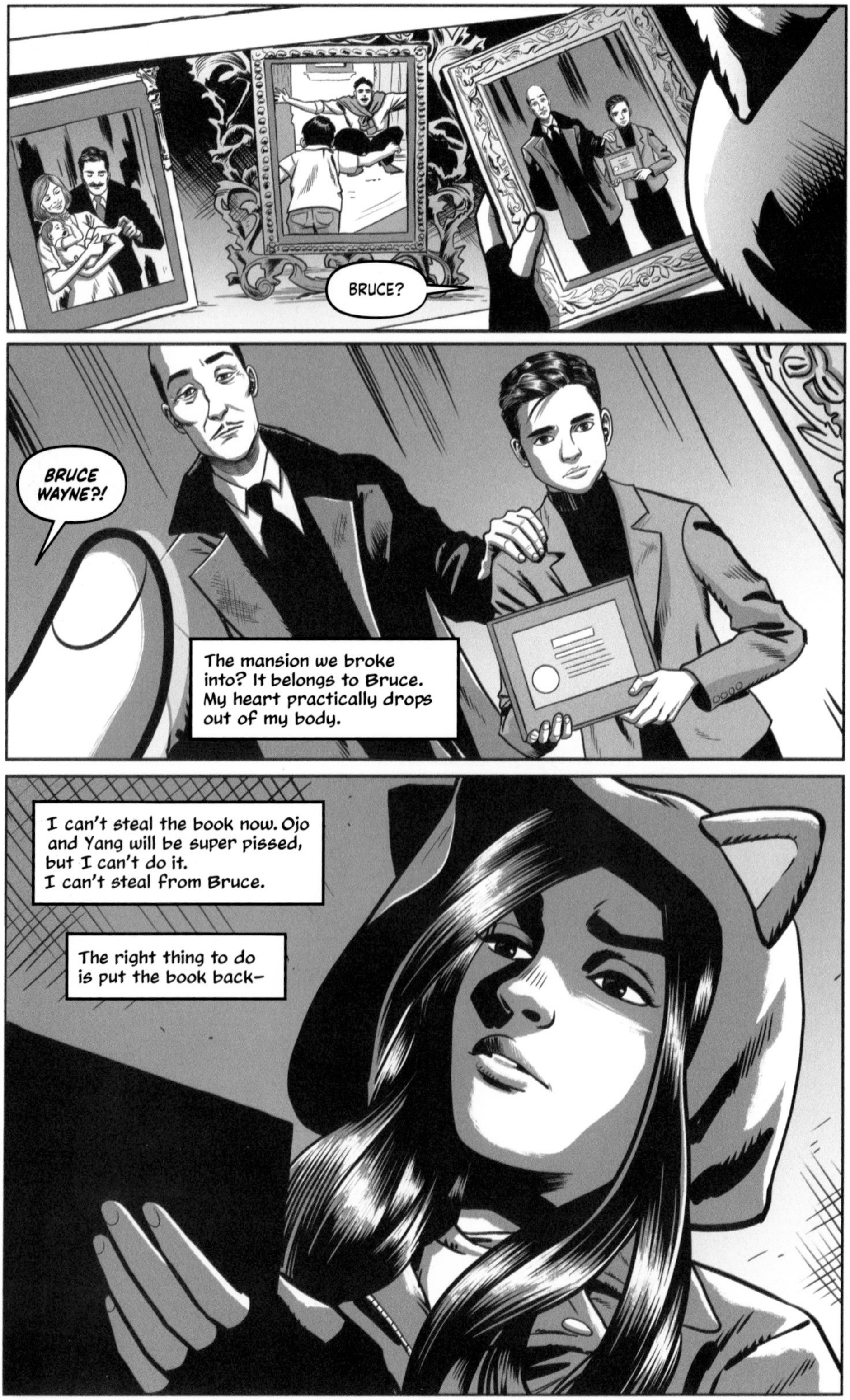
BRUCE?
BRUCE WAYNE?!
The mansion we broke into? It belongs to Bruce. My heart practically drops out of my body.
I can't steal the book now. Ojo and Yang will be super pissed, but I can't do it. I can't steal from Bruce.
The right thing to do is put the book back-

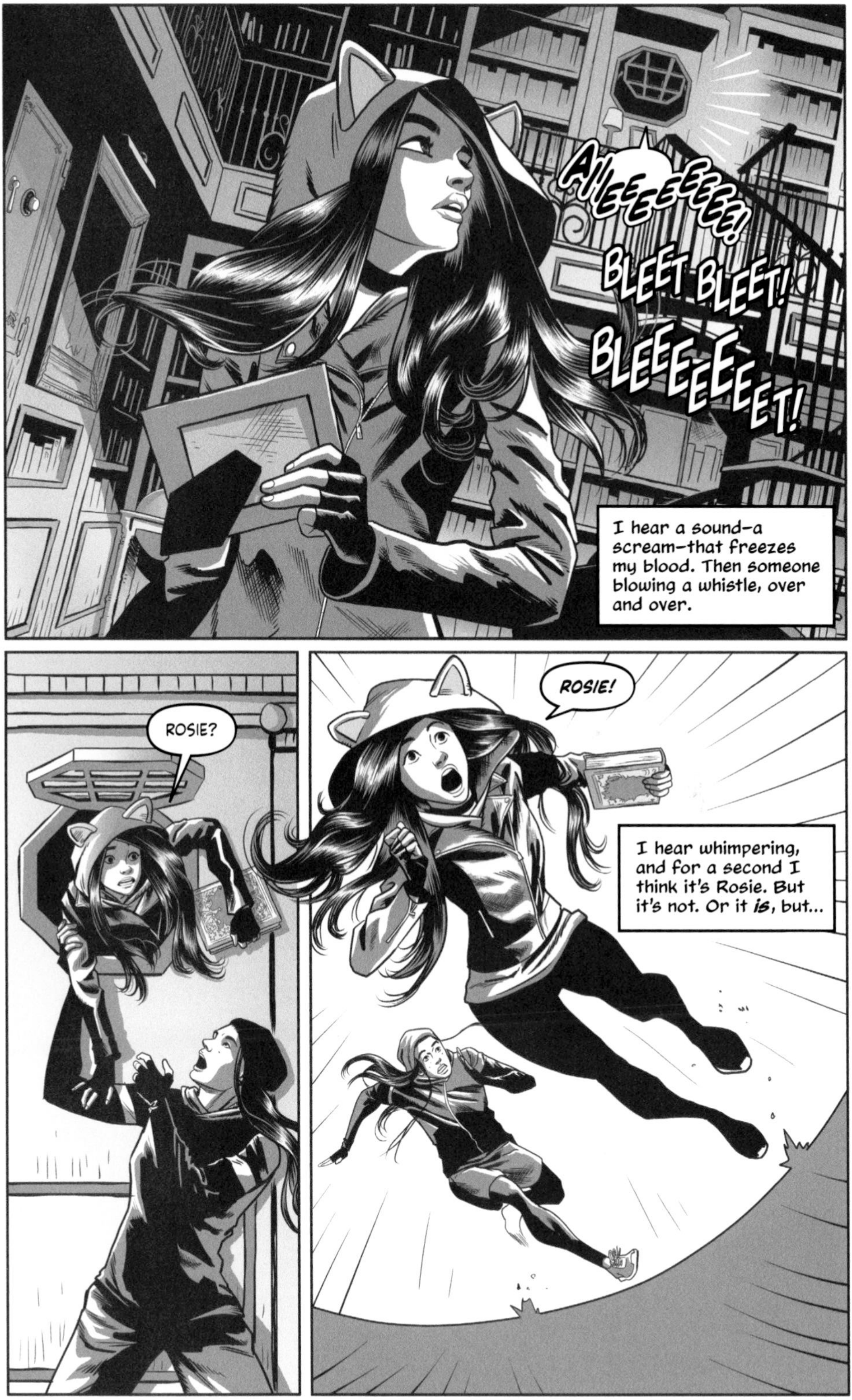
AIIEEEEEEEE!
BLEET BLEET!
BLEEEEEEET!
I hear a sound—a scream—that freezes my blood. Then someone blowing a whistle, over and over.
ROSIE?
ROSIE!
I hear whimpering, and for a second I think it's Rosie. But it's not. Or it *is*, but...

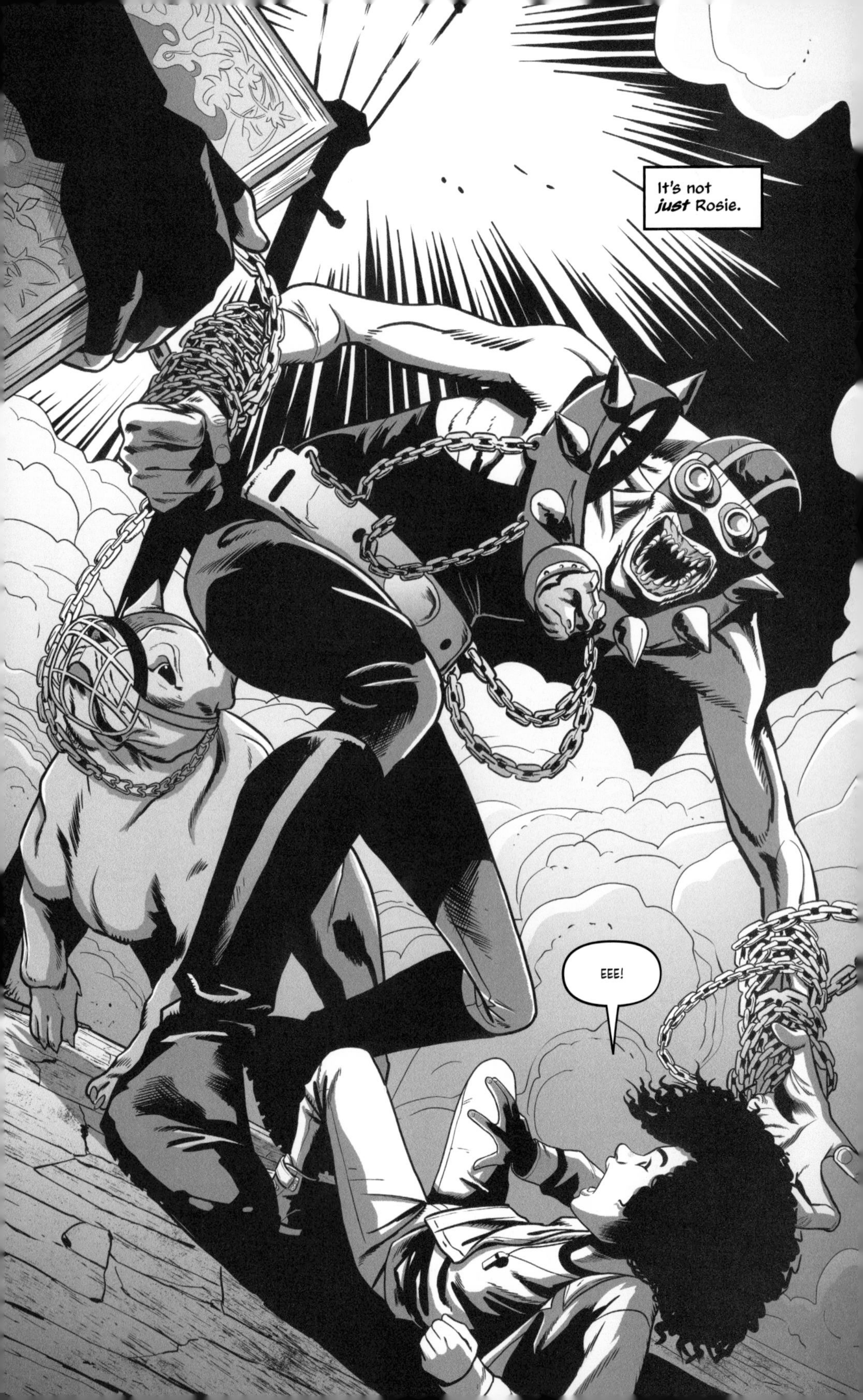
It's not *just* Rosie.
EEE!

CHISSY FIT

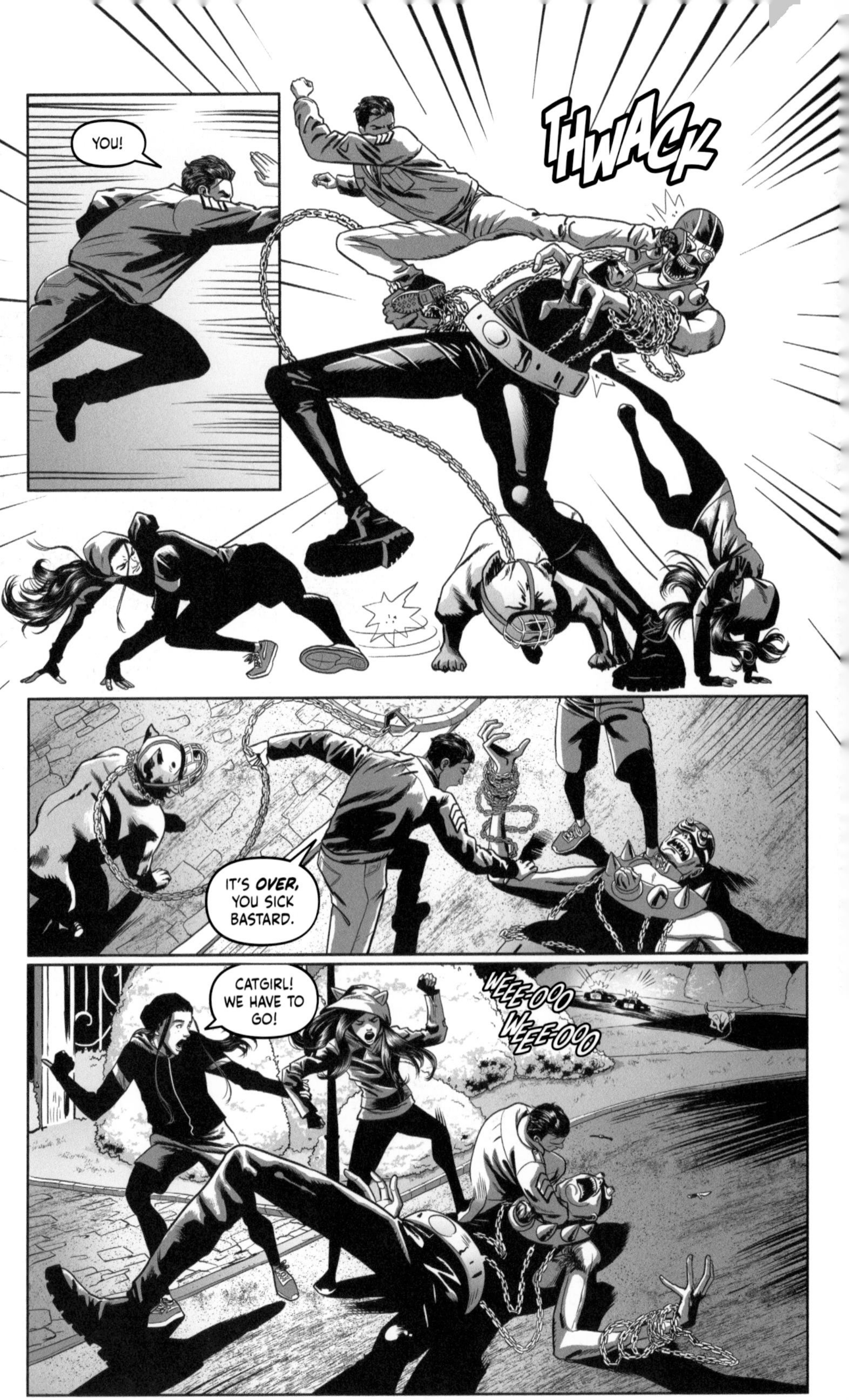
YOU!
THWACK
IT'S OVER, YOU SICK BASTARD.
CATGIRL! WE HAVE TO GO!
WEEE-OOO
WEEE-OOO

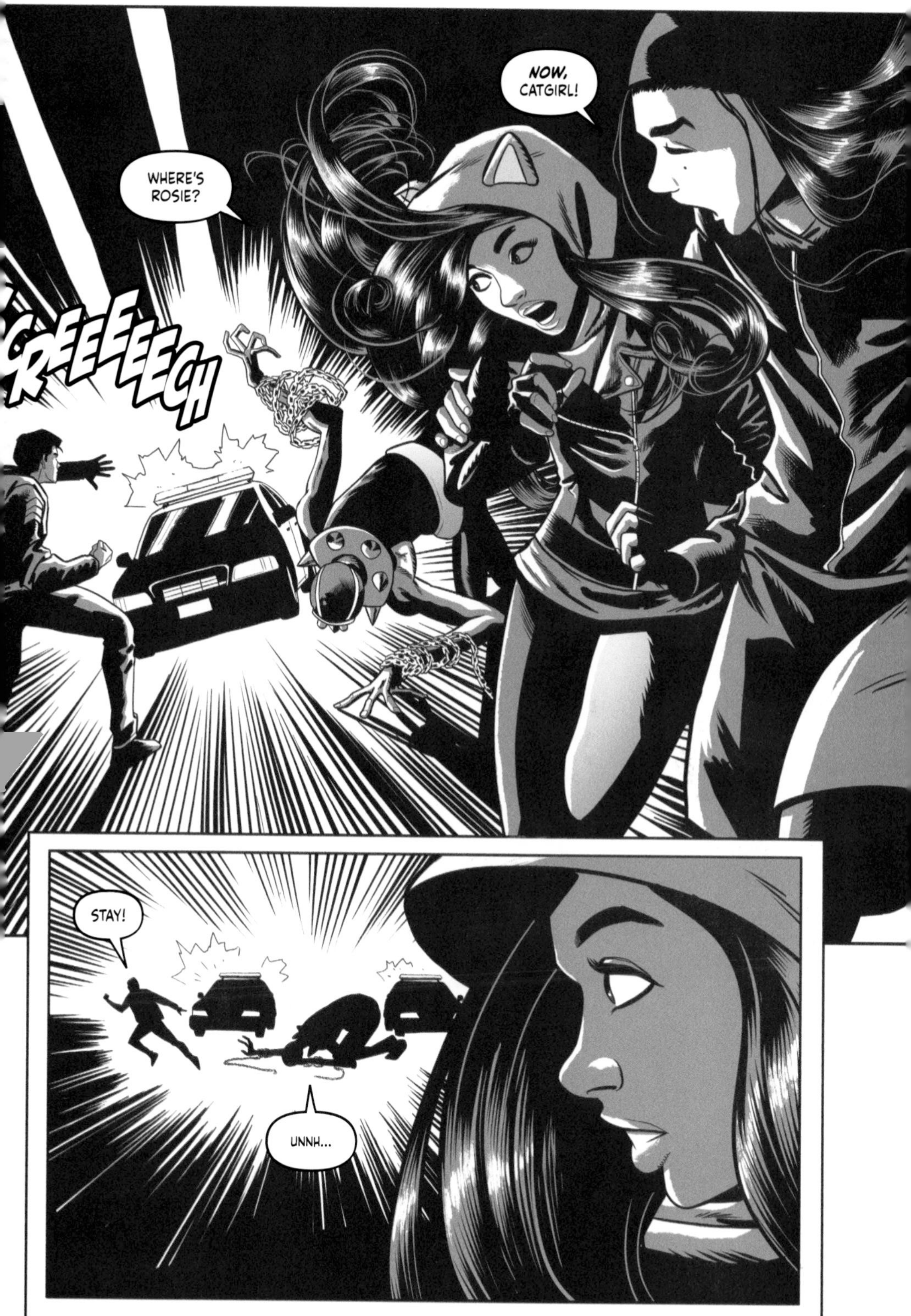
WHERE'S ROSIE?
NOW, CATGIRL!
SCREEEEECH
STAY!
UNNH...

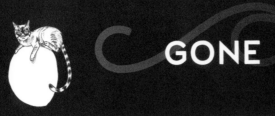

GONE

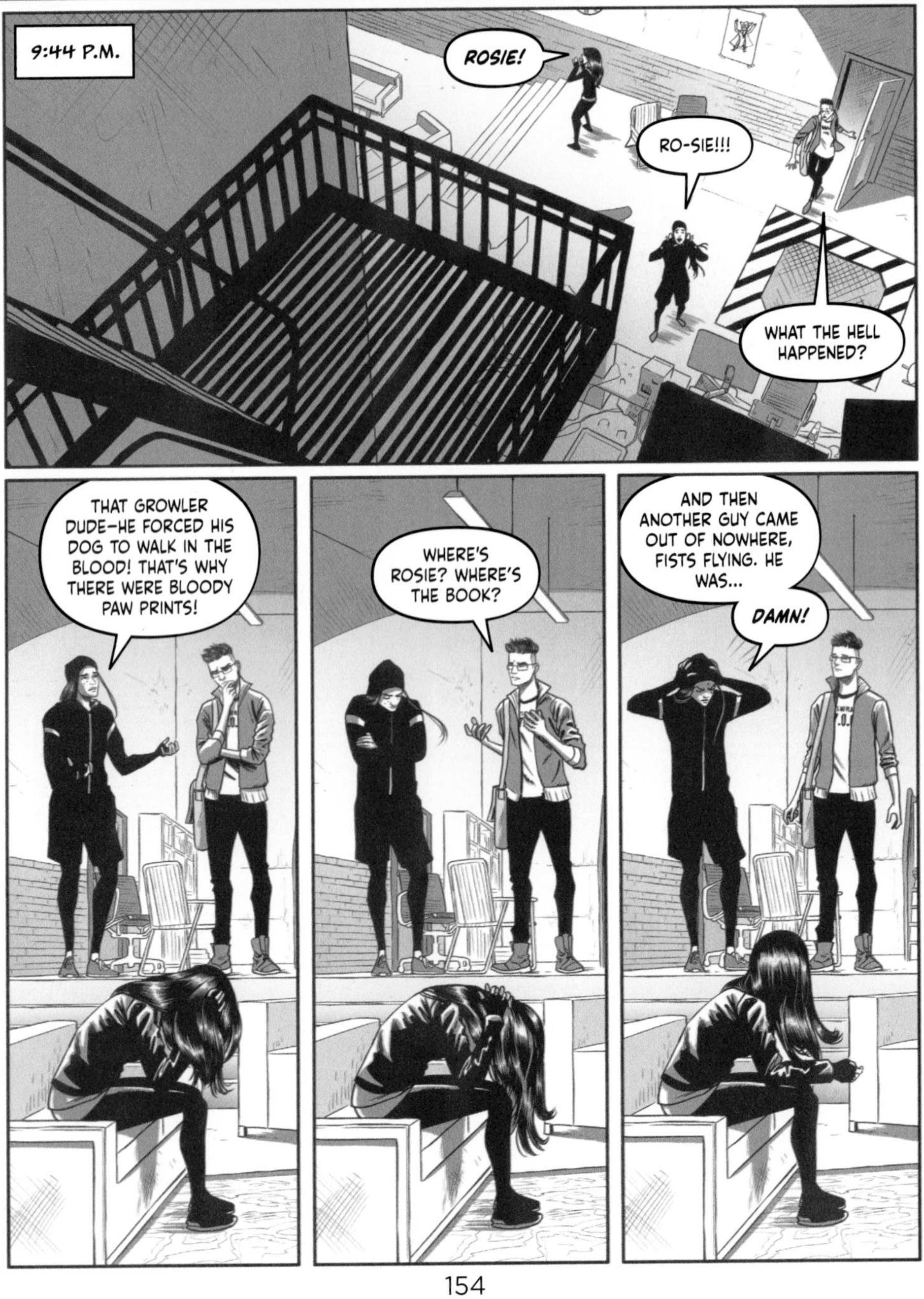

9:44 P.M.
ROSIE!
RO-SIE!!!
WHAT THE HELL HAPPENED?
THAT GROWLER DUDE—HE FORCED HIS DOG TO WALK IN THE BLOOD! THAT'S WHY THERE WERE BLOODY PAW PRINTS!
WHERE'S ROSIE? WHERE'S THE BOOK?
AND THEN ANOTHER GUY CAME OUT OF NOWHERE, FISTS FLYING. HE WAS...
DAMN!

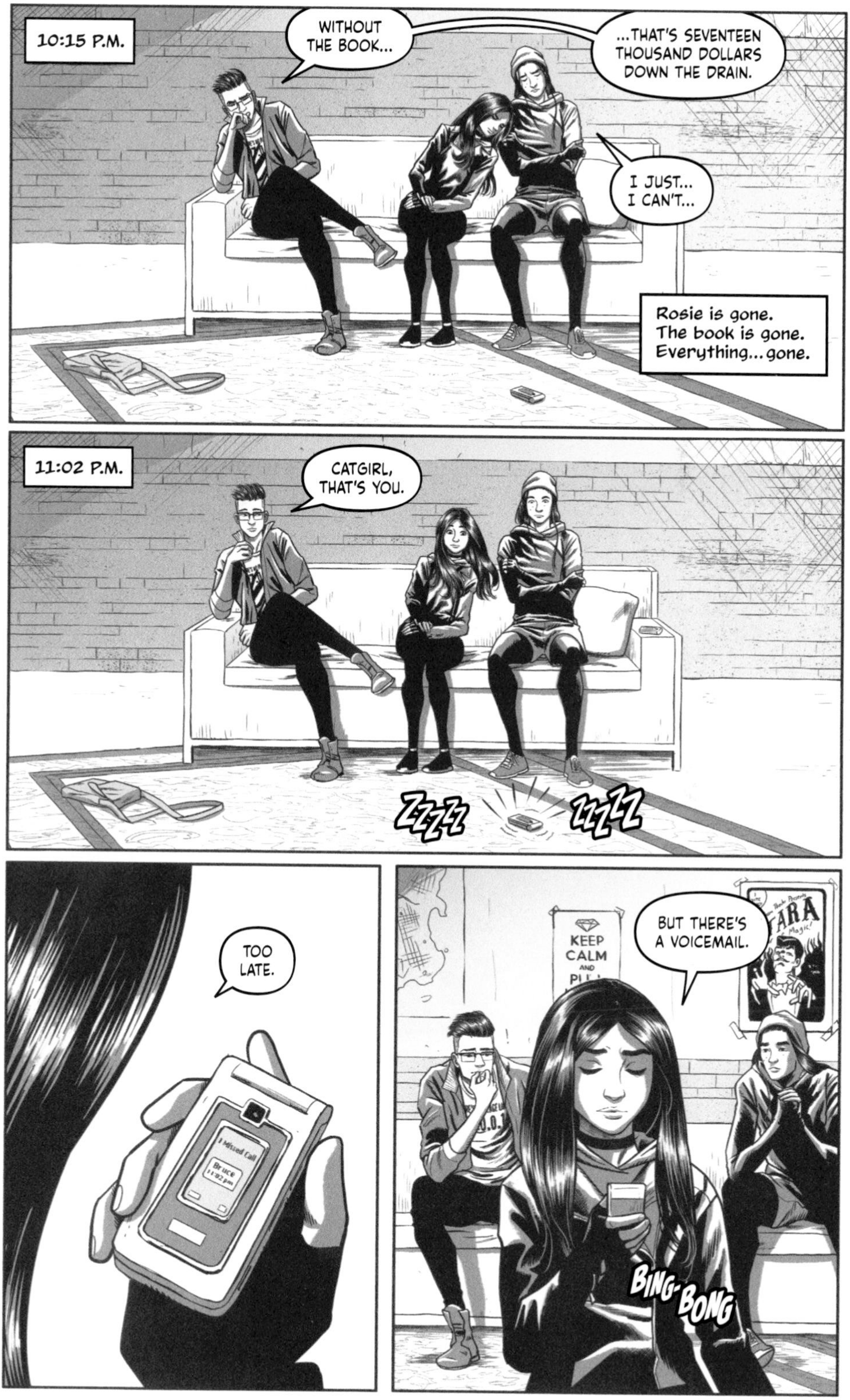
10:15 P.M.
WITHOUT THE BOOK...
...THAT'S SEVENTEEN THOUSAND DOLLARS DOWN THE DRAIN.
I JUST... I CAN'T...
Rosie is gone. The book is gone. Everything...gone.
11:02 P.M.
CATGIRL, THAT'S YOU.
ZZZZZ
ZZZZZ
TOO LATE.
KEEP CALM
BUT THERE'S A VOICEMAIL.
BING-BONG

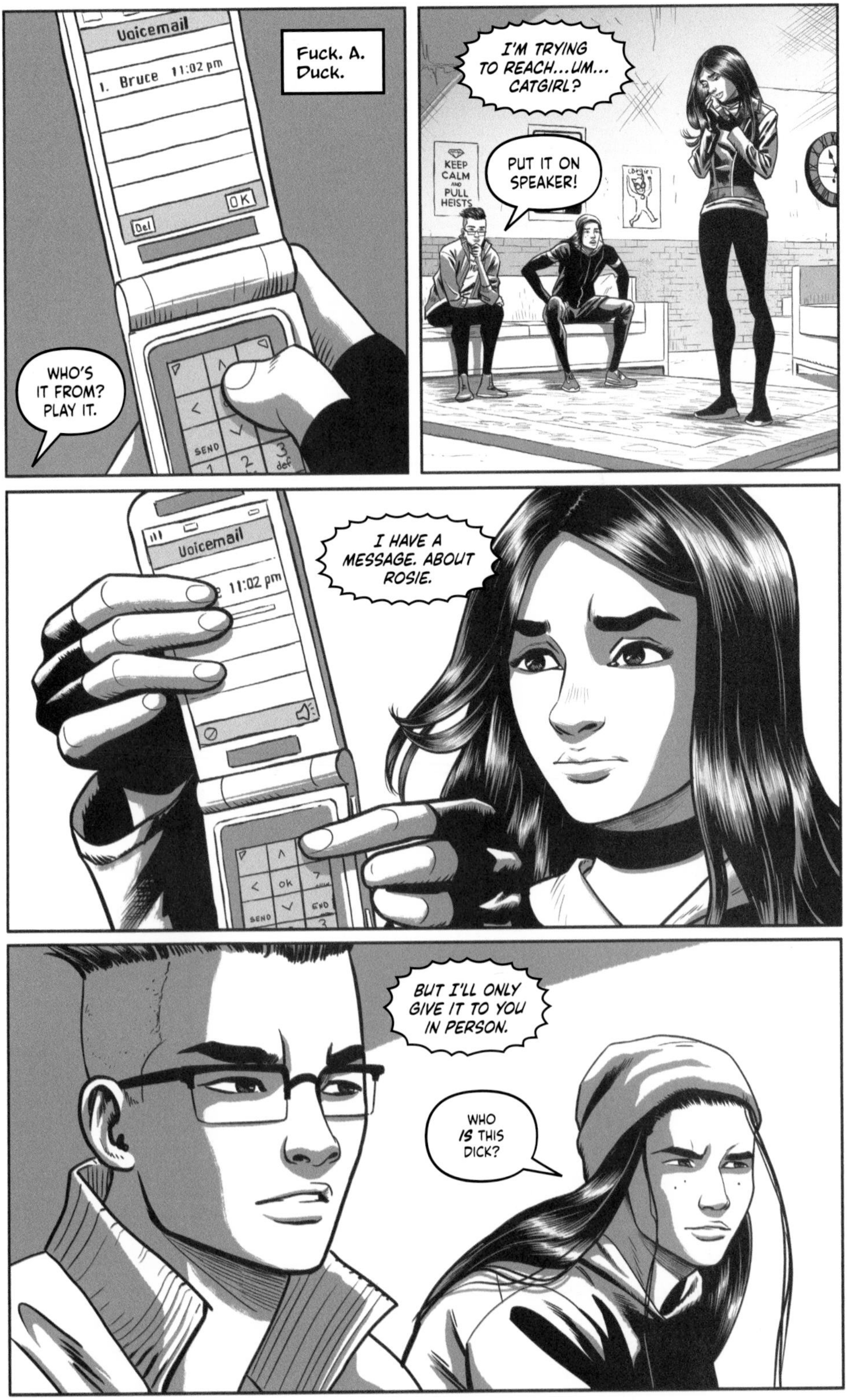
Voicemail
1. Bruce 11:02 pm
OK
Del
Fuck. A. Duck.
WHO'S IT FROM? PLAY IT.
I'M TRYING TO REACH...UM... CATGIRL?
KEEP CALM AND PULL HEISTS
PUT IT ON SPEAKER!
Voicemail
11:02 pm
I HAVE A MESSAGE. ABOUT ROSIE.
BUT I'LL ONLY GIVE IT TO YOU IN PERSON.
WHO *IS* THIS DICK?

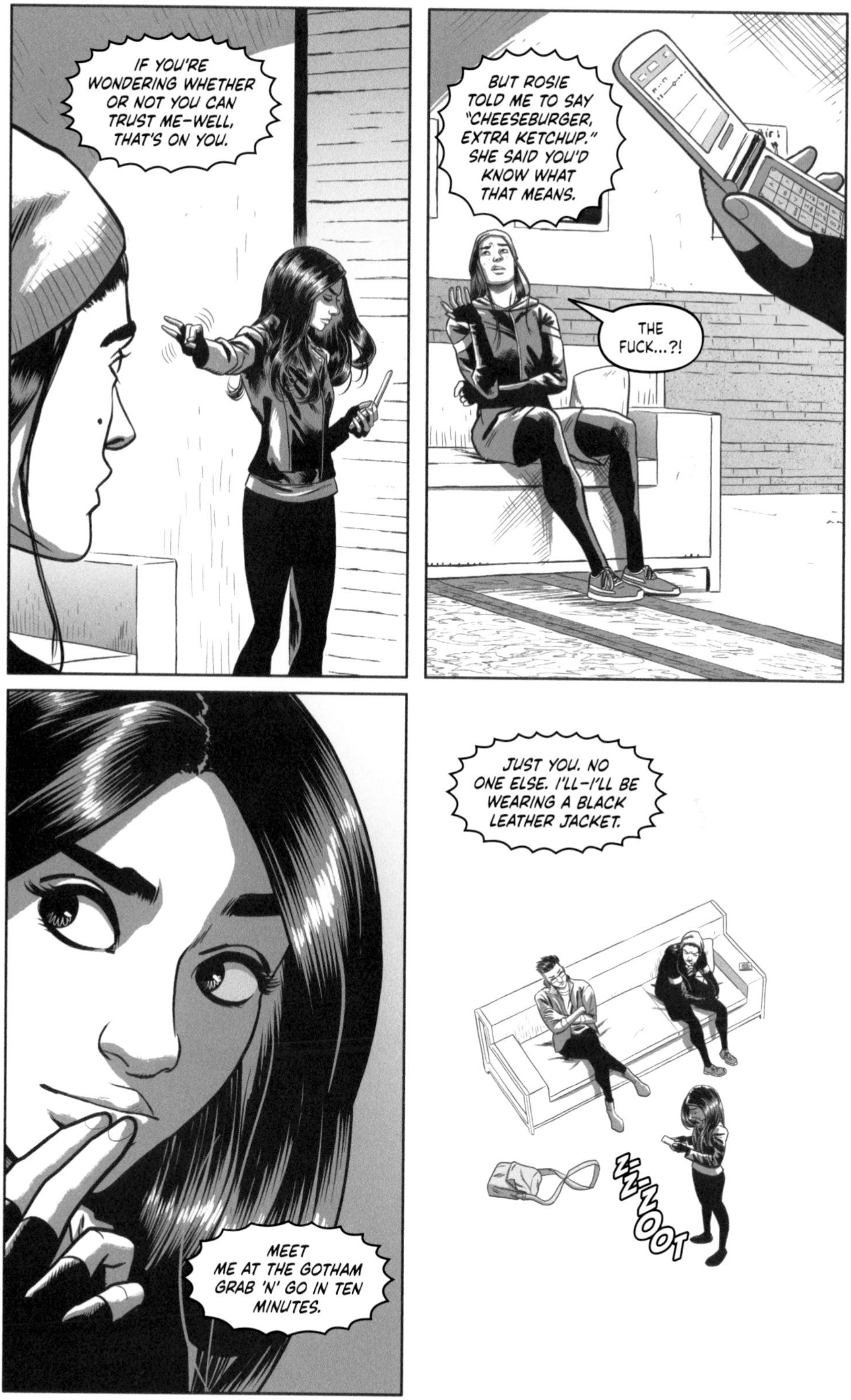
IF YOU'RE WONDERING WHETHER OR NOT YOU CAN TRUST ME—WELL, THAT'S ON YOU.
BUT ROSIE TOLD ME TO SAY "CHEESEBURGER, EXTRA KETCHUP." SHE SAID YOU'D KNOW WHAT THAT MEANS.
THE FUCK...?!
MEET ME AT THE GOTHAM GRAB 'N' GO IN TEN MINUTES.
JUST YOU. NO ONE ELSE. I'LL—I'LL BE WEARING A BLACK LEATHER JACKET.
Z-ZOOT

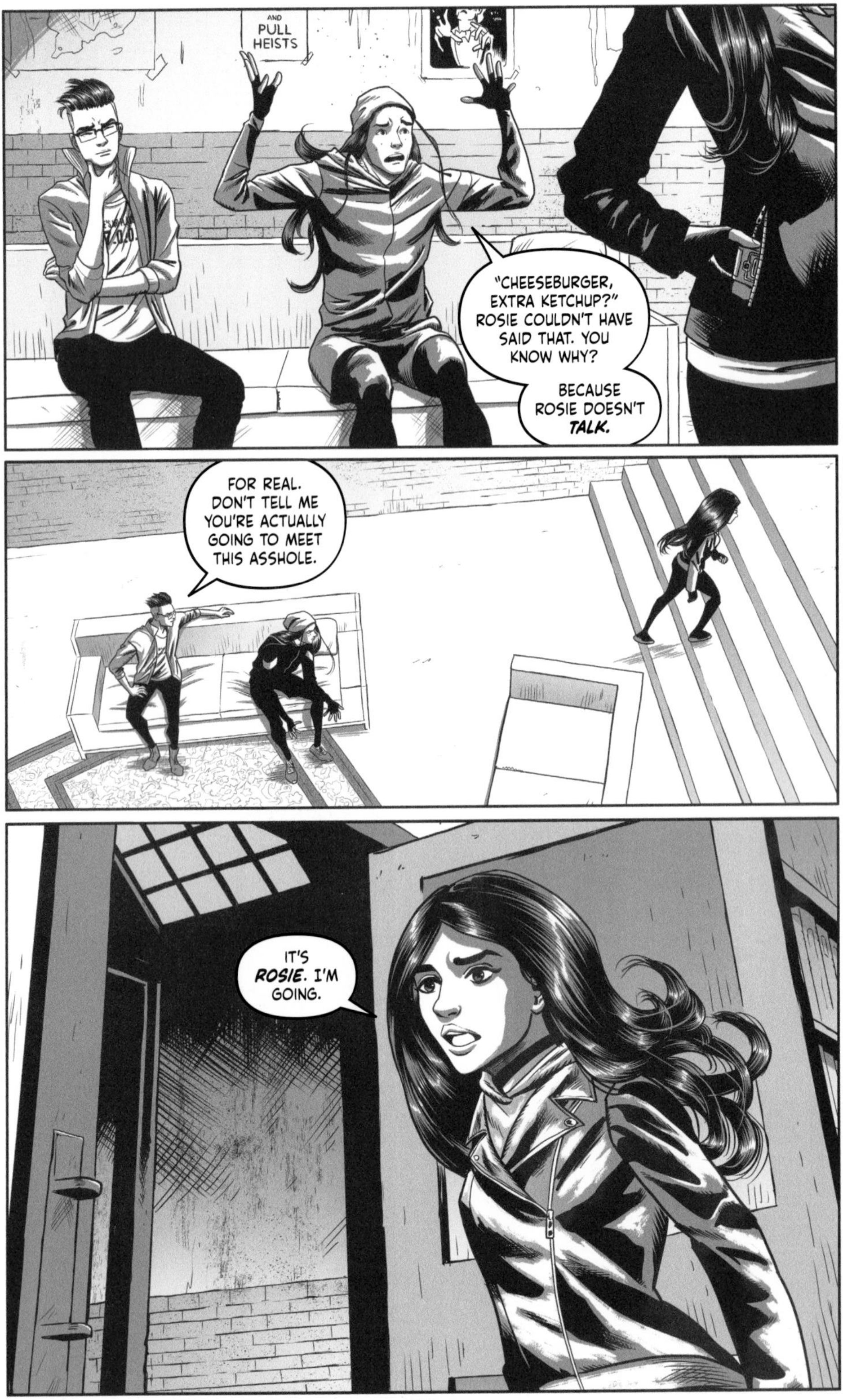
AND PULL HEISTS
"CHEESEBURGER, EXTRA KETCHUP?" ROSIE COULDN'T HAVE SAID THAT. YOU KNOW WHY?
BECAUSE ROSIE DOESN'T ***TALK.***
FOR REAL. DON'T TELL ME YOU'RE ACTUALLY GOING TO MEET THIS ASSHOLE.
IT'S ***ROSIE***. I'M GOING.

COLD NOSE, WARM HEART?

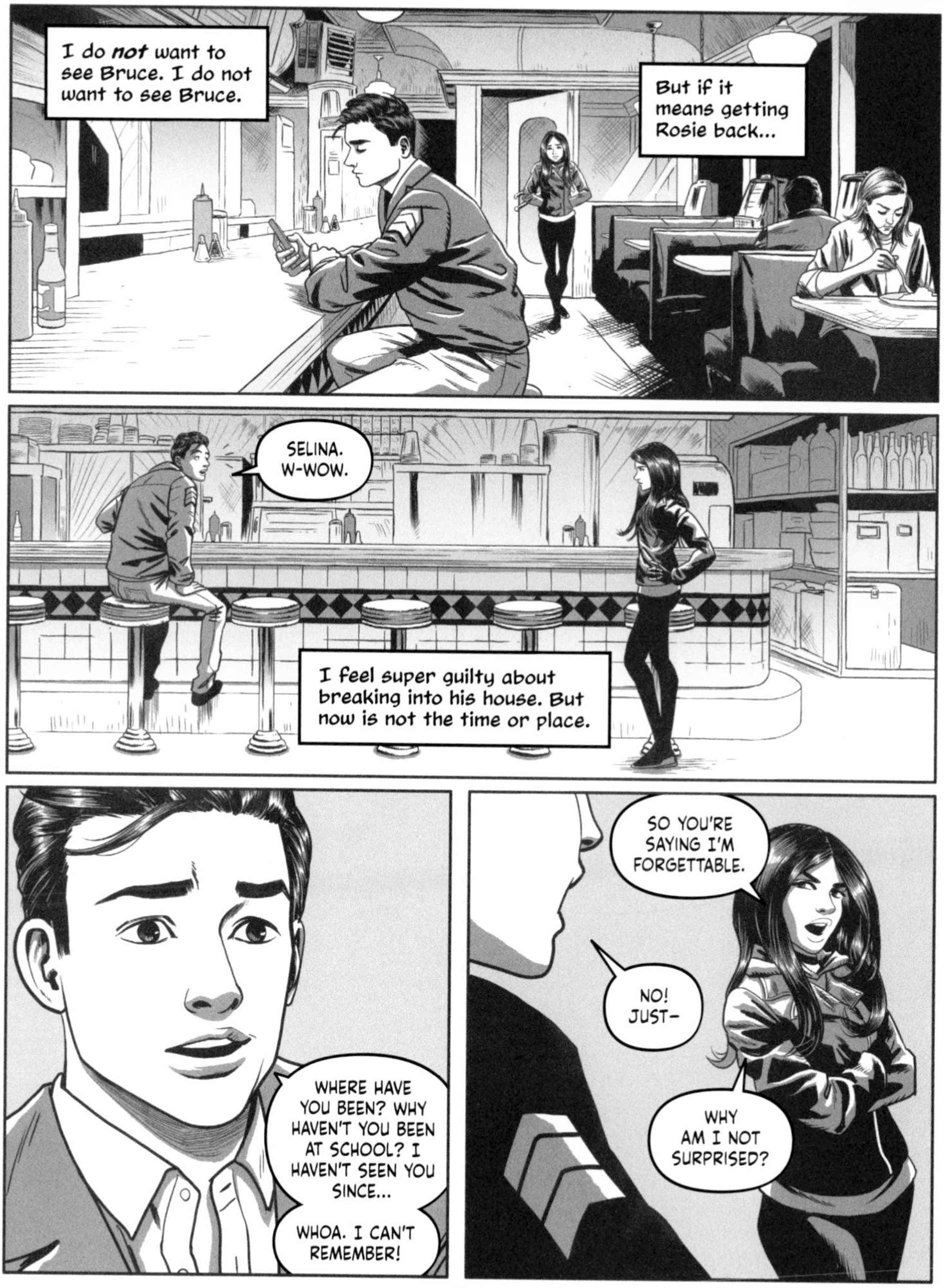

I do *not* want to see Bruce. I do not want to see Bruce.
But if it means getting Rosie back...
SELINA. W-WOW.
I feel super guilty about breaking into his house. But now is not the time or place.
WHERE HAVE YOU BEEN? WHY HAVEN'T YOU BEEN AT SCHOOL? I HAVEN'T SEEN YOU SINCE...
WHOA. I CAN'T REMEMBER!
SO YOU'RE SAYING I'M FORGETTABLE.
NO! JUST-
WHY AM I NOT SURPRISED?

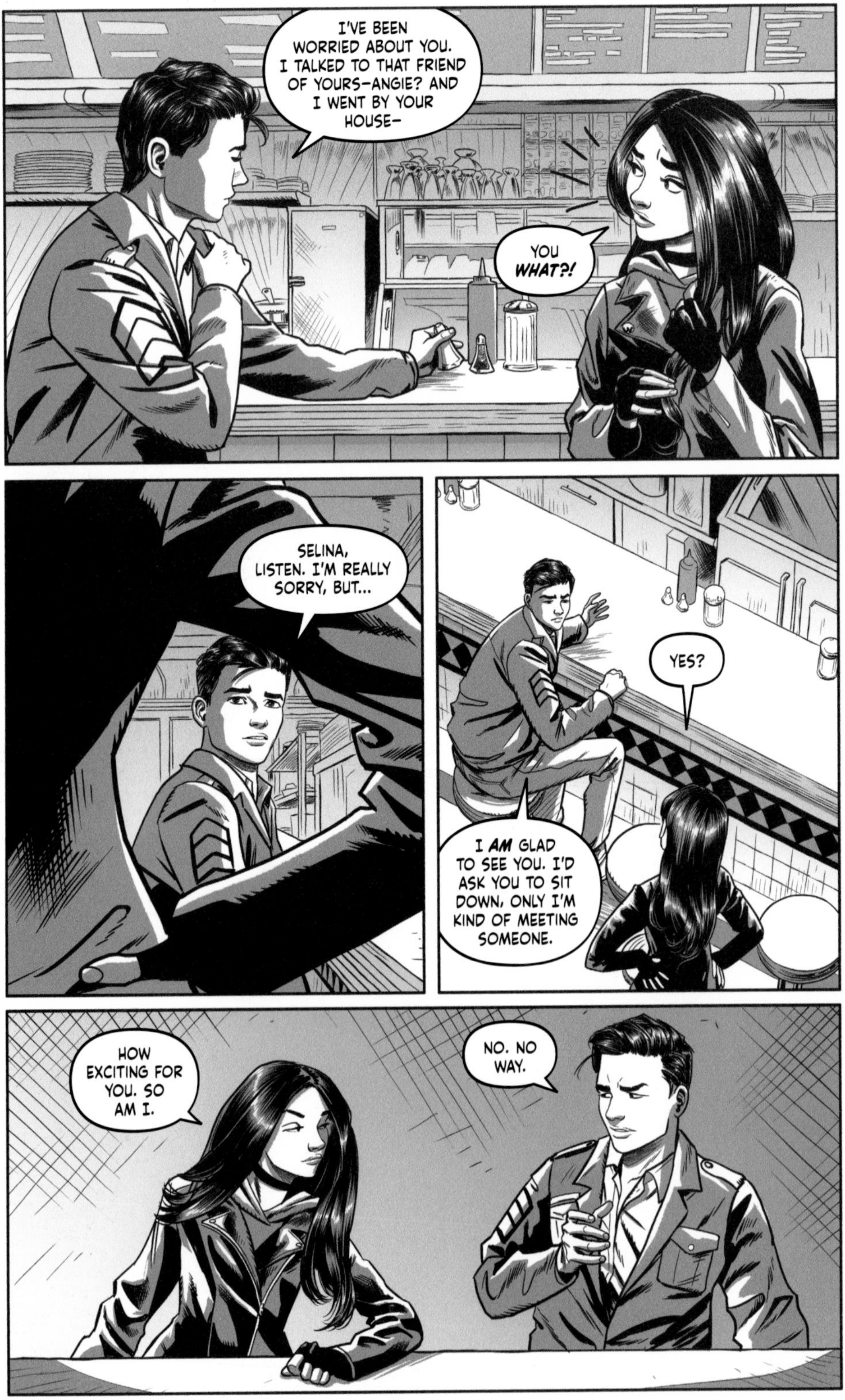
I'VE BEEN WORRIED ABOUT YOU. I TALKED TO THAT FRIEND OF YOURS—ANGIE? AND I WENT BY YOUR HOUSE—
YOU *WHAT?!*
SELINA, LISTEN. I'M REALLY SORRY, BUT...
YES?
I *AM* GLAD TO SEE YOU. I'D ASK YOU TO SIT DOWN, ONLY I'M KIND OF MEETING SOMEONE.
HOW EXCITING FOR YOU. SO AM I.
NO. NO WAY.

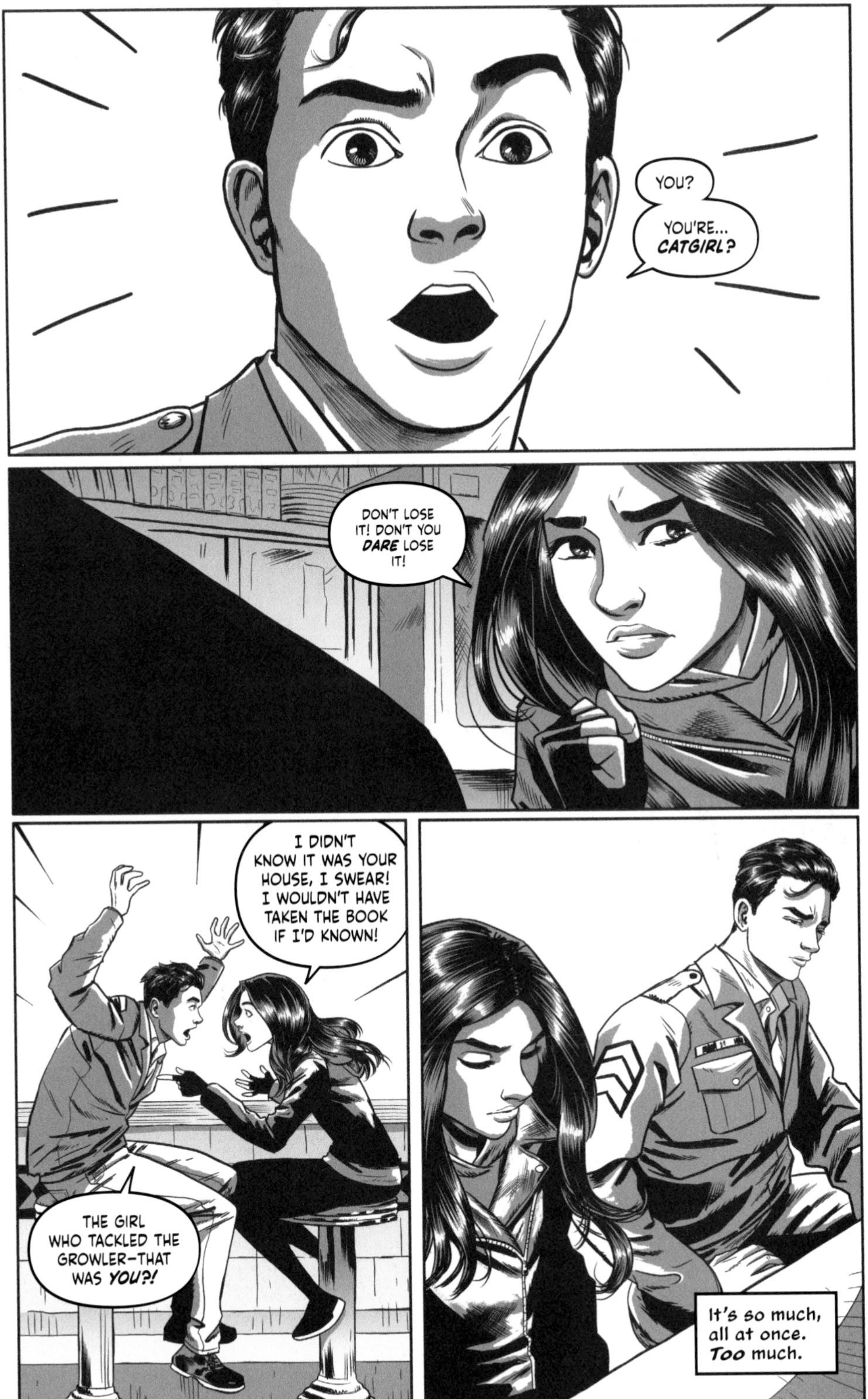
YOU?
YOU'RE... CATGIRL?
DON'T LOSE IT! DON'T YOU DARE LOSE IT!
I DIDN'T KNOW IT WAS YOUR HOUSE, I SWEAR! I WOULDN'T HAVE TAKEN THE BOOK IF I'D KNOWN!
THE GIRL WHO TACKLED THE GROWLER—THAT WAS YOU?!
It's so much, all at once. Too much.

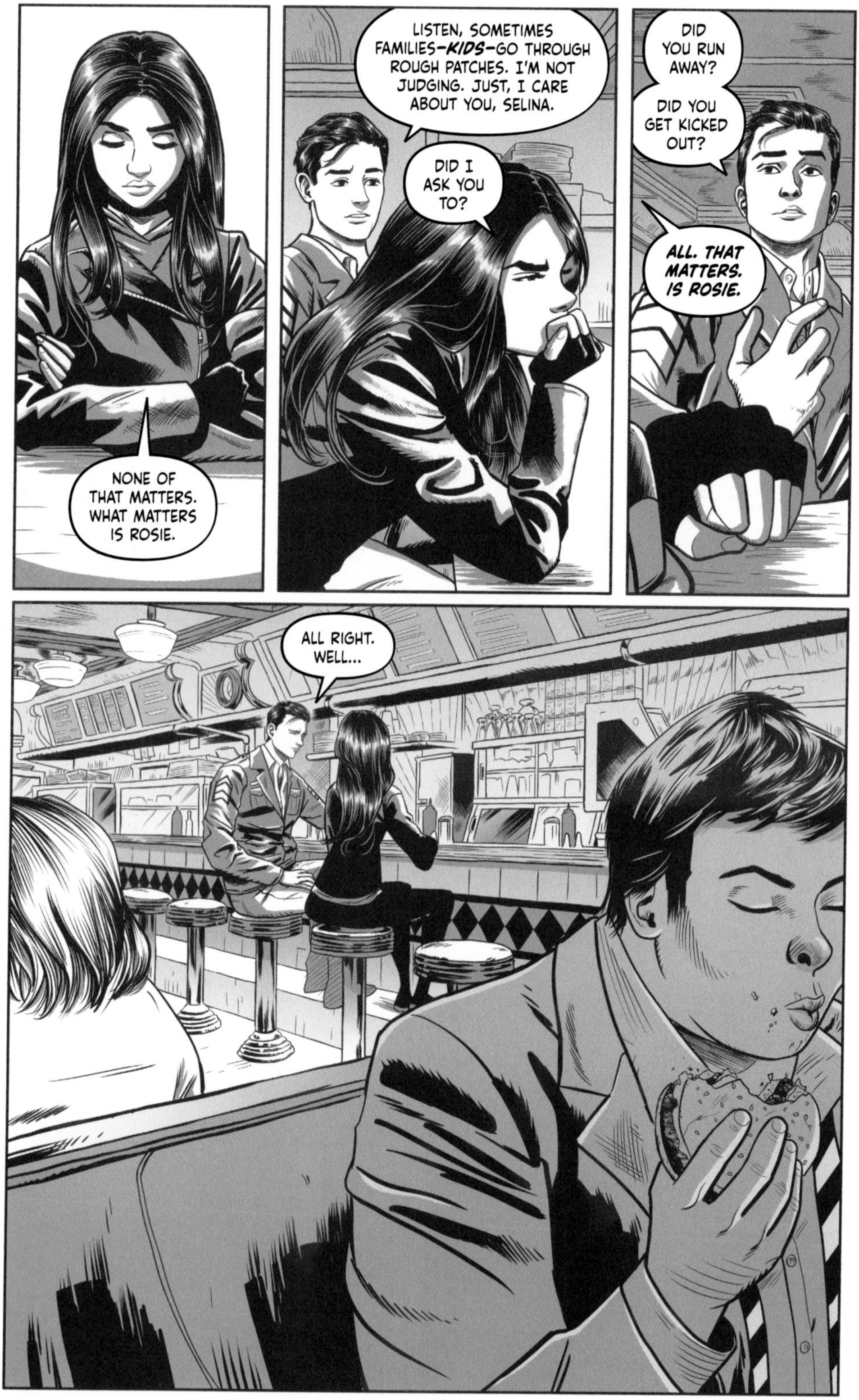
NONE OF THAT MATTERS. WHAT MATTERS IS ROSIE.
LISTEN, SOMETIMES FAMILIES--KIDS--GO THROUGH ROUGH PATCHES. I'M NOT JUDGING. JUST, I CARE ABOUT YOU, SELINA.
DID I ASK YOU TO?
DID YOU RUN AWAY?
DID YOU GET KICKED OUT?
ALL. THAT MATTERS. IS ROSIE.
ALL RIGHT. WELL...

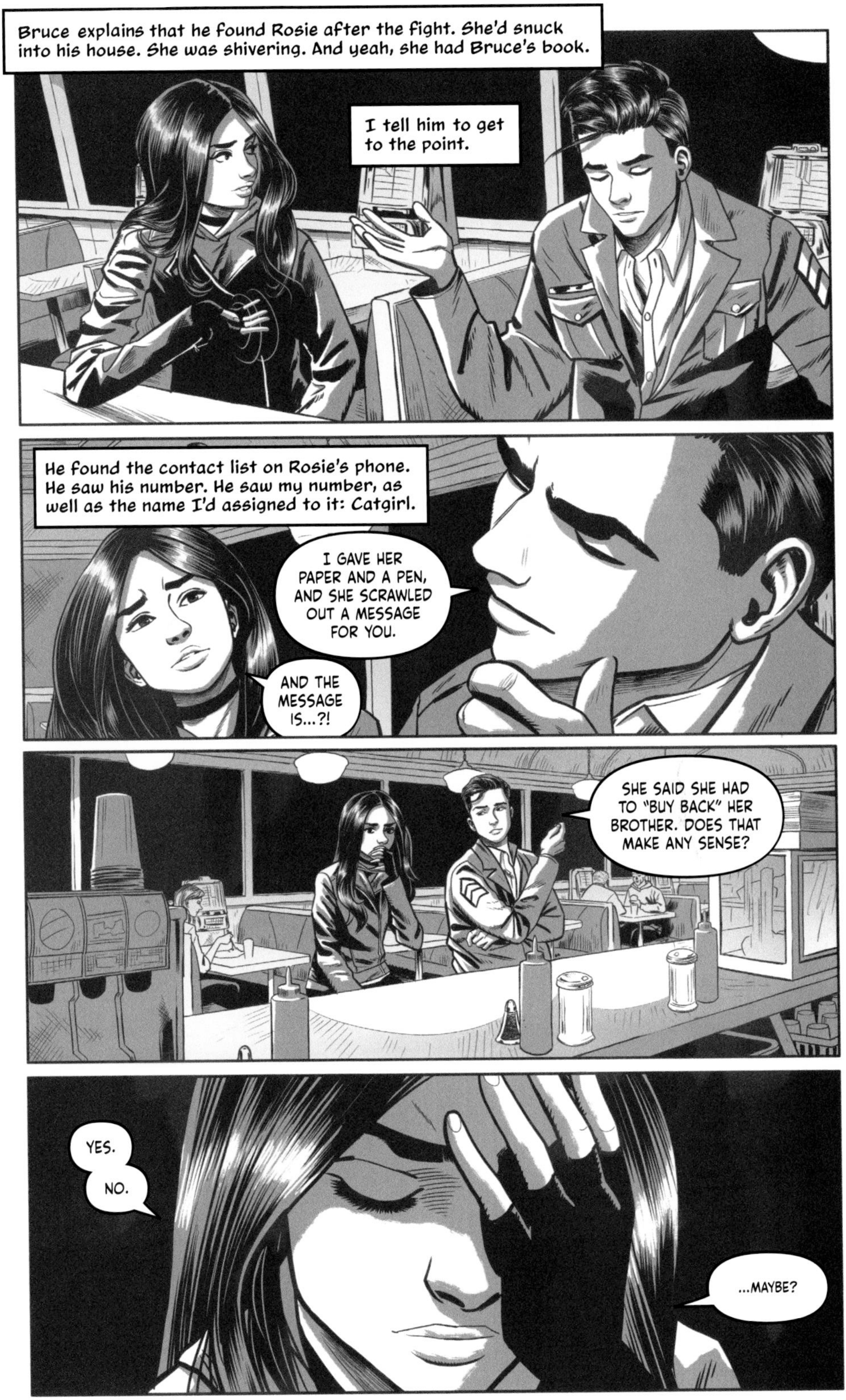
Bruce explains that he found Rosie after the fight. She'd snuck into his house. She was shivering. And yeah, she had Bruce's book.
I tell him to get to the point.
He found the contact list on Rosie's phone. He saw his number. He saw my number, as well as the name I'd assigned to it: Catgirl.
I GAVE HER PAPER AND A PEN, AND SHE SCRAWLED OUT A MESSAGE FOR YOU.
AND THE MESSAGE IS...?!
SHE SAID SHE HAD TO "BUY BACK" HER BROTHER. DOES THAT MAKE ANY SENSE?
YES.
NO.
...MAYBE?

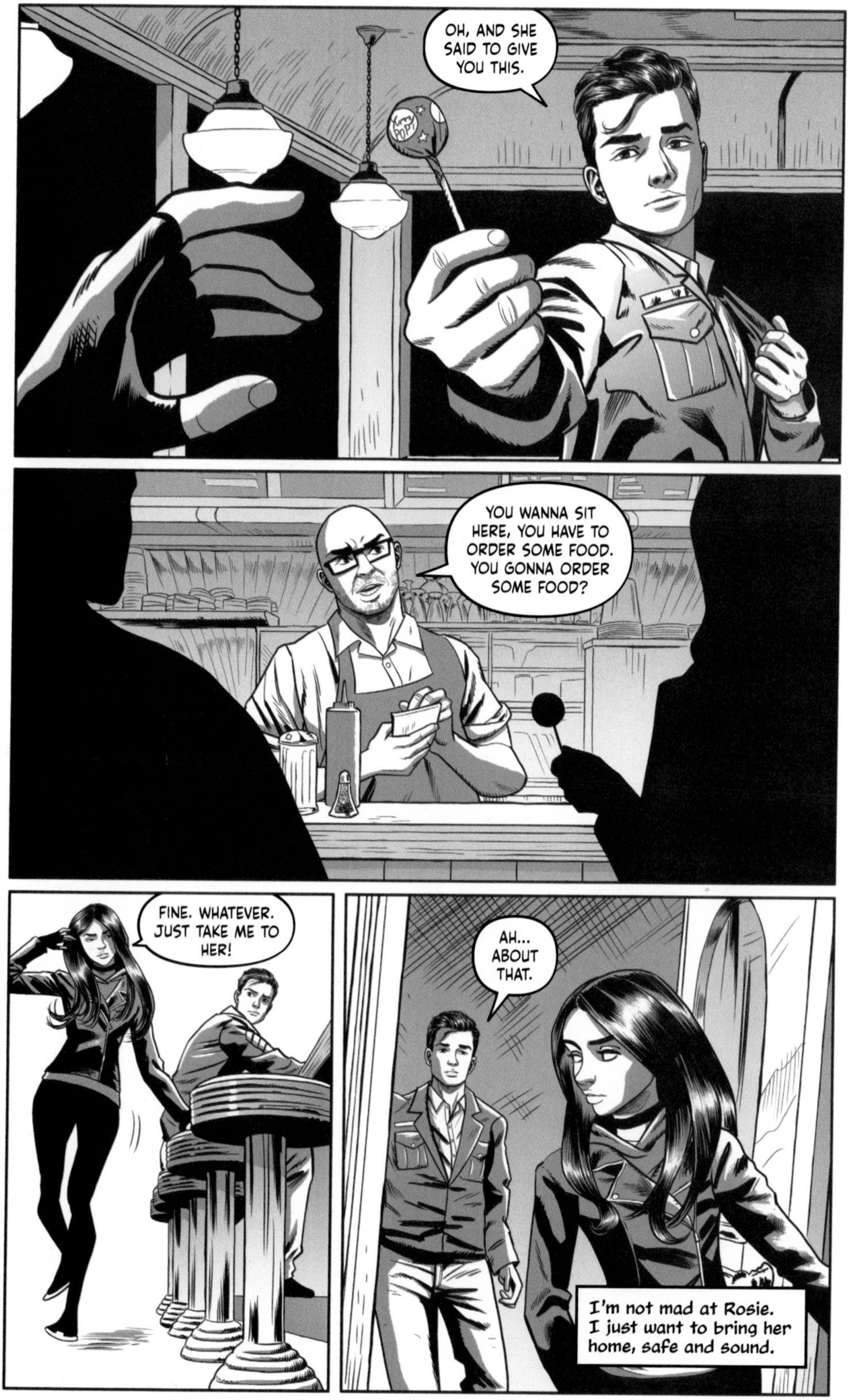
OH, AND SHE SAID TO GIVE YOU THIS.
YOU WANNA SIT HERE, YOU HAVE TO ORDER SOME FOOD. YOU GONNA ORDER SOME FOOD?
FINE. WHATEVER. JUST TAKE ME TO HER!
AH... ABOUT THAT.
I'm not mad at Rosie. I just want to bring her home, safe and sound.

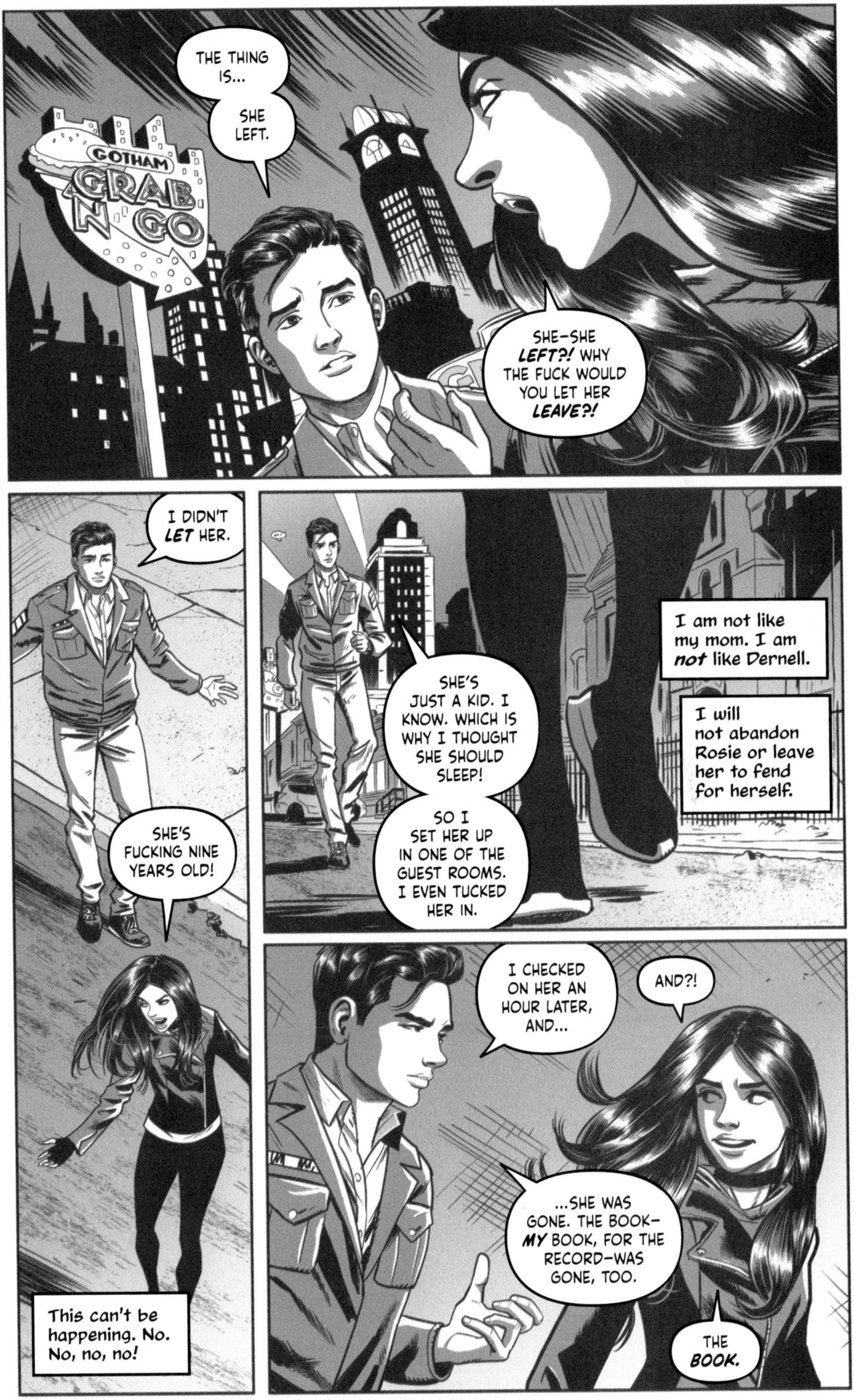
THE THING IS...
SHE LEFT.
GOTHAM GRAB N GO
SHE–SHE LEFT?! WHY THE FUCK WOULD YOU LET HER LEAVE?!
I DIDN'T LET HER.
SHE'S FUCKING NINE YEARS OLD!
This can't be happening. No. No, no, no!
SHE'S JUST A KID. I KNOW. WHICH IS WHY I THOUGHT SHE SHOULD SLEEP!
SO I SET HER UP IN ONE OF THE GUEST ROOMS. I EVEN TUCKED HER IN.
I am not like my mom. I am not like Dernell.
I will not abandon Rosie or leave her to fend for herself.
I CHECKED ON HER AN HOUR LATER, AND...
AND?!
...SHE WAS GONE. THE BOOK–MY BOOK, FOR THE RECORD–WAS GONE, TOO.
THE BOOK.

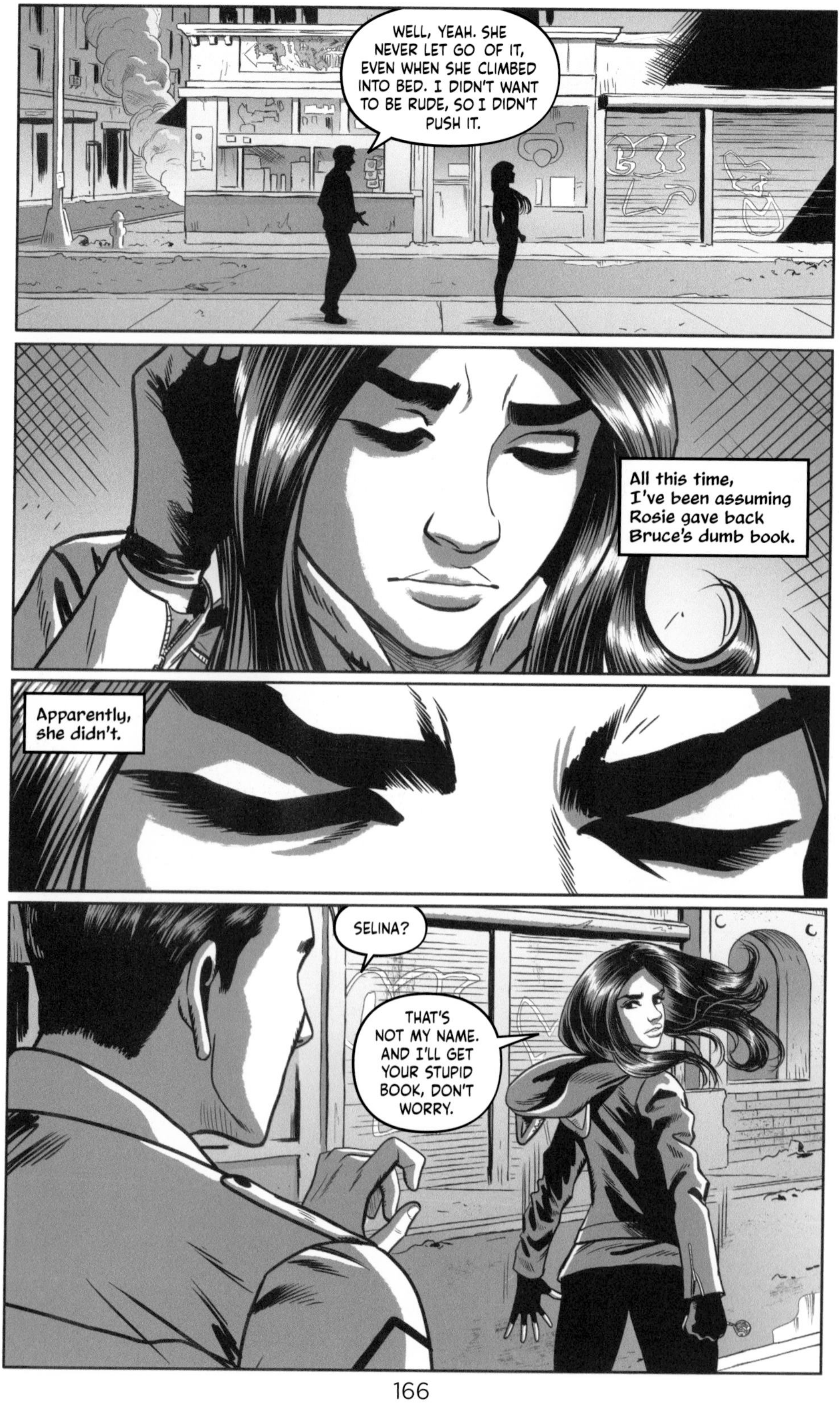
WELL, YEAH. SHE NEVER LET GO OF IT, EVEN WHEN SHE CLIMBED INTO BED. I DIDN'T WANT TO BE RUDE, SO I DIDN'T PUSH IT.
All this time, I've been assuming Rosie gave back Bruce's dumb book.
Apparently, she didn't.
SELINA?
THAT'S NOT MY NAME. AND I'LL GET YOUR STUPID BOOK, DON'T WORRY.

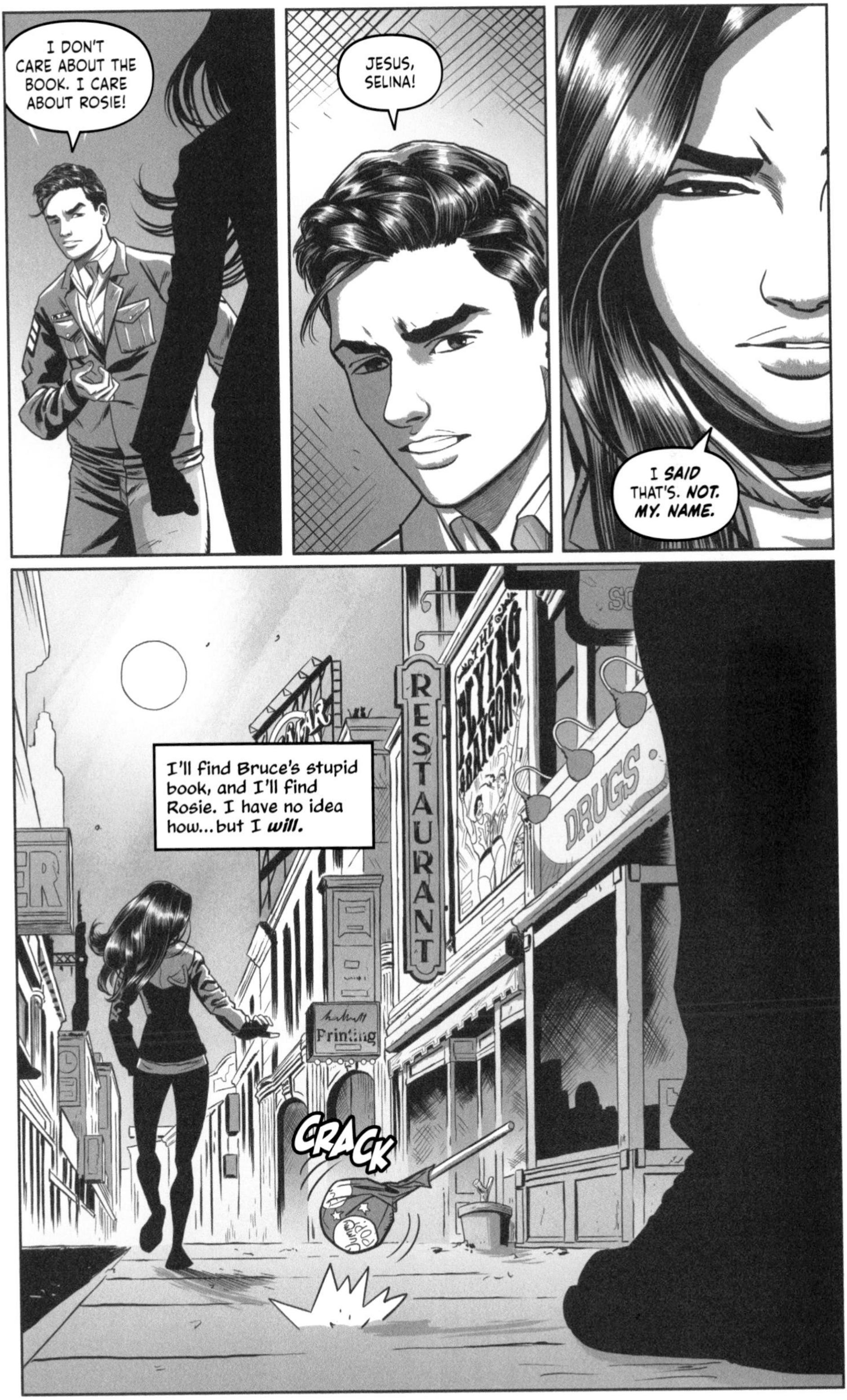
I DON'T CARE ABOUT THE BOOK. I CARE ABOUT ROSIE!
JESUS, SELINA!
I *SAID* THAT'S. ***NOT. MY. NAME.***
RESTAURANT
THE FLYING GRAYSONS
DRUGS
Printing
I'll find Bruce's stupid book, and I'll find Rosie. I have no idea how...but I ***will.***
CRACK

Under the Bright White Moon

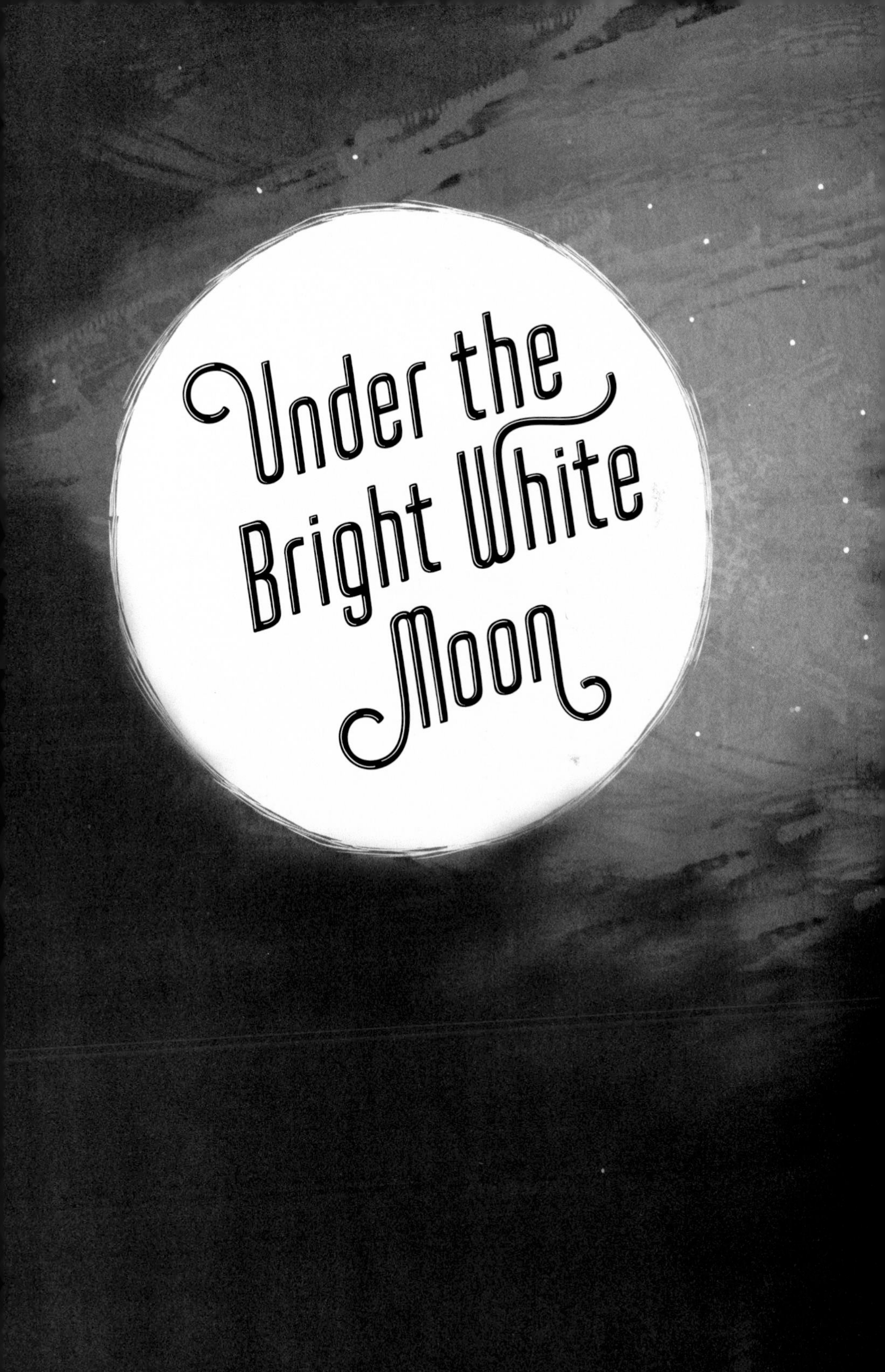

SEARCH AND RESCUE

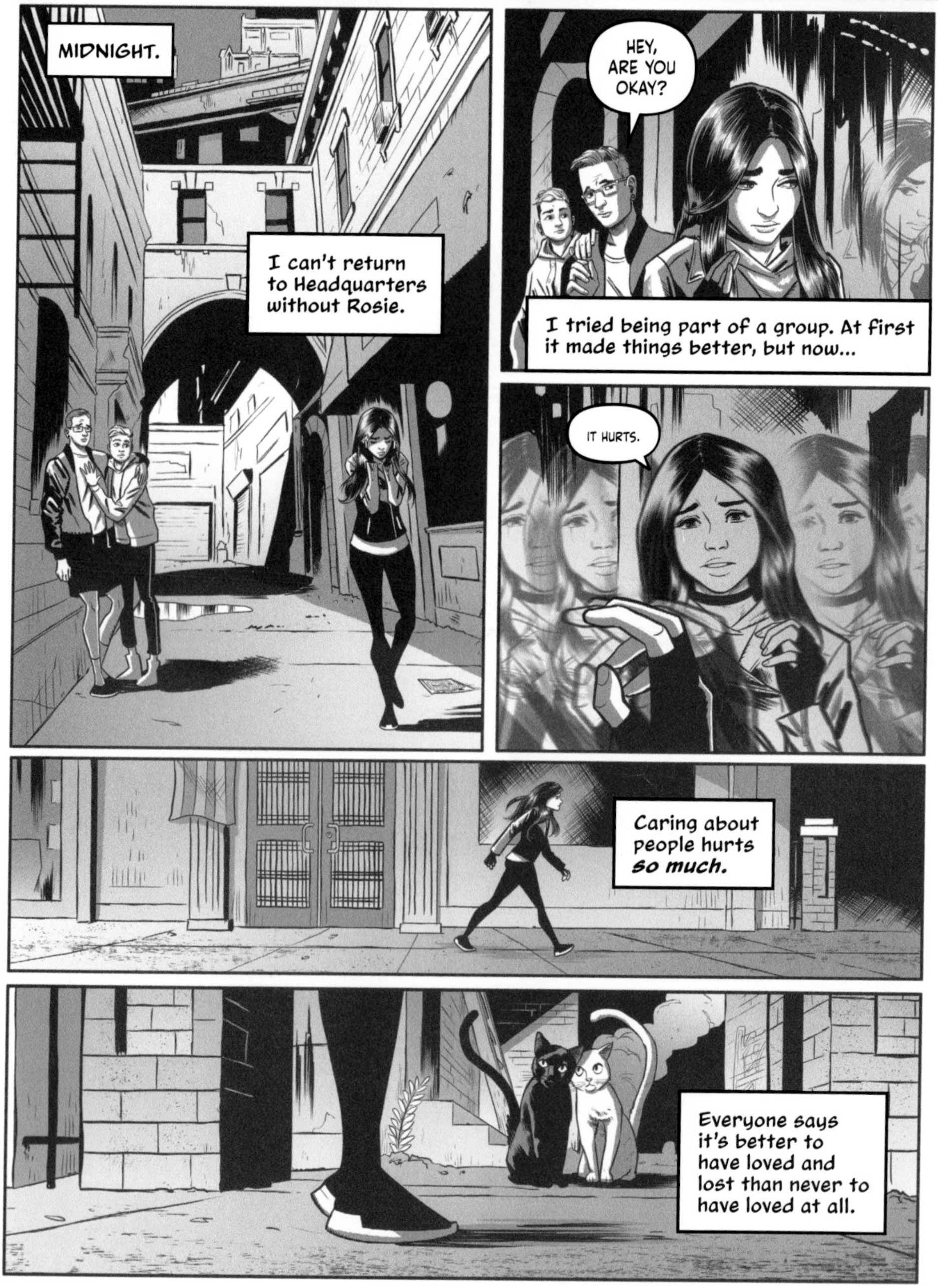
MIDNIGHT.
I can't return to Headquarters without Rosie.
HEY, ARE YOU OKAY?
I tried being part of a group. At first it made things better, but now...
IT HURTS.
Caring about people hurts *so much.*
Everyone says it's better to have loved and lost than never to have loved at all.

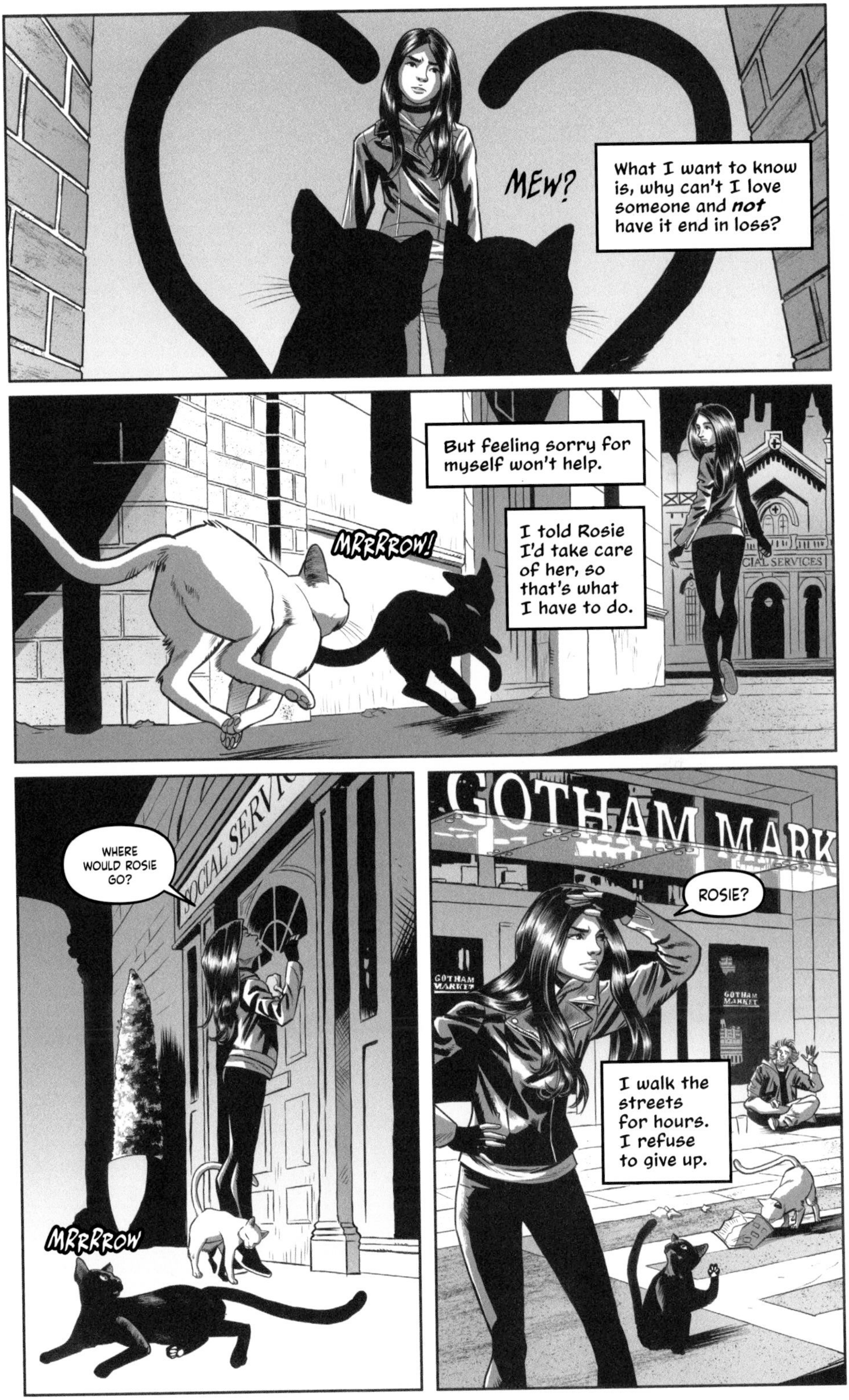
MEW?
What I want to know is, why can't I love someone and *not* have it end in loss?
But feeling sorry for myself won't help.
I told Rosie I'd take care of her, so that's what I have to do.
MRRRROW!
CIAL SERVICES
WHERE WOULD ROSIE GO?
SOCIAL SERVIC
MRRRROW
GOTHAM MARK
ROSIE?
GOTHAM MARKET
GOTHAM MARKET
I walk the streets for hours. I refuse to give up.

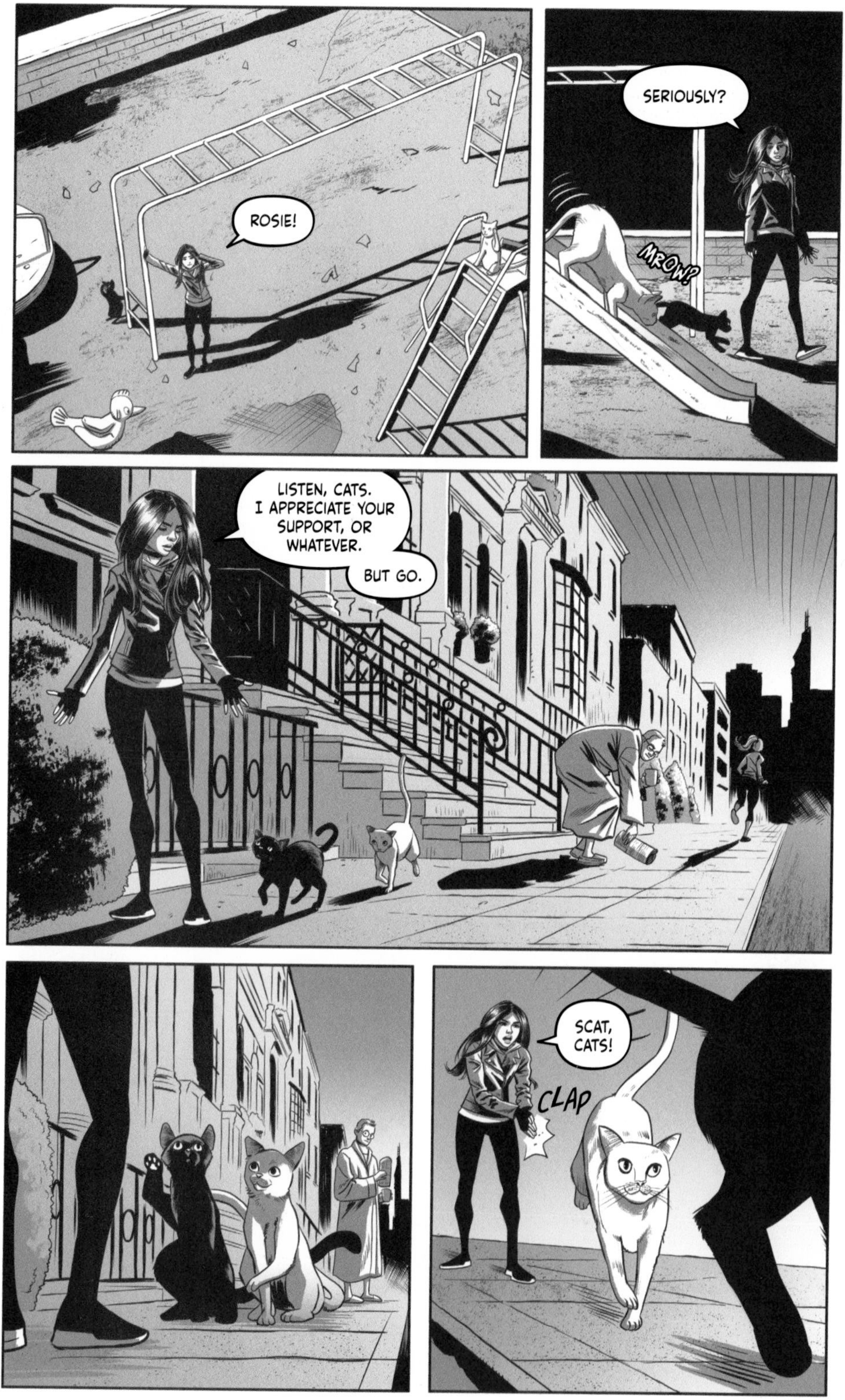
ROSIE!
SERIOUSLY?
MROW?
LISTEN, CATS. I APPRECIATE YOUR SUPPORT, OR WHATEVER.
BUT GO.
SCAT, CATS!
CLAP

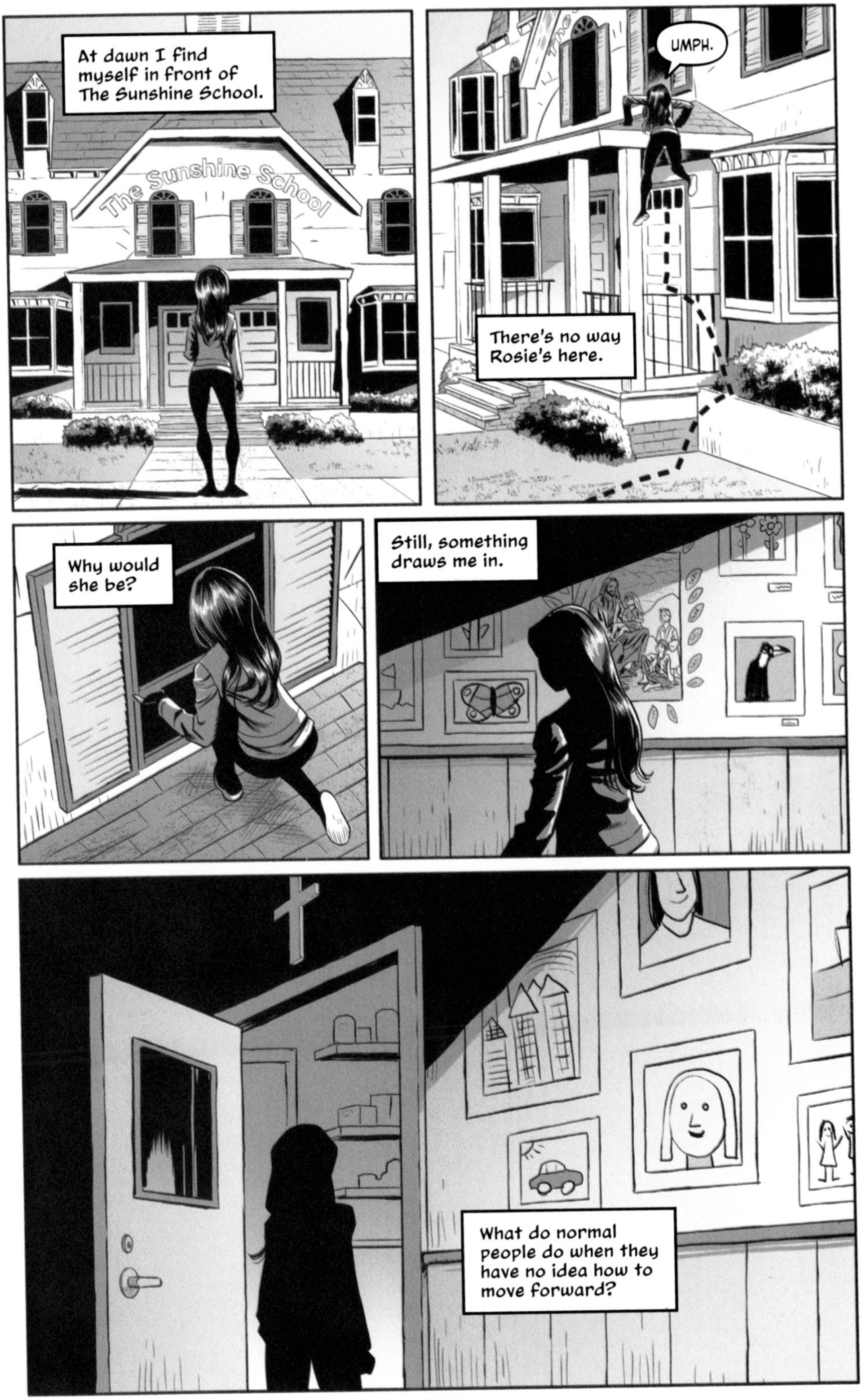
At dawn I find myself in front of The Sunshine School.
The Sunshine School
UMPH.
There's no way Rosie's here.
Why would she be?
Still, something draws me in.
What do normal people do when they have no idea how to move forward?

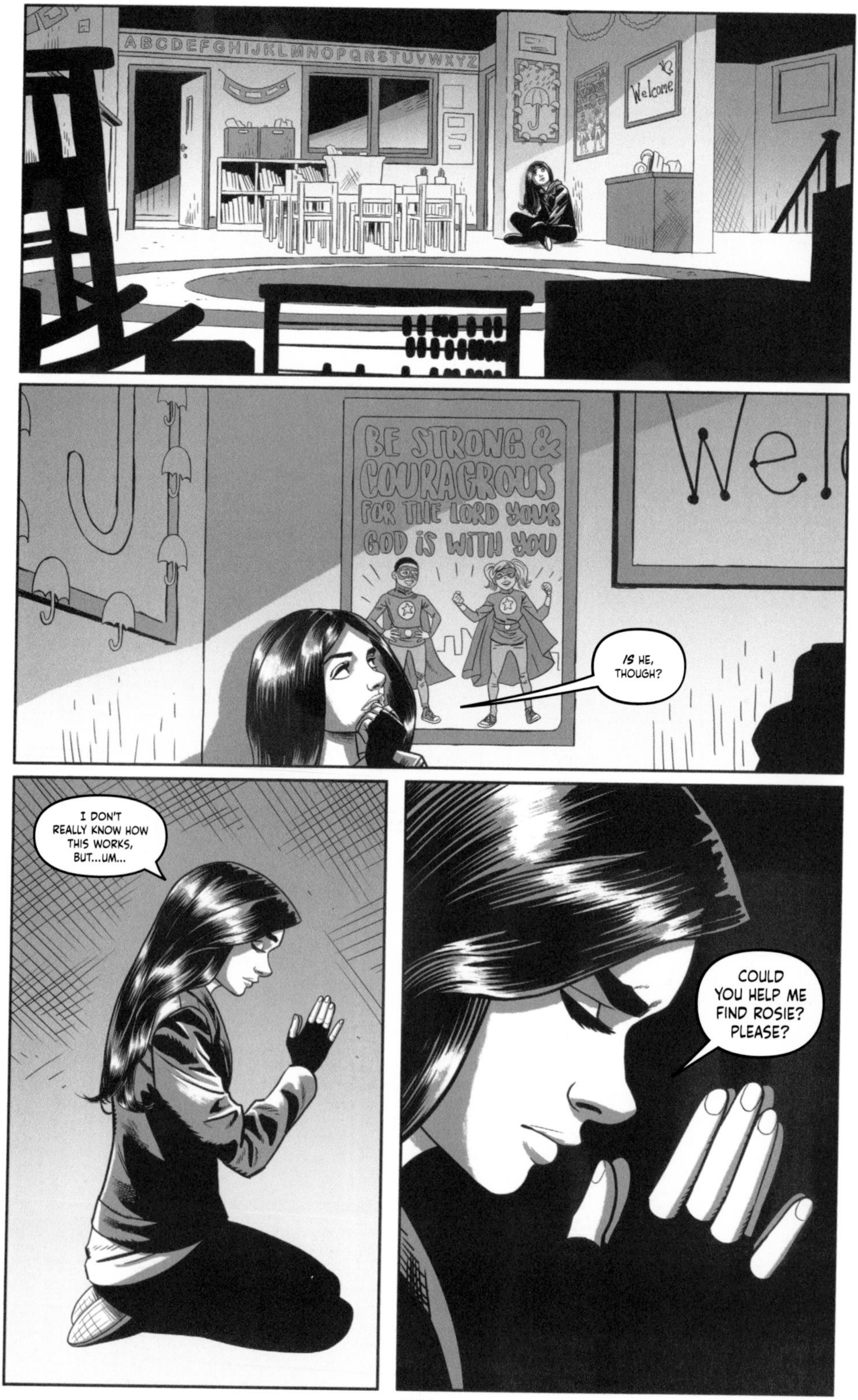
ABCDEFGHIJKLMNOPQRSTUVWXYZ
Welcome
BE STRONG & COURAGEOUS FOR THE LORD YOUR GOD IS WITH YOU
IS HE, THOUGH?
I DON'T REALLY KNOW HOW THIS WORKS, BUT...UM...
COULD YOU HELP ME FIND ROSIE? PLEASE?

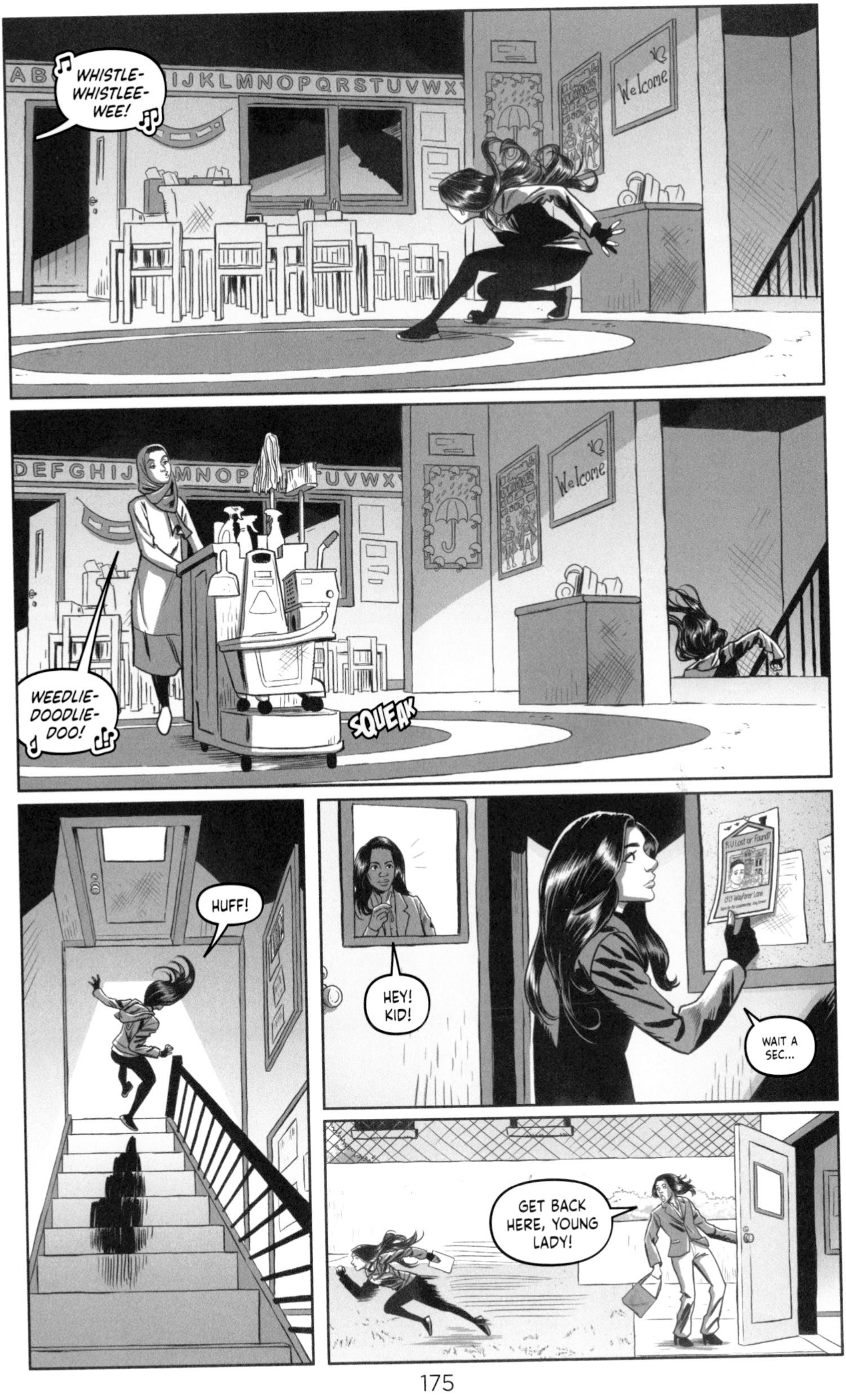
WHISTLE-WHISTLEE-WEE!
WEEDLIE-DOODLIE-DOO!
SQUEAK
HUFF!
HEY! KID!
WAIT A SEC...
GET BACK HERE, YOUNG LADY!

THE DOG POUND

THE BOY ON THIS FLYER, THERE'S SOMETHING ABOUT HIS EYES...

AND WHAT'S UP WITH REACHING OUT TO "LOST" KIDS?

R U Lost or Found?

1313 W...

Maybe it's the little boy. Maybe it's the way my chest tightens. But I can't help but wonder... would Rosie be sucked in by this?

I SHOULD TEXT BRUCE.

I SHOULD ABSOLUTELY *NOT* TEXT BRUCE.

GRRR.

1313 Wayfarer L...
me for th...mpanionship, s...

Message
To: Bruce
I think I know where Rosie is. Meet me at 1313 Wayfarer Lane

Send   Back

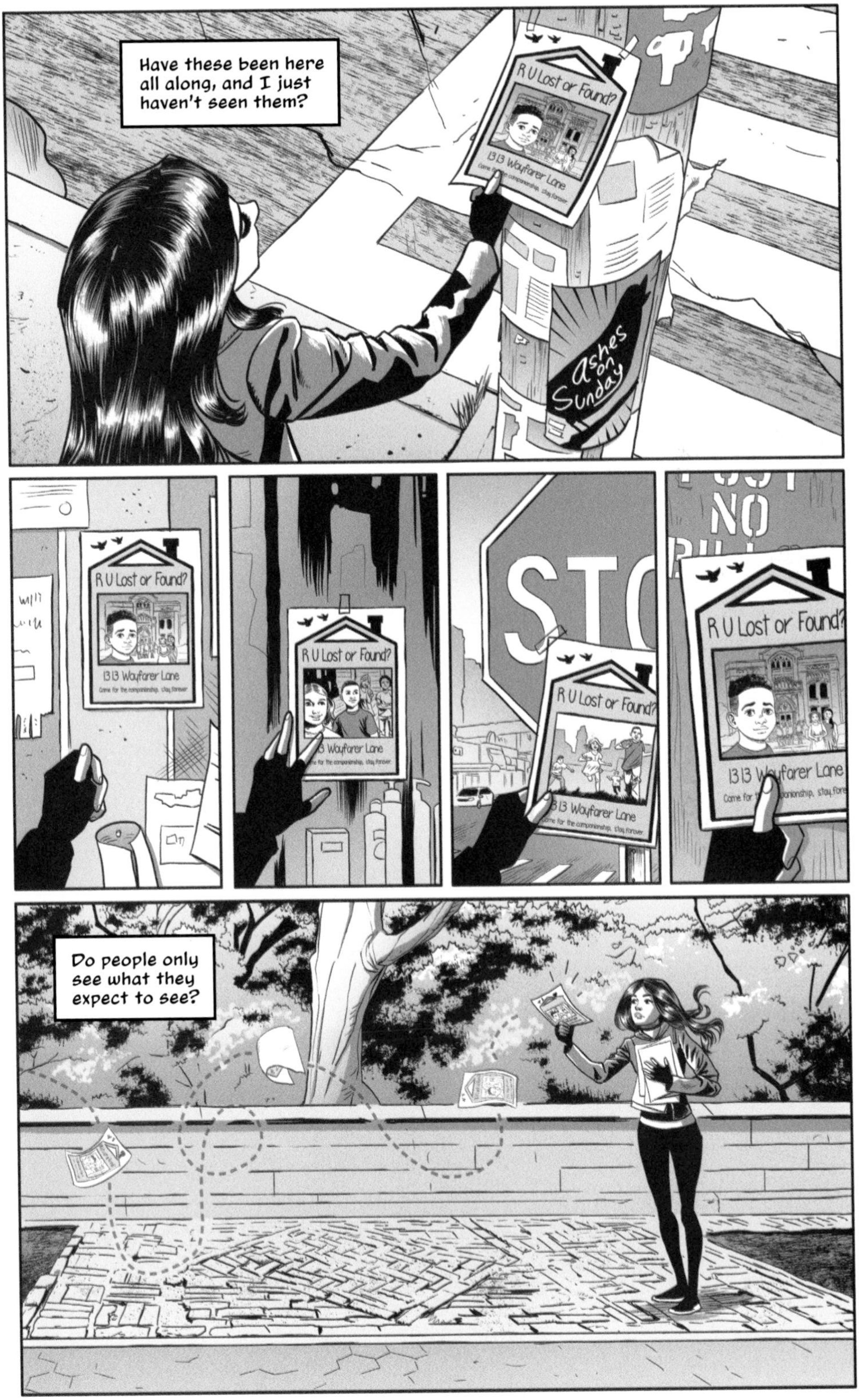
Have these been here all along, and I just haven't seen them?
R U Lost or Found?
1313 Wayfarer Lane
ashes on Sunday
R U Lost or Found?
1313 Wayfarer Lane
R U Lost or Found?
R U Lost or Found?
R U Lost or Found?
Do people only see what they expect to see?

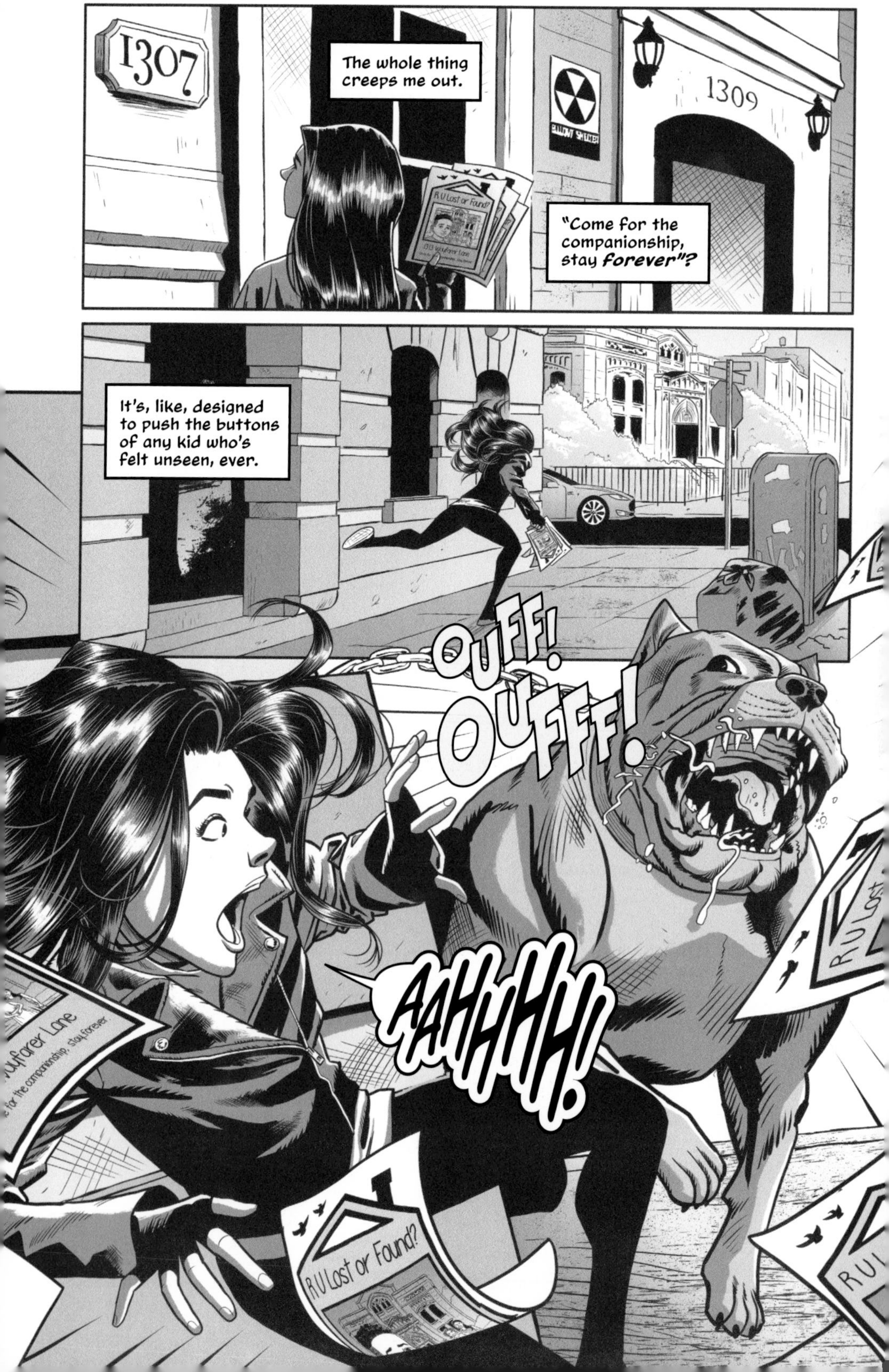
1307
The whole thing creeps me out.
1309
"Come for the companionship, stay *forever*"?
It's, like, designed to push the buttons of any kid who's felt unseen, ever.
OUFF! OUFFF!
AAHHHH!
R U Lost or Found?

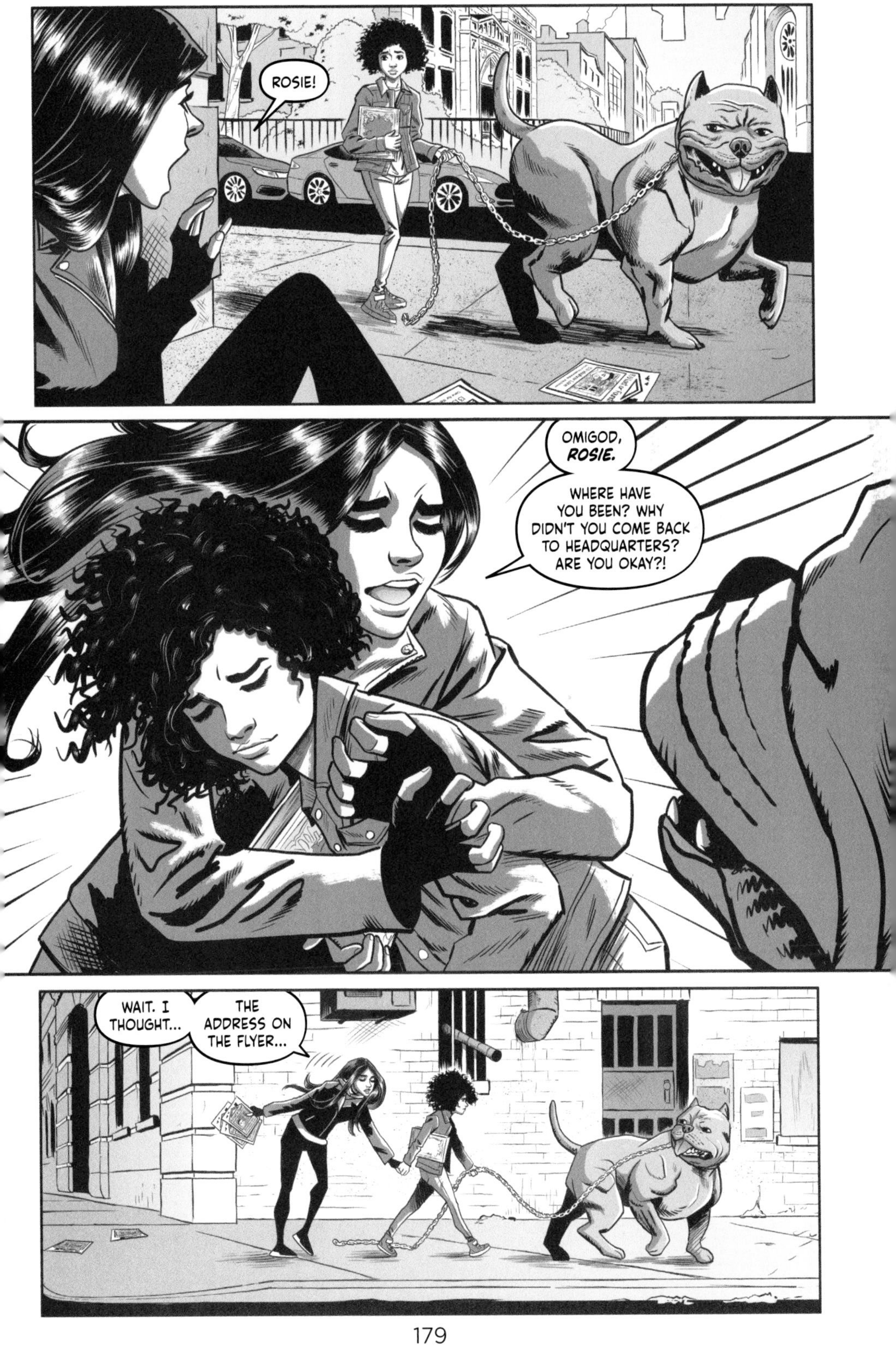
ROSIE!
OMIGOD, ROSIE.
WHERE HAVE YOU BEEN? WHY DIDN'T YOU COME BACK TO HEADQUARTERS? ARE YOU OKAY?!
WAIT. I THOUGHT...
THE ADDRESS ON THE FLYER...

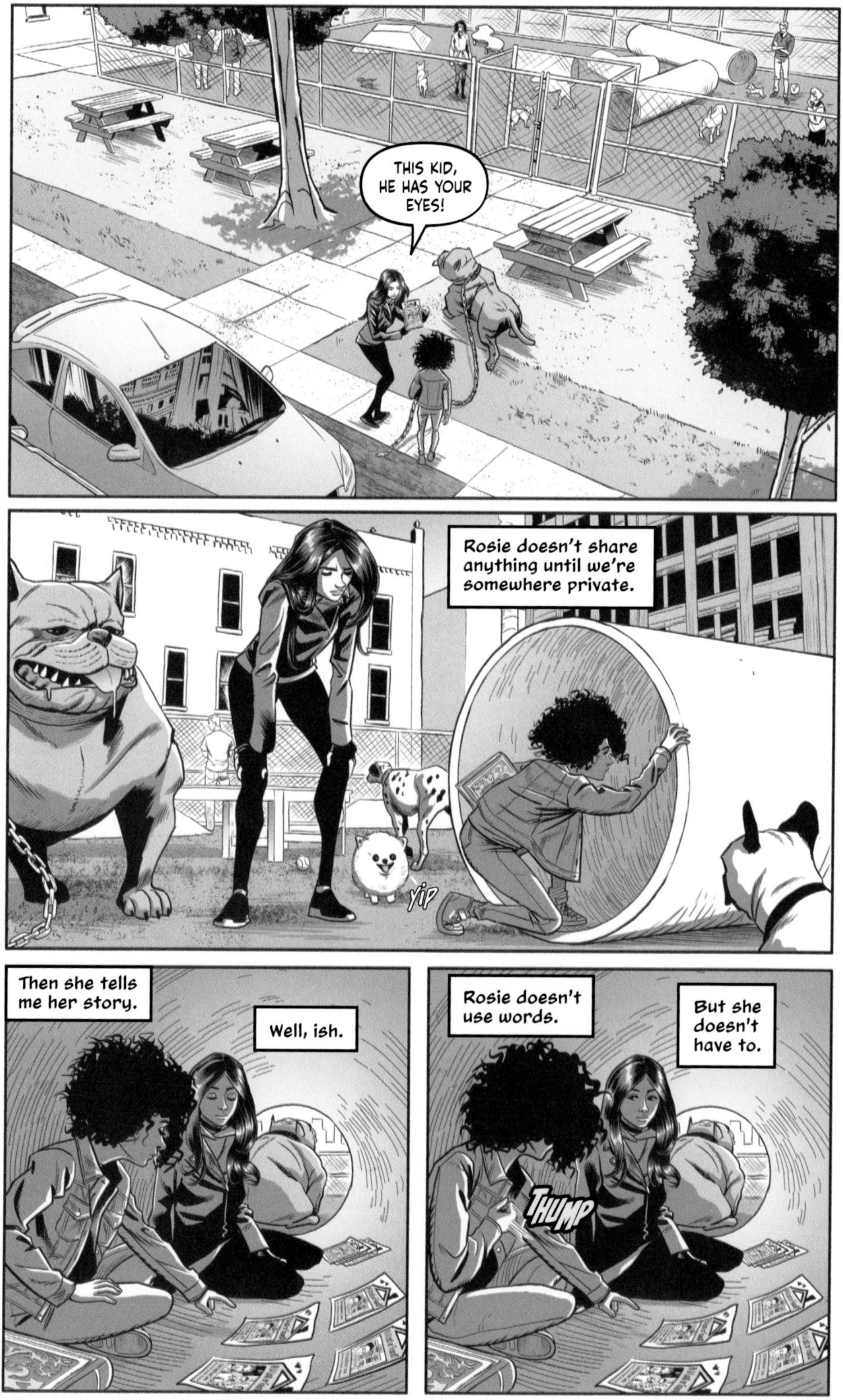
THIS KID, HE HAS YOUR EYES!
Rosie doesn't share anything until we're somewhere private.
YIP
Then she tells me her story.
Well, ish.
Rosie doesn't use words.
But she doesn't have to.
THUMP

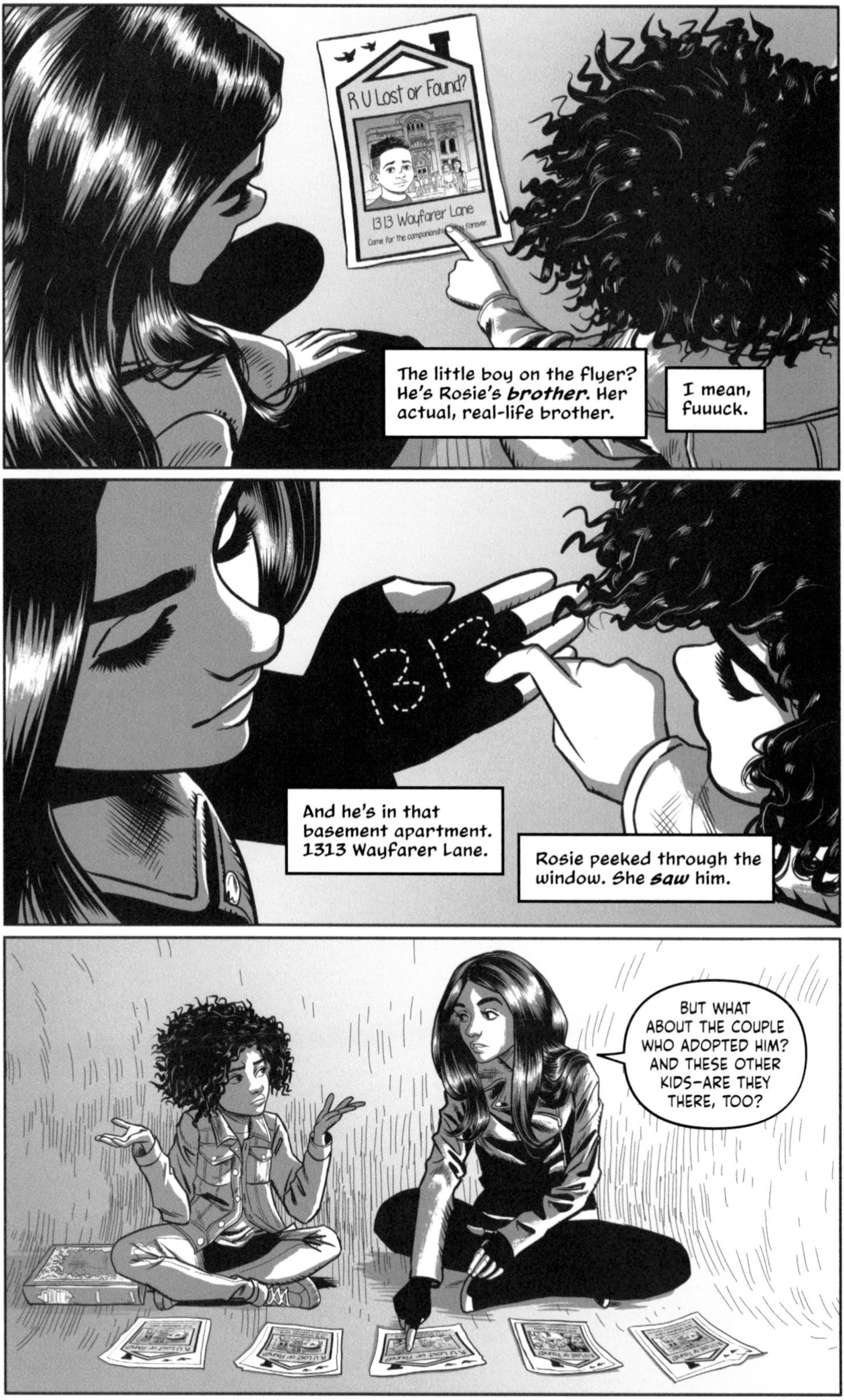
R U Lost or Found?
1313 Wayfarer Lane
The little boy on the flyer? He's Rosie's ***brother***. Her actual, real-life brother.
I mean, fuuuck.
1313
And he's in that basement apartment. 1313 Wayfarer Lane.
Rosie peeked through the window. She ***saw*** him.
BUT WHAT ABOUT THE COUPLE WHO ADOPTED HIM? AND THESE OTHER KIDS—ARE THEY THERE, TOO?

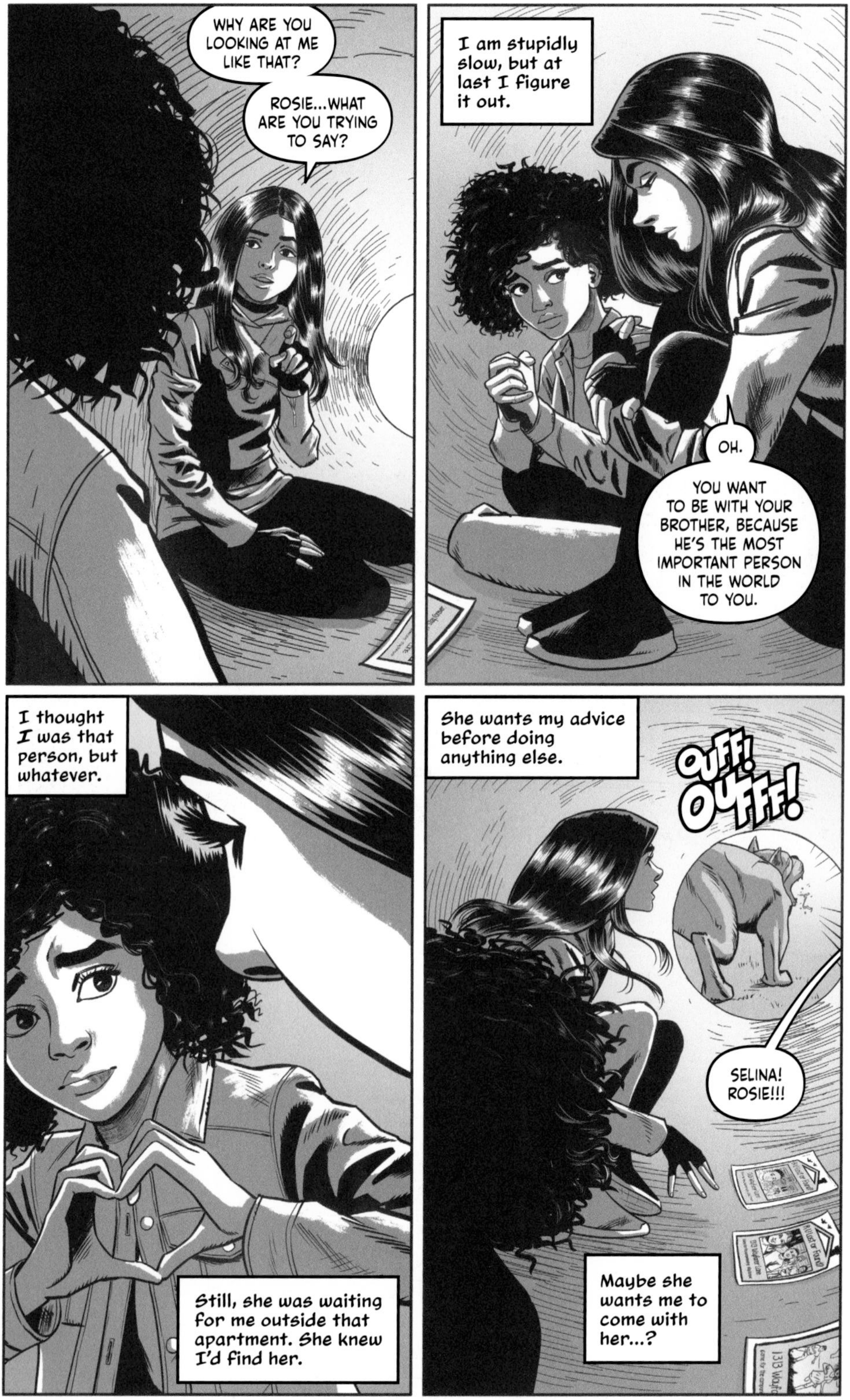
WHY ARE YOU LOOKING AT ME LIKE THAT?
ROSIE...WHAT ARE YOU TRYING TO SAY?
I am stupidly slow, but at last I figure it out.
OH.
YOU WANT TO BE WITH YOUR BROTHER, BECAUSE HE'S THE MOST IMPORTANT PERSON IN THE WORLD TO YOU.
I thought I was that person, but whatever.
Still, she was waiting for me outside that apartment. She knew I'd find her.
She wants my advice before doing anything else.
OUFF! OUFFF!
SELINA! ROSIE!!!
Maybe she wants me to come with her...?

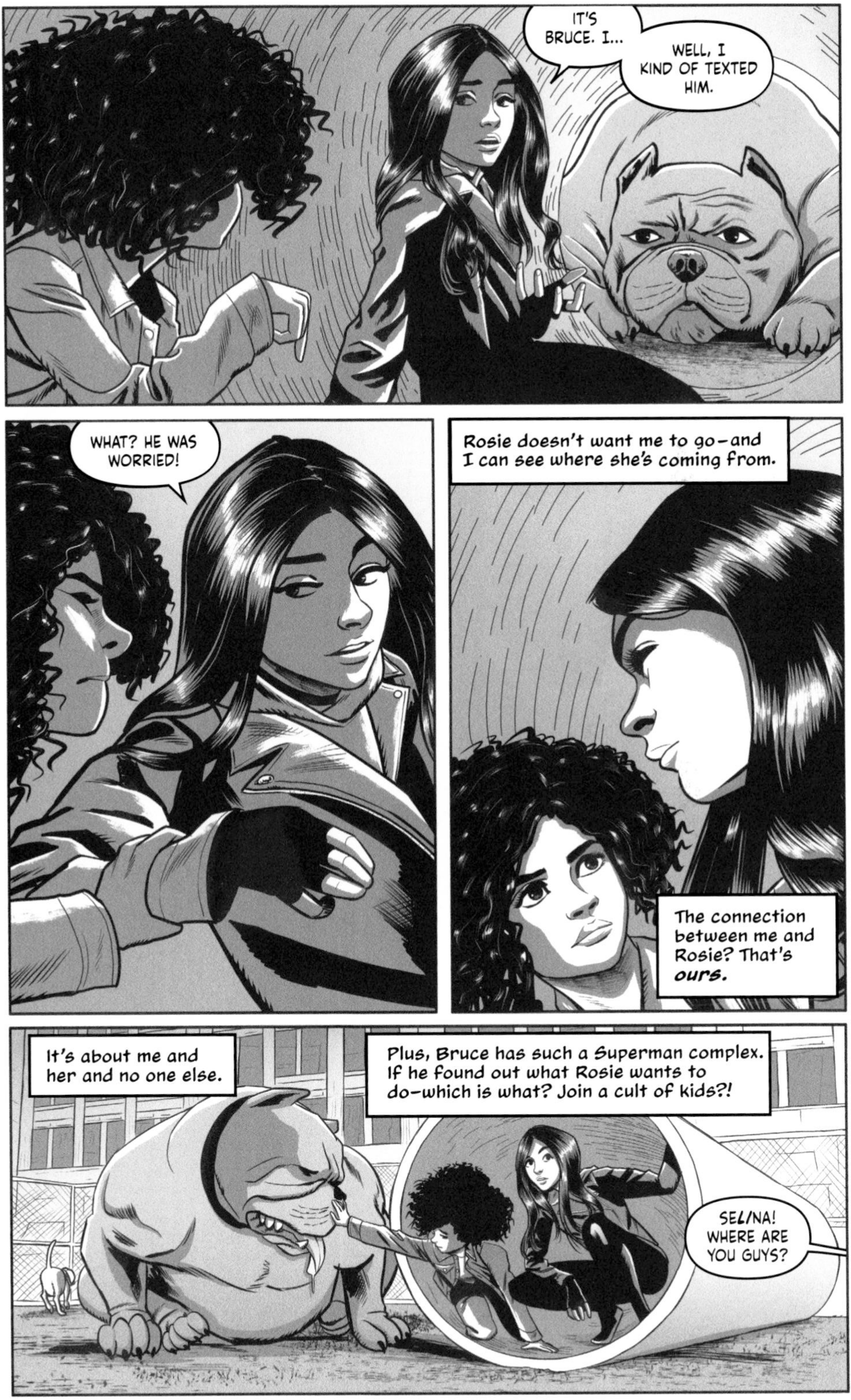
IT'S BRUCE. I...
WELL, I KIND OF TEXTED HIM.
WHAT? HE WAS WORRIED!
Rosie doesn't want me to go—and I can see where she's coming from.
The connection between me and Rosie? That's ***ours.***
It's about me and her and no one else.
Plus, Bruce has such a Superman complex. If he found out what Rosie wants to do—which is what? Join a cult of kids?!
SEL*I*NA! WHERE ARE YOU GUYS?

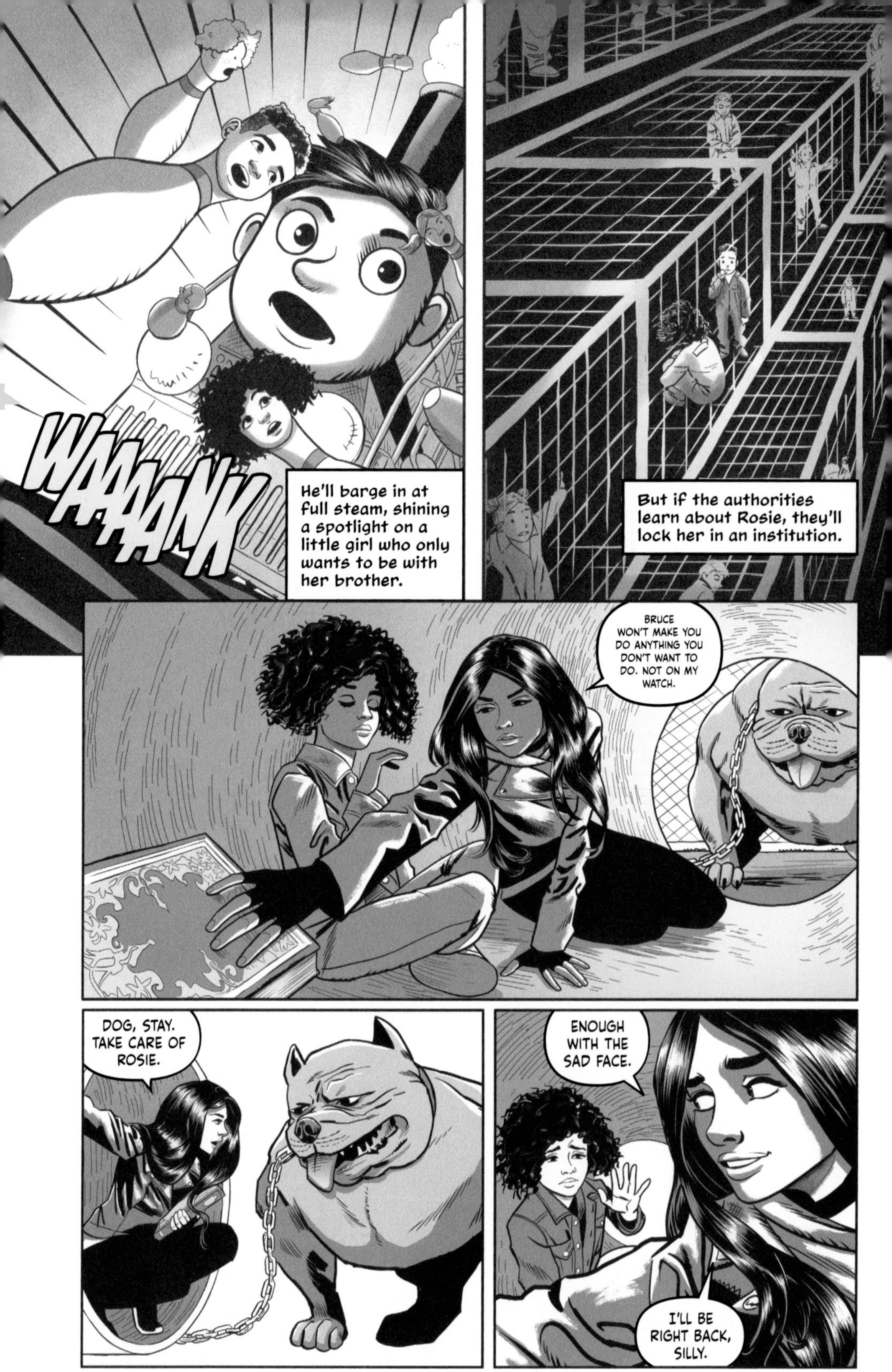
WAAAANK
He'll barge in at full steam, shining a spotlight on a little girl who only wants to be with her brother.
But if the authorities learn about Rosie, they'll lock her in an institution.
BRUCE WON'T MAKE YOU DO ANYTHING YOU DON'T WANT TO DO. NOT ON MY WATCH.
DOG, STAY. TAKE CARE OF ROSIE.
ENOUGH WITH THE SAD FACE.
I'LL BE RIGHT BACK, SILLY.

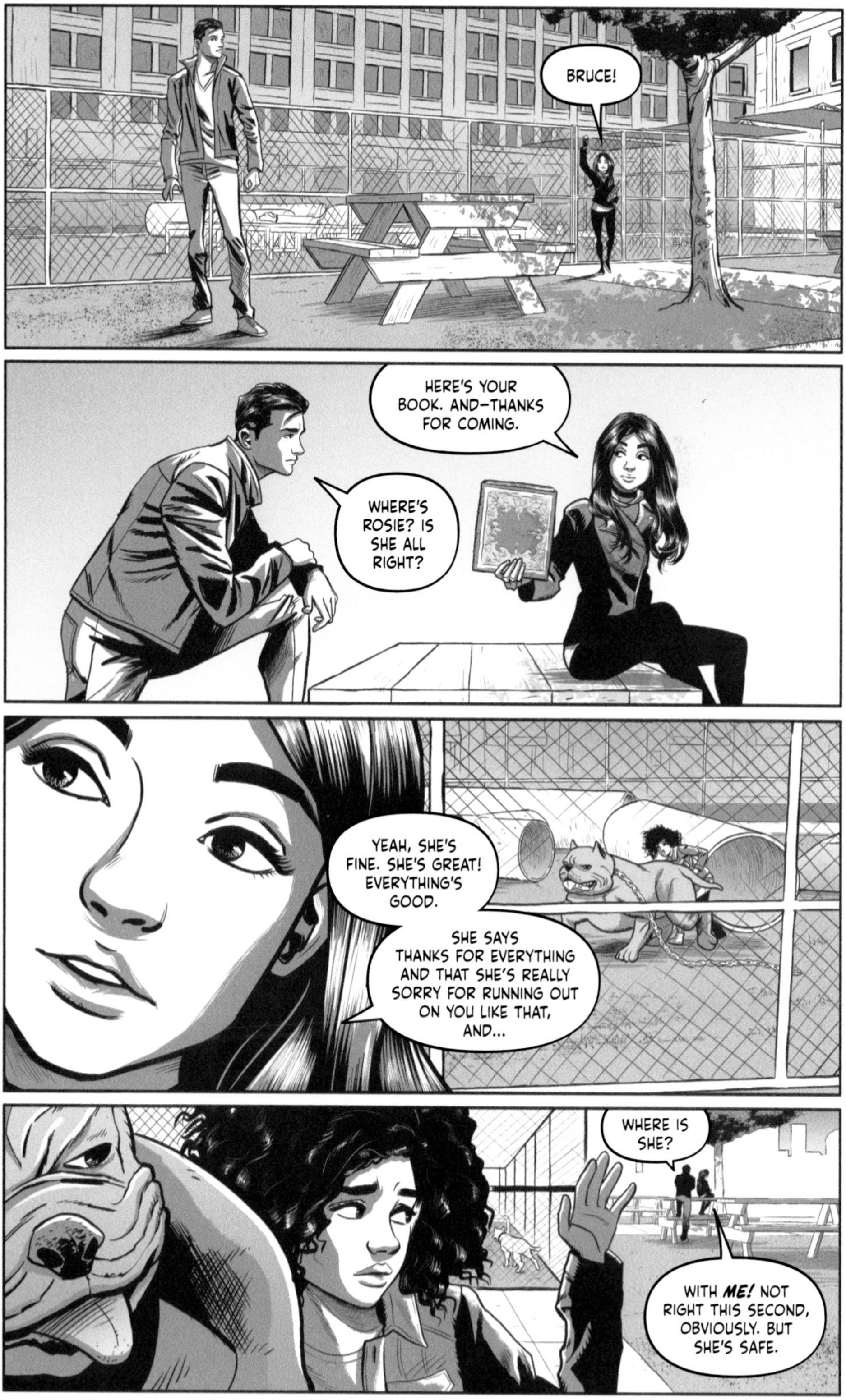
BRUCE!
HERE'S YOUR BOOK. AND—THANKS FOR COMING.
WHERE'S ROSIE? IS SHE ALL RIGHT?
YEAH, SHE'S FINE. SHE'S GREAT! EVERYTHING'S GOOD.
SHE SAYS THANKS FOR EVERYTHING AND THAT SHE'S REALLY SORRY FOR RUNNING OUT ON YOU LIKE THAT, AND...
WHERE IS SHE?
WITH *ME!* NOT RIGHT THIS SECOND, OBVIOUSLY. BUT SHE'S SAFE.

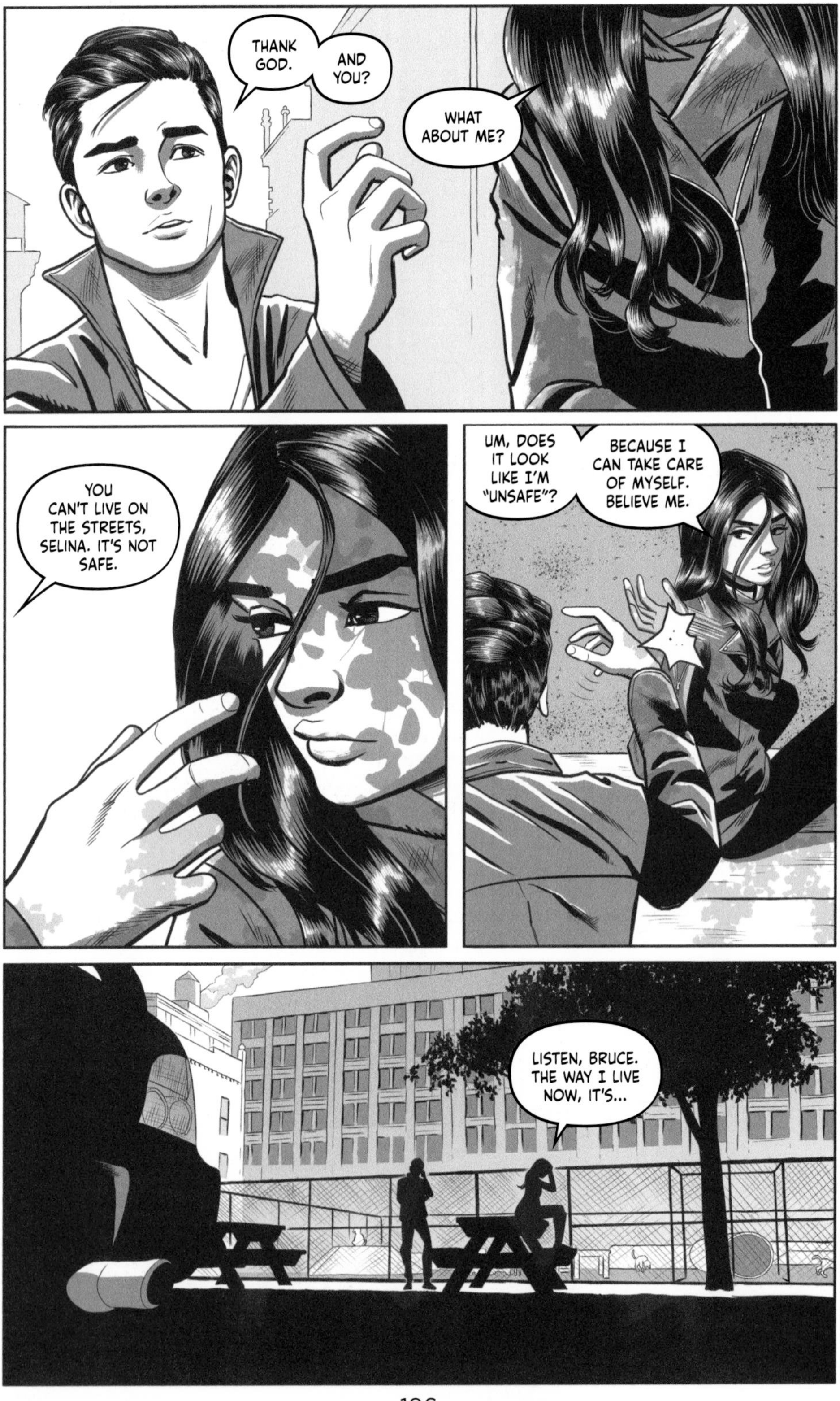
THANK GOD.
AND YOU?
WHAT ABOUT ME?
YOU CAN'T LIVE ON THE STREETS, SELINA. IT'S NOT SAFE.
UM, DOES IT LOOK LIKE I'M "UNSAFE"?
BECAUSE I CAN TAKE CARE OF MYSELF. BELIEVE ME.
LISTEN, BRUCE. THE WAY I LIVE NOW, IT'S...

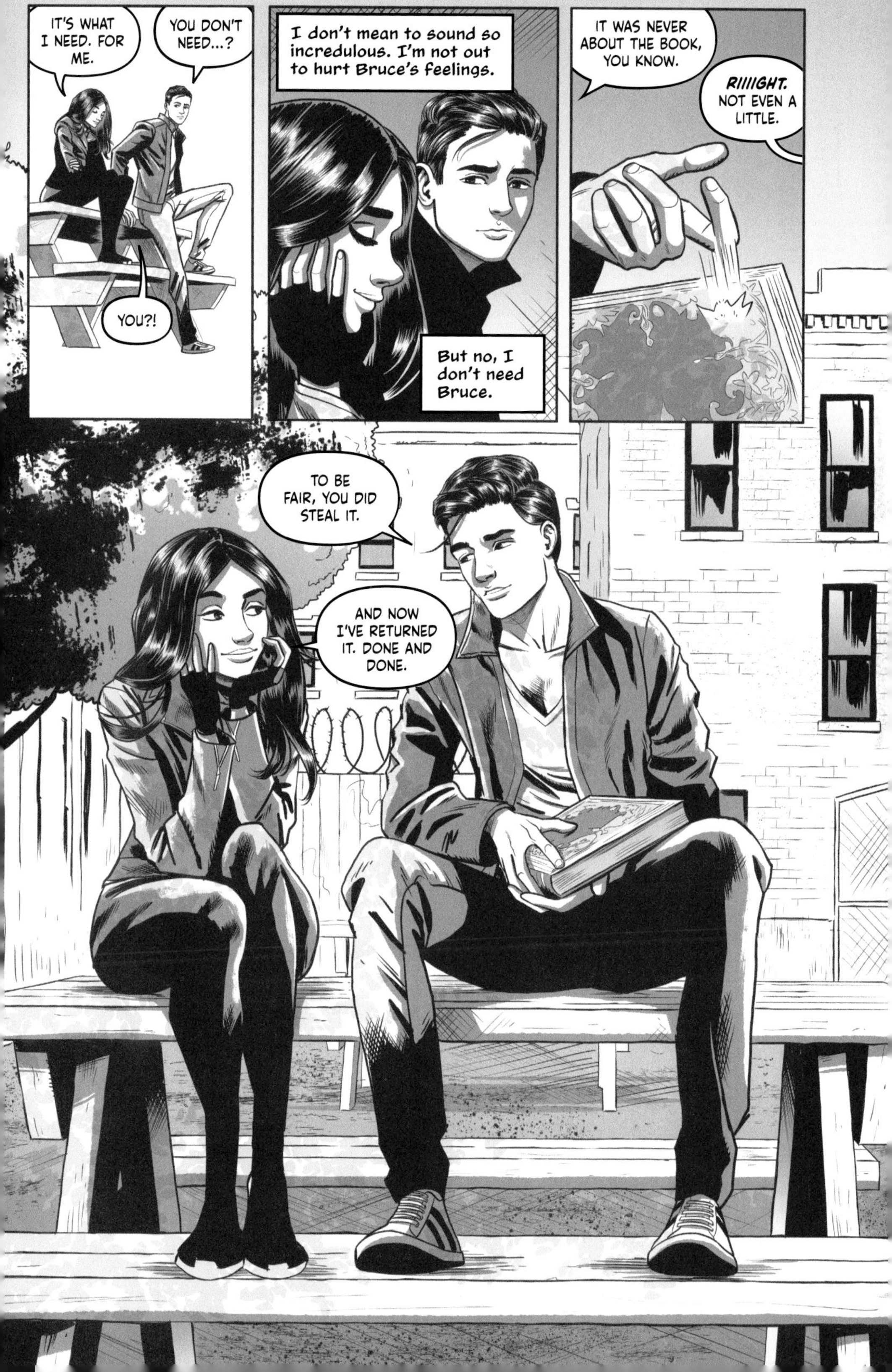
IT'S WHAT I NEED. FOR ME.
YOU DON'T NEED...?
YOU?!
I don't mean to sound so incredulous. I'm not out to hurt Bruce's feelings.
But no, I don't need Bruce.
IT WAS NEVER ABOUT THE BOOK, YOU KNOW.
RIIIIGHT. NOT EVEN A LITTLE.
TO BE FAIR, YOU DID STEAL IT.
AND NOW I'VE RETURNED IT. DONE AND DONE.

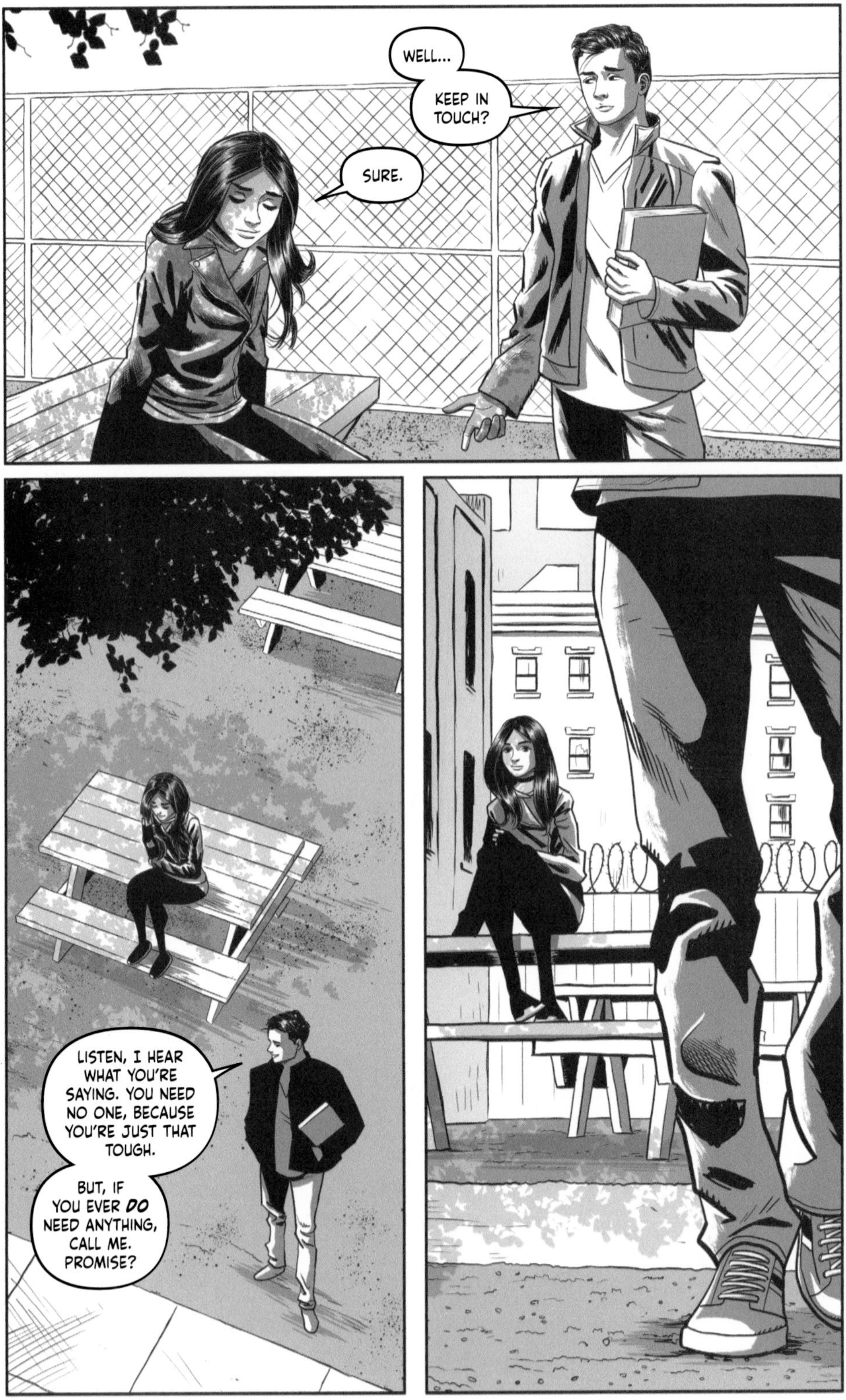
WELL...
KEEP IN TOUCH?
SURE.
LISTEN, I HEAR WHAT YOU'RE SAYING. YOU NEED NO ONE, BECAUSE YOU'RE JUST THAT TOUGH.
BUT, IF YOU EVER *DO* NEED ANYTHING, CALL ME. PROMISE?

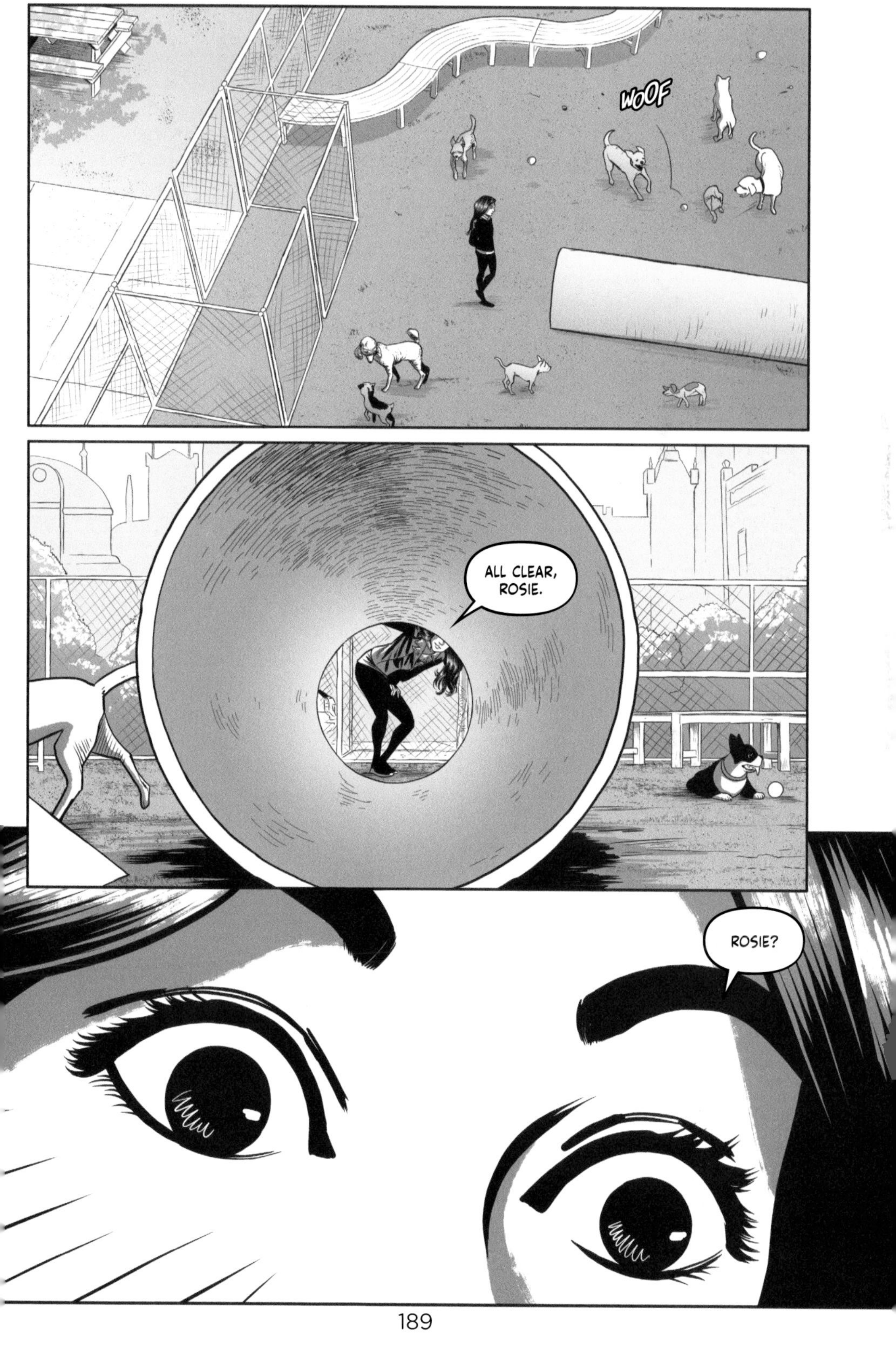
WOOF
ALL CLEAR, ROSIE.
ROSIE?

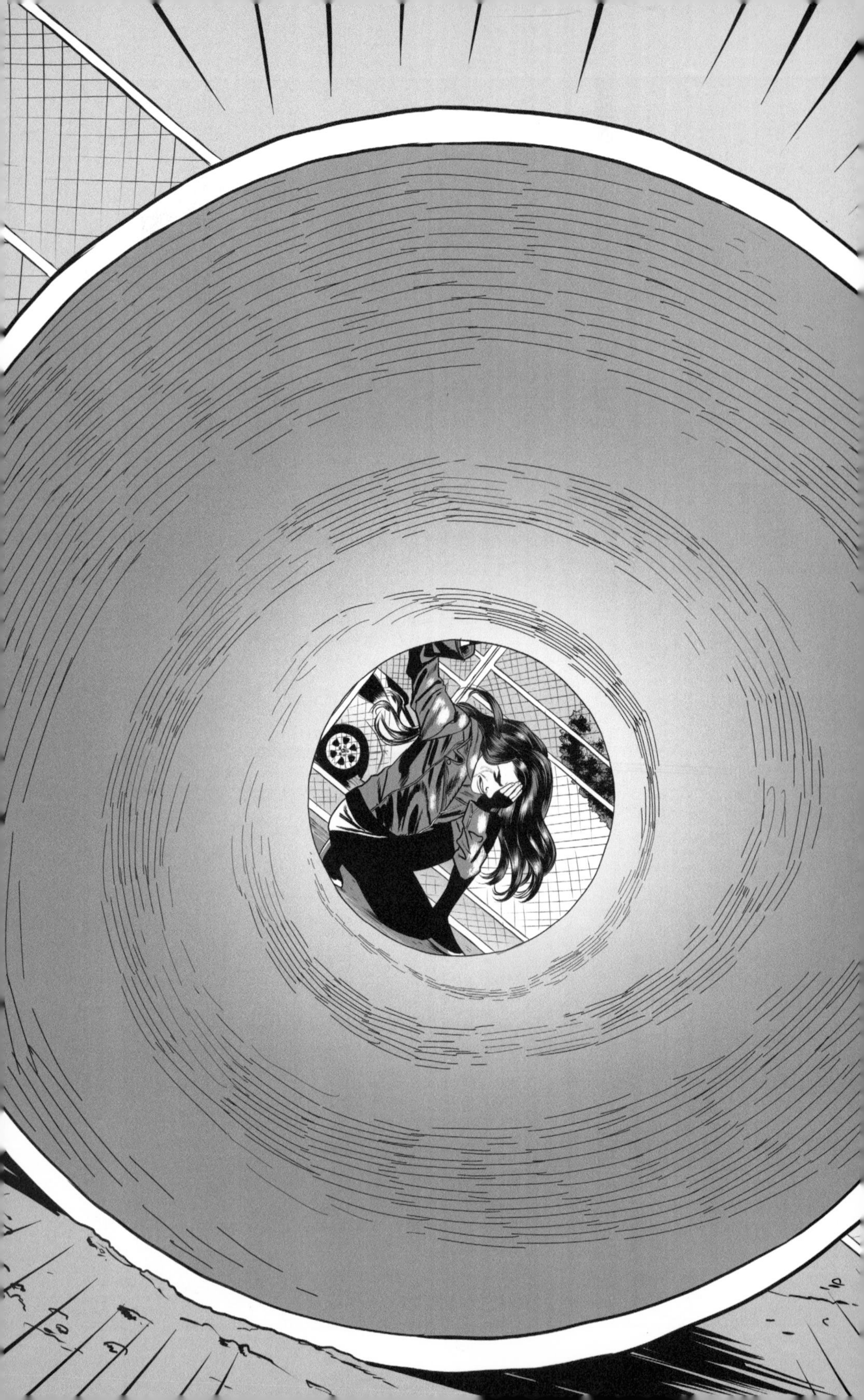

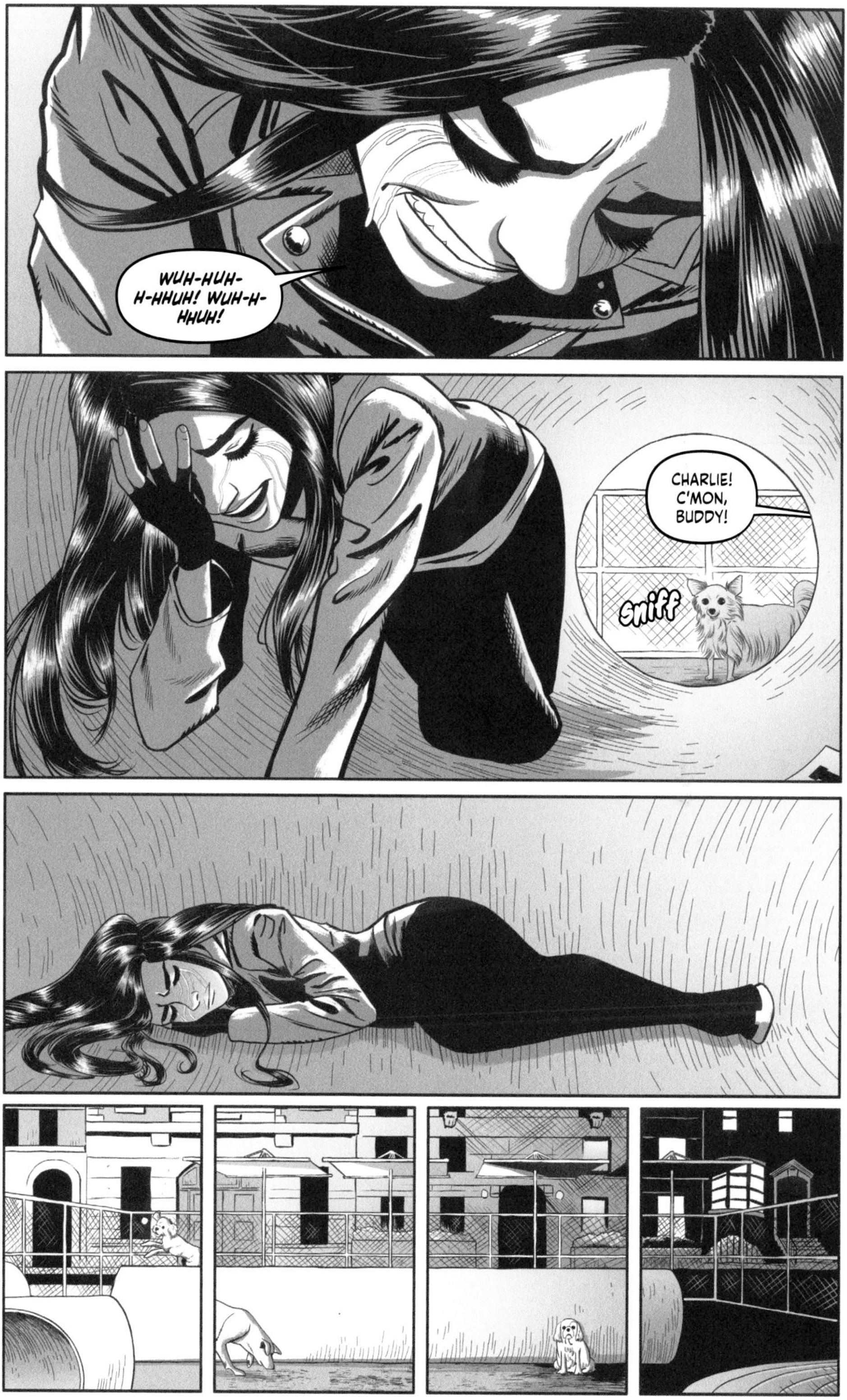
WUH-HUH-H-HHUH! WUH-H-HHUH!
CHARLIE! C'MON, BUDDY!
Sniff

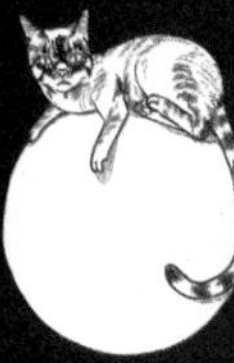

IT'S NOT THE SIZE OF THE ~~DOG~~ CAT IN THE FIGHT

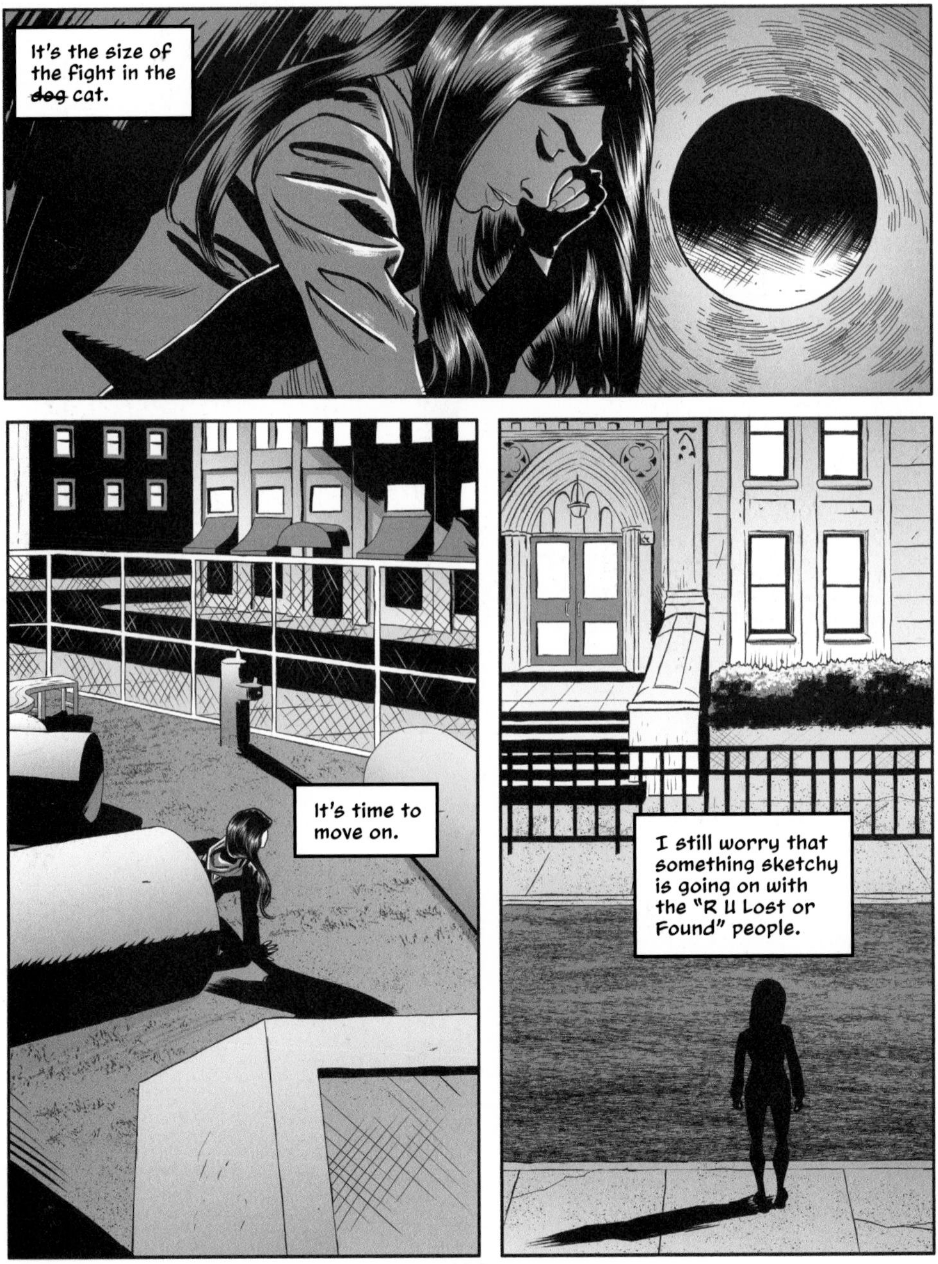

It's the size of the fight in the ~~dog~~ cat.
It's time to move on.
I still worry that something sketchy is going on with the "R U Lost or Found" people.

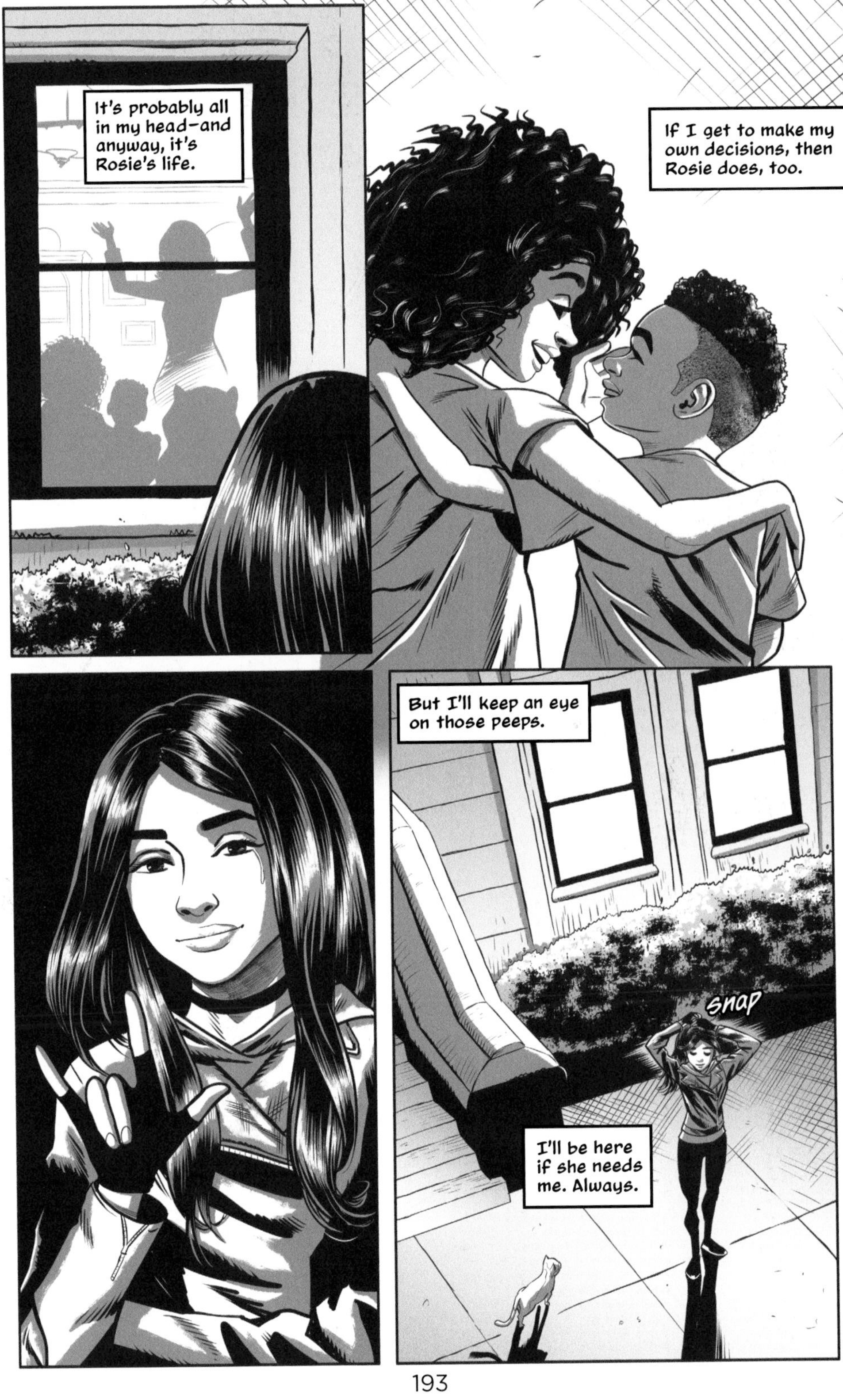

It's probably all in my head—and anyway, it's Rosie's life.
If I get to make my own decisions, then Rosie does, too.
But I'll keep an eye on those peeps.
SNAP
I'll be here if she needs me. Always.

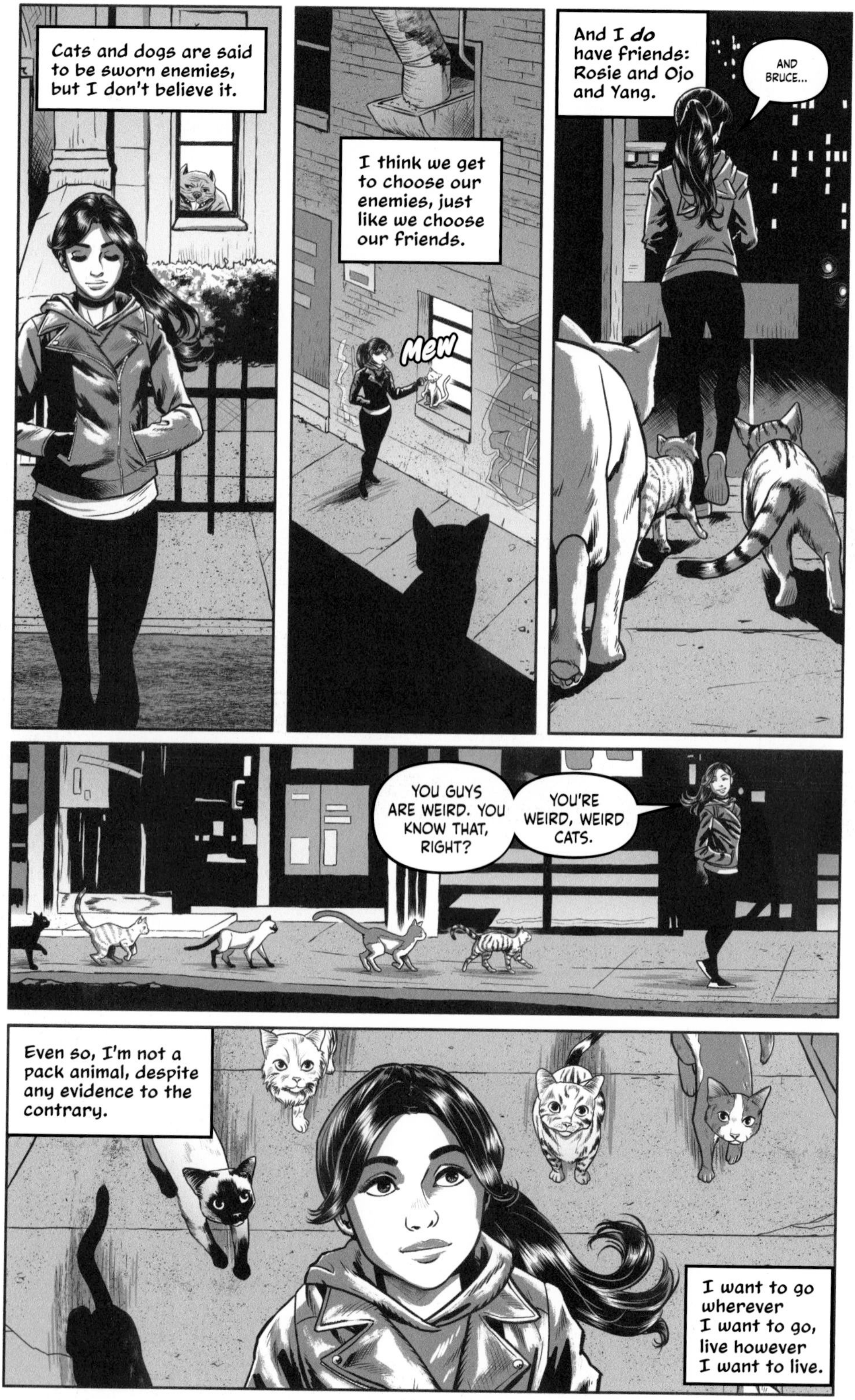
Cats and dogs are said to be sworn enemies, but I don't believe it.
I think we get to choose our enemies, just like we choose our friends.
Mew
And I *do* have friends: Rosie and Ojo and Yang.
AND BRUCE...
YOU GUYS ARE WEIRD. YOU KNOW THAT, RIGHT?
YOU'RE WEIRD, WEIRD CATS.
Even so, I'm not a pack animal, despite any evidence to the contrary.
I want to go wherever I want to go, live however I want to live.

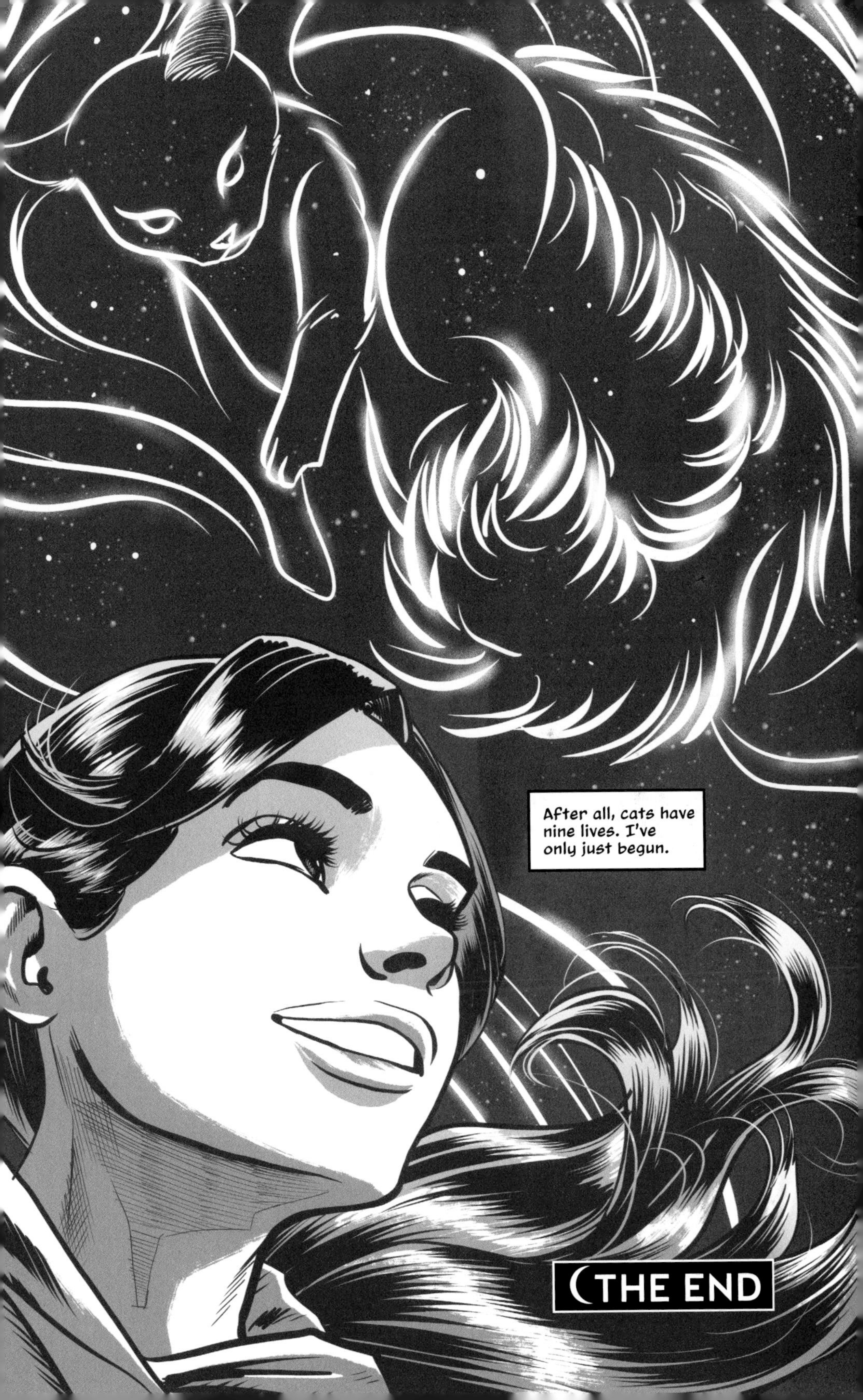
After all, cats have nine lives. I've only just begun.
THE END

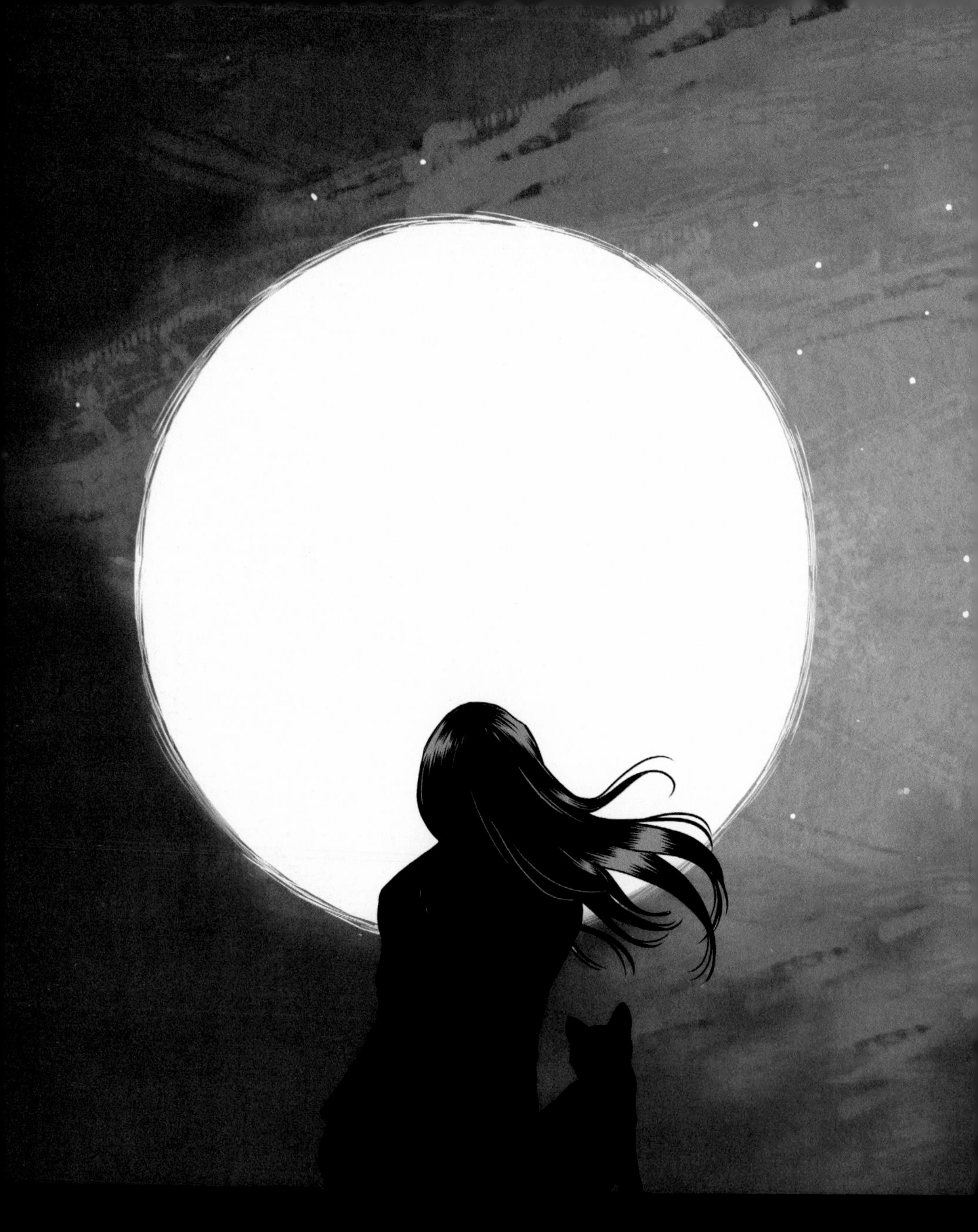

BEHIND THE SCENES

Resources for Suicide Prevention

If you are in danger of acting on suicidal thoughts or are in any other life-threatening crisis, please call emergency services in your area (9-1-1 in the U.S.) or go to your nearest hospital emergency room. By no means exhaustive, below is a list of resources for help dealing with suicide.

National Suicide Prevention Lifeline
Available 24 hours a day, 7 days a week.
Phone: 1-800-273-8255
Website: https://suicidepreventionlifeline.org
Online chat: chat.suicidepreventionlifeline.org/gethelp/lifelinechat.aspx

Crisis Text Line
According to the Crisis Text Line's website at https://www.crisistextline.org, if you text 741741 anywhere, anytime, you can receive a confidential text from a live, trained crisis counselor from their secure platform within minutes.
Text: 741741

The Trevor Project
A helpline for LGBT youth.
Phone: 1-866-488-7386
Website: https://www.thetrevorproject.org
Online chat: https://www.thetrevorproject.org/get-help-now

Trans Lifeline
A hotline for transgender people. The volunteers and staff are themselves transgender.
Phone (U.S.) 1-877-565-8860/(Canada) 1-877-330-6366
Website: https://www.translifeline.org

International Hotlines
The above hotlines are based in the U.S. and Canada. A list of international suicide hotlines is listed at http://www.suicide.org/international-suicide-hotlines.html, compiled by Suicide.org. Another list can be found at https://www.iasp.info/index.php, compiled by the International Association for Suicide Prevention.

Chronic Suicide Support Forum
This site offers an opportunity for supportive group discussion about chronic suicidal thoughts, with others who have experienced them as well. It is part of the site chronicsuicidesupport.com.
Message Board: https://chronicsuicidesupport.com/forum/

Online Suicide Help Wiki
This site contains lists of sites, in addition to those listed above, that offer discussion via instant messaging, chat rooms, email, text, and online support groups.
Website: https://unsuicide.org/suicide-help/

Resources for Stopping Domestic Violence

If you are in danger or are experiencing a life-threatening crisis, please call emergency services in your area (9-1-1 in the U.S.) or go to your nearest hospital emergency room.
By no means exhaustive, below is a list of resources for help dealing with domestic abuse.

The National Domestic Violence Hotline
Phone: 1-800-799-7233 or TTY 1-800-787-3224
Website: https://www.cdc.gov/violenceprevention/youthviolence/index.html
Online Chat: https://www.thehotline.org

National Teen Dating Abuse Helpline
Phone: 1-866-331-9474 or TTY 1-866-331-8453
Website: https://www.loveisrespect.org
Online Chat: http://www.loveisrespect.org/get-help/contact-us/chat-with-us
Text: "loveis" to 22522

National Sexual Assault Hotline (RAINN)
Phone: 1-800-656-4673
Website: https://ohl.rainn.org/online/
Online Chat: https://hotline.rainn.org/online/

Stalking Resource Center
Website: http://victimsofcrime.org/our-programs/stalking-resource-center

Resources for Avoiding Self-Harm

Self-Injury Outreach and Support (SIOS)
Website: http://sioutreach.org

The Trevor Project
A helpline for LGBT youth.
Phone: 1-866-488-7386
Website: https://www.thetrevorproject.org/trvr_support_center/self-injury
Online chat: https://www.thetrevorproject.org/get-help-now

To Write Love on Her Arms
A nonprofit movement dedicated to presenting hope and finding help for people struggling with depression, addiction, self-injury, and suicide.
Website: https://twloha.com/find-help/help-by-topic/self-injury/
Text: "TWLOHA" to 741741

National Alliance on Mental Illness
Website: https://www.nami.org/learn-more/mental-health-conditions/related-conditions/self-harm
Phone: 1-800-950-NAMI
Text: "NAMI" to 741741

Resources for Stopping Animal Cruelty

If you have found a stray or injured animal, please call your local animal care and control agency immediately. To report a case of animal cruelty, neglect, or abuse, please contact your local law enforcement agency.

Humane Society

Website: https://www.humanesociety.org/resources/report-animal-cruelty
Phone: 1-866-720-2676

ASPCA

Website: https://www.aspca.org/take-action/report-animal-cruelty

ASPCAPro

8 Tips for Reporting Animal Cruelty: https://www.aspcapro.org/resource/8-tips-reporting-animal-cruelty

Save Them All

Website: https://resources.bestfriends.org/article/animal-cruelty-and-abuse-or-neglect

Character designs by Isaac Goodhart

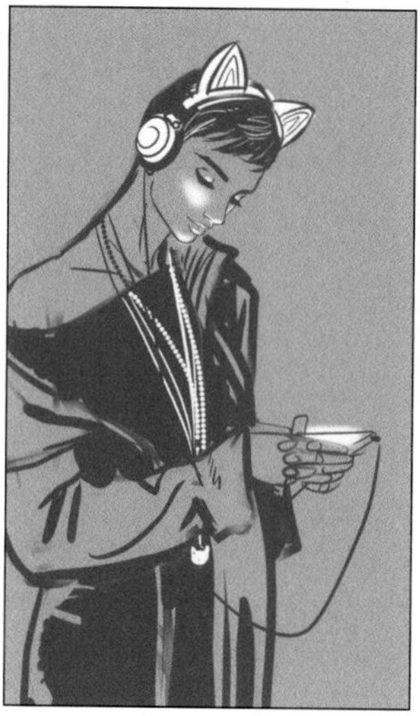

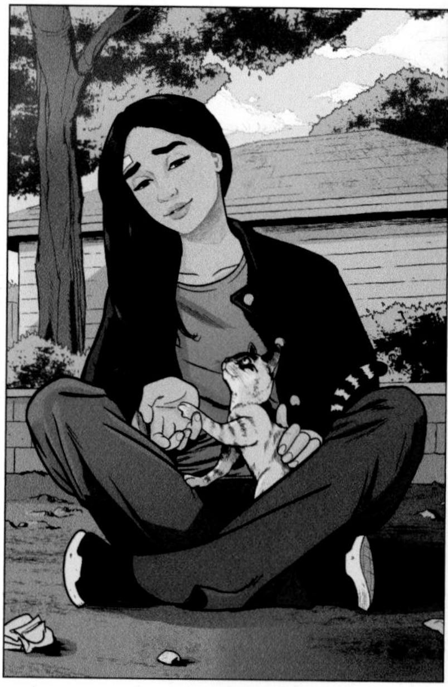

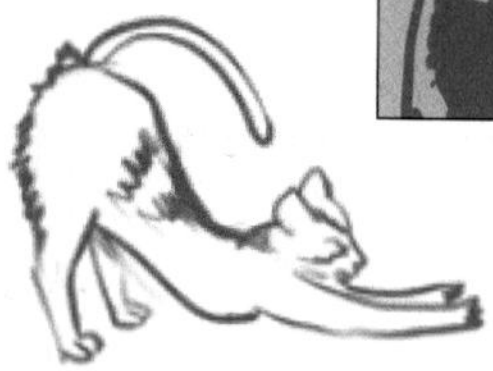

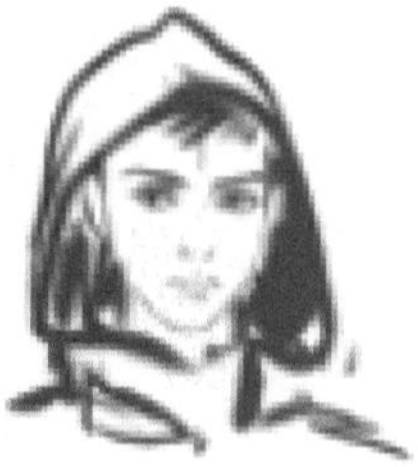

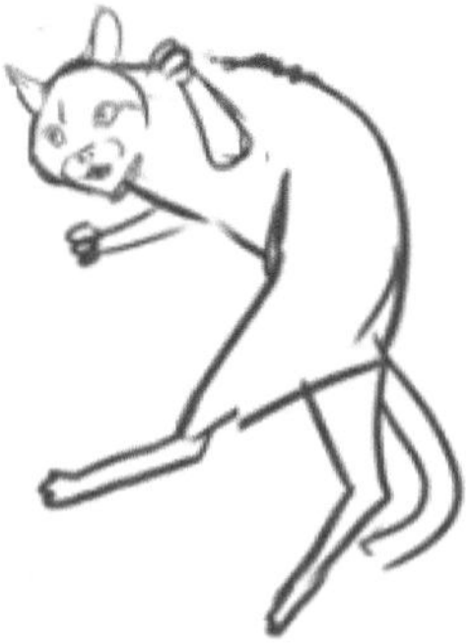

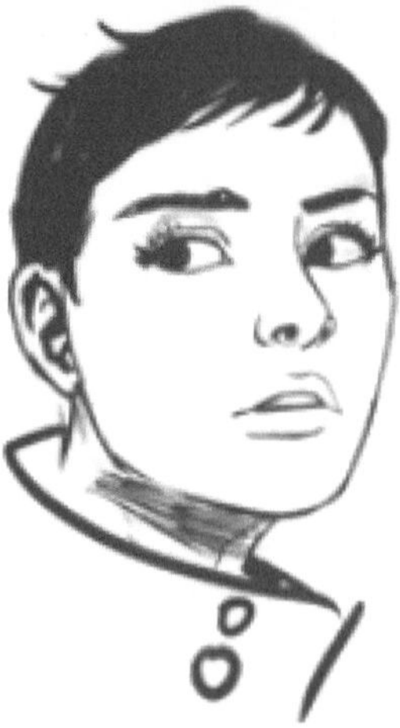

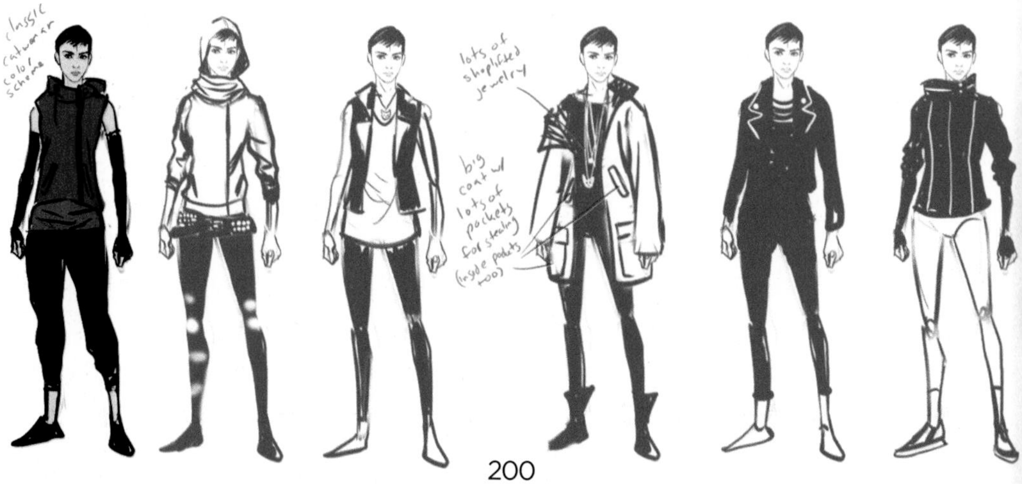
classic catwoman color scheme
lots of shoplifted jewelry
big coat w/ lots of pockets for stealing (inside pockets too)

AUTHOR LAUREN MYRACLE AND ARTIST ISAAC GOODHART INTERVIEW...
EACH OTHER.

When we asked Lauren and Isaac to interview each other about the process of making this book, they pulled out their phones and dove right in! Here's their text interview below:

Lauren Myracle: Hello, friend! You ready to get this party going?

Isaac Goodhart: Let's do it!

Lauren: You know what's cool? We've never met, so we've yet to talk face to face. This chat is our first-ever time to TALK in real time, you and I!

So here's a question for you. As a writer, and definitely not an artist, I was trained to always, always let the artist do his/her own thing with little input/guidance from me. But it seems as if in the comic book world, there is perhaps a slightly different...starting place of assumptions, since I kind of got to tell you what to draw.

How do you see this particular job of illustrating a graphic novel? Because not only are you getting "direction" from me, but shit, Catwoman already existed before we came along! How do you put all that aside and find a way to dive in on your own?

Isaac: That's a good question. Honestly, when our editors first talked to me about the book, I instinctually thought of a handful of artists who would do a good (better?) job. I thought of maybe tailoring my style to look more like those other artists, even. But when I asked for examples of what the other artists in our line were doing, Bobbie told me they wanted me for a reason and to trust my instincts. That was probably the most helpful thing she said early on.

Lauren: OH MY GOD I LOVE THIS SO MUCH.

Isaac: And once we were day-in-day-out grinding, I didn't have time to second-guess anything! So there was no time to really worry or do anything except go!

Lauren: Isaac. See how genuine and true you are? Mr. G, you are the real deal. I am so glad you didn't "tailor" your style, period.

Also, thank you for not giving Selina big boobs. Really!

Speaking of...did knowing that we were creating a story for a younger set of readers influence your art? Did you have to tone down the sexy?

Isaac: Hm, style-wise I don't think I had to alter anything. I just wanted to draw high school as close to how I remembered it as I could. I was aware that we were drawing for a younger audience, so I thought of the books I loved the most when I was in high school and why. What appealed to me about the art I liked. I definitely have my influences!

Lauren: I really like what you said earlier about the day-in-day-out grinding. That part of this job blew me away. DC is so frickin' fast and on top of things! And the collaboration that was involved between the two of us and Bobbie and Diego, solving problems and making changes almost in real time, I loved that. That is NOT typical of the writing projects I'm usually involved with. Is that quick-quick-quick collaborative pace normal for you?

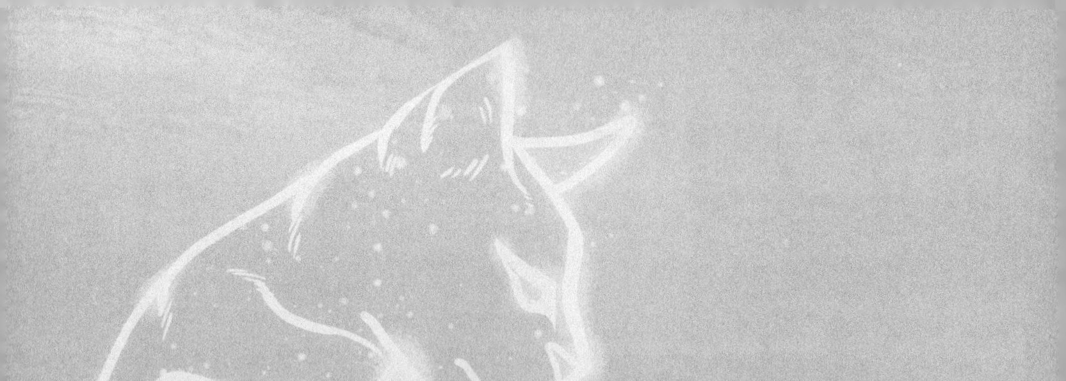

Isaac: Our pace on UNDER THE MOON has been typical for me in my relatively short comic book career. But I hear legends of comic book artists with weekends off and vacation time!! To be honest, if DC gave me another six months to complete the book, I would have taken every minute of those six months to draw and redraw, futzing away until the deadline. As they say, art is never finished, only abandoned. That's the real reason it takes a long time to finish the art in a comic. Perfectionist artists!

Lauren: "Art is never finished, only abandoned." See, I've never heard that before, but yes, absolutely true for novels as well. But again, one of the cool things about working with you is getting a glimpse of your world, the world of an illustrator. Let's see, here's one that all writers will recognize, but maybe it's new to you? You tell me: "Kill your darlings."

Isaac: Oh yeah! To me that's something to urge me to erase a whole figure or face and redraw it. Sometimes a drawing can be good but doesn't "work." So kill your darlings. And redraw them!

Lauren: Yup. For me, it's: "Don't be precious. If you're in love with a bit of prose, odds are you're holding on to it just because you're in love with it, not because it serves the novel."

Isaac: Okay, Lauren, a question for you. I loved your script. But beyond that, I was really impressed with how well-paced and structured it was into comics format. How did you learn how to write specifically for comics?

Lauren: Ohhhh, Isaac, that makes me so happy! Your encouragement from the get-go, once we persuaded Bobbie to let us talk to each other (☺), meant the world to me.

Because you ARE a comic book dude. I am not, or rather I wasn't then, a comic book lady. Like you, I was plagued by doubts at the onset, because who was I to deign to write a graphic novel script? And for Catwoman?! Though I will always call our Selina Catgirl. She. Is. Not. Yet. A woman!

But Bobbie sent me sample scripts, which were super helpful. And then I learned that Scrivener has a "comic script" template, which was also super helpful as it made the formatting of the script manageable. And I got to sit in on two online tutorials, one led by Mariko Tamaki and the other led by Gene Yang. (!!!! I mean, right?!!!!!)

Isaac: Right! How long did it take you to script the book?

Lauren: When I was writing my initial pitch for Bobbie, I worked feverishly and in a possessed sort of way for two weeks. But then the cool thing was, I had a frickin' outline for the whole book! DC made me do that, made me take that approach, and I sure see the merit in it. After that, I guess it took about three months to get a full first draft completed.

And after that, it just became a matter of telling this story, our story, about Selina in the format of a script, if that makes sense. The storytelling itself isn't any different from writing a novel—

except, hmm. That's not true. The panel-by-panel demands made me a better writer, for sure, because I had to come up with ACTION for every fricking panel. I mean, good lord. Where are all the lovely scenes of high schoolers just sitting around TALKING? I guess there's a reason literary fiction doesn't translate well to graphic novels!

KK, one more question each?

Isaac: Yeah!

Lauren: Who's your fave character in UTM? And which character are you the most like?

Oops. That was two!

Isaac: I have a question I've always wanted to ask: What was your relationship to Catwoman and comics in general before DC contacted you? Did you read any comics growing up? Or watch any of the movies?

Oops, that was three.

Lauren: Ha! Excellent.

I watched all the movies, absolutely. And loved them. And thought Catwoman was fierce and sexy and strong and feminine. She always, always held an allure for me. But I never read any of the comics about her or about Bruce or anyone in the DC world. I, ah, read Richie Rich! And Archie! And Casper the Ghost!

Until working with DC, my relationship with graphic novels was influenced by the fact that I wanted words words words, I wanted to gobble any story down, I didn't want to linger over drawings. Or maybe I didn't want to have to interpret the drawings? Maybe words, for me, zoom straight into my brain in the way that drawings do for you?

I guess I was the opposite of dyslexic, and not in a way that reflects well on me. Like, I wasn't patient enough to sit down and savor a graphic novel, which was my loss.

Because once I dove into the genre...damn. Well, you know. It was just a matter of slowing down and ENJOYING the journey all along!

Isaac: My favorite character is Selina. I'm the most like her by a mile. Like Selina, I've had some difficult relationships in my family. I dealt with stresses and tough times like she does. I always made sure to present a good front. And like her, I've always had a very strong sense of identity. And that's why I was always so independent. Although for me, I was always the "comic book kid" in school! I do have a soft spot for Ojo. I think life would be easier if I had more of his happy-go-lucky attitude!

Lauren: Awwww! Perfect!

And, dear Isaac, it's a wrap! Yeah?

Isaac: I believe so!

Lauren: Sending hugs and kisses and high fives! You rock!!! Bye for now, friend!

Isaac: Bye! This was fun. Let's do it again sometime!!

Lauren: Yessir! +salutes+ Anytime.

LAUREN MYRACLE

is the bestselling author of many books for children and young adults,
including the acclaimed Internet Girls books *ttyl*, *ttfn*, and *l8r, g8r*. *ttyl* and
ttfn are *New York Times* bestsellers, and *ttyl* was the first book to be written
entirely in instant message. Lauren is also the author of the popular
Winnie Years middle grade series. Lauren grew up in Atlanta, Georgia,
and earned a BA in English and psychology from the University of North
Carolina at Chapel Hill. She later earned an MA in English from Colorado
State University, where she taught for two years, and an MFA in writing for
children and young adults from Vermont College.

ISAAC GOODHART

is a 2010 graduate of the School of Visual Arts with a BFA in cartooning. He got his start in comics in 2014 as one of the winners of the Top Cow Talent Hunt. After drawing *Artifacts* #38, he moved on to illustrating Matt Hawkins' *Postal* for 26 consecutive issues. He has also contributed to *Love Is Love*, *Rat Queens* webcomics, and *Welcome to Showside*.

special sneak preview

#1 *NEW YORK TIMES* & *USA TODAY* BESTSELLING CO-AUTHOR OF *BEAUTIFUL CREATURES*

KAMI GARCIA

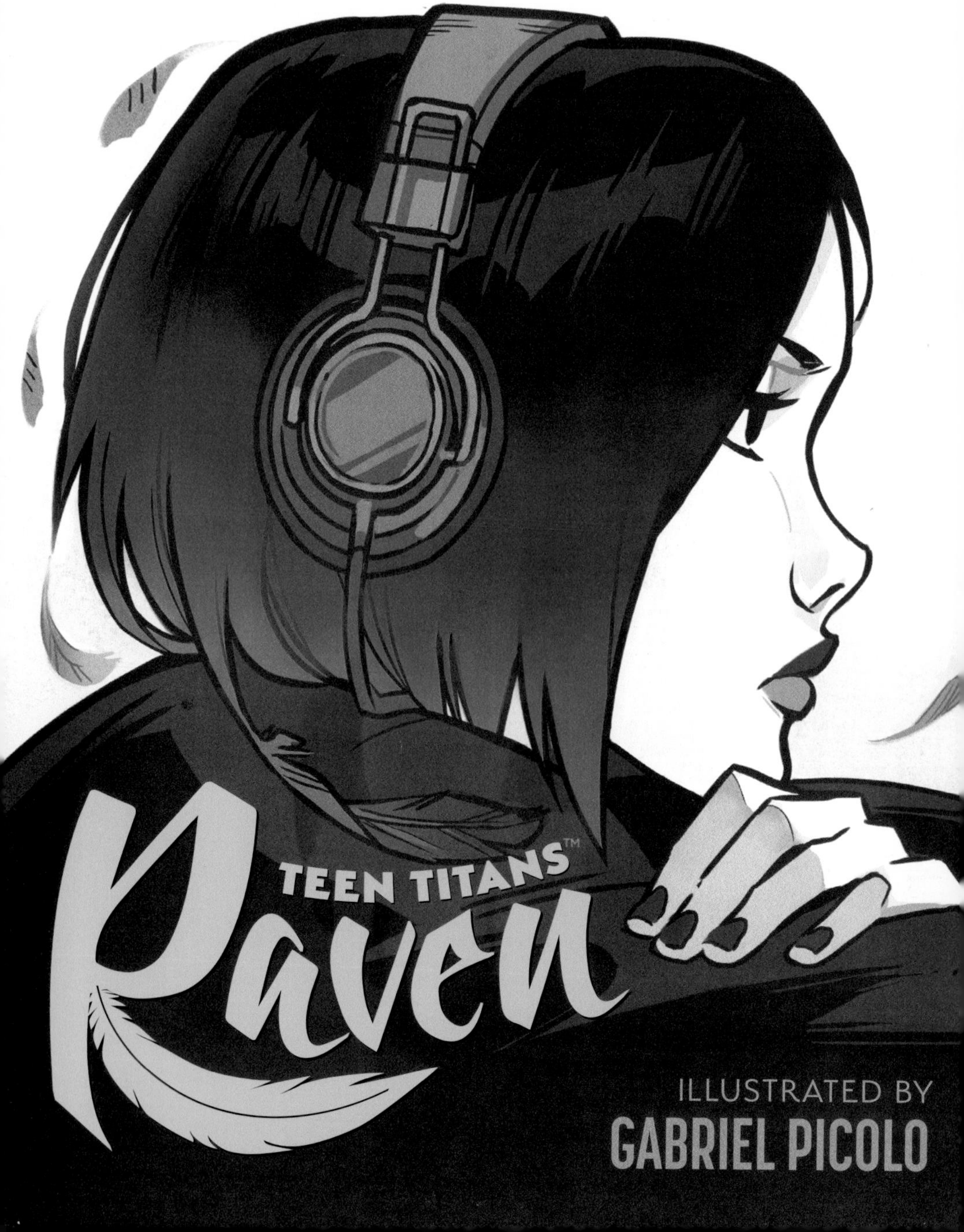
TEEN TITANS™
Raven
ILLUSTRATED BY
GABRIEL PICOLO

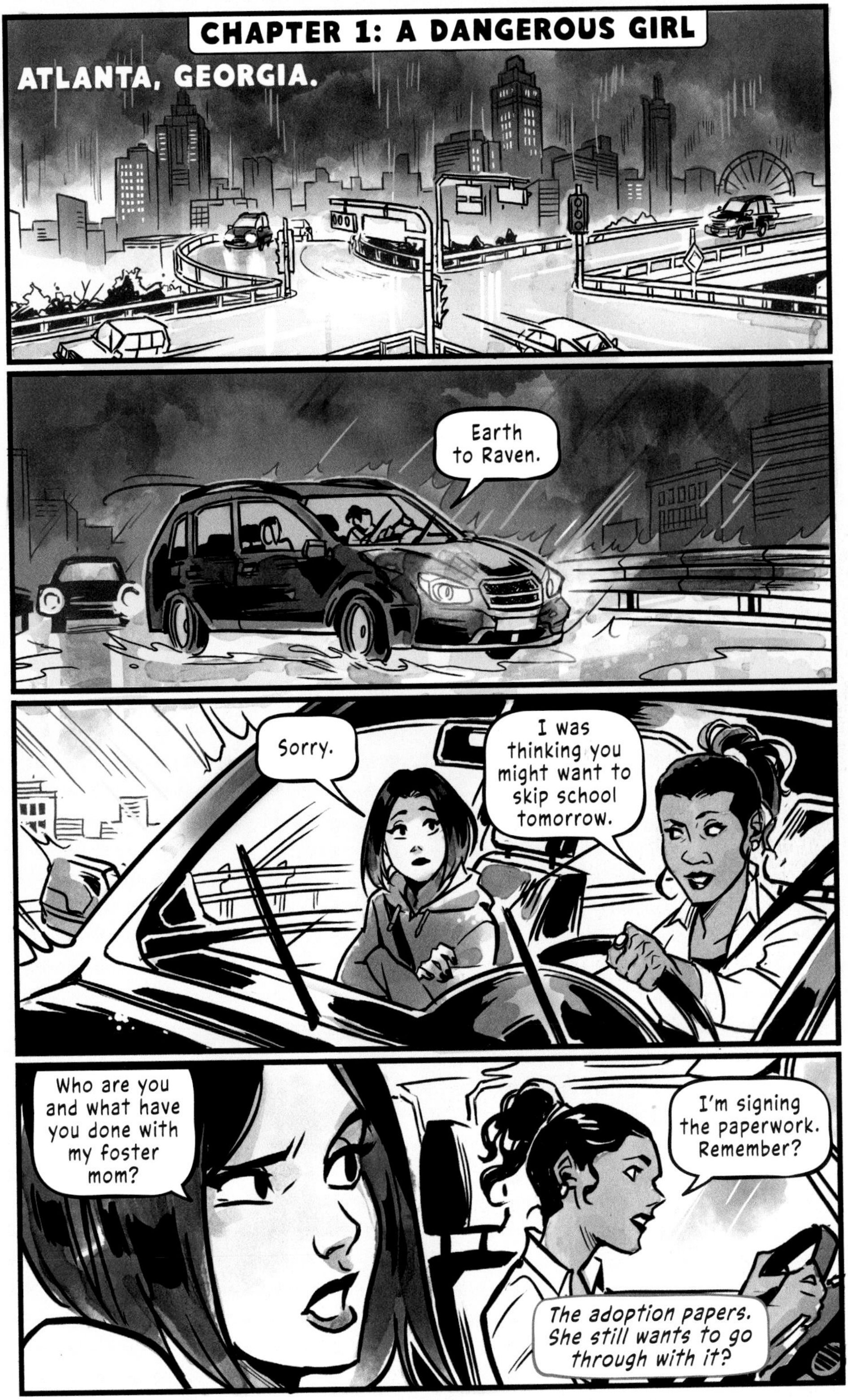
CHAPTER 1: A DANGEROUS GIRL
ATLANTA, GEORGIA.
Earth to Raven.
Sorry.
I was thinking you might want to skip school tomorrow.
Who are you and what have you done with my foster mom?
I'm signing the paperwork. Remember?
The adoption papers. She still wants to go through with it?

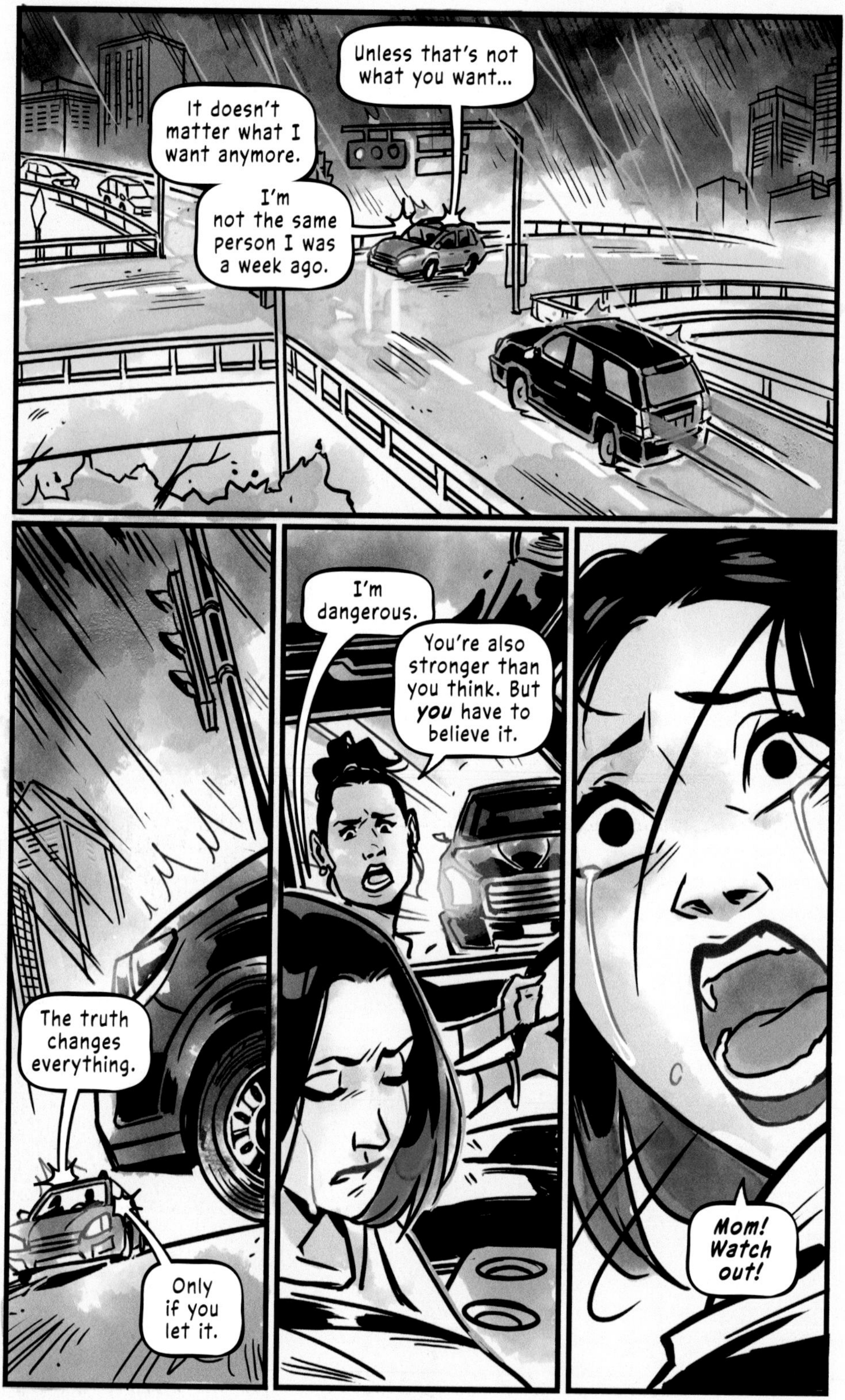
It doesn't matter what I want anymore.
Unless that's not what you want...
I'm not the same person I was a week ago.
The truth changes everything.
Only if you let it.
I'm dangerous.
You're also stronger than you think. But *you* have to believe it.
Mom! Watch out!

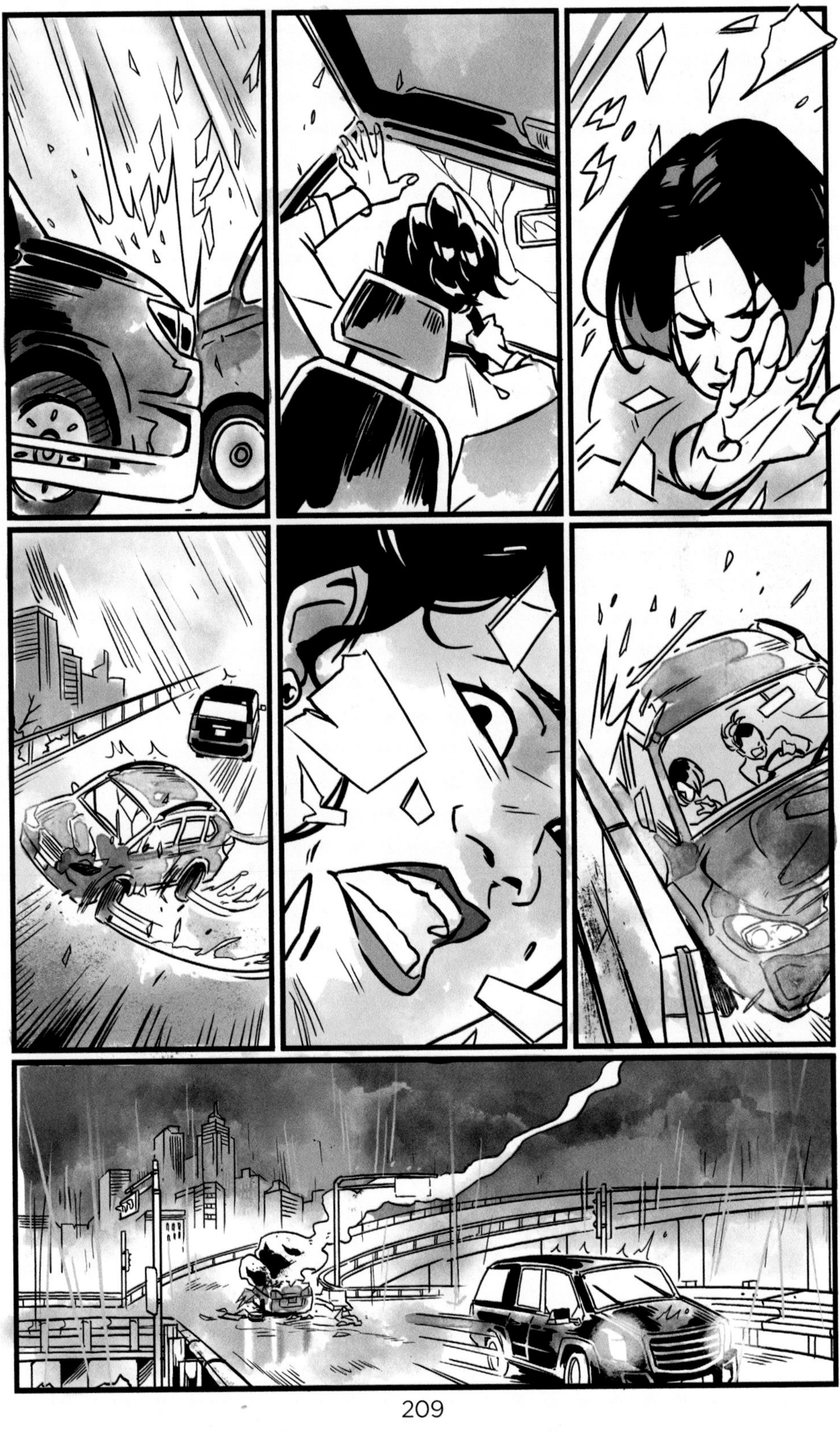

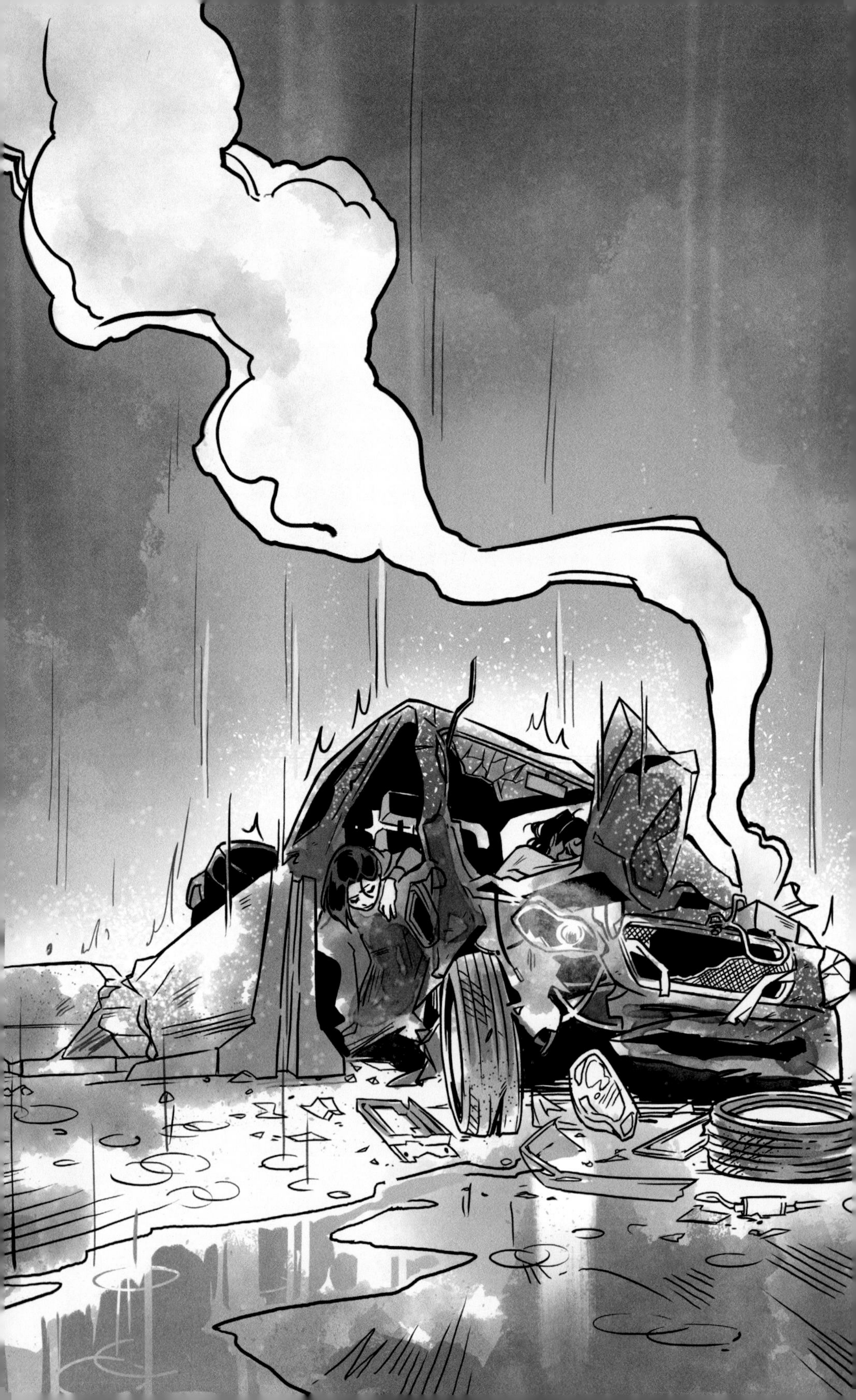

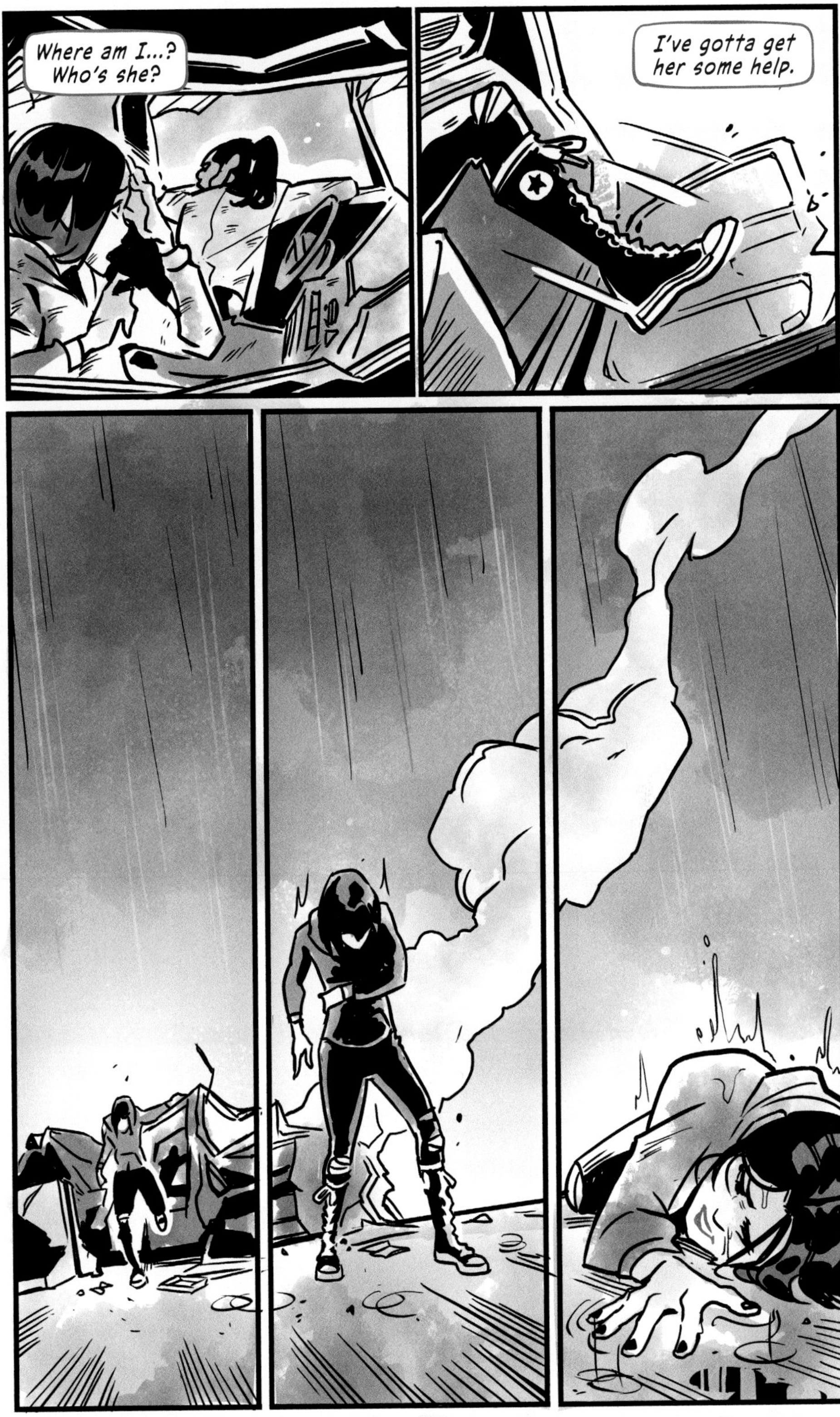
Where am I...? Who's she?
I've gotta get her some help.

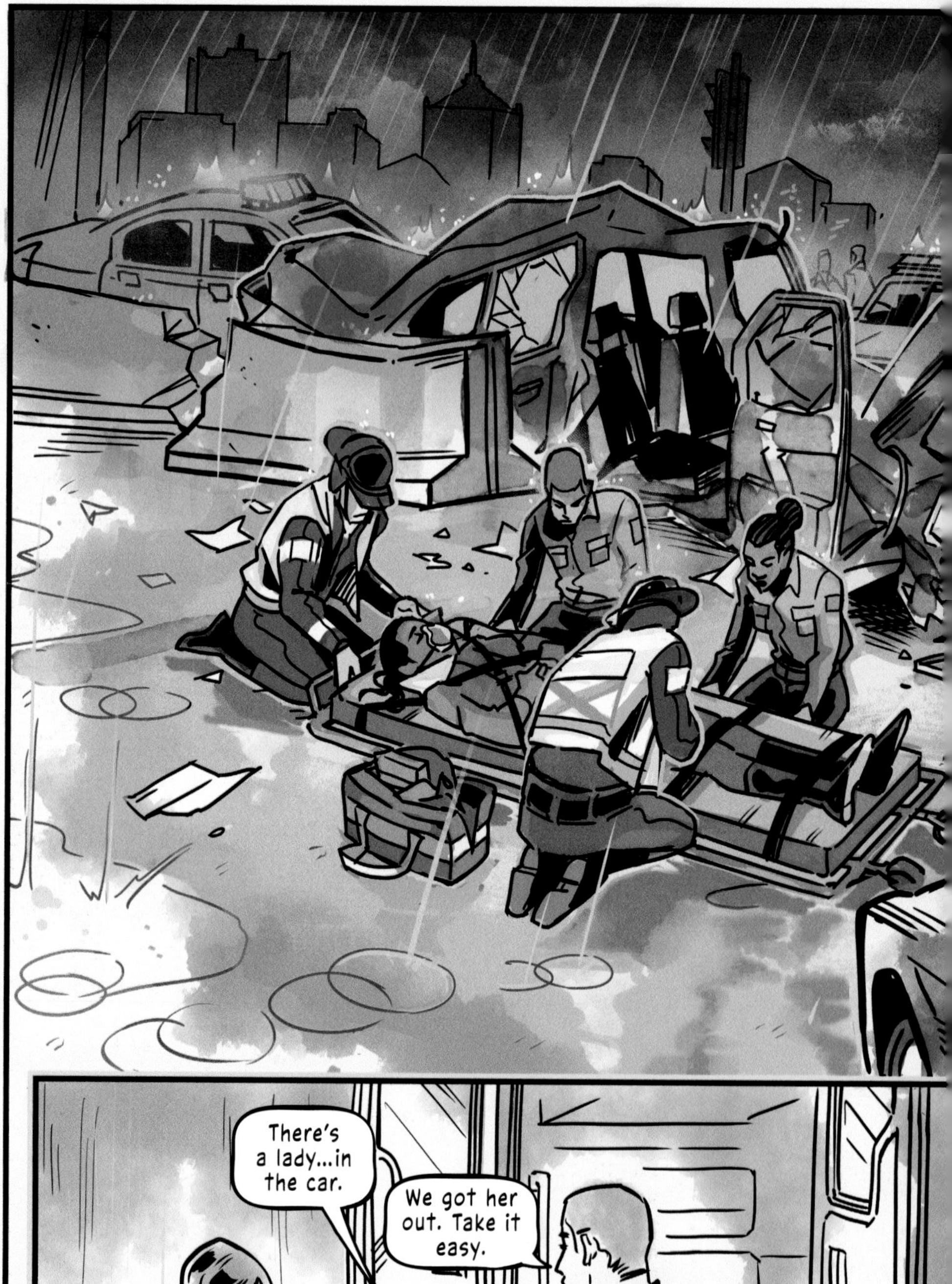

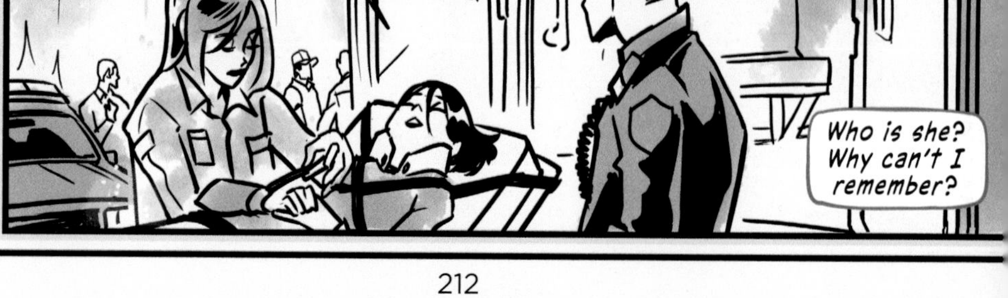
There's a lady...in the car.
We got her out. Take it easy.
Who is she? Why can't I remember?

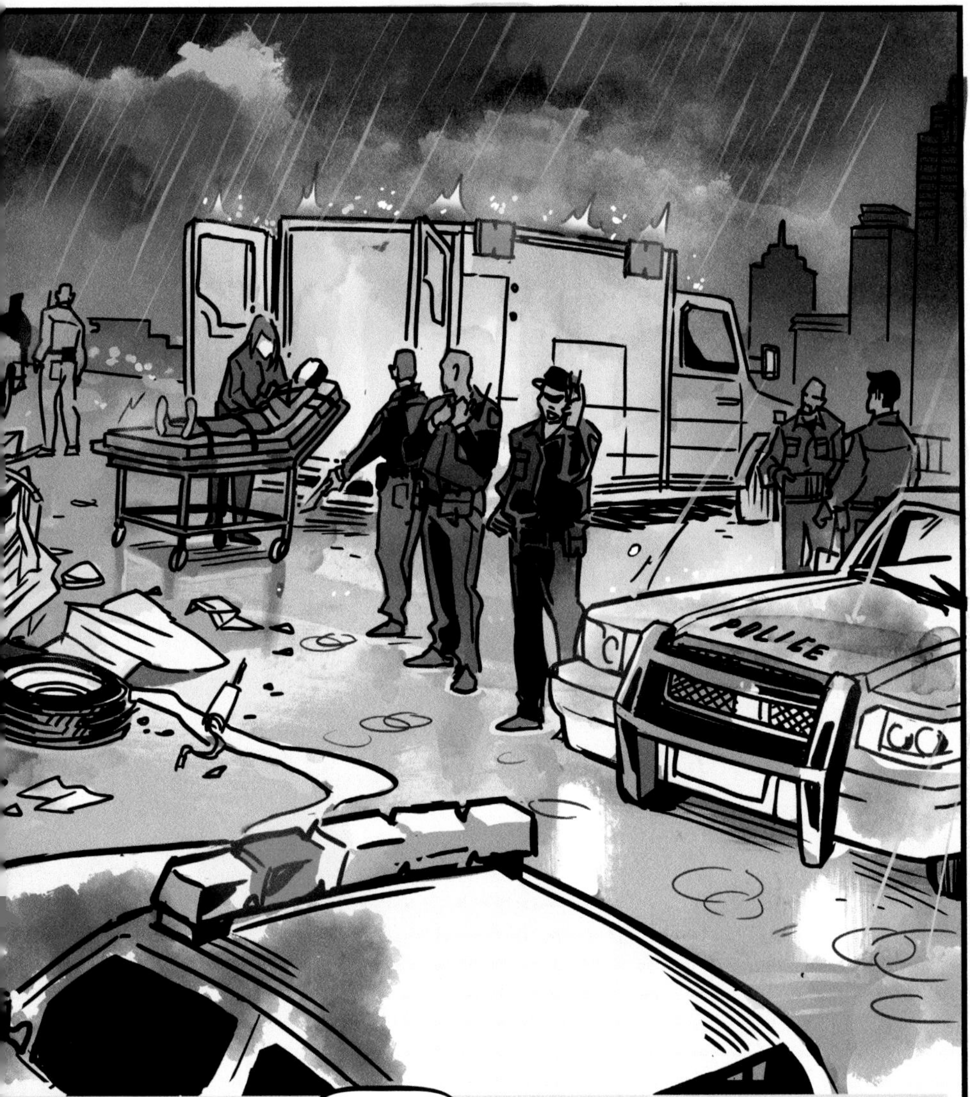

POLICE

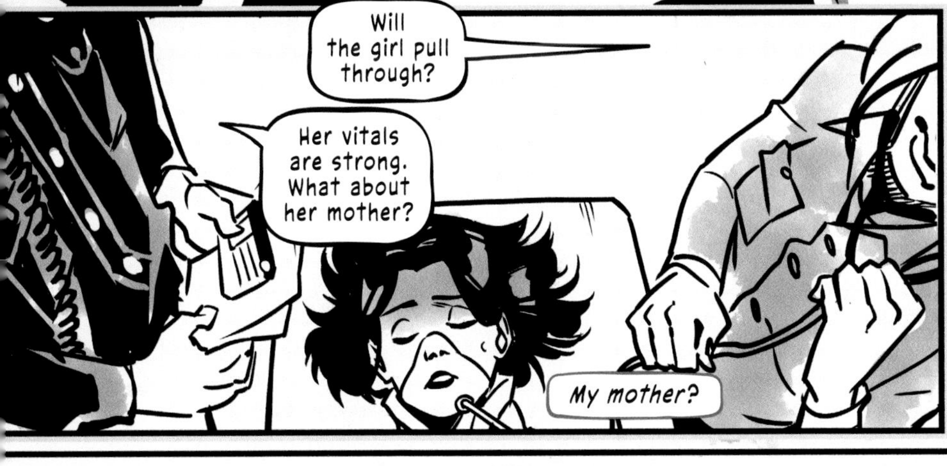

Will the girl pull through?
Her vitals are strong. What about her mother?
My mother?

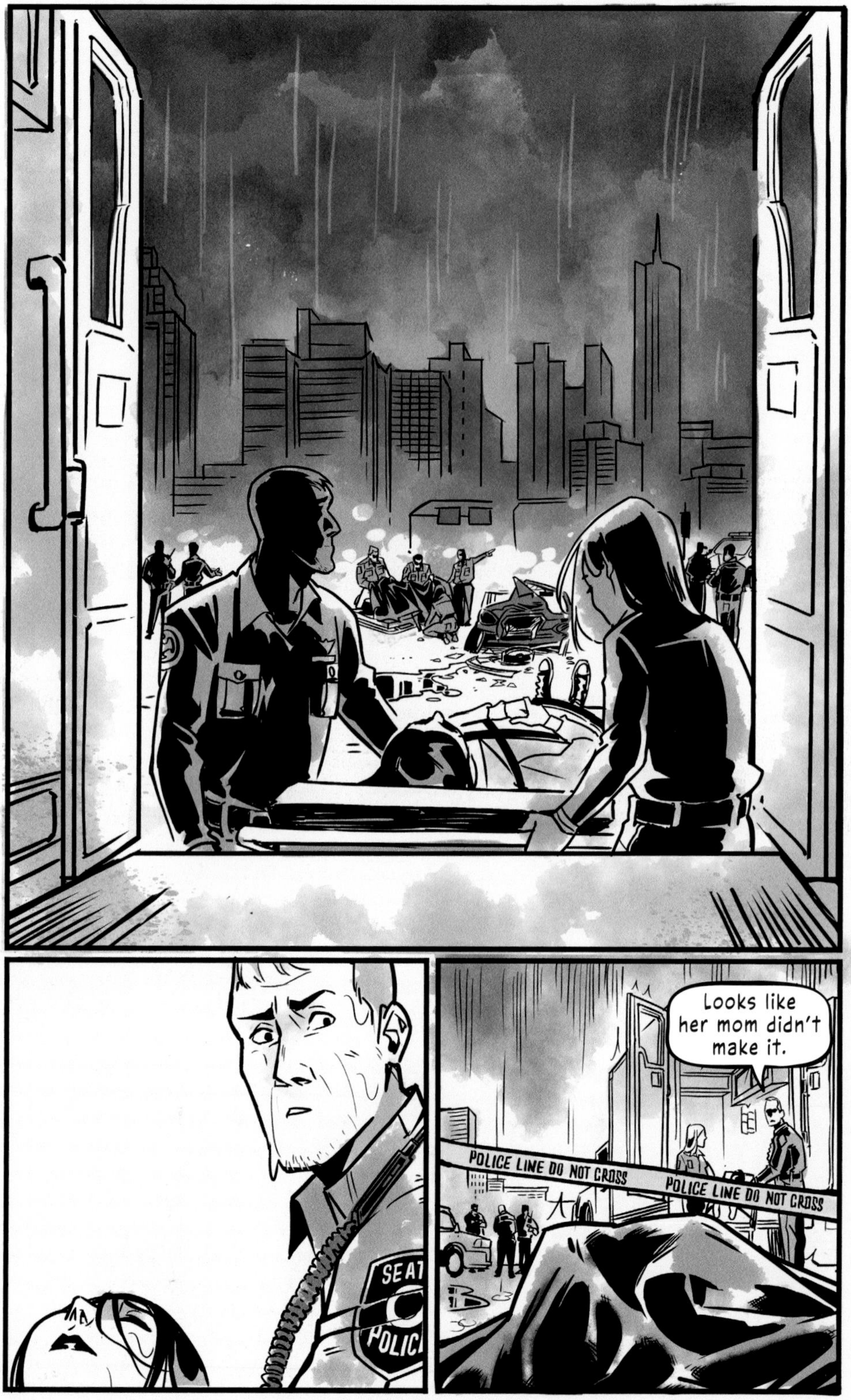
SEAT
POLIC
Looks like her mom didn't make it.
POLICE LINE DO NOT CROSS
POLICE LINE DO NOT CROSS

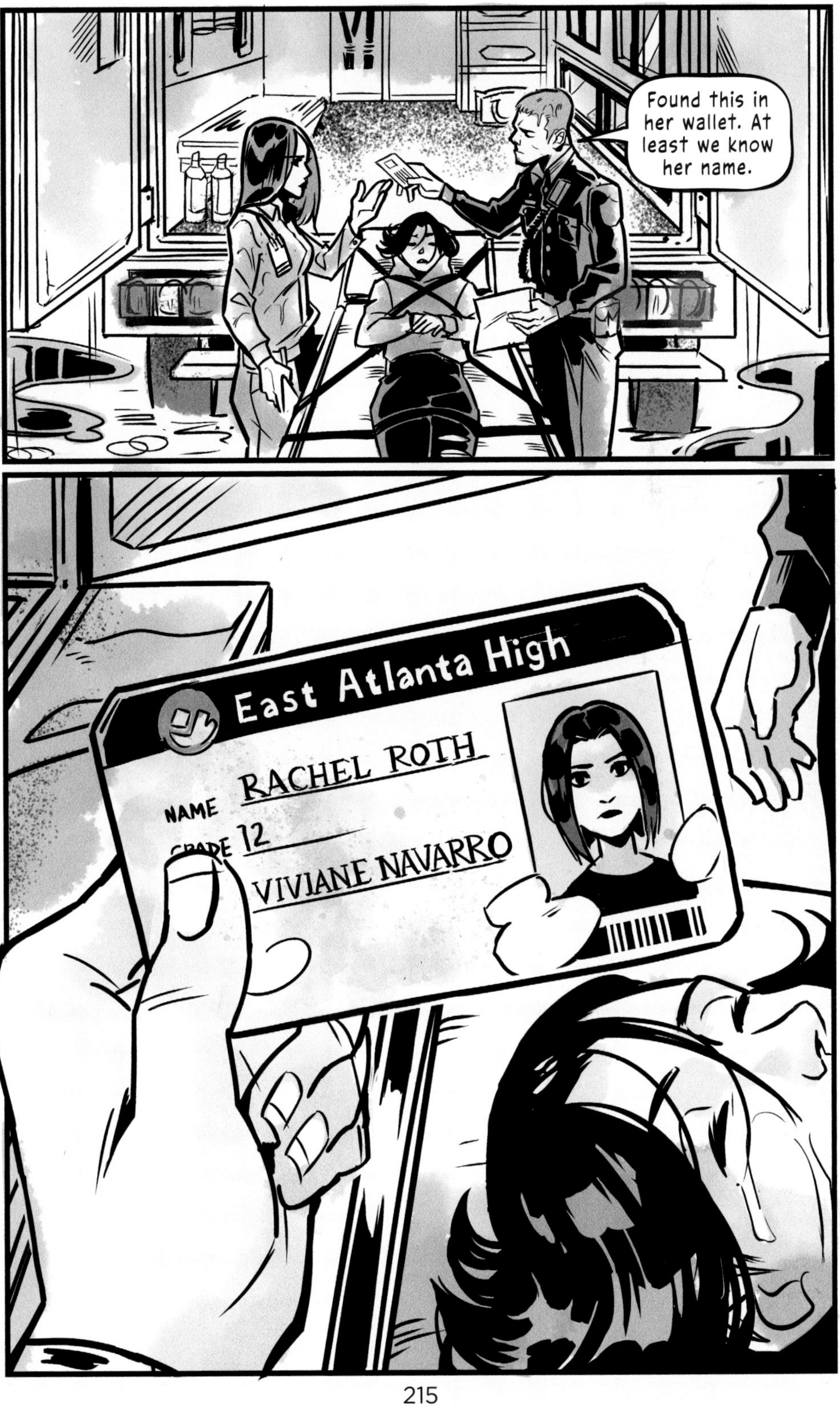
Found this in her wallet. At least we know her name.
East Atlanta High
RACHEL ROTH
NAME
12
VIVIANE NAVARRO

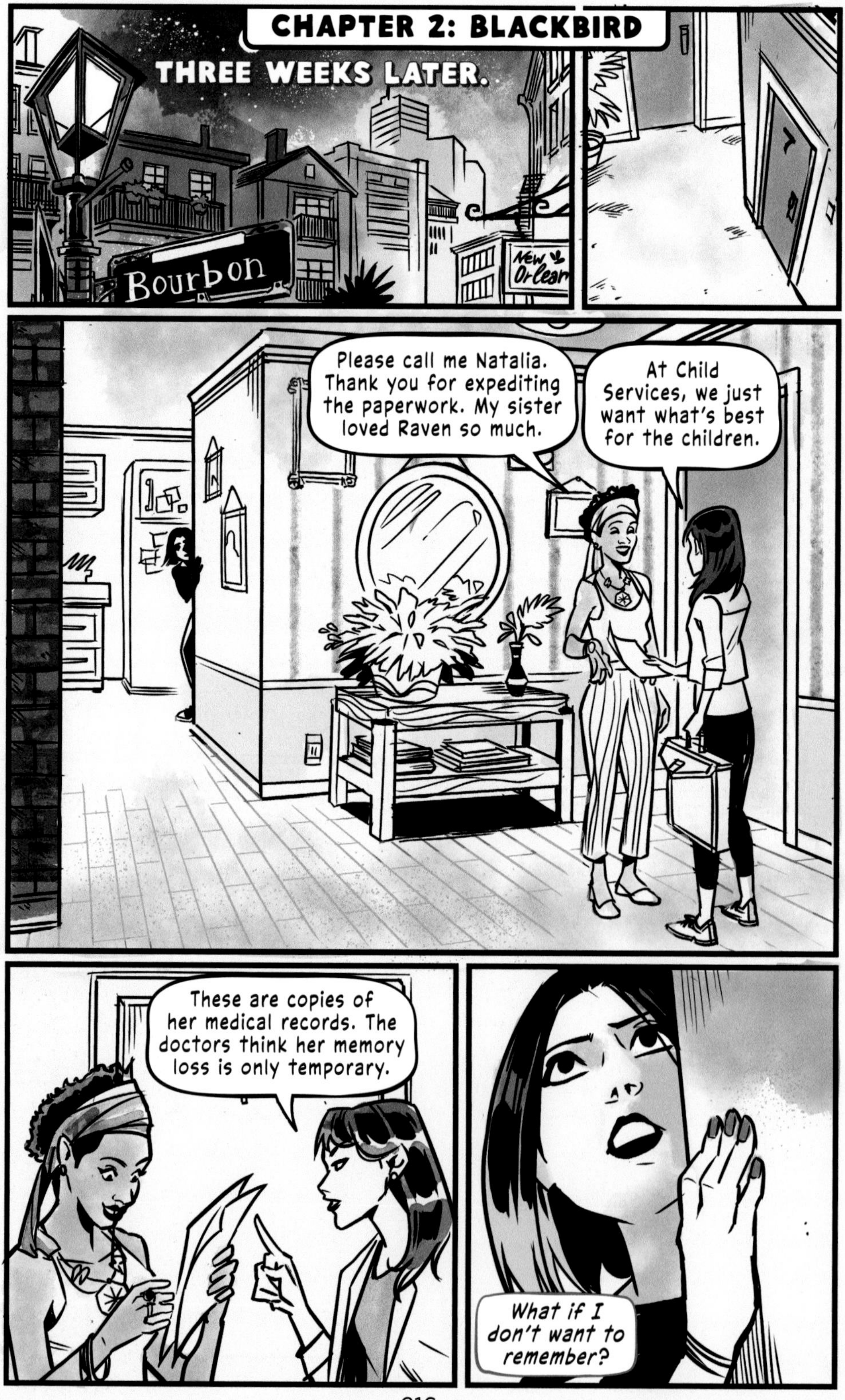
CHAPTER 2: BLACKBIRD
THREE WEEKS LATER.
Bourbon
Please call me Natalia. Thank you for expediting the paperwork. My sister loved Raven so much.
At Child Services, we just want what's best for the children.
These are copies of her medical records. The doctors think her memory loss is only temporary.
What if I don't want to remember?

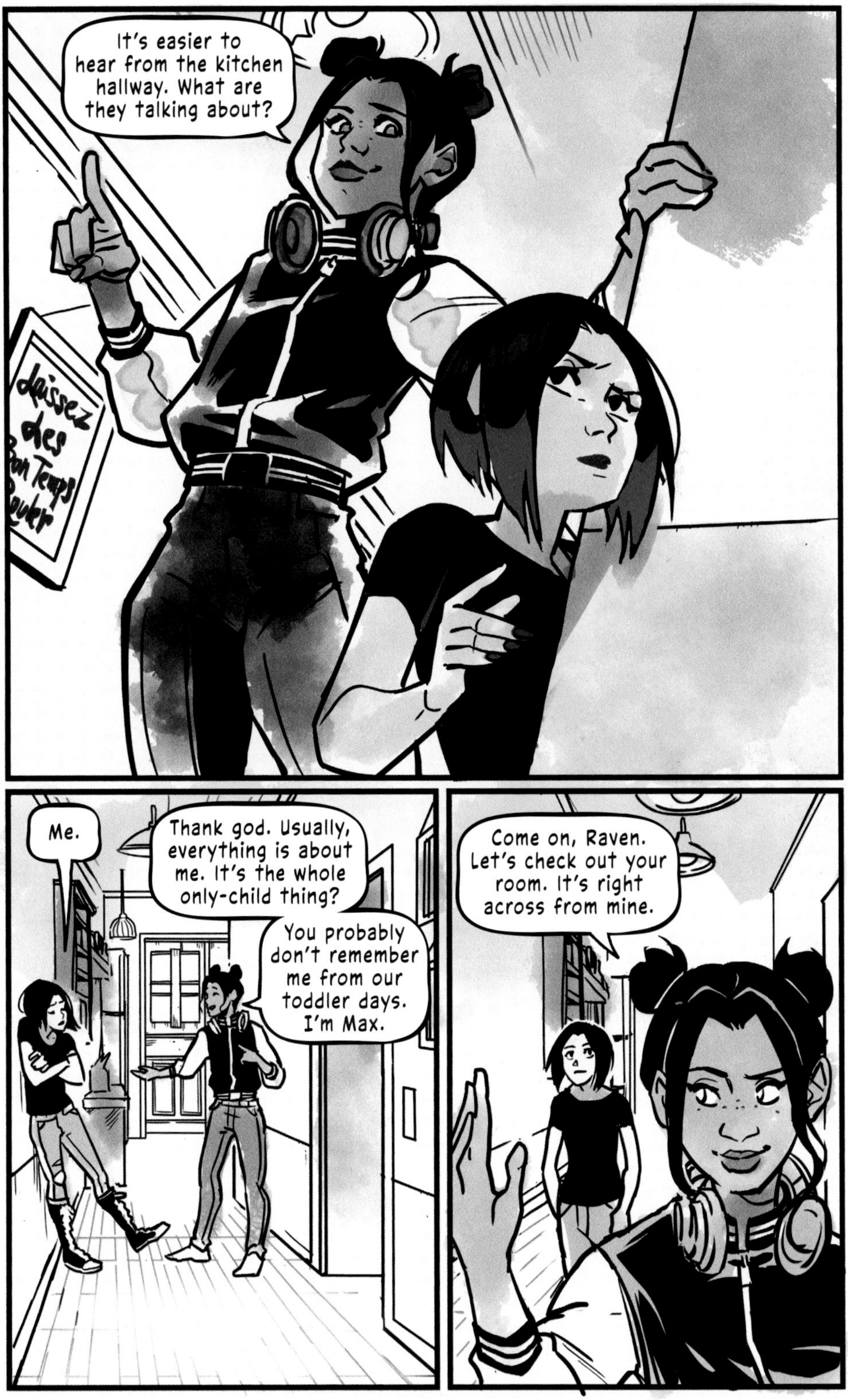
It's easier to hear from the kitchen hallway. What are they talking about?
Laissez des Bon Temps Rouler
Me.
Thank god. Usually, everything is about me. It's the whole only-child thing?
You probably don't remember me from our toddler days. I'm Max.
Come on, Raven. Let's check out your room. It's right across from mine.

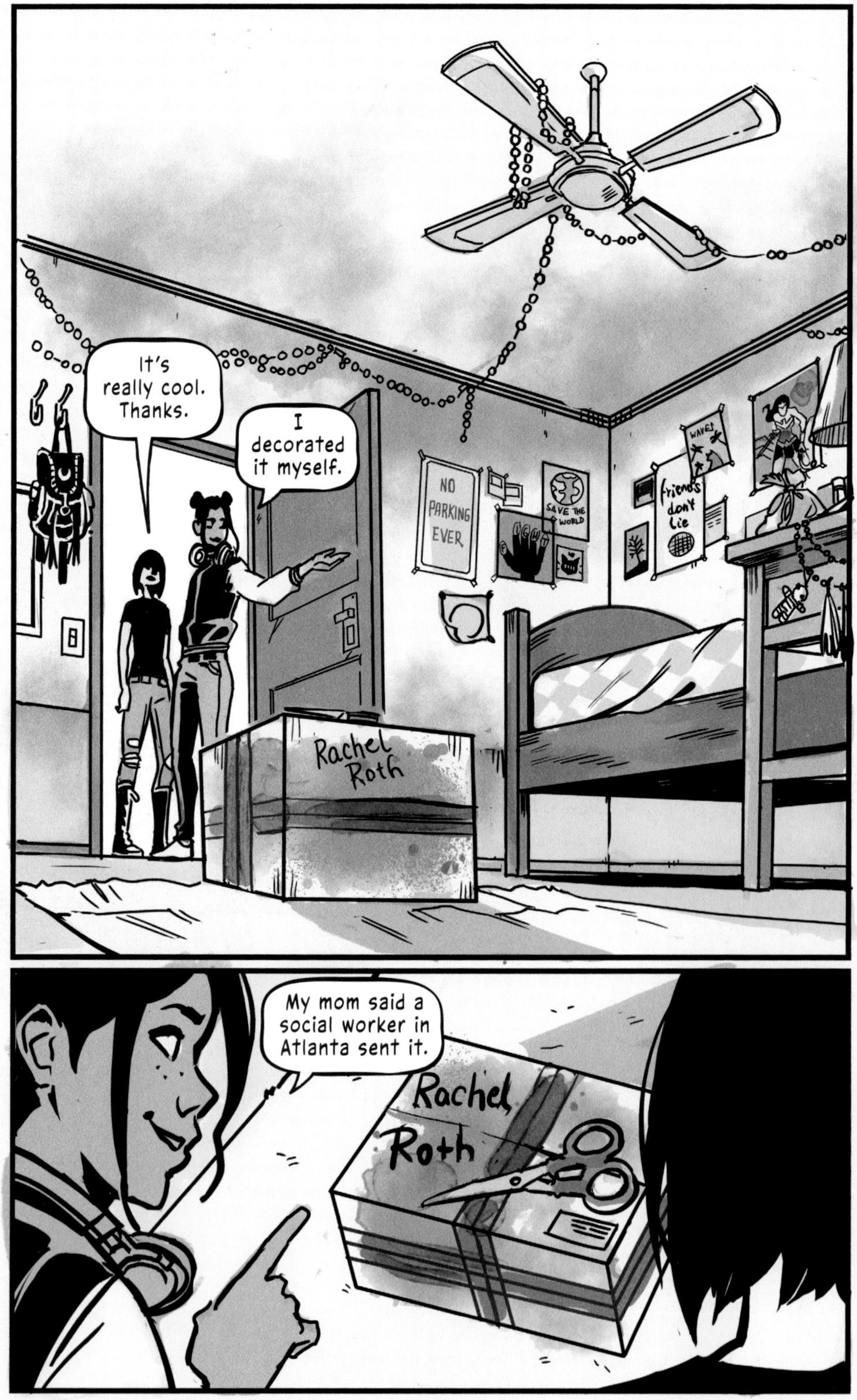
It's really cool. Thanks.
I decorated it myself.
NO PARKING EVER
SAVE THE WORLD
WAVES
friends don't lie
Rachel Roth
My mom said a social worker in Atlanta sent it.
Rachel Roth

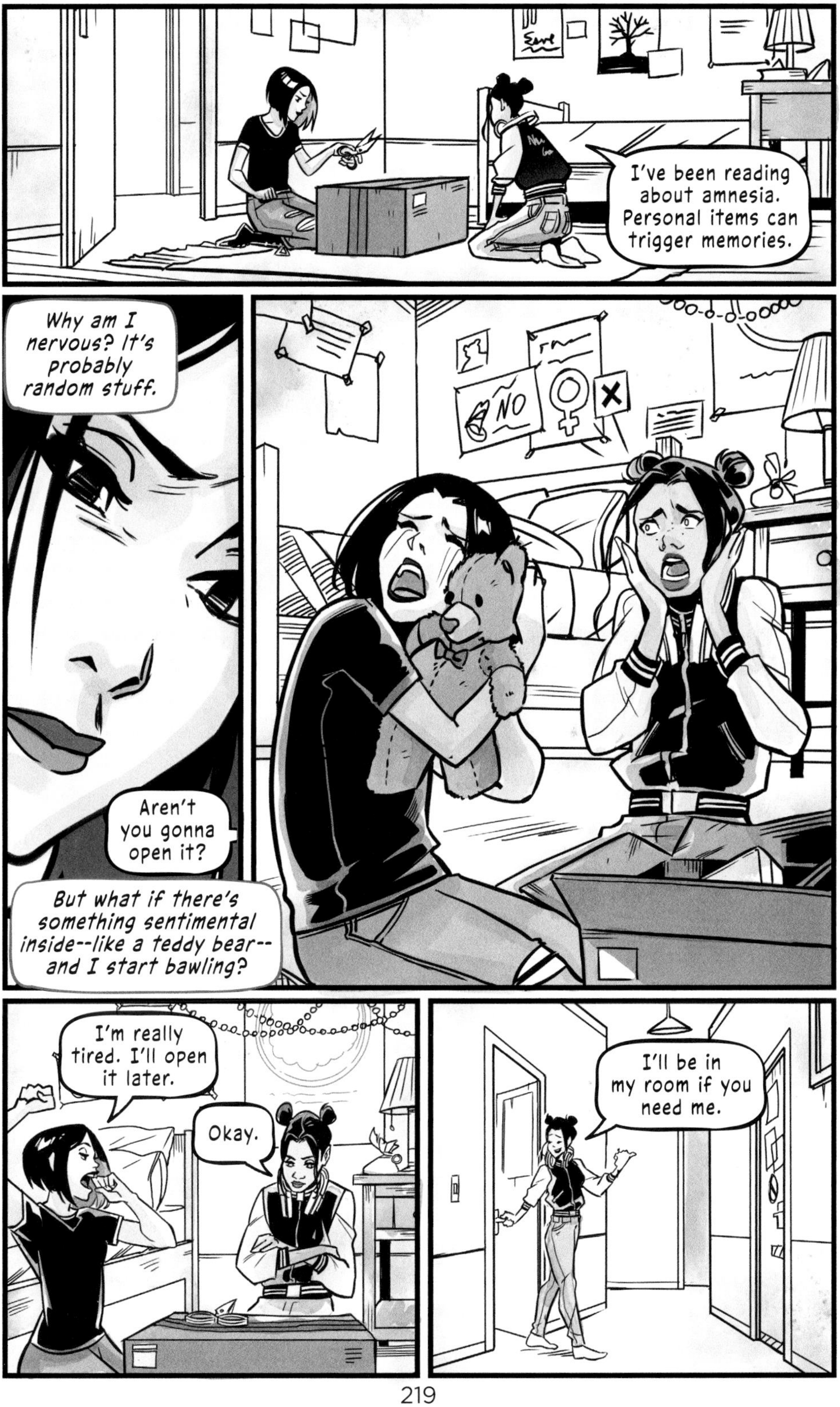
I've been reading about amnesia. Personal items can trigger memories.
Why am I nervous? It's probably random stuff.
Aren't you gonna open it?
But what if there's something sentimental inside--like a teddy bear--and I start bawling?
NO
I'm really tired. I'll open it later.
Okay.
I'll be in my room if you need me.

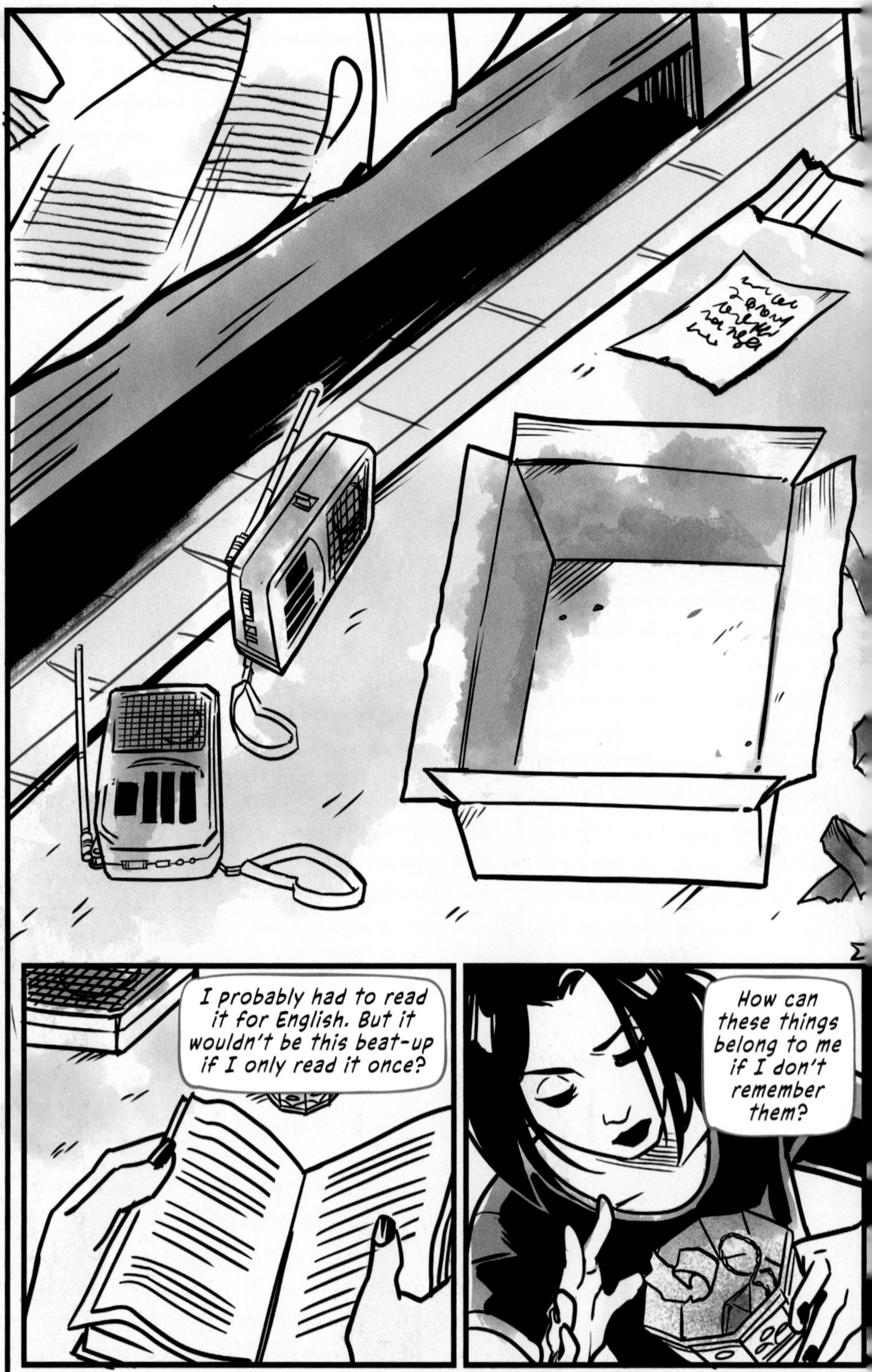
I probably had to read it for English. But it wouldn't be this beat-up if I only read it once?
How can these things belong to me if I don't remember them?

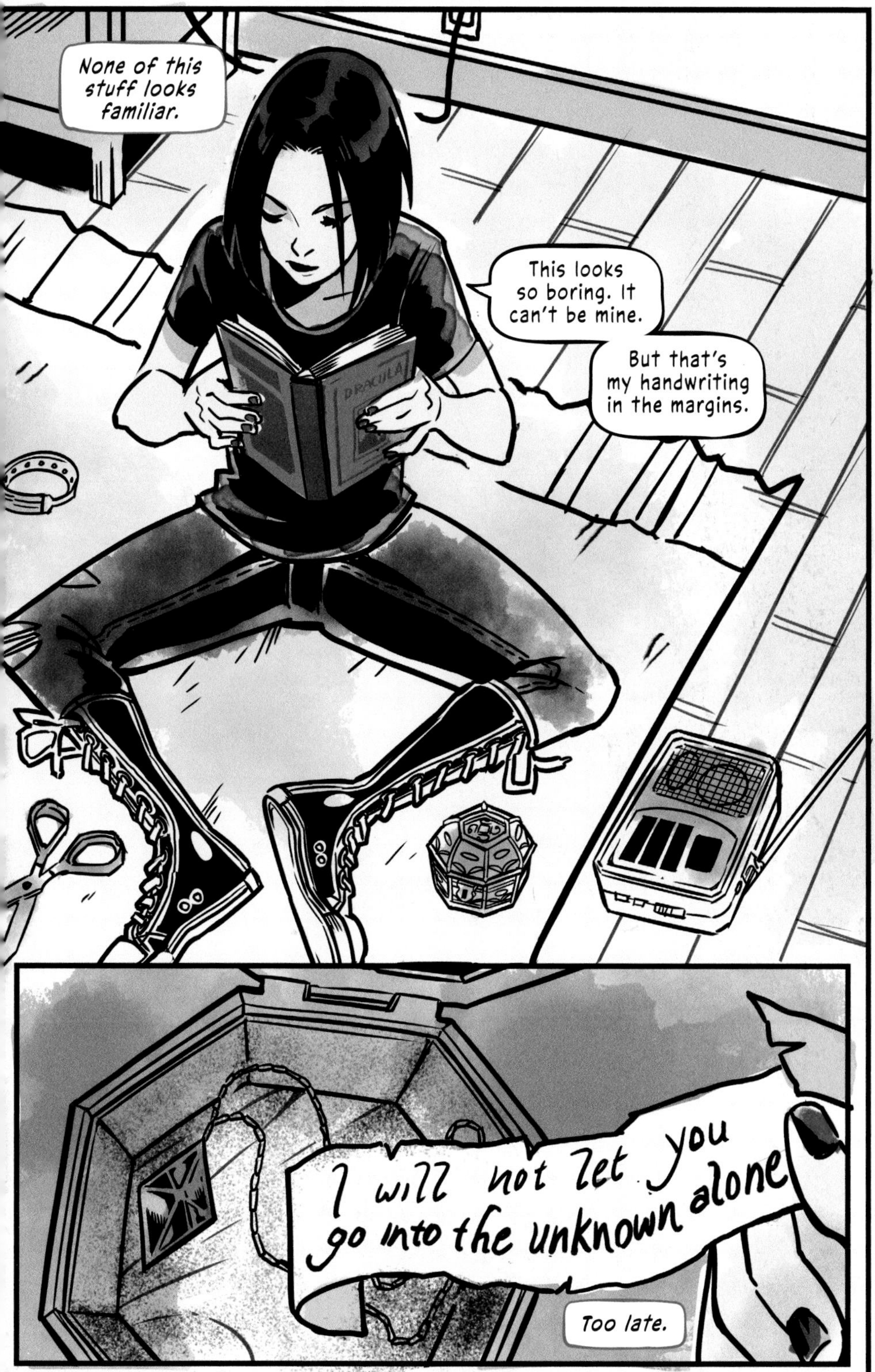
None of this stuff looks familiar.
This looks so boring. It can't be mine.
But that's my handwriting in the margins.
DRACULA
I will not let you go into the unknown alone
Too late.

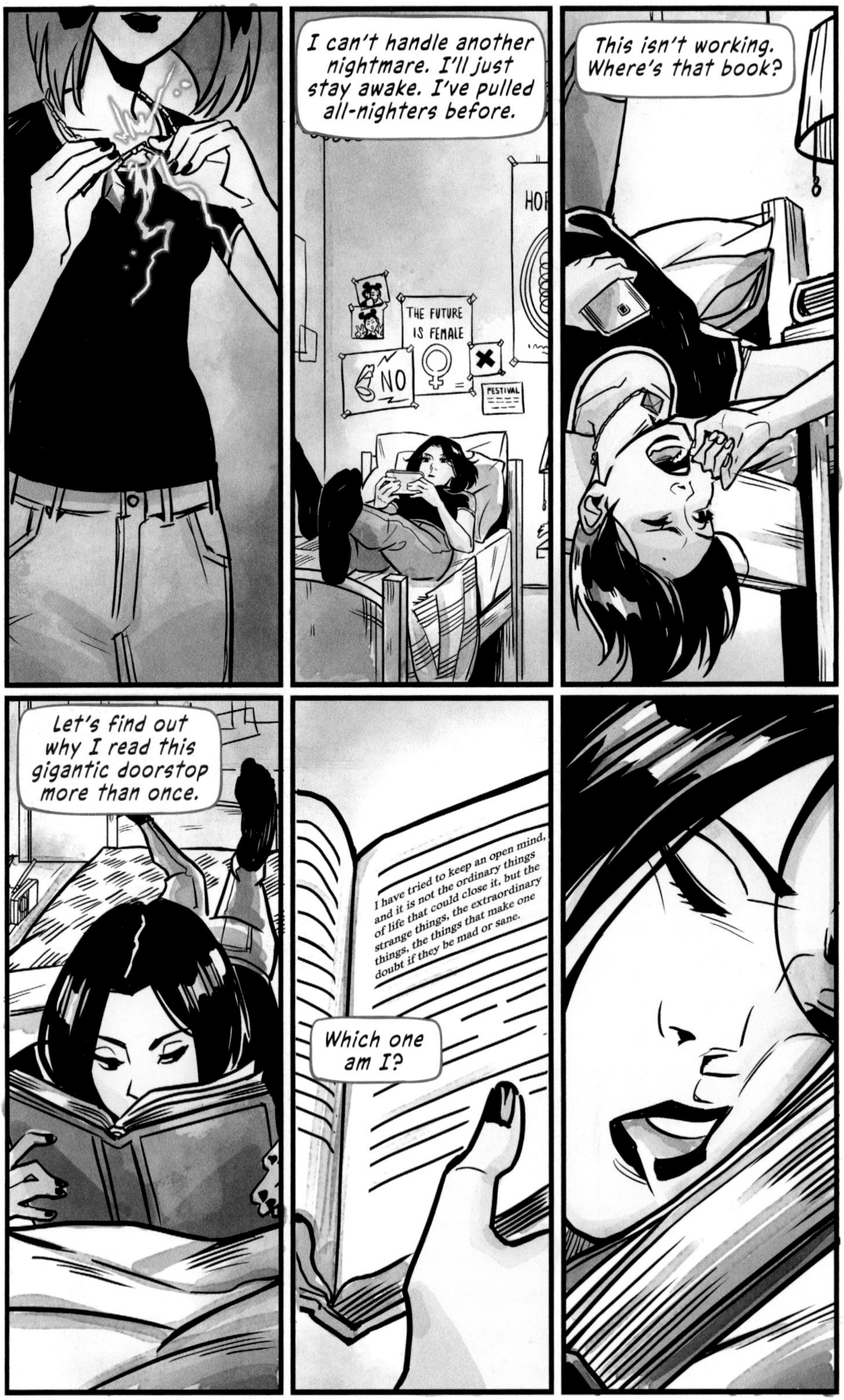
I can't handle another nightmare. I'll just stay awake. I've pulled all-nighters before.
THE FUTURE IS FEMALE
NO
FESTIVAL
This isn't working. Where's that book?
Let's find out why I read this gigantic doorstop more than once.
I have tried to keep an open mind, and it is not the ordinary things of life that could close it, but the strange things, the extraordinary things, the things that make one doubt if they be mad or sane.
Which one am I?

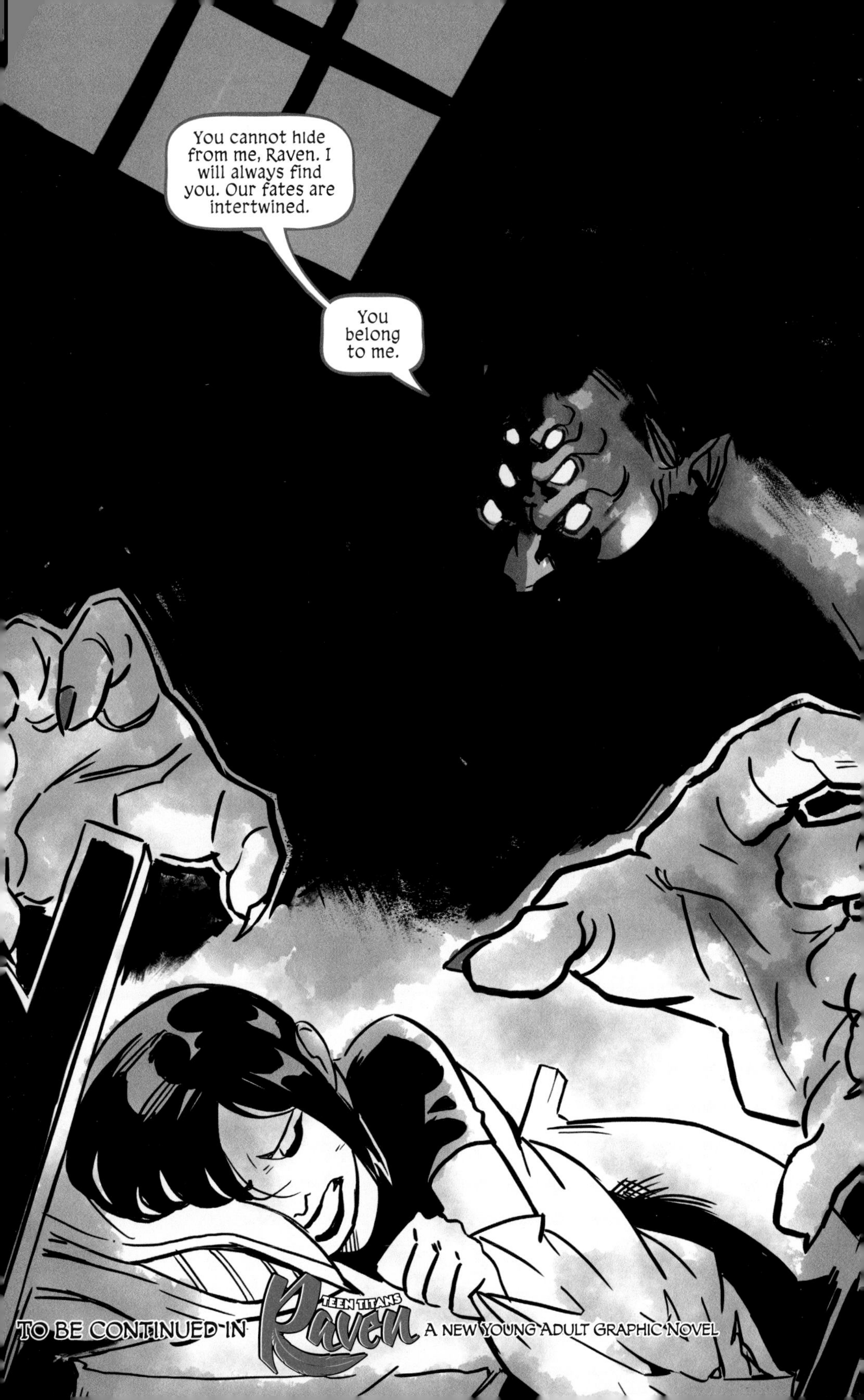
You cannot hide from me, Raven. I will always find you. Our fates are intertwined.
You belong to me.
TO BE CONTINUED IN TEEN TITANS Raven A NEW YOUNG ADULT GRAPHIC NOVEL

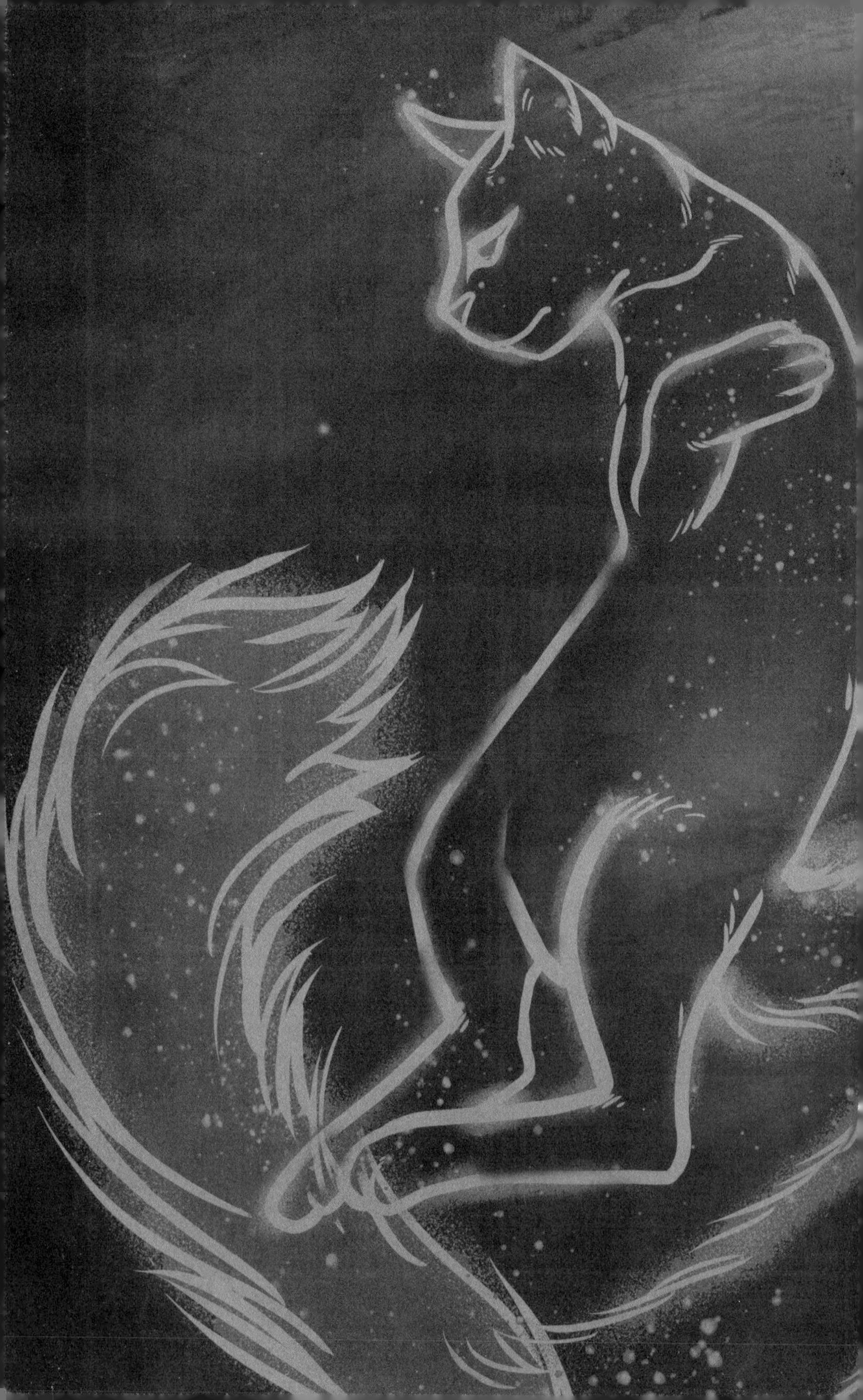